THE HEROES OF OLYMPUS

Book Two

THE SON OF NEPTUNE

THE GRAPHIC NOVEL

by

RICK RIORDAN

Adapted by
ROBERT VENDITTI

Art by
ANTOINE DODÉ

Color by
ORPHEUS COLLAR

Lettering by
CHRIS DICKEY

DISNEP · HYPERION
Los Angeles   New York

Adapted from the novel
The Heroes of Olympus, Book Two: *The Son of Neptune*

Text copyright © 2017 by Rick Riordan
Illustrations copyright © 2017 Disney Enterprises, Inc.

First Edition, February 2017
1 3 5 7 9 10 8 6 4 2

FAC-008598-17006
Printed in the United States of America

Text is set in Minion Pro and Lithos from Fontspring
Designed by Jim Titus

Library of Congress Cataloging-in-Publication Data

Names: Venditti, Robert, author. | Riordan, Rick. Son of Neptune. | Disney
Enterprises (1996-)
Title: The son of Neptune : the graphic novel / by Rick Riordan ; adapted by
Robert Venditti ; illustrations Disney Enterprises, Inc.
Description: First edition. | New York : Disney/Hyperion, [2016] | Series:
The heroes of Olympus ; book 2 | Summary: Demigod Percy Jackson, still
with no memory, and his new friends from Camp Jupiter, Hazel and Frank, go
on a quest to free Death, but their bigger task is to unite the Greek and
Roman camps so that the Prophecy of Seven can be fulfilled.
Identifiers: LCCN 2015031231| ISBN 9781484716212 (hardcover) | ISBN
9781484723036 (pbk.)
Subjects: LCSH: Mythology, Roman--Juvenile fiction. | Mythology,
Greek—Juvenile fiction. | Graphic novels. | CYAC: Graphic novels. |
Mythology, Roman—Fiction. | Mythology, Greek—Fiction. | Camps—Fiction.
| Hera (Greek deity)—Fiction. | Gaia (Greek deity)—Fiction. |
Monsters—Fiction. | Prophecies—Fiction. | Riordan, Rick. Son of
Neptune—Adaptations.
Classification: LCC PZ7.7.V48 So 2016 | DDC 741.5973—dc23
LC record available at https://lccn.loc.gov/2015031231

ISBN (hardcover) 978-1-4847-1621-2
ISBN (paperback) 978-1-4847-2303-6

Reinforced binding
Visit www.RickRiordan.com
And www.DisneyBooks.com

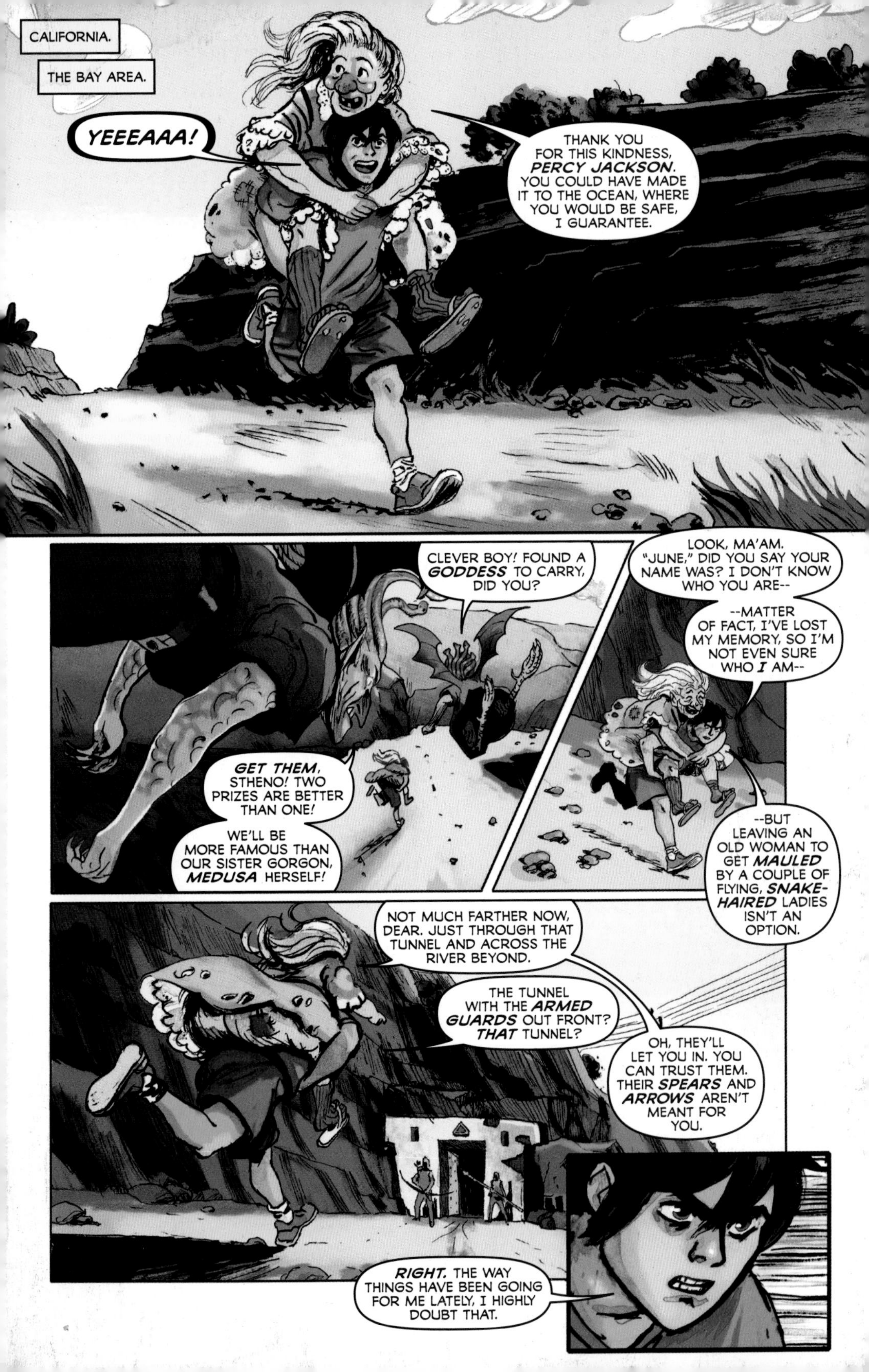
CALIFORNIA.
THE BAY AREA.
YEEEAAA!
THANK YOU FOR THIS KINDNESS, PERCY JACKSON. YOU COULD HAVE MADE IT TO THE OCEAN, WHERE YOU WOULD BE SAFE, I GUARANTEE.
CLEVER BOY! FOUND A GODDESS TO CARRY, DID YOU?
GET THEM, STHENO! TWO PRIZES ARE BETTER THAN ONE!
WE'LL BE MORE FAMOUS THAN OUR SISTER GORGON, MEDUSA HERSELF!
LOOK, MA'AM. "JUNE," DID YOU SAY YOUR NAME WAS? I DON'T KNOW WHO YOU ARE--
--MATTER OF FACT, I'VE LOST MY MEMORY, SO I'M NOT EVEN SURE WHO I AM--
--BUT LEAVING AN OLD WOMAN TO GET MAULED BY A COUPLE OF FLYING, SNAKE-HAIRED LADIES ISN'T AN OPTION.
NOT MUCH FARTHER NOW, DEAR. JUST THROUGH THAT TUNNEL AND ACROSS THE RIVER BEYOND.
THE TUNNEL WITH THE ARMED GUARDS OUT FRONT? THAT TUNNEL?
OH, THEY'LL LET YOU IN. YOU CAN TRUST THEM. THEIR SPEARS AND ARROWS AREN'T MEANT FOR YOU.
RIGHT. THE WAY THINGS HAVE BEEN GOING FOR ME LATELY, I HIGHLY DOUBT THAT.

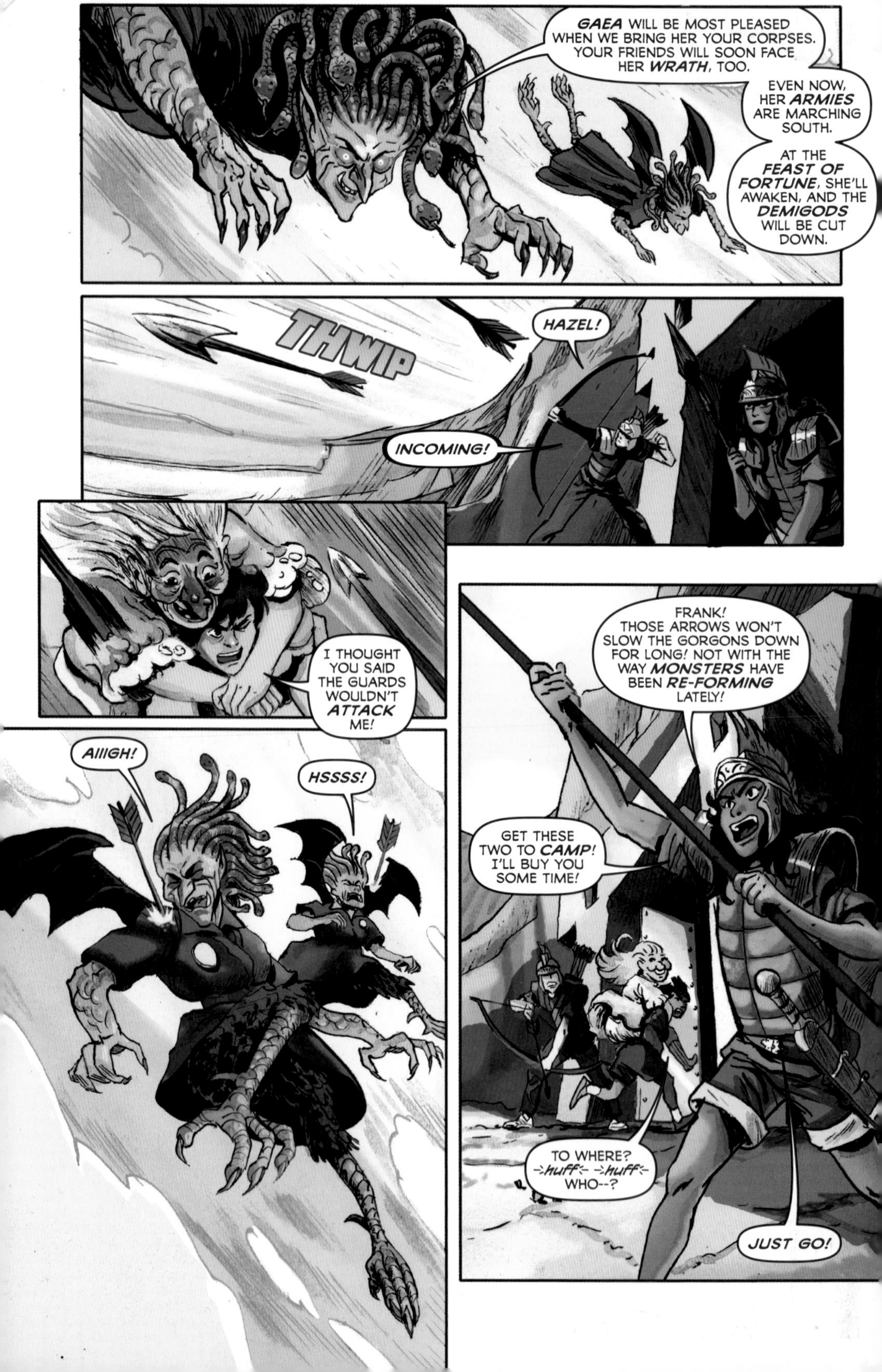
GAEA WILL BE MOST PLEASED WHEN WE BRING HER YOUR CORPSES. YOUR FRIENDS WILL SOON FACE HER WRATH, TOO.
EVEN NOW, HER ARMIES ARE MARCHING SOUTH.
AT THE FEAST OF FORTUNE, SHE'LL AWAKEN, AND THE DEMIGODS WILL BE CUT DOWN.
THWIP
HAZEL!
INCOMING!
I THOUGHT YOU SAID THE GUARDS WOULDN'T ATTACK ME!
FRANK! THOSE ARROWS WON'T SLOW THE GORGONS DOWN FOR LONG! NOT WITH THE WAY MONSTERS HAVE BEEN RE-FORMING LATELY!
AIIIGH!
HSSSS!
GET THESE TWO TO CAMP! I'LL BUY YOU SOME TIME!
TO WHERE? huff huff WHO--?
JUST GO!

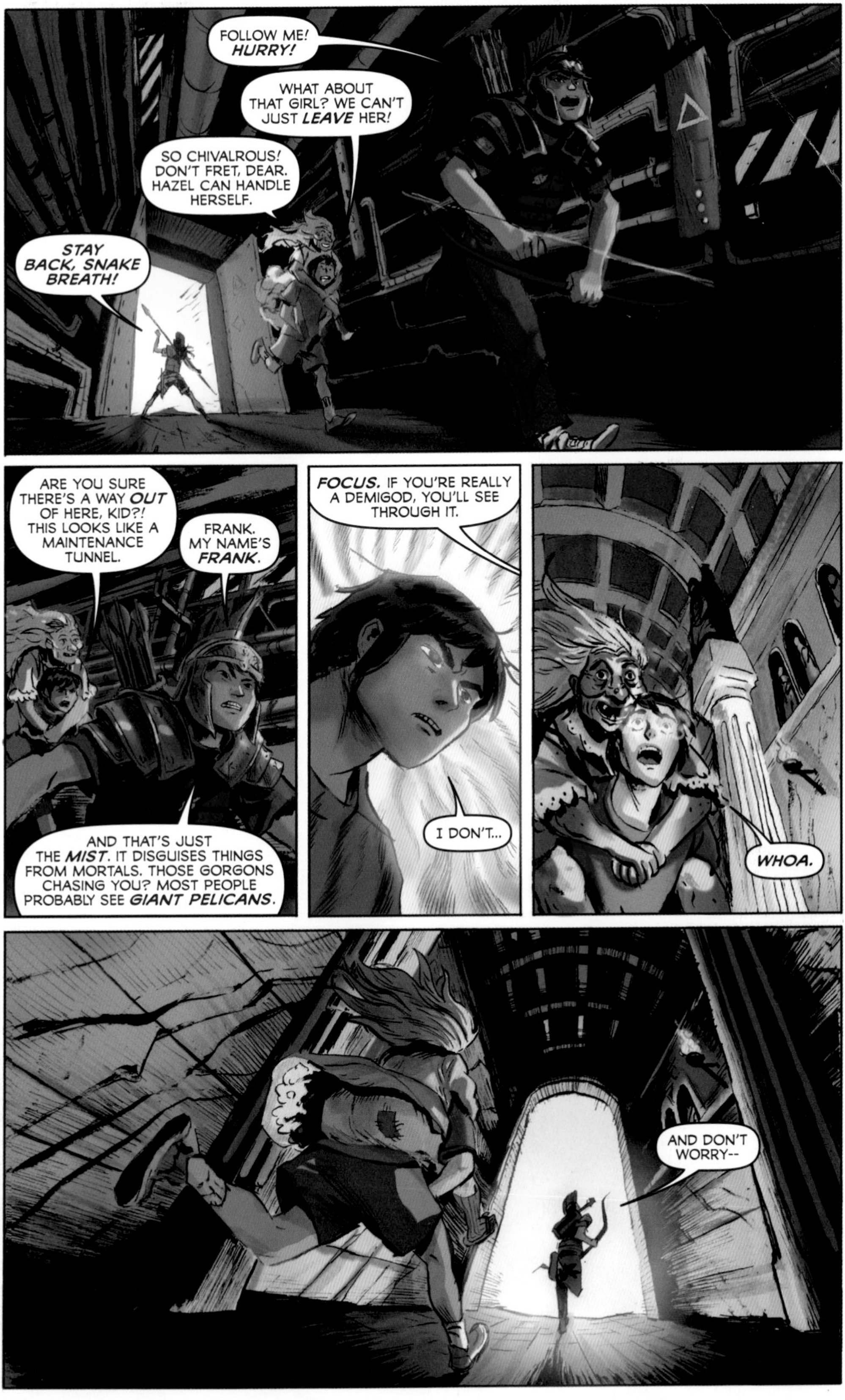
FOLLOW ME! HURRY!
WHAT ABOUT THAT GIRL? WE CAN'T JUST LEAVE HER!
SO CHIVALROUS! DON'T FRET, DEAR. HAZEL CAN HANDLE HERSELF.
STAY BACK, SNAKE BREATH!
ARE YOU SURE THERE'S A WAY OUT OF HERE, KID?! THIS LOOKS LIKE A MAINTENANCE TUNNEL.
FRANK. MY NAME'S FRANK.
AND THAT'S JUST THE MIST. IT DISGUISES THINGS FROM MORTALS. THOSE GORGONS CHASING YOU? MOST PEOPLE PROBABLY SEE GIANT PELICANS.
FOCUS. IF YOU'RE REALLY A DEMIGOD, YOU'LL SEE THROUGH IT.
I DON'T...
WHOA.
AND DON'T WORRY--

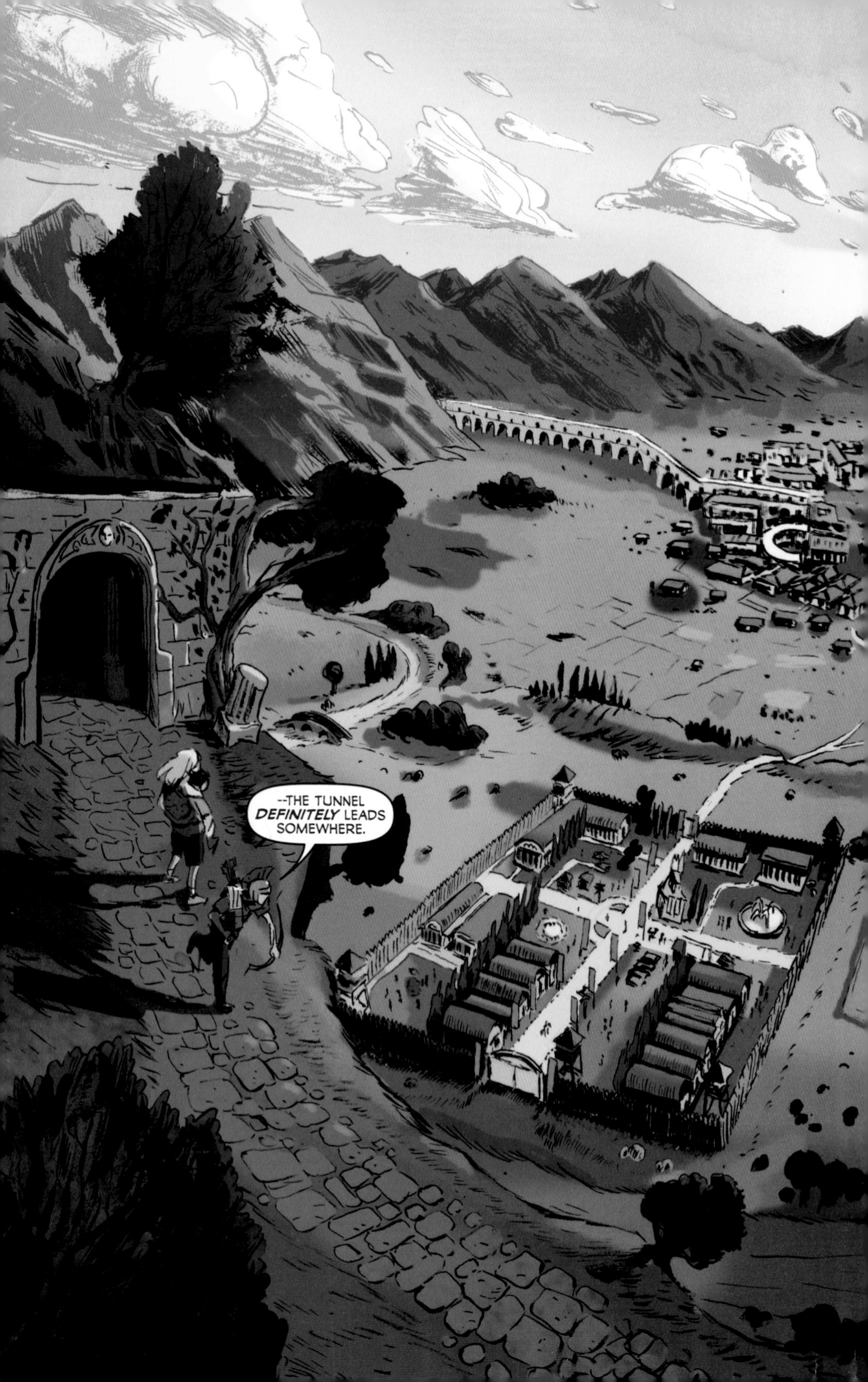
--THE TUNNEL DEFINITELY LEADS SOMEWHERE.

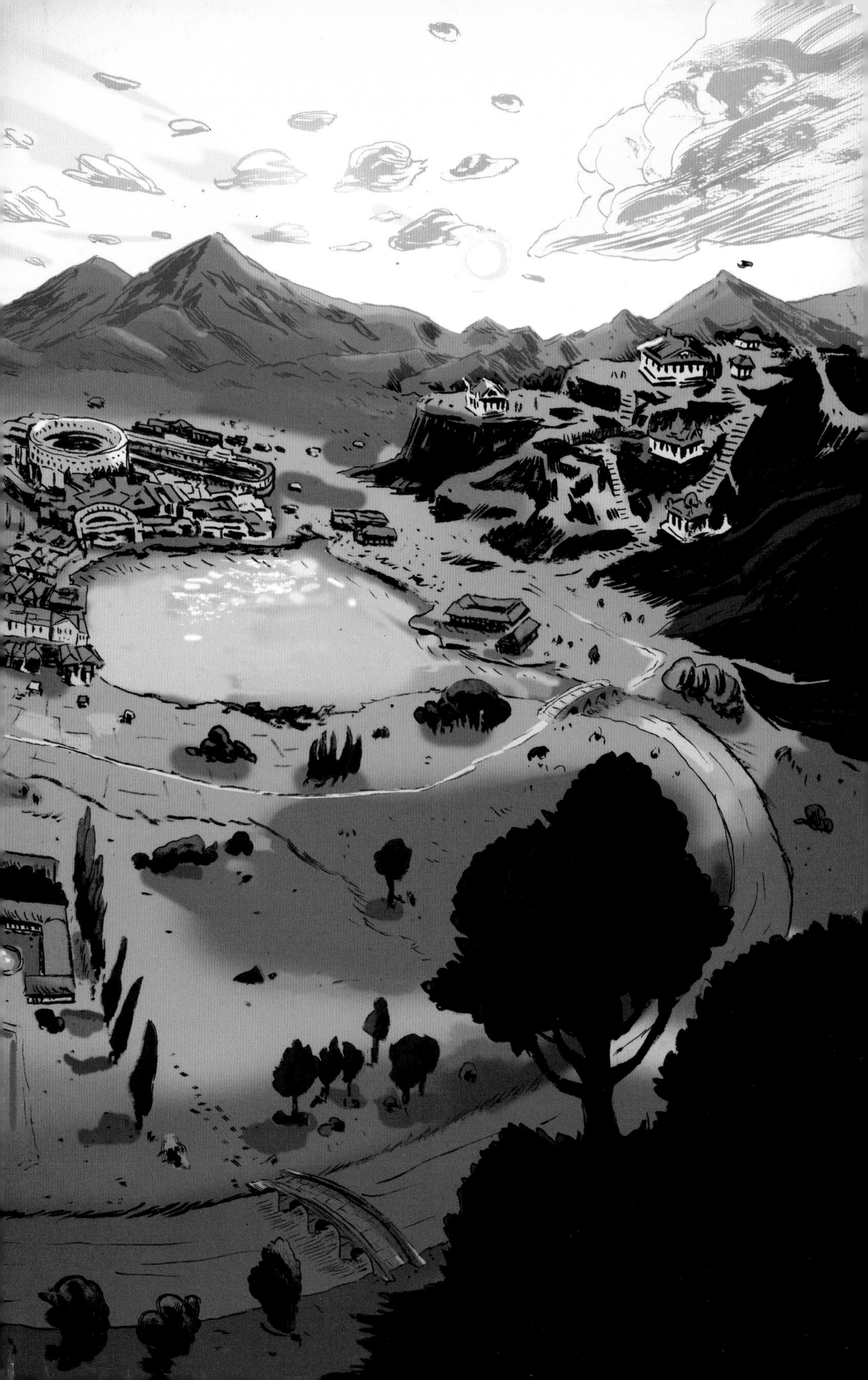

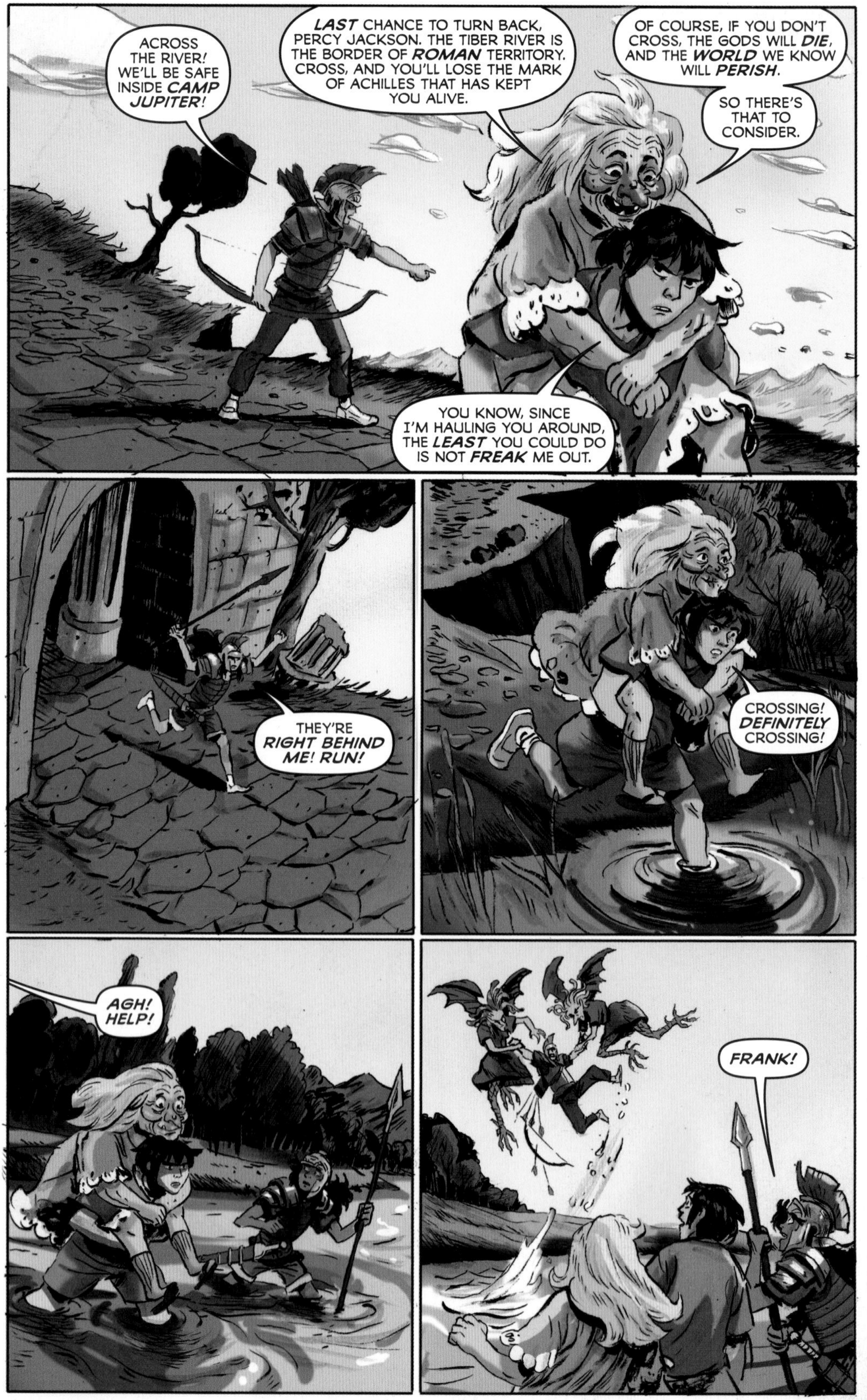
ACROSS THE RIVER! WE'LL BE SAFE INSIDE CAMP JUPITER!
LAST CHANCE TO TURN BACK, PERCY JACKSON. THE TIBER RIVER IS THE BORDER OF ROMAN TERRITORY. CROSS, AND YOU'LL LOSE THE MARK OF ACHILLES THAT HAS KEPT YOU ALIVE.
OF COURSE, IF YOU DON'T CROSS, THE GODS WILL DIE, AND THE WORLD WE KNOW WILL PERISH.
SO THERE'S THAT TO CONSIDER.
YOU KNOW, SINCE I'M HAULING YOU AROUND, THE LEAST YOU COULD DO IS NOT FREAK ME OUT.
THEY'RE RIGHT BEHIND ME! RUN!
CROSSING! DEFINITELY CROSSING!
AGH! HELP!
FRANK!

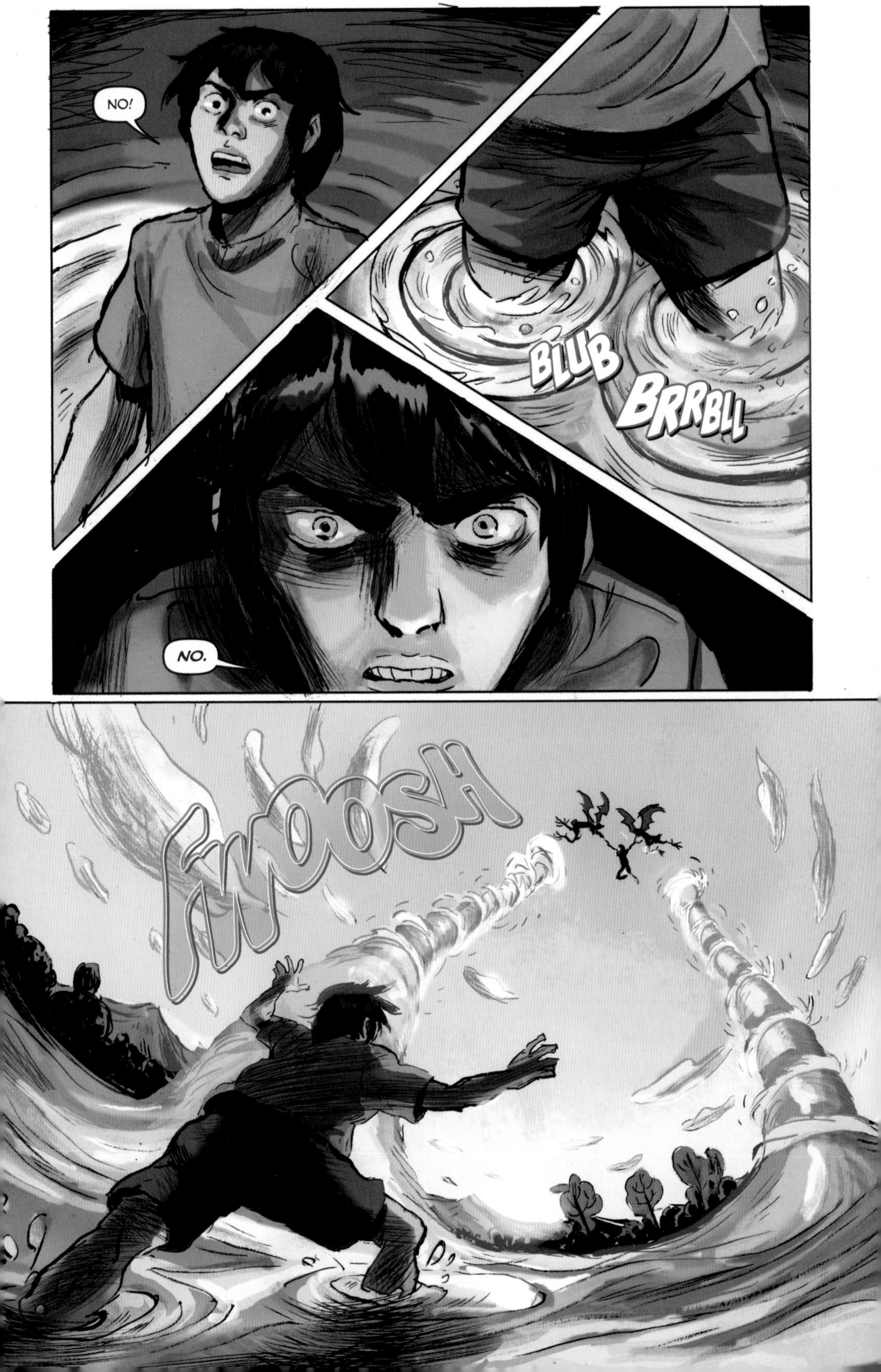
NO!
BLUB
BRRBLL
NO.
FWOOSH

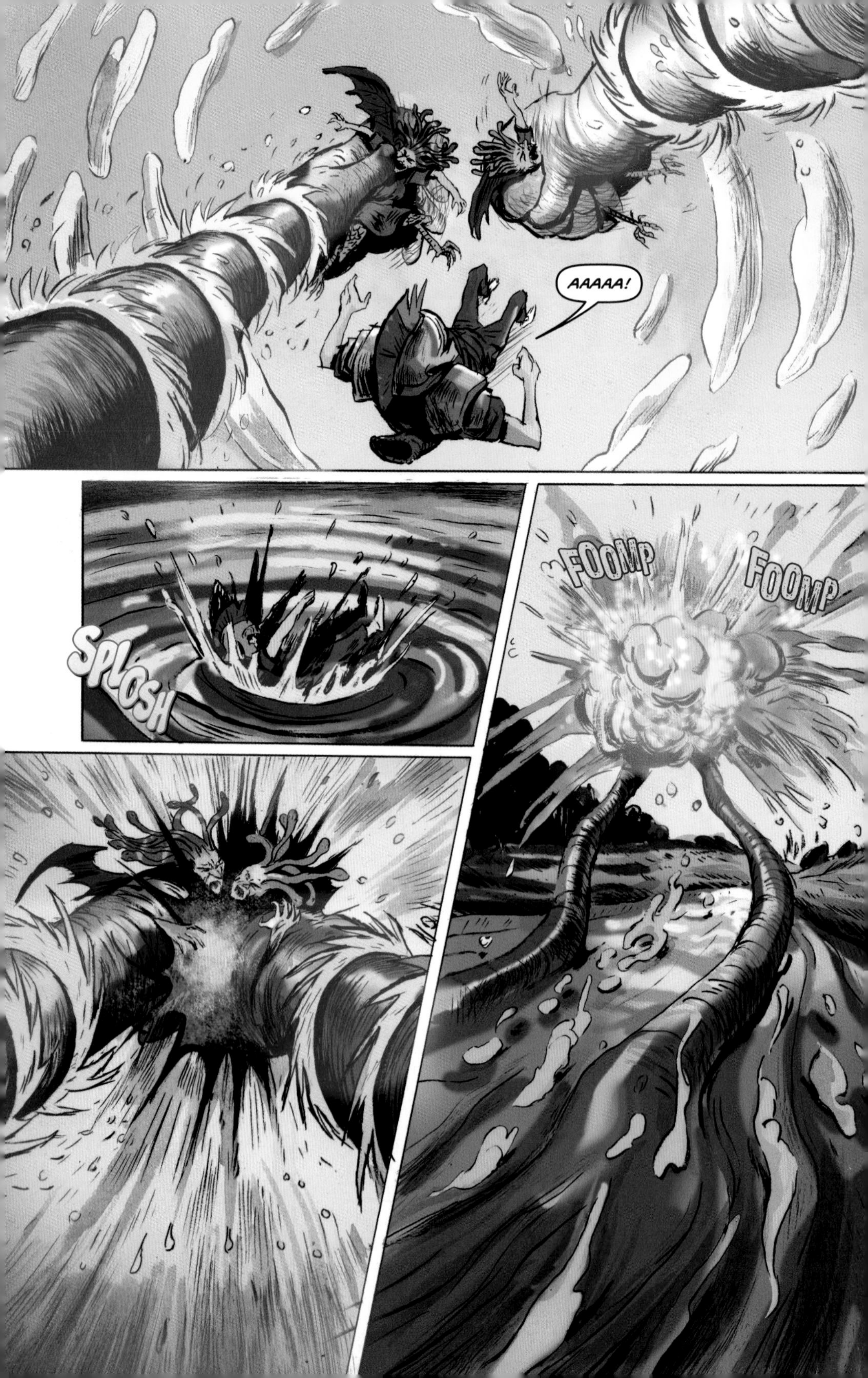
AAAAA!
SPLOSH
FOOMP
FOOMP

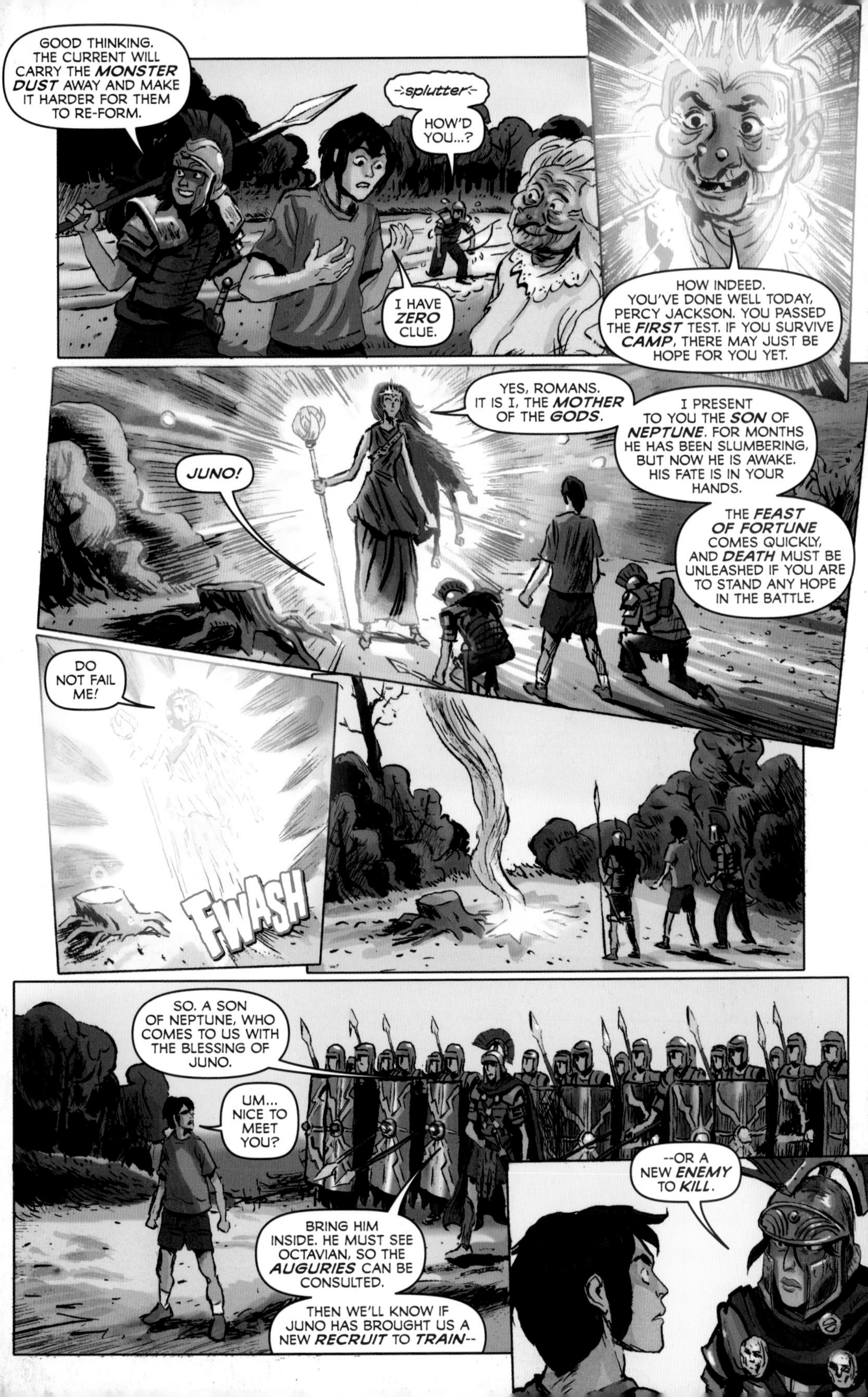
GOOD THINKING. THE CURRENT WILL CARRY THE MONSTER DUST AWAY AND MAKE IT HARDER FOR THEM TO RE-FORM.
splutter
HOW'D YOU...?
I HAVE ZERO CLUE.
HOW INDEED. YOU'VE DONE WELL TODAY, PERCY JACKSON. YOU PASSED THE FIRST TEST. IF YOU SURVIVE CAMP, THERE MAY JUST BE HOPE FOR YOU YET.
JUNO!
YES, ROMANS. IT IS I, THE MOTHER OF THE GODS.
I PRESENT TO YOU THE SON OF NEPTUNE. FOR MONTHS HE HAS BEEN SLUMBERING, BUT NOW HE IS AWAKE. HIS FATE IS IN YOUR HANDS.
THE FEAST OF FORTUNE COMES QUICKLY, AND DEATH MUST BE UNLEASHED IF YOU ARE TO STAND ANY HOPE IN THE BATTLE.
DO NOT FAIL ME!
FWASH
SO. A SON OF NEPTUNE, WHO COMES TO US WITH THE BLESSING OF JUNO.
UM... NICE TO MEET YOU?
BRING HIM INSIDE. HE MUST SEE OCTAVIAN, SO THE AUGURIES CAN BE CONSULTED.
THEN WE'LL KNOW IF JUNO HAS BROUGHT US A NEW RECRUIT TO TRAIN--
--OR A NEW ENEMY TO KILL.

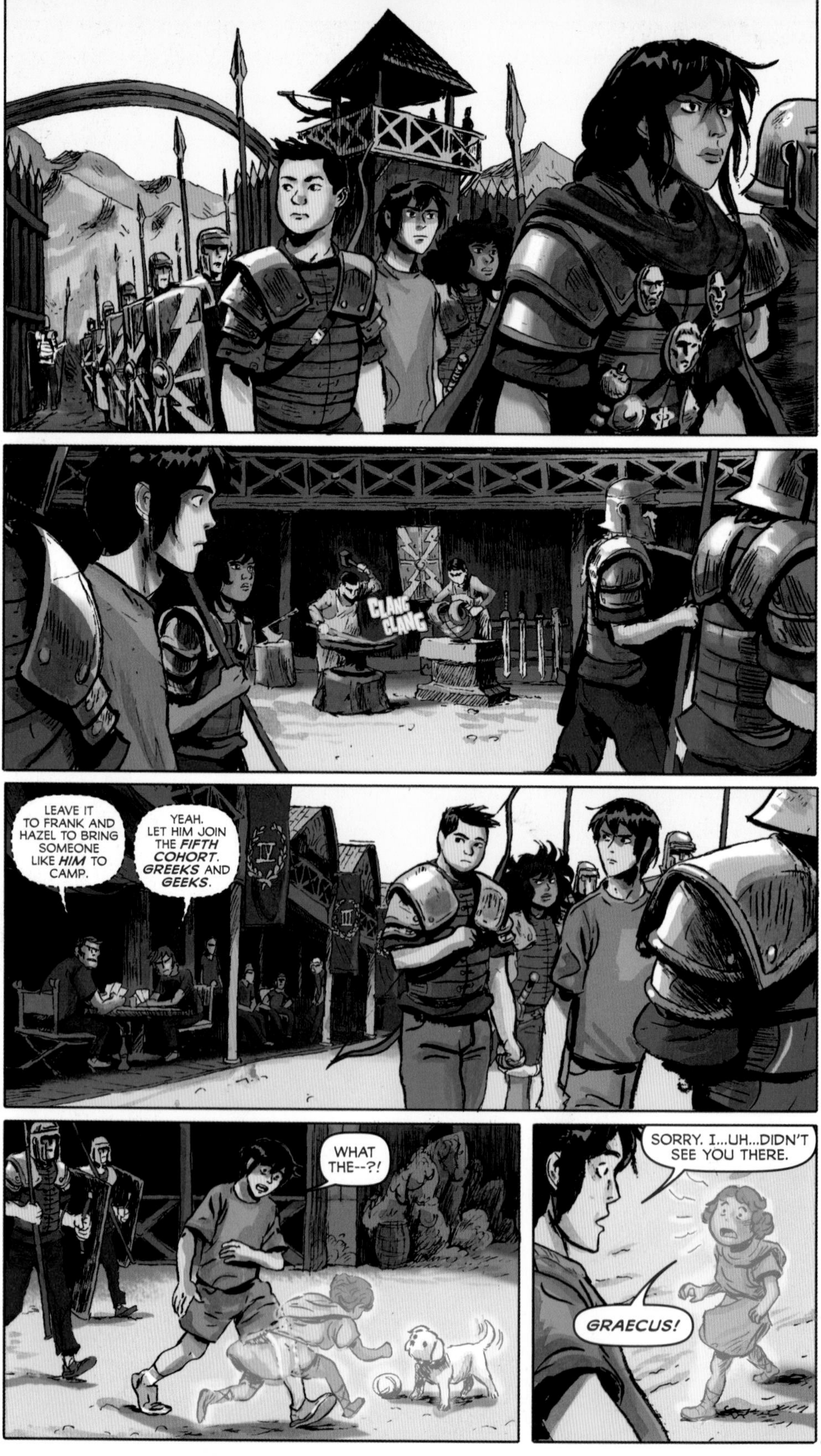
CLANG CLANG
LEAVE IT TO FRANK AND HAZEL TO BRING SOMEONE LIKE *HIM* TO CAMP.
YEAH. LET HIM JOIN THE *FIFTH COHORT*. *GREEKS* AND *GEEKS*.
WHAT THE--?!
SORRY. I...UH...DIDN'T SEE YOU THERE.
GRAECUS!

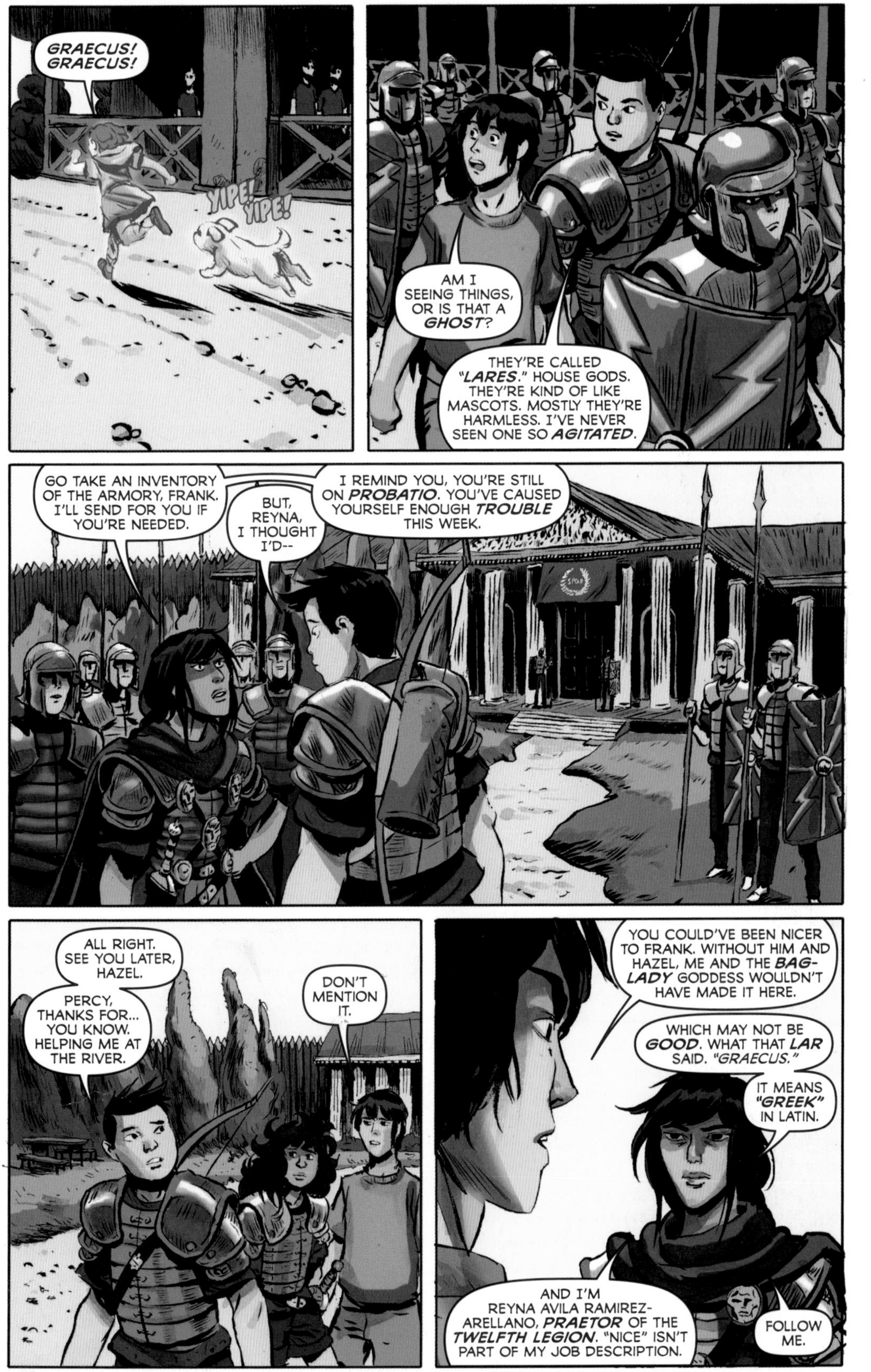
GRAECUS! GRAECUS!
YIPE! YIPE!
AM I SEEING THINGS, OR IS THAT A GHOST?
THEY'RE CALLED "LARES." HOUSE GODS. THEY'RE KIND OF LIKE MASCOTS. MOSTLY THEY'RE HARMLESS. I'VE NEVER SEEN ONE SO AGITATED.
GO TAKE AN INVENTORY OF THE ARMORY, FRANK. I'LL SEND FOR YOU IF YOU'RE NEEDED.
BUT, REYNA, I THOUGHT I'D--
I REMIND YOU, YOU'RE STILL ON PROBATIO. YOU'VE CAUSED YOURSELF ENOUGH TROUBLE THIS WEEK.
ALL RIGHT. SEE YOU LATER, HAZEL.
PERCY, THANKS FOR... YOU KNOW. HELPING ME AT THE RIVER.
DON'T MENTION IT.
YOU COULD'VE BEEN NICER TO FRANK. WITHOUT HIM AND HAZEL, ME AND THE BAG-LADY GODDESS WOULDN'T HAVE MADE IT HERE.
WHICH MAY NOT BE GOOD. WHAT THAT LAR SAID. "GRAECUS."
IT MEANS "GREEK" IN LATIN.
AND I'M REYNA AVILA RAMIREZ-ARELLANO, PRAETOR OF THE TWELFTH LEGION. "NICE" ISN'T PART OF MY JOB DESCRIPTION.
FOLLOW ME.

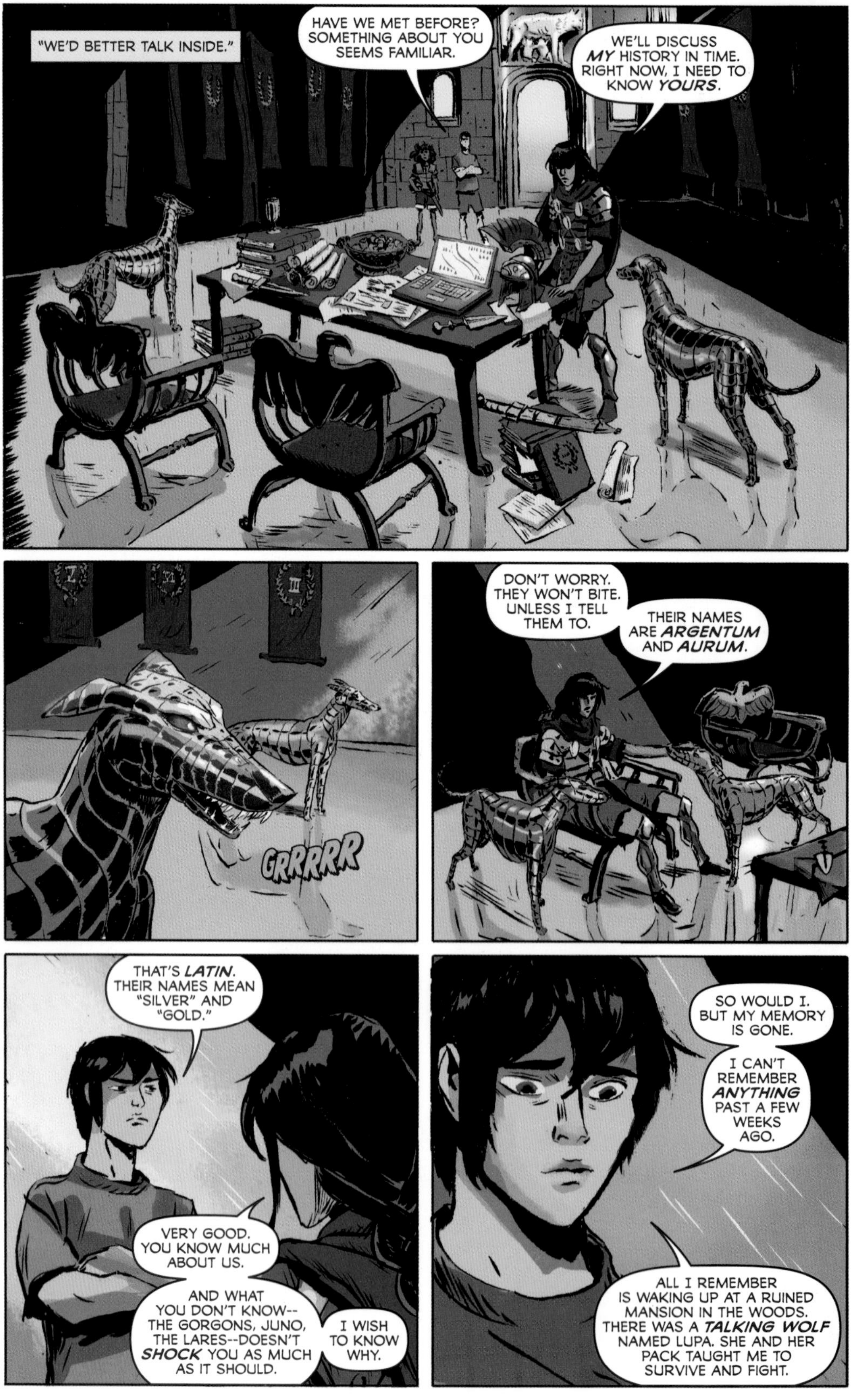
"WE'D BETTER TALK INSIDE."
HAVE WE MET BEFORE? SOMETHING ABOUT YOU SEEMS FAMILIAR.
WE'LL DISCUSS MY HISTORY IN TIME. RIGHT NOW, I NEED TO KNOW YOURS.
GRRRRR
DON'T WORRY. THEY WON'T BITE. UNLESS I TELL THEM TO.
THEIR NAMES ARE ARGENTUM AND AURUM.
THAT'S LATIN. THEIR NAMES MEAN "SILVER" AND "GOLD."
VERY GOOD. YOU KNOW MUCH ABOUT US.
AND WHAT YOU DON'T KNOW-- THE GORGONS, JUNO, THE LARES--DOESN'T SHOCK YOU AS MUCH AS IT SHOULD.
I WISH TO KNOW WHY.
SO WOULD I. BUT MY MEMORY IS GONE.
I CAN'T REMEMBER ANYTHING PAST A FEW WEEKS AGO.
ALL I REMEMBER IS WAKING UP AT A RUINED MANSION IN THE WOODS. THERE WAS A TALKING WOLF NAMED LUPA. SHE AND HER PACK TAUGHT ME TO SURVIVE AND FIGHT.

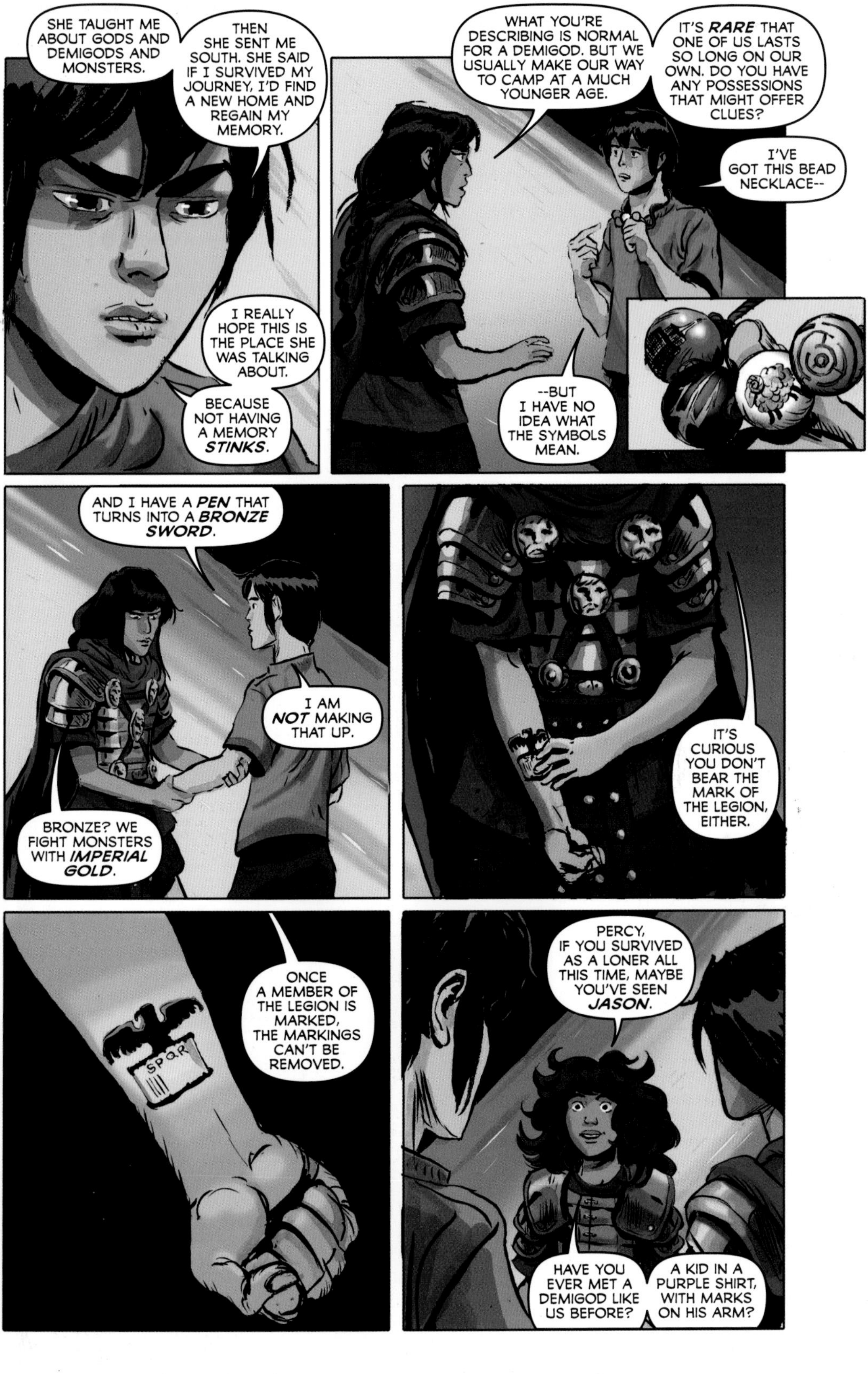
SHE TAUGHT ME ABOUT GODS AND DEMIGODS AND MONSTERS.
THEN SHE SENT ME SOUTH. SHE SAID IF I SURVIVED MY JOURNEY, I'D FIND A NEW HOME AND REGAIN MY MEMORY.
I REALLY HOPE THIS IS THE PLACE SHE WAS TALKING ABOUT.
BECAUSE NOT HAVING A MEMORY *STINKS*.
WHAT YOU'RE DESCRIBING IS NORMAL FOR A DEMIGOD. BUT WE USUALLY MAKE OUR WAY TO CAMP AT A MUCH YOUNGER AGE.
IT'S *RARE* THAT ONE OF US LASTS SO LONG ON OUR OWN. DO YOU HAVE ANY POSSESSIONS THAT MIGHT OFFER CLUES?
I'VE GOT THIS BEAD NECKLACE--
--BUT I HAVE NO IDEA WHAT THE SYMBOLS MEAN.
AND I HAVE A *PEN* THAT TURNS INTO A *BRONZE SWORD*.
I AM *NOT* MAKING THAT UP.
BRONZE? WE FIGHT MONSTERS WITH *IMPERIAL GOLD*.
IT'S CURIOUS YOU DON'T BEAR THE MARK OF THE LEGION, EITHER.
SPQR
ONCE A MEMBER OF THE LEGION IS MARKED, THE MARKINGS CAN'T BE REMOVED.
PERCY, IF YOU SURVIVED AS A LONER ALL THIS TIME, MAYBE YOU'VE SEEN *JASON*.
HAVE YOU EVER MET A DEMIGOD LIKE US BEFORE?
A KID IN A PURPLE SHIRT, WITH MARKS ON HIS ARM?

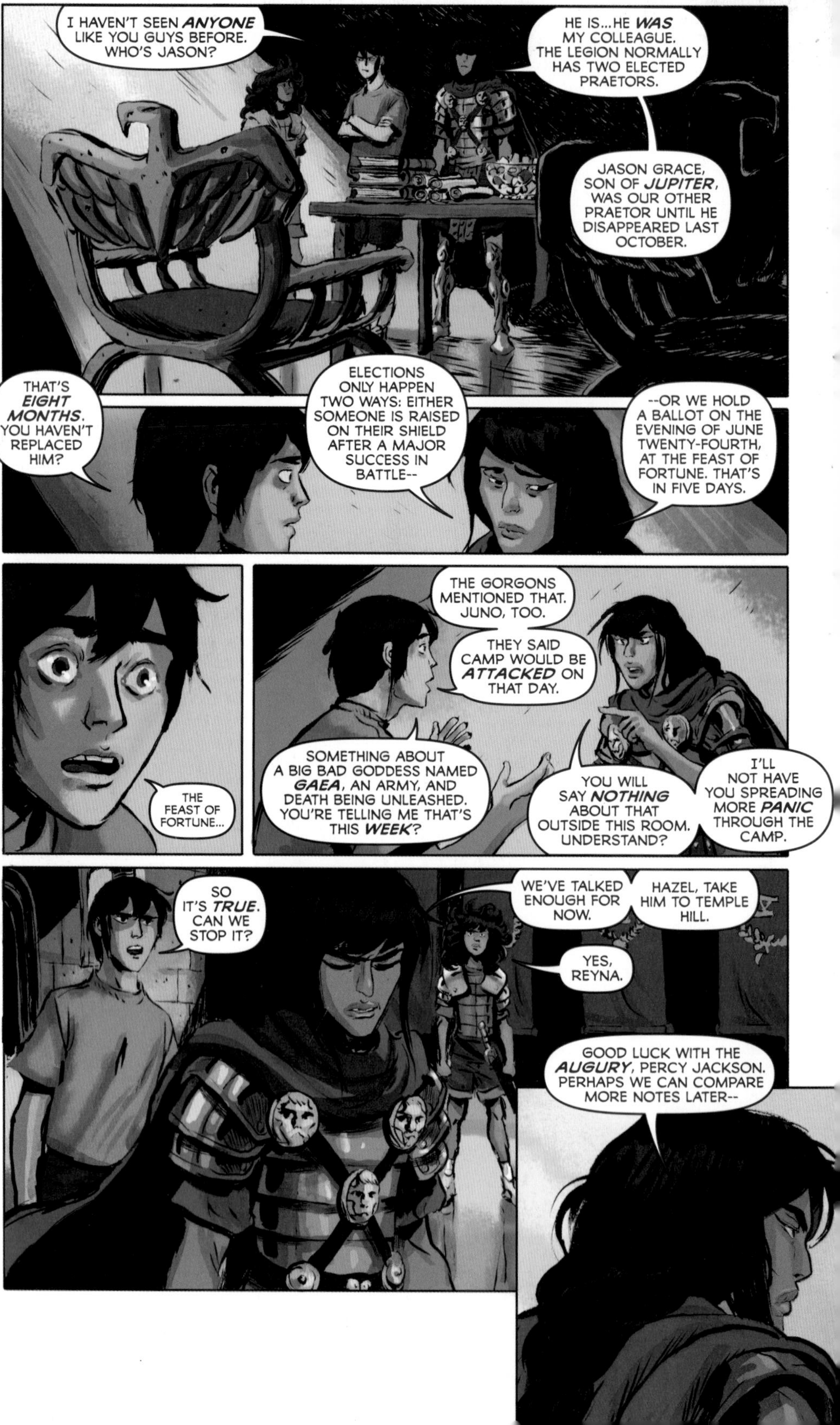
I HAVEN'T SEEN ANYONE LIKE YOU GUYS BEFORE. WHO'S JASON?
HE IS...HE WAS MY COLLEAGUE. THE LEGION NORMALLY HAS TWO ELECTED PRAETORS.
JASON GRACE, SON OF JUPITER, WAS OUR OTHER PRAETOR UNTIL HE DISAPPEARED LAST OCTOBER.
THAT'S EIGHT MONTHS. YOU HAVEN'T REPLACED HIM?
ELECTIONS ONLY HAPPEN TWO WAYS: EITHER SOMEONE IS RAISED ON THEIR SHIELD AFTER A MAJOR SUCCESS IN BATTLE--
--OR WE HOLD A BALLOT ON THE EVENING OF JUNE TWENTY-FOURTH, AT THE FEAST OF FORTUNE. THAT'S IN FIVE DAYS.
THE FEAST OF FORTUNE...
THE GORGONS MENTIONED THAT. JUNO, TOO.
THEY SAID CAMP WOULD BE ATTACKED ON THAT DAY.
SOMETHING ABOUT A BIG BAD GODDESS NAMED GAEA, AN ARMY, AND DEATH BEING UNLEASHED. YOU'RE TELLING ME THAT'S THIS WEEK?
YOU WILL SAY NOTHING ABOUT THAT OUTSIDE THIS ROOM. UNDERSTAND?
I'LL NOT HAVE YOU SPREADING MORE PANIC THROUGH THE CAMP.
SO IT'S TRUE. CAN WE STOP IT?
WE'VE TALKED ENOUGH FOR NOW.
HAZEL, TAKE HIM TO TEMPLE HILL.
YES, REYNA.
GOOD LUCK WITH THE AUGURY, PERCY JACKSON. PERHAPS WE CAN COMPARE MORE NOTES LATER--

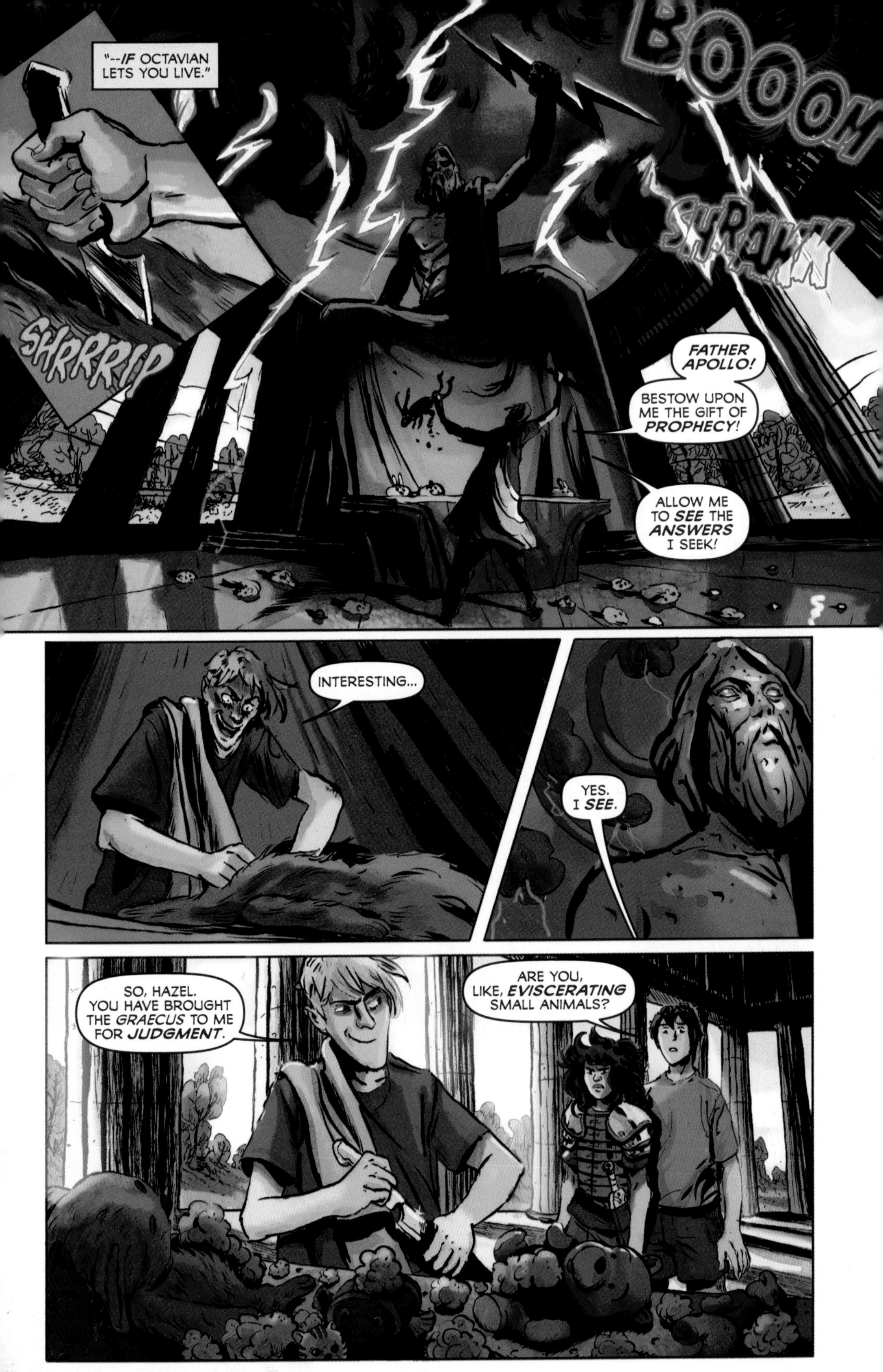
"--*IF* OCTAVIAN LETS YOU LIVE."
SHRRRIP
BOOOOM
SHRAWW
FATHER APOLLO!
BESTOW UPON ME THE GIFT OF ***PROPHECY***!
ALLOW ME TO ***SEE*** THE ***ANSWERS*** I SEEK!
INTERESTING...
YES. I ***SEE***.
SO, HAZEL. YOU HAVE BROUGHT THE *GRAECUS* TO ME FOR ***JUDGMENT***.
ARE YOU, LIKE, ***EVISCERATING*** SMALL ANIMALS?

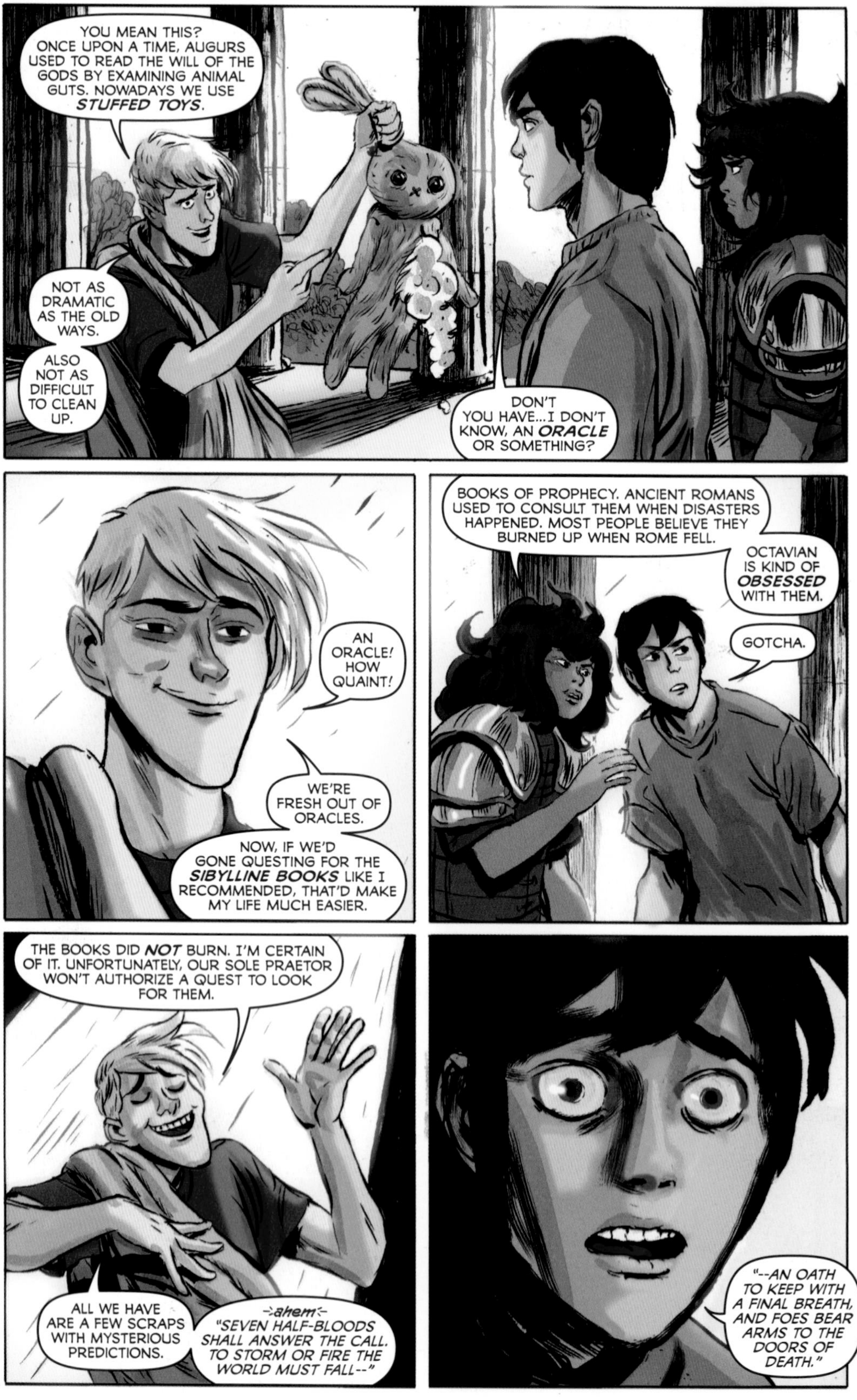
YOU MEAN THIS? ONCE UPON A TIME, AUGURS USED TO READ THE WILL OF THE GODS BY EXAMINING ANIMAL GUTS. NOWADAYS WE USE STUFFED TOYS.
NOT AS DRAMATIC AS THE OLD WAYS.
ALSO NOT AS DIFFICULT TO CLEAN UP.
DON'T YOU HAVE...I DON'T KNOW, AN ORACLE OR SOMETHING?
AN ORACLE! HOW QUAINT!
WE'RE FRESH OUT OF ORACLES.
NOW, IF WE'D GONE QUESTING FOR THE SIBYLLINE BOOKS LIKE I RECOMMENDED, THAT'D MAKE MY LIFE MUCH EASIER.
BOOKS OF PROPHECY. ANCIENT ROMANS USED TO CONSULT THEM WHEN DISASTERS HAPPENED. MOST PEOPLE BELIEVE THEY BURNED UP WHEN ROME FELL.
OCTAVIAN IS KIND OF OBSESSED WITH THEM.
GOTCHA.
THE BOOKS DID NOT BURN. I'M CERTAIN OF IT. UNFORTUNATELY, OUR SOLE PRAETOR WON'T AUTHORIZE A QUEST TO LOOK FOR THEM.
ALL WE HAVE ARE A FEW SCRAPS WITH MYSTERIOUS PREDICTIONS.
-ahem- "SEVEN HALF-BLOODS SHALL ANSWER THE CALL. TO STORM OR FIRE THE WORLD MUST FALL--"
"--AN OATH TO KEEP WITH A FINAL BREATH, AND FOES BEAR ARMS TO THE DOORS OF DEATH."

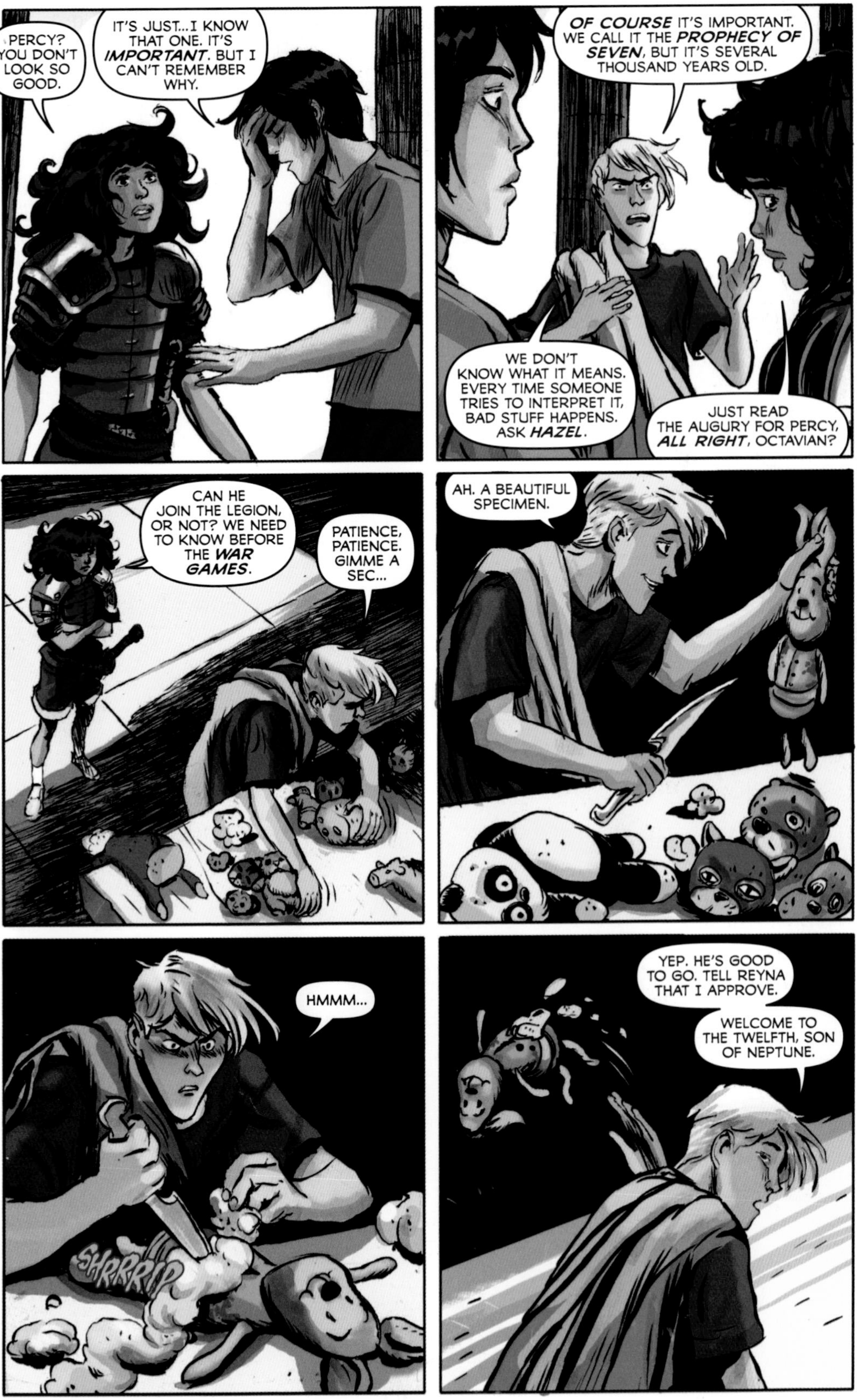
PERCY? YOU DON'T LOOK SO GOOD.
IT'S JUST...I KNOW THAT ONE. IT'S IMPORTANT. BUT I CAN'T REMEMBER WHY.
OF COURSE IT'S IMPORTANT. WE CALL IT THE PROPHECY OF SEVEN, BUT IT'S SEVERAL THOUSAND YEARS OLD.
WE DON'T KNOW WHAT IT MEANS. EVERY TIME SOMEONE TRIES TO INTERPRET IT, BAD STUFF HAPPENS. ASK HAZEL.
JUST READ THE AUGURY FOR PERCY, ALL RIGHT, OCTAVIAN?
CAN HE JOIN THE LEGION, OR NOT? WE NEED TO KNOW BEFORE THE WAR GAMES.
PATIENCE, PATIENCE. GIMME A SEC...
AH. A BEAUTIFUL SPECIMEN.
HMMM...
SHRRRIP
YEP. HE'S GOOD TO GO. TELL REYNA THAT I APPROVE.
WELCOME TO THE TWELFTH, SON OF NEPTUNE.

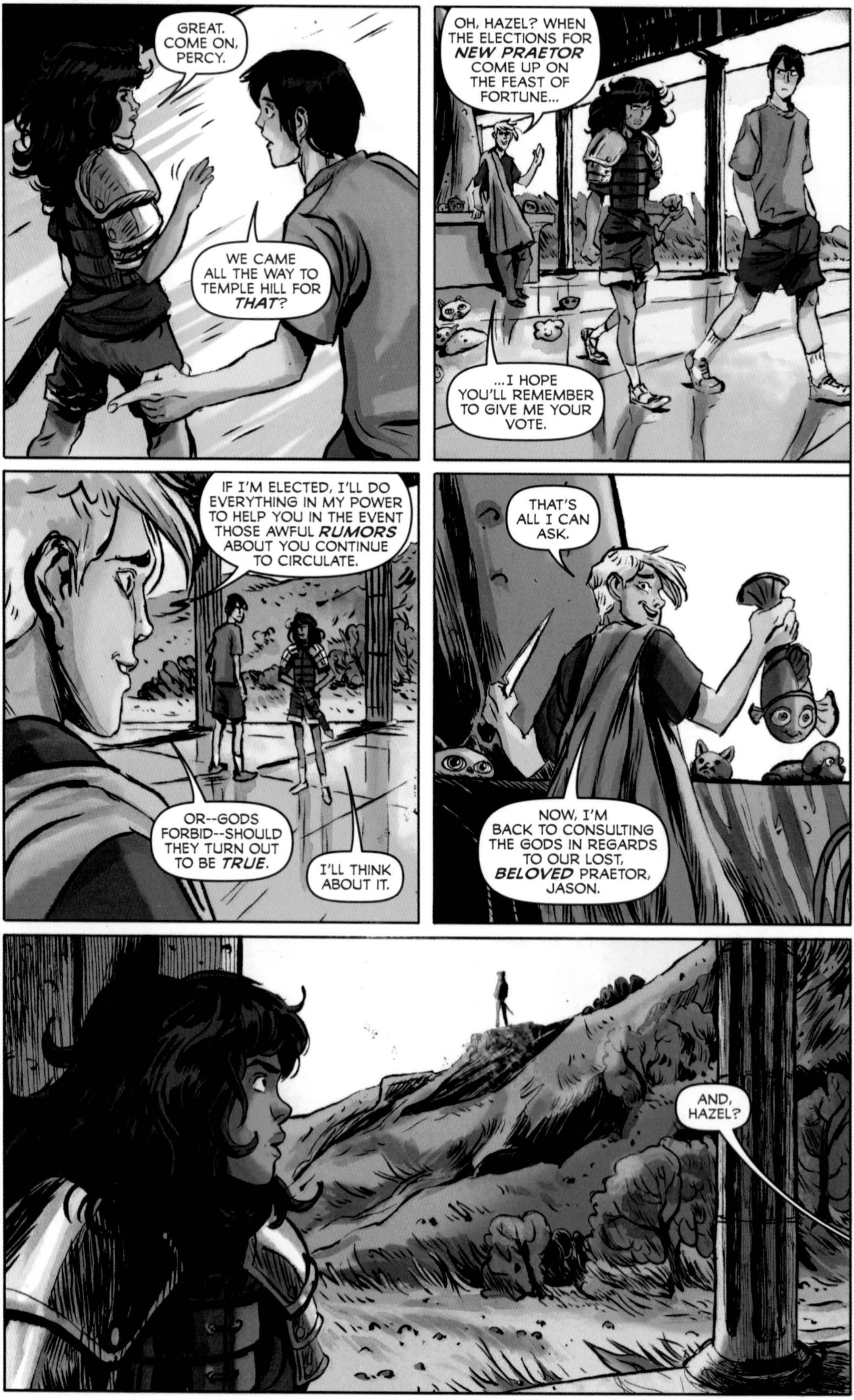
GREAT. COME ON, PERCY.
WE CAME ALL THE WAY TO TEMPLE HILL FOR *THAT*?
OH, HAZEL? WHEN THE ELECTIONS FOR ***NEW PRAETOR*** COME UP ON THE FEAST OF FORTUNE...
...I HOPE YOU'LL REMEMBER TO GIVE ME YOUR VOTE.
IF I'M ELECTED, I'LL DO EVERYTHING IN MY POWER TO HELP YOU IN THE EVENT THOSE AWFUL ***RUMORS*** ABOUT YOU CONTINUE TO CIRCULATE.
OR--GODS FORBID--SHOULD THEY TURN OUT TO BE *TRUE*.
I'LL THINK ABOUT IT.
THAT'S ALL I CAN ASK.
NOW, I'M BACK TO CONSULTING THE GODS IN REGARDS TO OUR LOST, ***BELOVED*** PRAETOR, JASON.
AND, HAZEL?

"SAY HI TO YOUR *BROTHER* FOR ME."

NICO? WHAT ARE YOU DOING HERE?

GOOD TO SEE YOU, TOO, SIS--

OH.

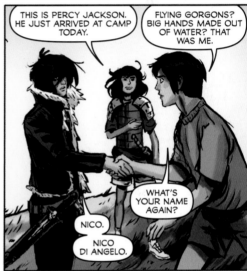

THIS IS PERCY JACKSON. HE JUST ARRIVED AT CAMP TODAY.

FLYING GORGONS? BIG HANDS MADE OUT OF WATER? THAT WAS ME.

WHAT'S YOUR NAME AGAIN?

NICO.

NICO DI ANGELO.

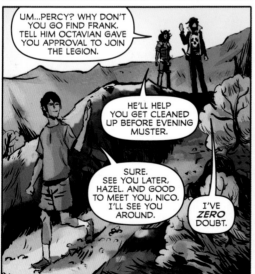

UM...PERCY? WHY DON'T YOU GO FIND FRANK. TELL HIM OCTAVIAN GAVE YOU APPROVAL TO JOIN THE LEGION.

HE'LL HELP YOU GET CLEANED UP BEFORE EVENING MUSTER.

SURE. SEE YOU LATER, HAZEL. AND GOOD TO MEET YOU, NICO. I'LL SEE YOU AROUND.

I'VE *ZERO* DOUBT.

YOU *RECOGNIZE* HIM, DON'T YOU? YOU'VE MET HIM BEFORE.

PERCY JACKSON.

HAZEL, I HAVE TO BE CAREFUL WHAT I SAY. SOME SECRETS NEED TO *STAY* SECRET. IMPORTANT THINGS ARE AT WORK HERE.

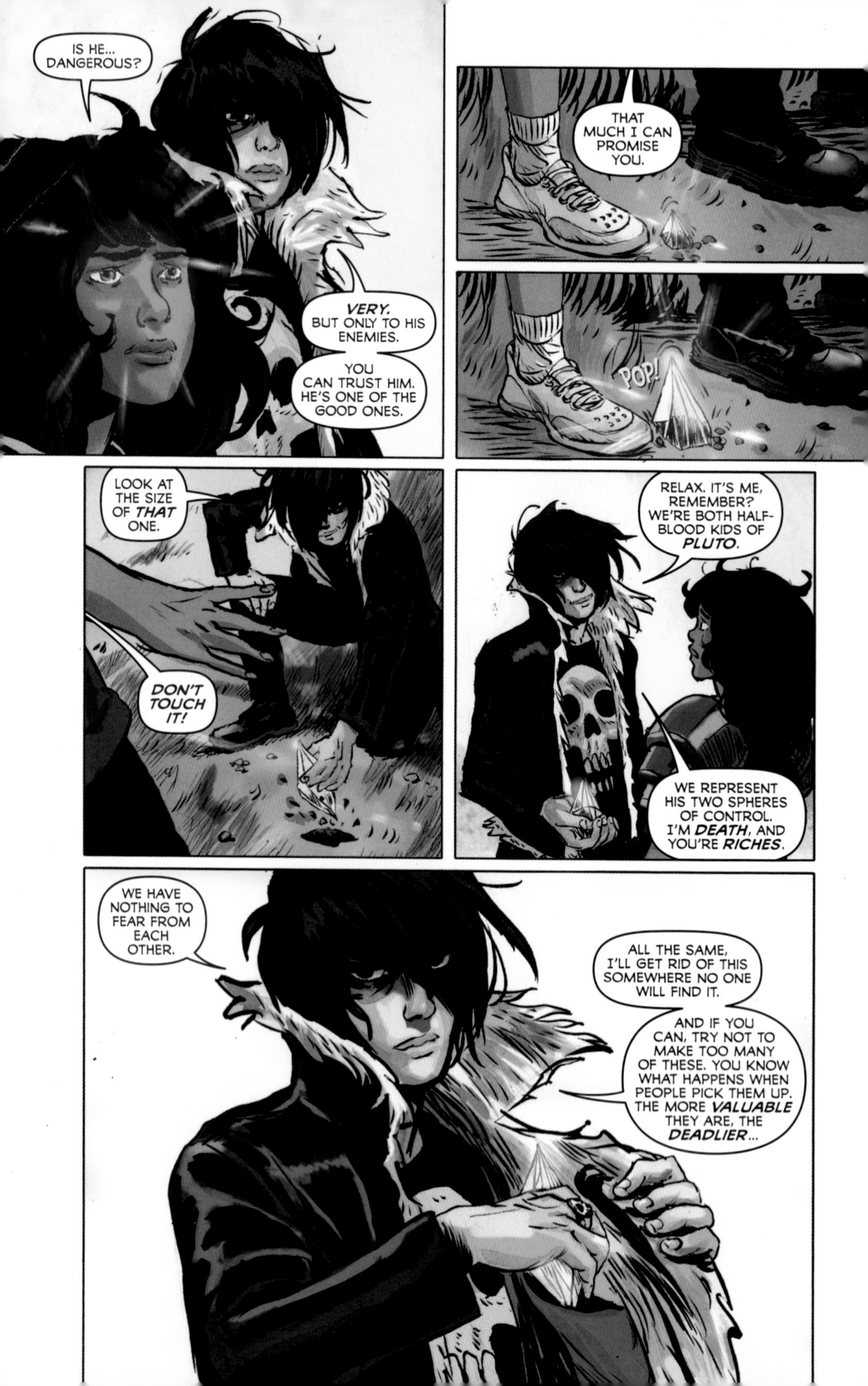
IS HE... DANGEROUS?
VERY. BUT ONLY TO HIS ENEMIES.
YOU CAN TRUST HIM. HE'S ONE OF THE GOOD ONES.
THAT MUCH I CAN PROMISE YOU.
POP!
LOOK AT THE SIZE OF THAT ONE.
DON'T TOUCH IT!
RELAX. IT'S ME, REMEMBER? WE'RE BOTH HALF-BLOOD KIDS OF PLUTO.
WE REPRESENT HIS TWO SPHERES OF CONTROL. I'M DEATH, AND YOU'RE RICHES.
WE HAVE NOTHING TO FEAR FROM EACH OTHER.
ALL THE SAME, I'LL GET RID OF THIS SOMEWHERE NO ONE WILL FIND IT.
AND IF YOU CAN, TRY NOT TO MAKE TOO MANY OF THESE. YOU KNOW WHAT HAPPENS WHEN PEOPLE PICK THEM UP. THE MORE VALUABLE THEY ARE, THE DEADLIER...

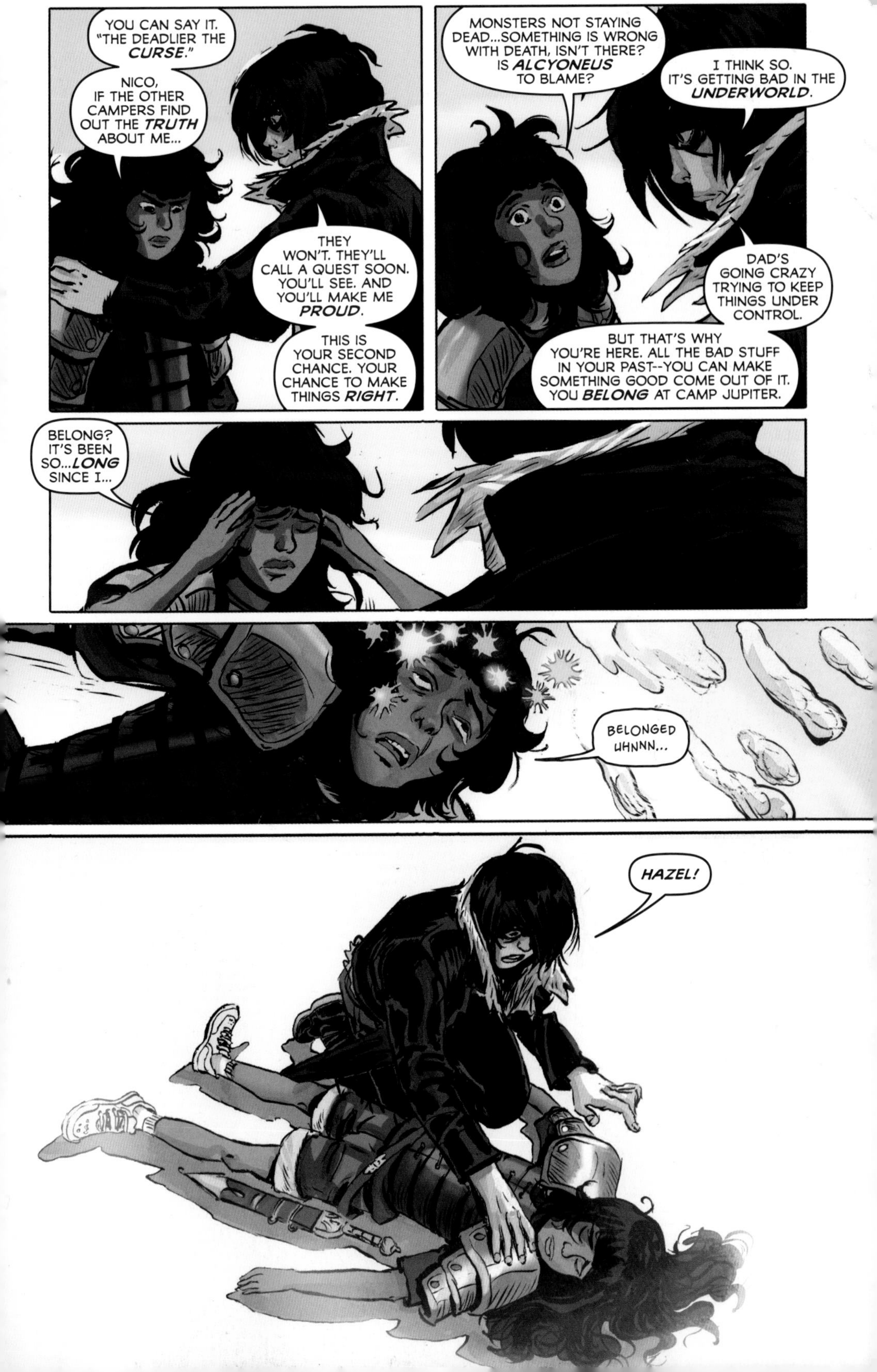
YOU CAN SAY IT. "THE DEADLIER THE CURSE."
NICO, IF THE OTHER CAMPERS FIND OUT THE TRUTH ABOUT ME...
THEY WON'T. THEY'LL CALL A QUEST SOON. YOU'LL SEE. AND YOU'LL MAKE ME PROUD.
THIS IS YOUR SECOND CHANCE. YOUR CHANCE TO MAKE THINGS RIGHT.
MONSTERS NOT STAYING DEAD...SOMETHING IS WRONG WITH DEATH, ISN'T THERE? IS ALCYONEUS TO BLAME?
I THINK SO. IT'S GETTING BAD IN THE UNDERWORLD.
DAD'S GOING CRAZY TRYING TO KEEP THINGS UNDER CONTROL.
BUT THAT'S WHY YOU'RE HERE. ALL THE BAD STUFF IN YOUR PAST--YOU CAN MAKE SOMETHING GOOD COME OUT OF IT. YOU BELONG AT CAMP JUPITER.
BELONG? IT'S BEEN SO...LONG SINCE I...
BELONGED UHNNN...
HAZEL!

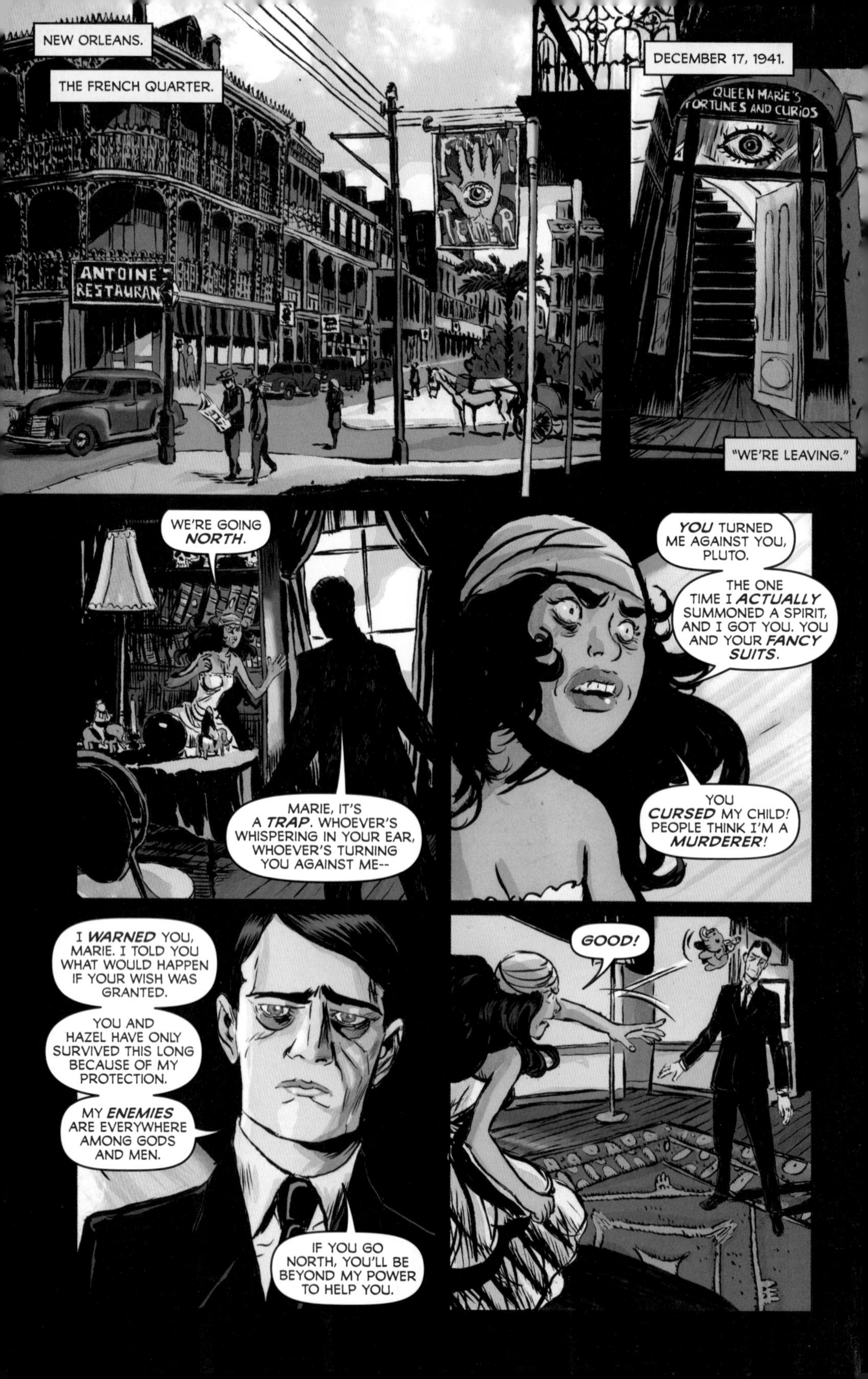
NEW ORLEANS.
THE FRENCH QUARTER.
DECEMBER 17, 1941.
ANTOINE'S RESTAURAN
QUEEN MARIE'S FORTUNES AND CURIOS
"WE'RE LEAVING."
WE'RE GOING NORTH.
MARIE, IT'S A TRAP. WHOEVER'S WHISPERING IN YOUR EAR, WHOEVER'S TURNING YOU AGAINST ME--
YOU TURNED ME AGAINST YOU, PLUTO.
THE ONE TIME I ACTUALLY SUMMONED A SPIRIT, AND I GOT YOU. YOU AND YOUR FANCY SUITS.
YOU CURSED MY CHILD! PEOPLE THINK I'M A MURDERER!
I WARNED YOU, MARIE. I TOLD YOU WHAT WOULD HAPPEN IF YOUR WISH WAS GRANTED.
YOU AND HAZEL HAVE ONLY SURVIVED THIS LONG BECAUSE OF MY PROTECTION.
MY ENEMIES ARE EVERYWHERE AMONG GODS AND MEN.
IF YOU GO NORTH, YOU'LL BE BEYOND MY POWER TO HELP YOU.
GOOD!

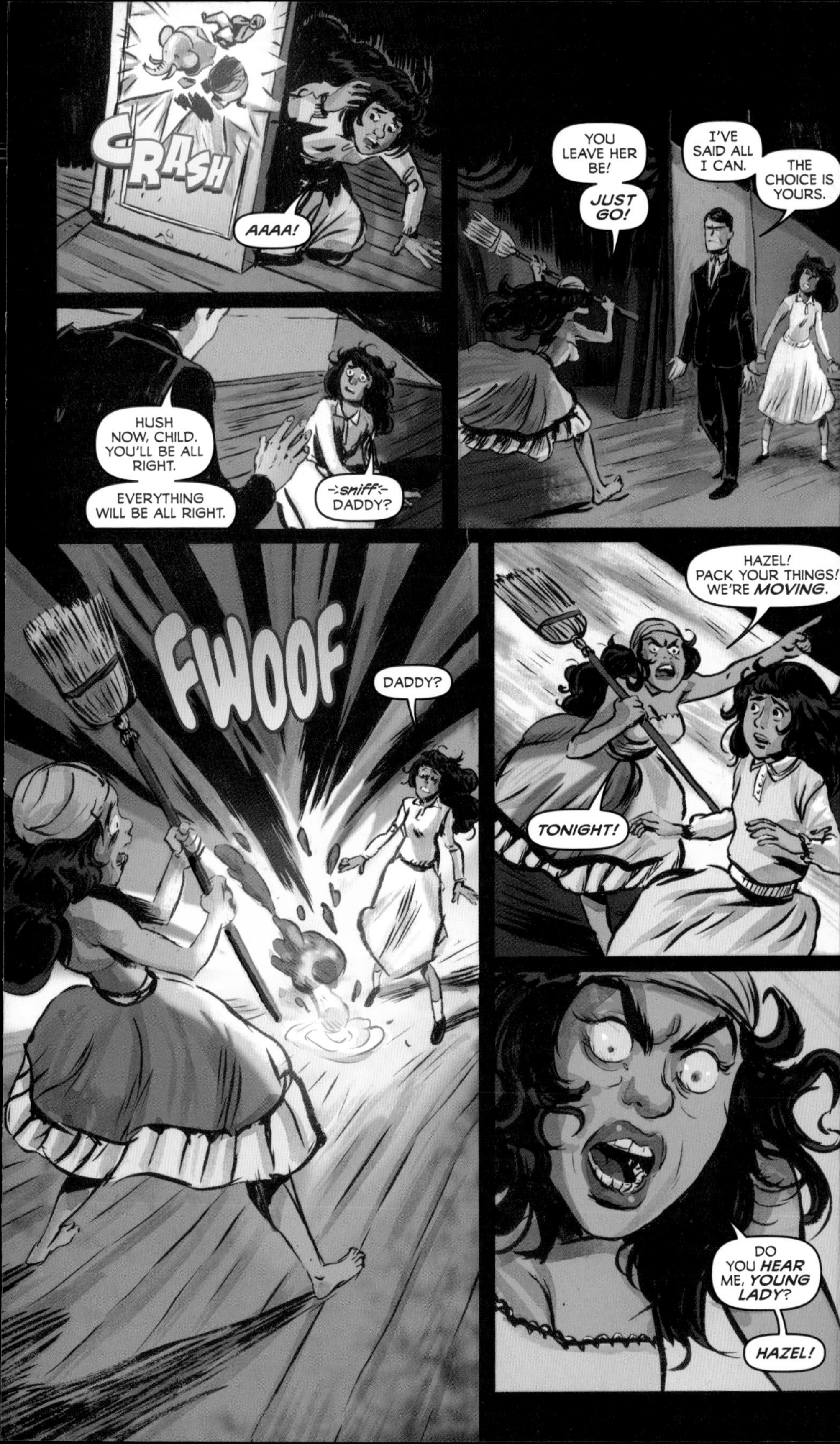
CRASH
AAAA!
HUSH NOW, CHILD. YOU'LL BE ALL RIGHT.
EVERYTHING WILL BE ALL RIGHT.
-sniff- DADDY?
YOU LEAVE HER BE! JUST GO!
I'VE SAID ALL I CAN.
THE CHOICE IS YOURS.
FWOOF
DADDY?
HAZEL! PACK YOUR THINGS! WE'RE MOVING.
TONIGHT!
DO YOU HEAR ME, YOUNG LADY?
HAZEL!

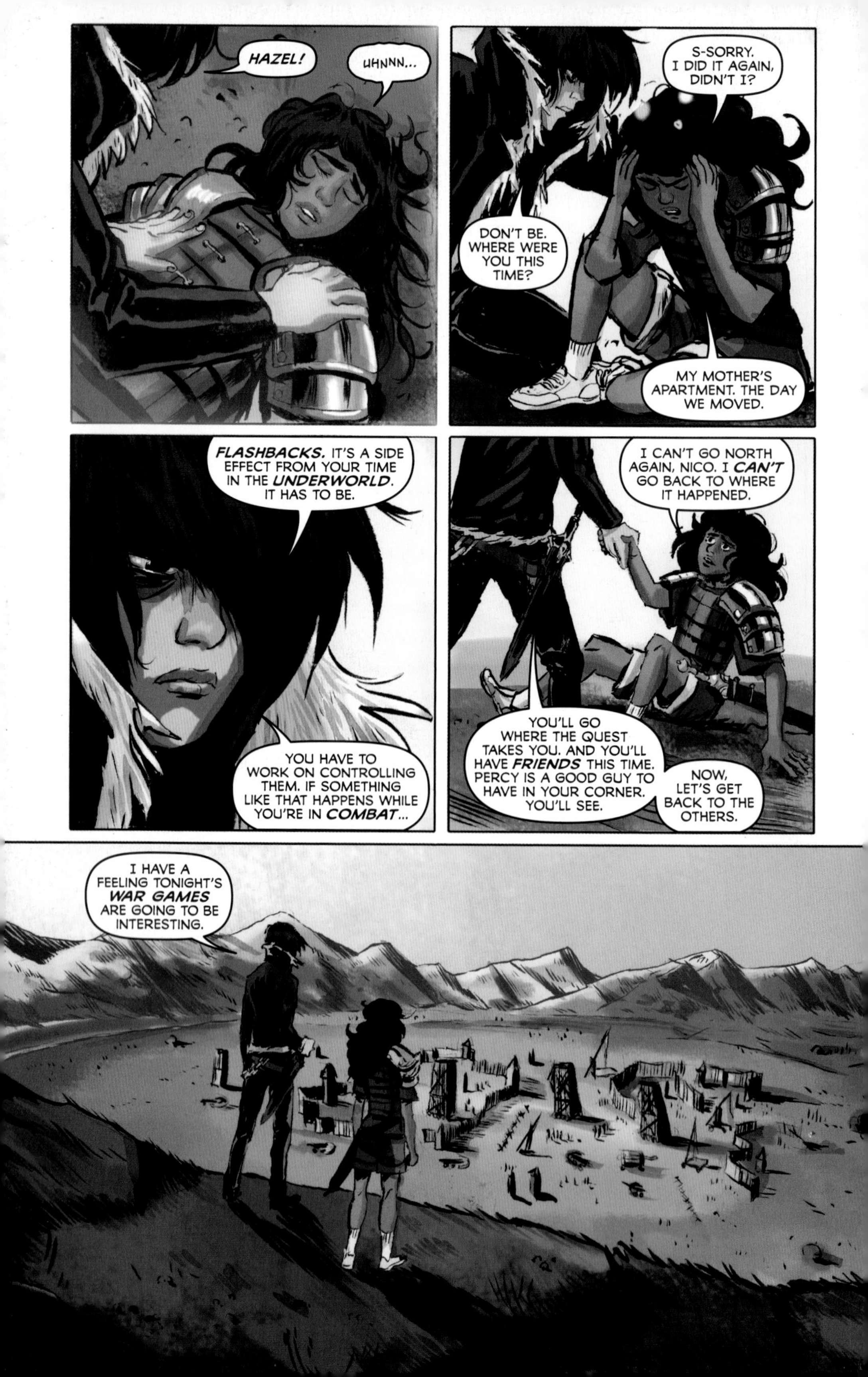
HAZEL!
UHNNN...
S-SORRY. I DID IT AGAIN, DIDN'T I?
DON'T BE. WHERE WERE YOU THIS TIME?
MY MOTHER'S APARTMENT. THE DAY WE MOVED.
FLASHBACKS. IT'S A SIDE EFFECT FROM YOUR TIME IN THE UNDERWORLD. IT HAS TO BE.
YOU HAVE TO WORK ON CONTROLLING THEM. IF SOMETHING LIKE THAT HAPPENS WHILE YOU'RE IN COMBAT...
I CAN'T GO NORTH AGAIN, NICO. I CAN'T GO BACK TO WHERE IT HAPPENED.
YOU'LL GO WHERE THE QUEST TAKES YOU. AND YOU'LL HAVE FRIENDS THIS TIME. PERCY IS A GOOD GUY TO HAVE IN YOUR CORNER. YOU'LL SEE.
NOW, LET'S GET BACK TO THE OTHERS.
I HAVE A FEELING TONIGHT'S WAR GAMES ARE GOING TO BE INTERESTING.

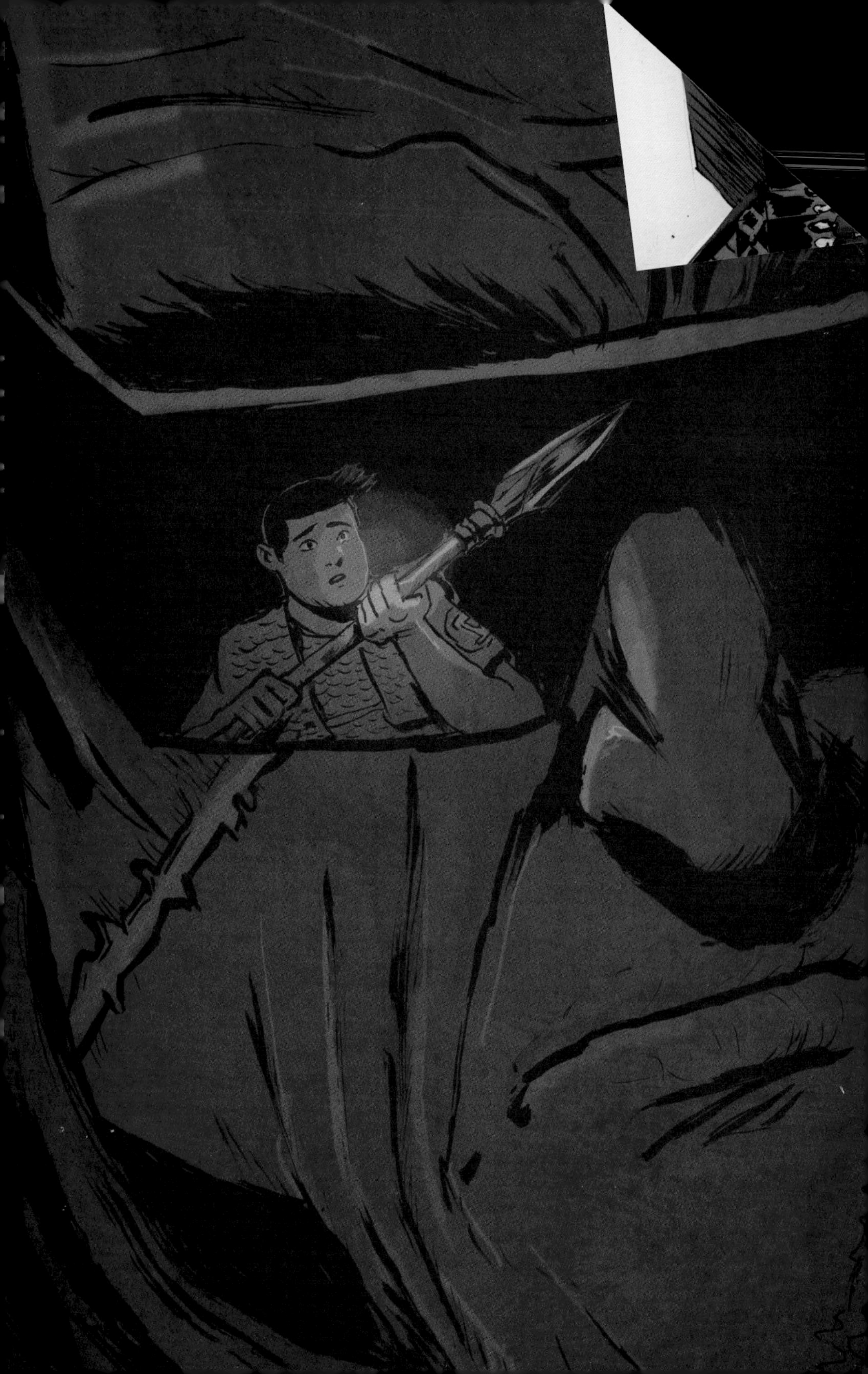

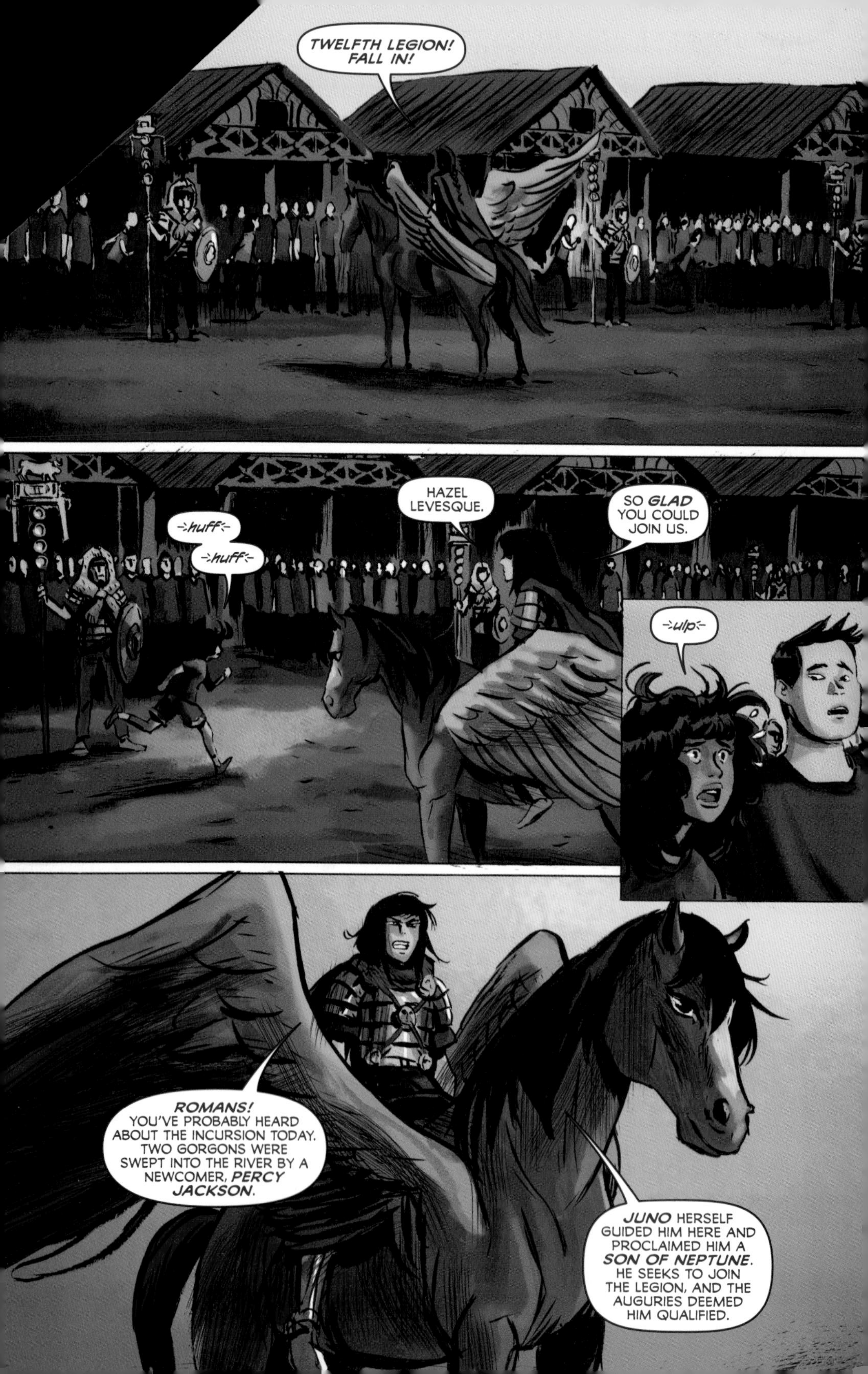
TWELFTH LEGION! FALL IN!
HAZEL LEVESQUE.
SO GLAD YOU COULD JOIN US.
-huff-
-huff-
-ulp-
ROMANS! YOU'VE PROBABLY HEARD ABOUT THE INCURSION TODAY. TWO GORGONS WERE SWEPT INTO THE RIVER BY A NEWCOMER, PERCY JACKSON.
JUNO HERSELF GUIDED HIM HERE AND PROCLAIMED HIM A SON OF NEPTUNE. HE SEEKS TO JOIN THE LEGION, AND THE AUGURIES DEEMED HIM QUALIFIED.

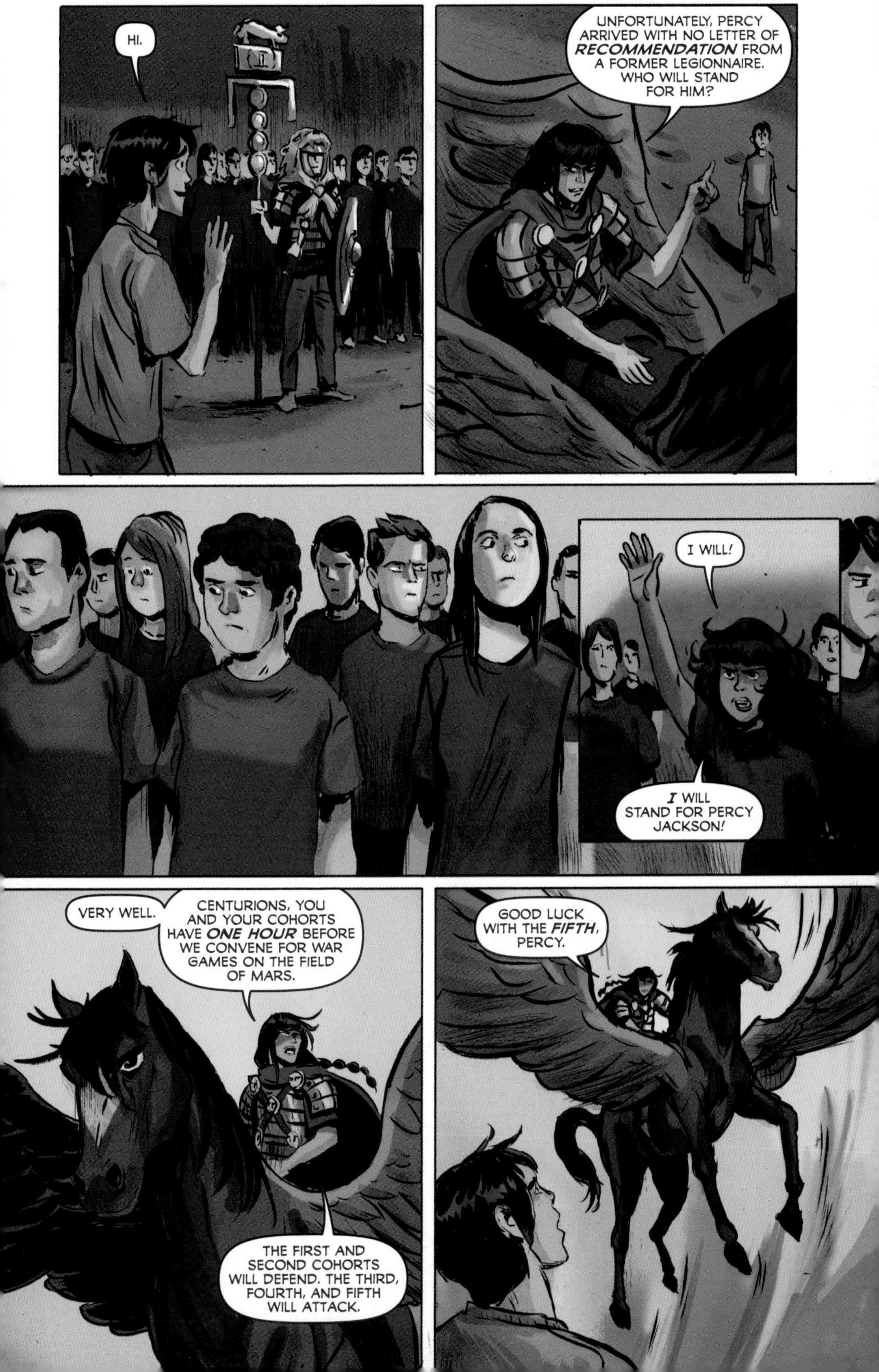
HI.
UNFORTUNATELY, PERCY ARRIVED WITH NO LETTER OF RECOMMENDATION FROM A FORMER LEGIONNAIRE. WHO WILL STAND FOR HIM?
I WILL!
I WILL STAND FOR PERCY JACKSON!
VERY WELL.
CENTURIONS, YOU AND YOUR COHORTS HAVE ONE HOUR BEFORE WE CONVENE FOR WAR GAMES ON THE FIELD OF MARS.
THE FIRST AND SECOND COHORTS WILL DEFEND. THE THIRD, FOURTH, AND FIFTH WILL ATTACK.
GOOD LUCK WITH THE FIFTH, PERCY.

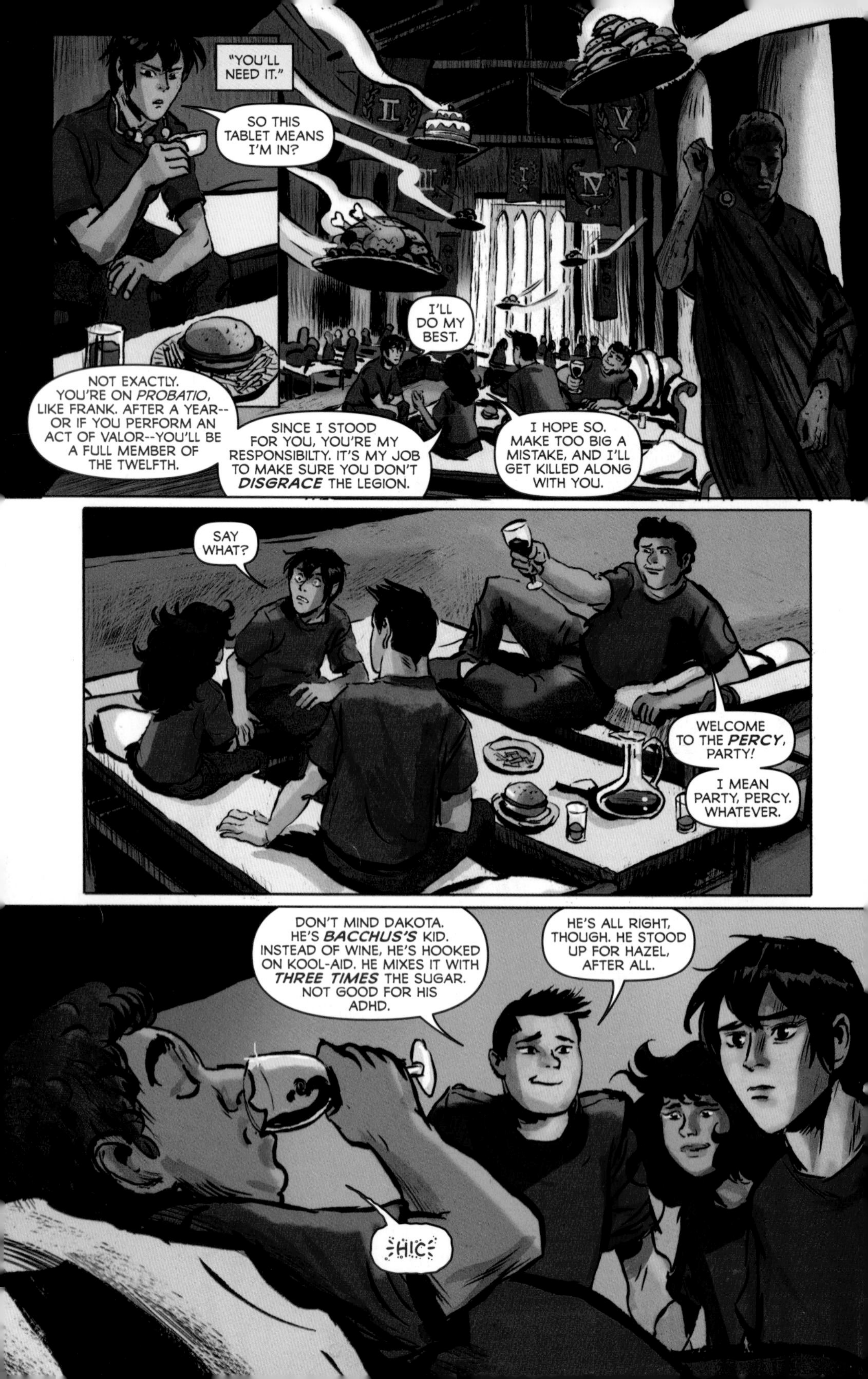
"YOU'LL NEED IT."
SO THIS TABLET MEANS I'M IN?
NOT EXACTLY. YOU'RE ON *PROBATIO*, LIKE FRANK. AFTER A YEAR--OR IF YOU PERFORM AN ACT OF VALOR--YOU'LL BE A FULL MEMBER OF THE TWELFTH.
SINCE I STOOD FOR YOU, YOU'RE MY RESPONSIBILTY. IT'S MY JOB TO MAKE SURE YOU DON'T **DISGRACE** THE LEGION.
I'LL DO MY BEST.
I HOPE SO. MAKE TOO BIG A MISTAKE, AND I'LL GET KILLED ALONG WITH YOU.
SAY WHAT?
WELCOME TO THE *PERCY*, PARTY!
I MEAN PARTY, PERCY. WHATEVER.
DON'T MIND DAKOTA. HE'S **BACCHUS'S** KID. INSTEAD OF WINE, HE'S HOOKED ON KOOL-AID. HE MIXES IT WITH ***THREE TIMES*** THE SUGAR. NOT GOOD FOR HIS ADHD.
HE'S ALL RIGHT, THOUGH. HE STOOD UP FOR HAZEL, AFTER ALL.
HIC

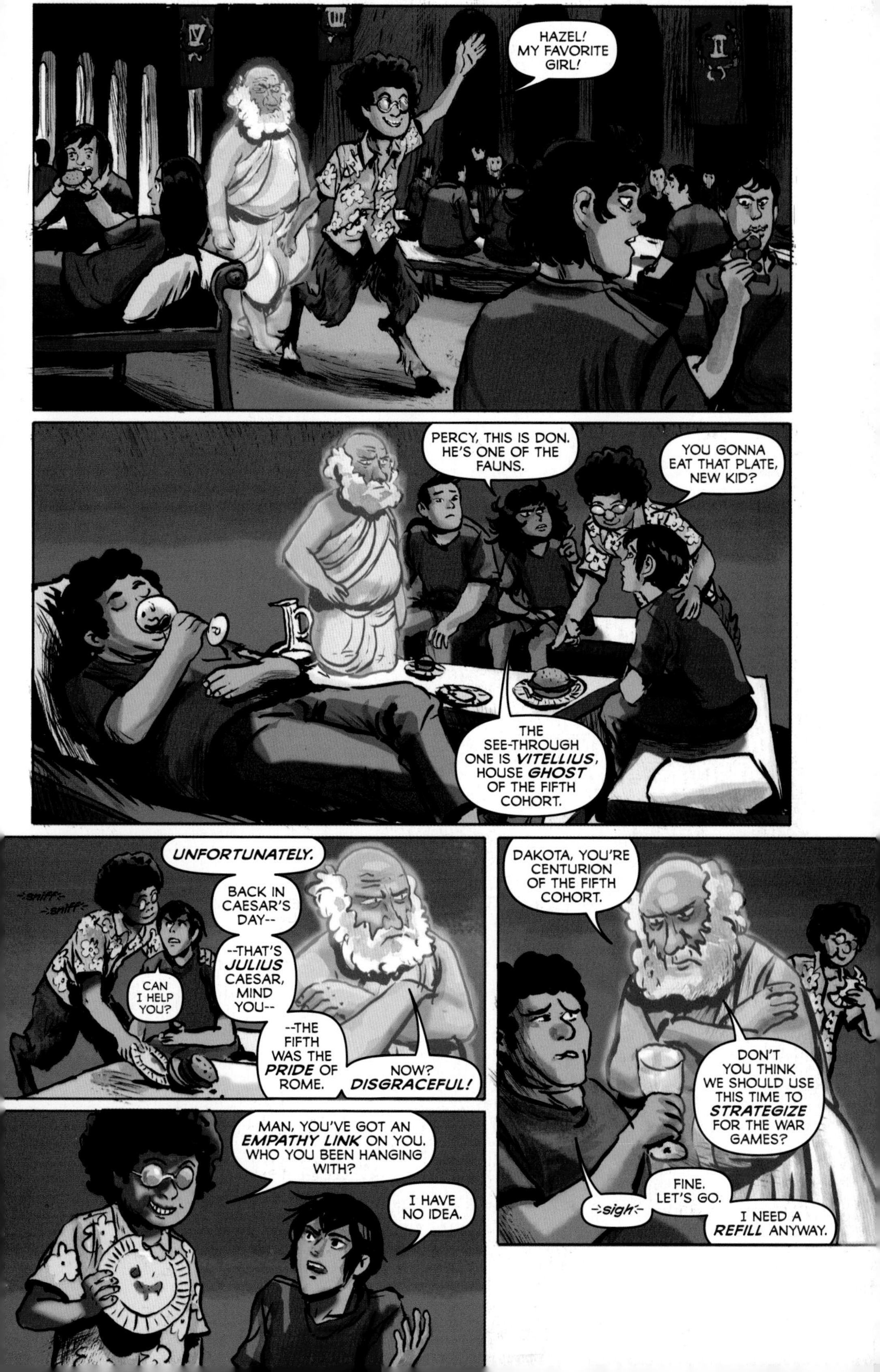
HAZEL! MY FAVORITE GIRL!
PERCY, THIS IS DON. HE'S ONE OF THE FAUNS.
YOU GONNA EAT THAT PLATE, NEW KID?
THE SEE-THROUGH ONE IS VITELLIUS, HOUSE GHOST OF THE FIFTH COHORT.
UNFORTUNATELY.
BACK IN CAESAR'S DAY--
--THAT'S JULIUS CAESAR, MIND YOU--
--THE FIFTH WAS THE PRIDE OF ROME.
NOW? DISGRACEFUL!
-sniff-
-sniff-
CAN I HELP YOU?
MAN, YOU'VE GOT AN EMPATHY LINK ON YOU. WHO YOU BEEN HANGING WITH?
I HAVE NO IDEA.
DAKOTA, YOU'RE CENTURION OF THE FIFTH COHORT.
DON'T YOU THINK WE SHOULD USE THIS TIME TO STRATEGIZE FOR THE WAR GAMES?
-sigh-
FINE. LET'S GO.
I NEED A REFILL ANYWAY.

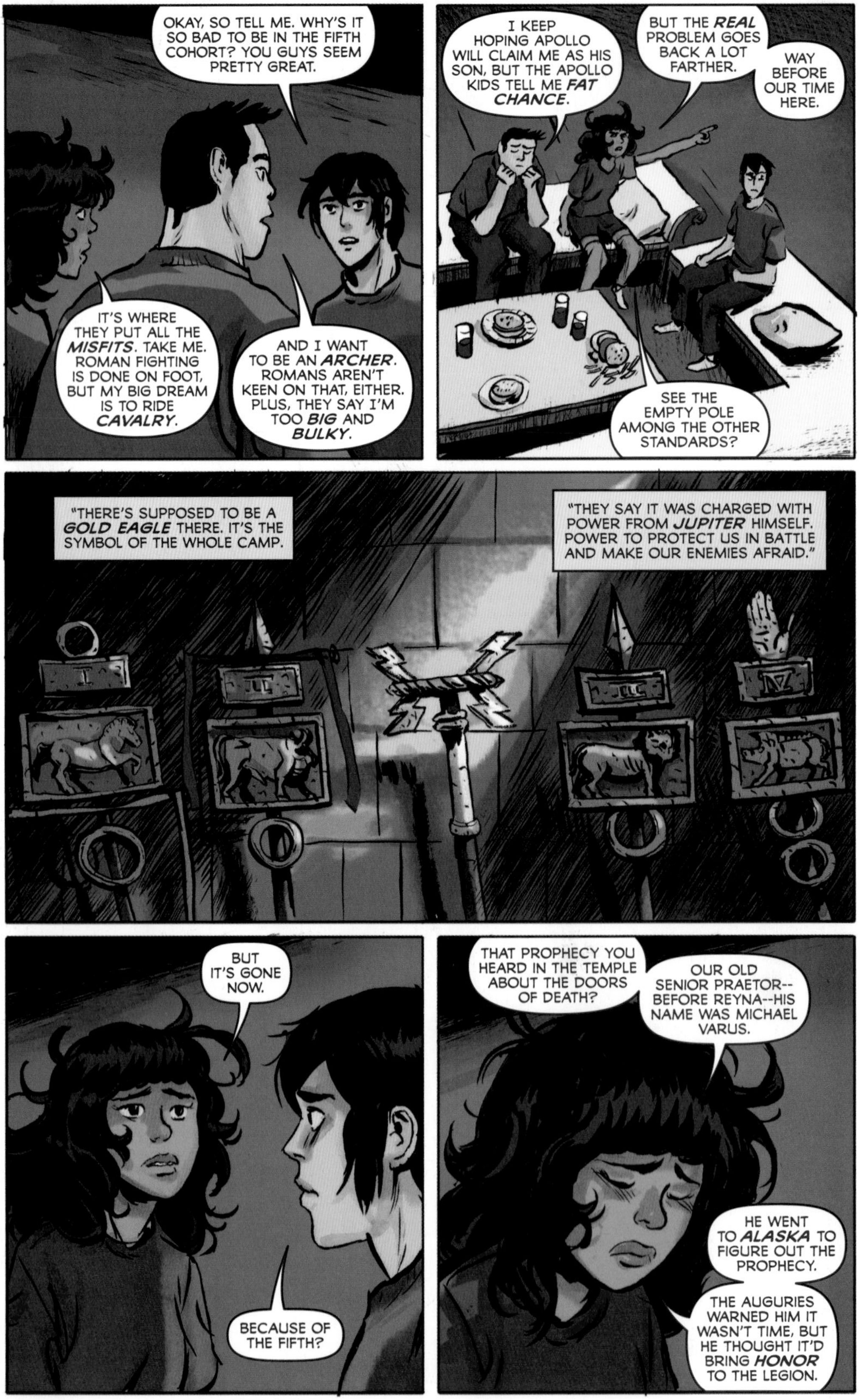
OKAY, SO TELL ME. WHY'S IT SO BAD TO BE IN THE FIFTH COHORT? YOU GUYS SEEM PRETTY GREAT.
IT'S WHERE THEY PUT ALL THE MISFITS. TAKE ME. ROMAN FIGHTING IS DONE ON FOOT, BUT MY BIG DREAM IS TO RIDE CAVALRY.
AND I WANT TO BE AN ARCHER. ROMANS AREN'T KEEN ON THAT, EITHER. PLUS, THEY SAY I'M TOO BIG AND BULKY.
I KEEP HOPING APOLLO WILL CLAIM ME AS HIS SON, BUT THE APOLLO KIDS TELL ME FAT CHANCE.
BUT THE REAL PROBLEM GOES BACK A LOT FARTHER.
WAY BEFORE OUR TIME HERE.
SEE THE EMPTY POLE AMONG THE OTHER STANDARDS?
"THERE'S SUPPOSED TO BE A GOLD EAGLE THERE. IT'S THE SYMBOL OF THE WHOLE CAMP.
"THEY SAY IT WAS CHARGED WITH POWER FROM JUPITER HIMSELF. POWER TO PROTECT US IN BATTLE AND MAKE OUR ENEMIES AFRAID."
BUT IT'S GONE NOW.
BECAUSE OF THE FIFTH?
THAT PROPHECY YOU HEARD IN THE TEMPLE ABOUT THE DOORS OF DEATH?
OUR OLD SENIOR PRAETOR--BEFORE REYNA--HIS NAME WAS MICHAEL VARUS.
HE WENT TO ALASKA TO FIGURE OUT THE PROPHECY.
THE AUGURIES WARNED HIM IT WASN'T TIME, BUT HE THOUGHT IT'D BRING HONOR TO THE LEGION.

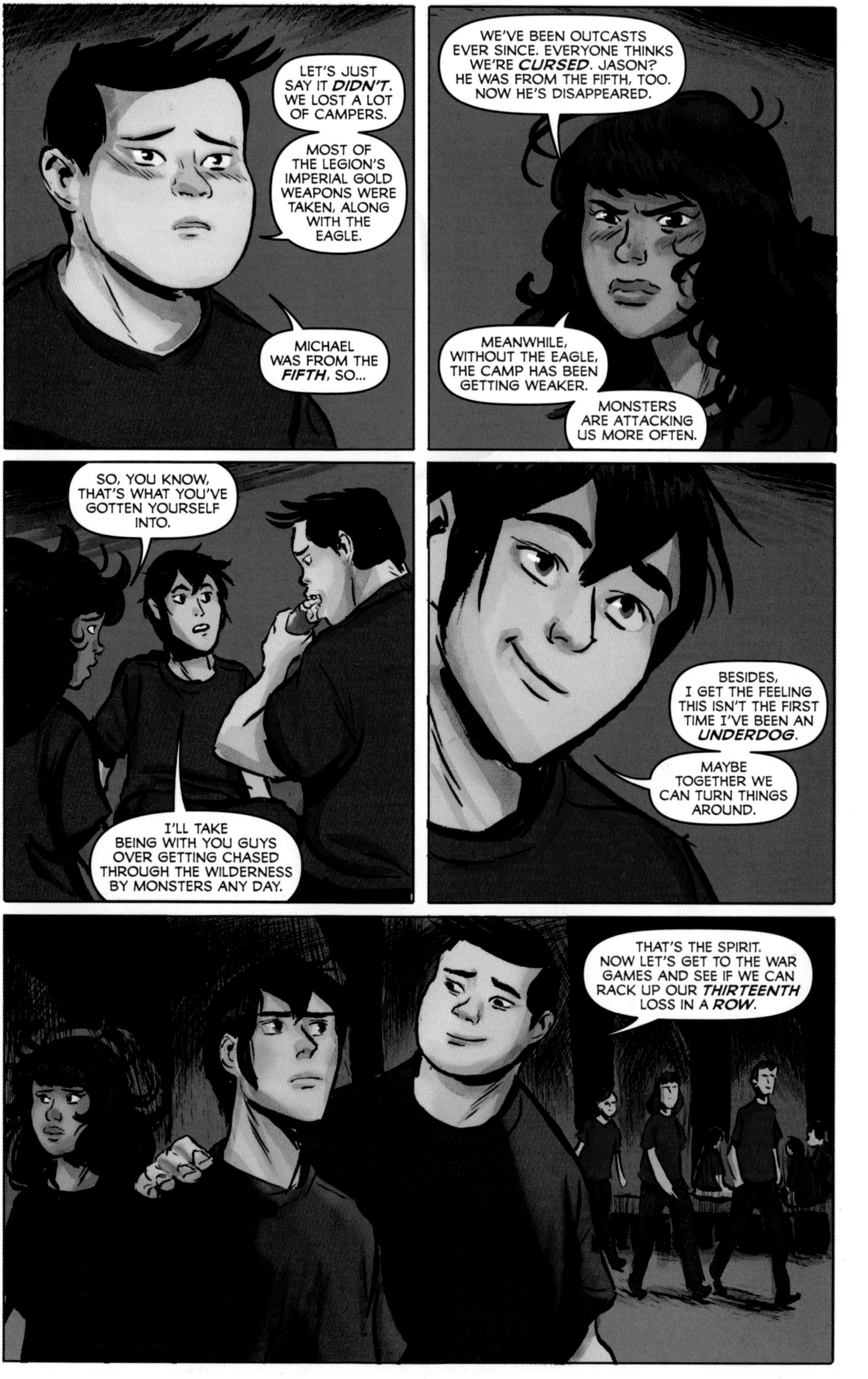
LET'S JUST SAY IT *DIDN'T*. WE LOST A LOT OF CAMPERS.
MOST OF THE LEGION'S IMPERIAL GOLD WEAPONS WERE TAKEN, ALONG WITH THE EAGLE.
MICHAEL WAS FROM THE *FIFTH*, SO...
WE'VE BEEN OUTCASTS EVER SINCE. EVERYONE THINKS WE'RE *CURSED*. JASON? HE WAS FROM THE FIFTH, TOO. NOW HE'S DISAPPEARED.
MEANWHILE, WITHOUT THE EAGLE, THE CAMP HAS BEEN GETTING WEAKER.
MONSTERS ARE ATTACKING US MORE OFTEN.
SO, YOU KNOW, THAT'S WHAT YOU'VE GOTTEN YOURSELF INTO.
I'LL TAKE BEING WITH YOU GUYS OVER GETTING CHASED THROUGH THE WILDERNESS BY MONSTERS ANY DAY.
BESIDES, I GET THE FEELING THIS ISN'T THE FIRST TIME I'VE BEEN AN *UNDERDOG*.
MAYBE TOGETHER WE CAN TURN THINGS AROUND.
THAT'S THE SPIRIT. NOW LET'S GET TO THE WAR GAMES AND SEE IF WE CAN RACK UP OUR *THIRTEENTH* LOSS IN A *ROW*.

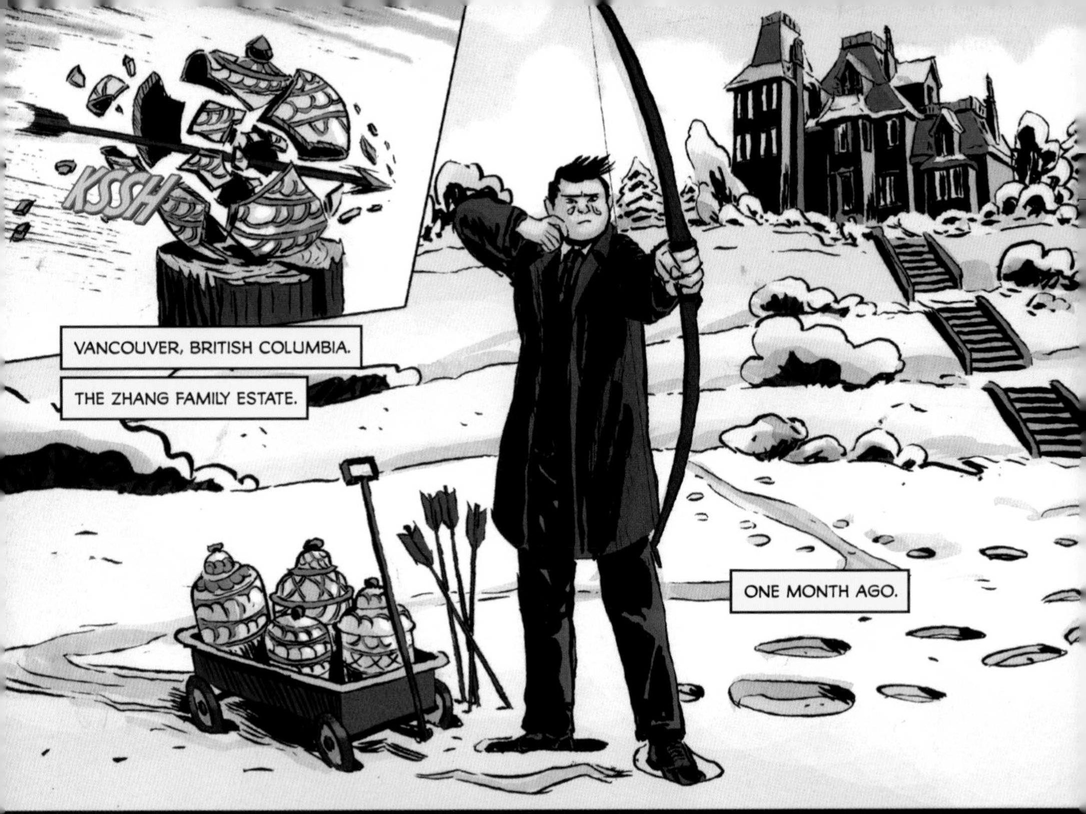
KSSH
VANCOUVER, BRITISH COLUMBIA.
THE ZHANG FAMILY ESTATE.
ONE MONTH AGO.

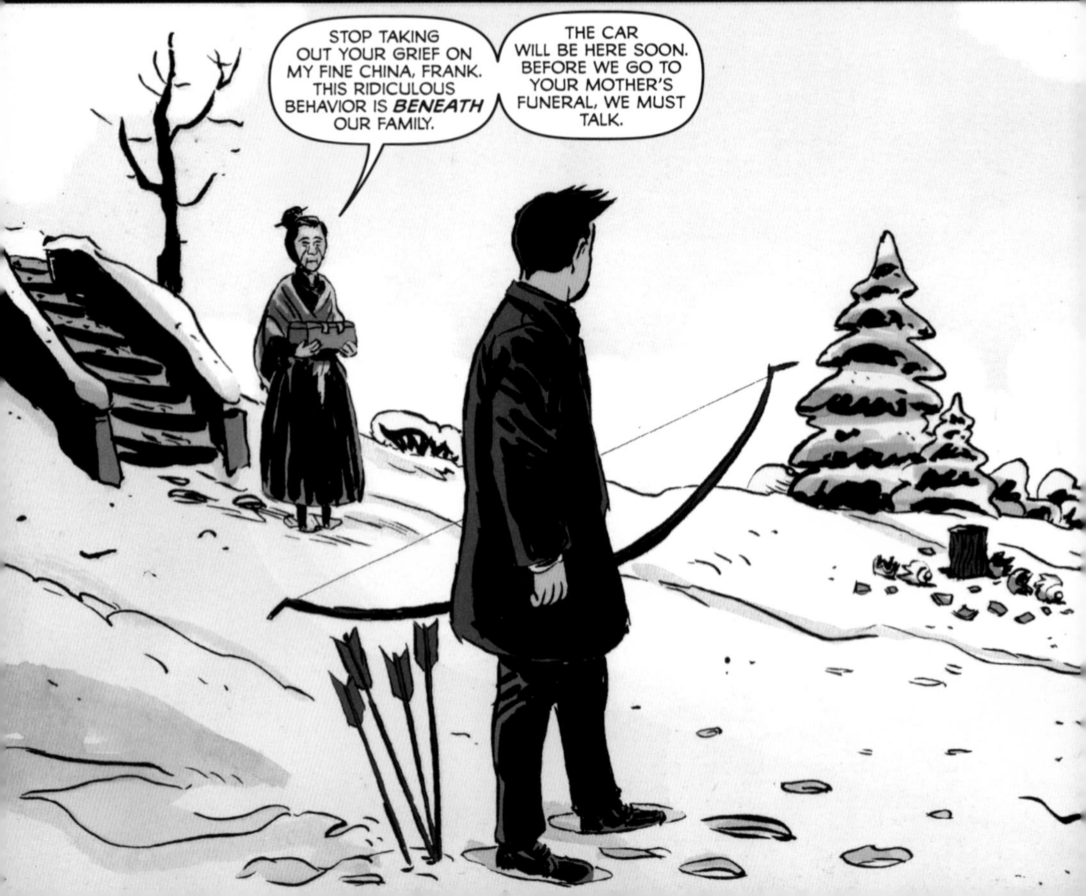
STOP TAKING OUT YOUR GRIEF ON MY FINE CHINA, FRANK. THIS RIDICULOUS BEHAVIOR IS BENEATH OUR FAMILY.
THE CAR WILL BE HERE SOON. BEFORE WE GO TO YOUR MOTHER'S FUNERAL, WE MUST TALK.

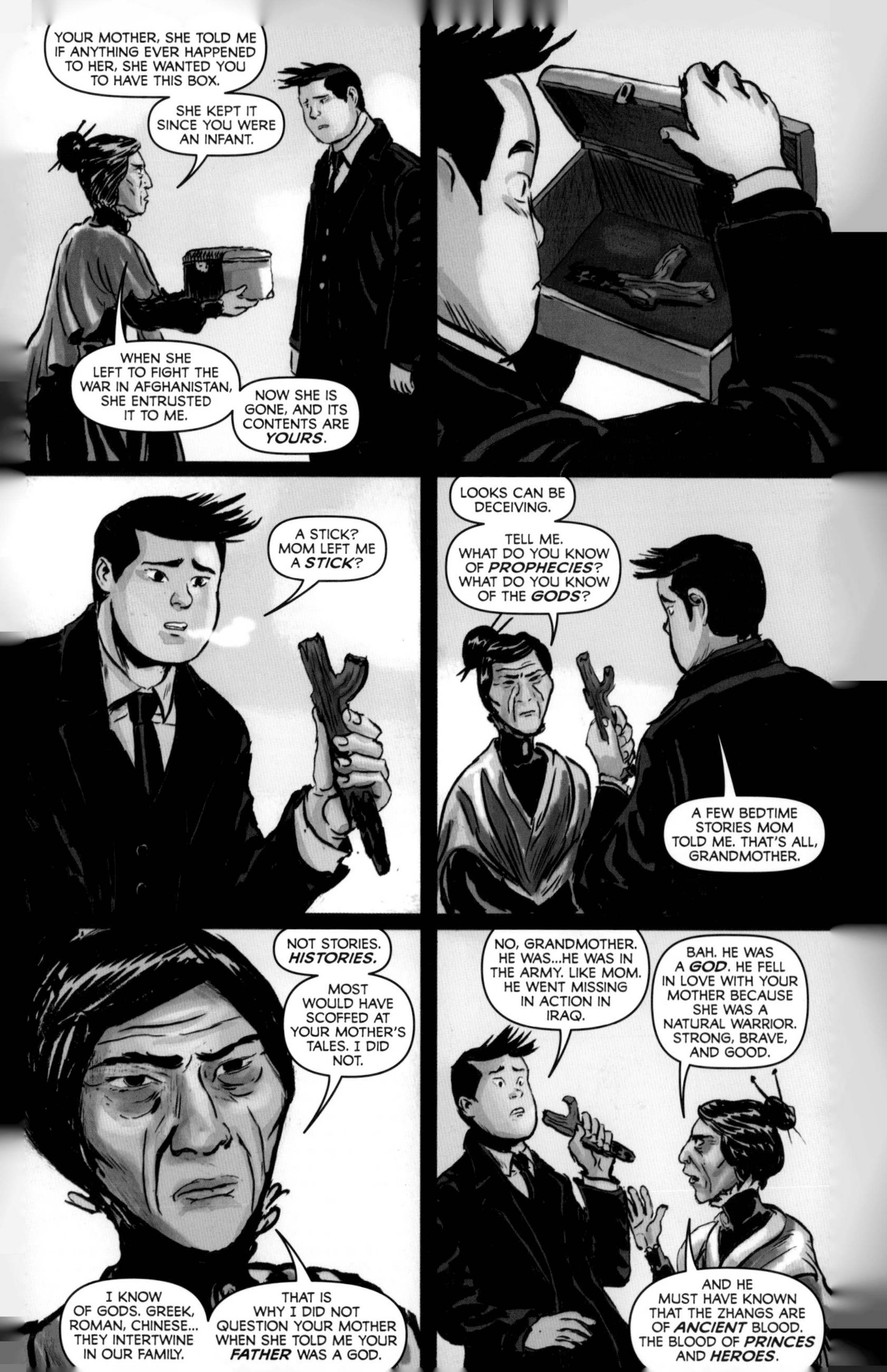
YOUR MOTHER, SHE TOLD ME IF ANYTHING EVER HAPPENED TO HER, SHE WANTED YOU TO HAVE THIS BOX.
SHE KEPT IT SINCE YOU WERE AN INFANT.
WHEN SHE LEFT TO FIGHT THE WAR IN AFGHANISTAN, SHE ENTRUSTED IT TO ME.
NOW SHE IS GONE, AND ITS CONTENTS ARE *YOURS*.
A STICK? MOM LEFT ME A *STICK*?
LOOKS CAN BE DECEIVING.
TELL ME. WHAT DO YOU KNOW OF *PROPHECIES*? WHAT DO YOU KNOW OF THE *GODS*?
A FEW BEDTIME STORIES MOM TOLD ME. THAT'S ALL, GRANDMOTHER.
NOT STORIES. *HISTORIES.*
MOST WOULD HAVE SCOFFED AT YOUR MOTHER'S TALES. I DID NOT.
I KNOW OF GODS. GREEK, ROMAN, CHINESE... THEY INTERTWINE IN OUR FAMILY.
THAT IS WHY I DID NOT QUESTION YOUR MOTHER WHEN SHE TOLD ME YOUR *FATHER* WAS A GOD.
NO, GRANDMOTHER. HE WAS...HE WAS IN THE ARMY. LIKE MOM. HE WENT MISSING IN ACTION IN IRAQ.
BAH. HE WAS A *GOD*. HE FELL IN LOVE WITH YOUR MOTHER BECAUSE SHE WAS A NATURAL WARRIOR. STRONG, BRAVE, AND GOOD.
AND HE MUST HAVE KNOWN THAT THE ZHANGS ARE OF *ANCIENT* BLOOD. THE BLOOD OF *PRINCES* AND *HEROES*.

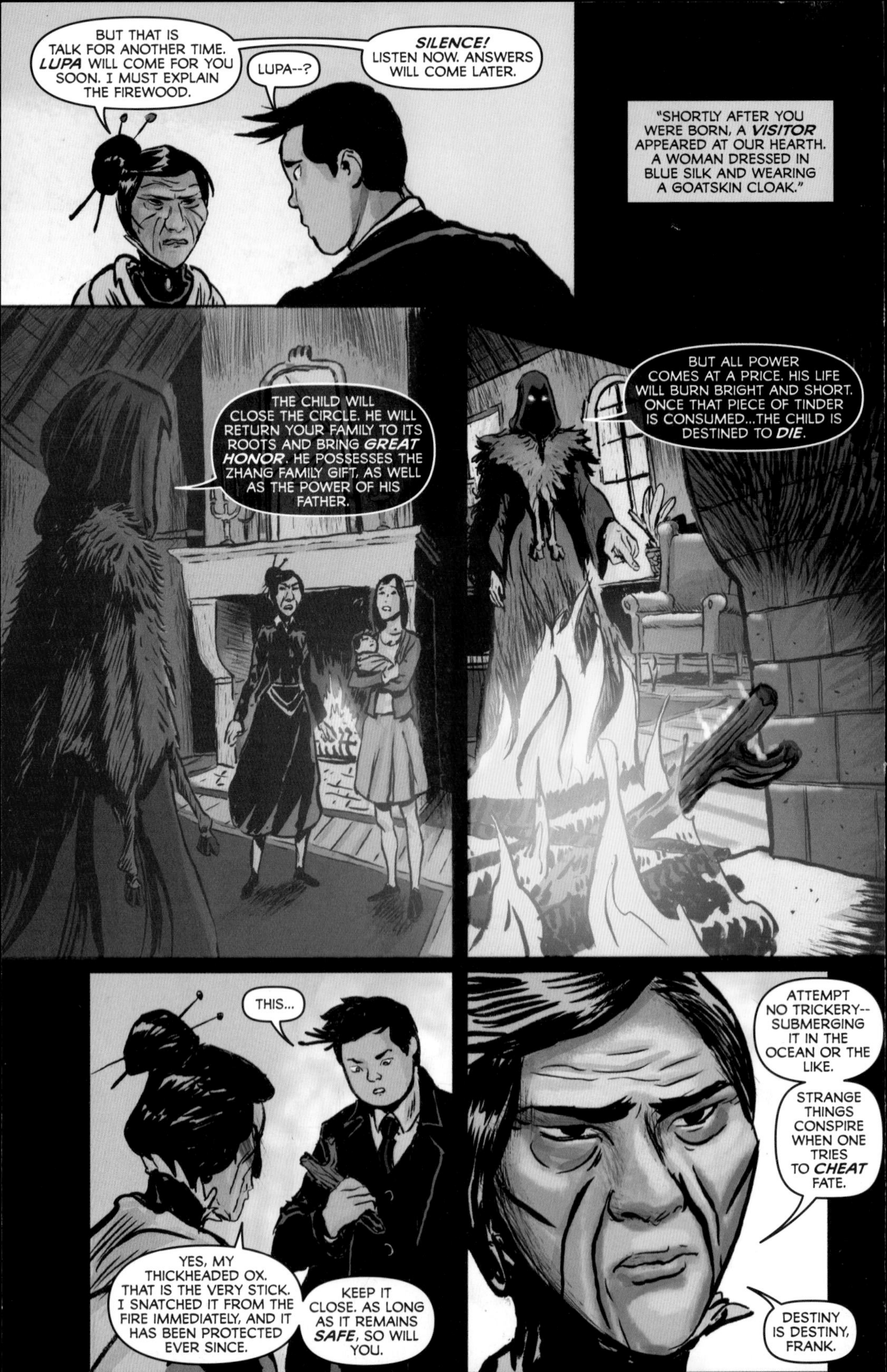
BUT THAT IS TALK FOR ANOTHER TIME. LUPA WILL COME FOR YOU SOON. I MUST EXPLAIN THE FIREWOOD.
LUPA--?
SILENCE! LISTEN NOW. ANSWERS WILL COME LATER.
"SHORTLY AFTER YOU WERE BORN, A VISITOR APPEARED AT OUR HEARTH. A WOMAN DRESSED IN BLUE SILK AND WEARING A GOATSKIN CLOAK."
THE CHILD WILL CLOSE THE CIRCLE. HE WILL RETURN YOUR FAMILY TO ITS ROOTS AND BRING GREAT HONOR. HE POSSESSES THE ZHANG FAMILY GIFT, AS WELL AS THE POWER OF HIS FATHER.
BUT ALL POWER COMES AT A PRICE. HIS LIFE WILL BURN BRIGHT AND SHORT. ONCE THAT PIECE OF TINDER IS CONSUMED...THE CHILD IS DESTINED TO DIE.
THIS...
YES, MY THICKHEADED OX. THAT IS THE VERY STICK. I SNATCHED IT FROM THE FIRE IMMEDIATELY, AND IT HAS BEEN PROTECTED EVER SINCE.
KEEP IT CLOSE. AS LONG AS IT REMAINS SAFE, SO WILL YOU.
ATTEMPT NO TRICKERY-- SUBMERGING IT IN THE OCEAN OR THE LIKE.
STRANGE THINGS CONSPIRE WHEN ONE TRIES TO CHEAT FATE.
DESTINY IS DESTINY, FRANK.

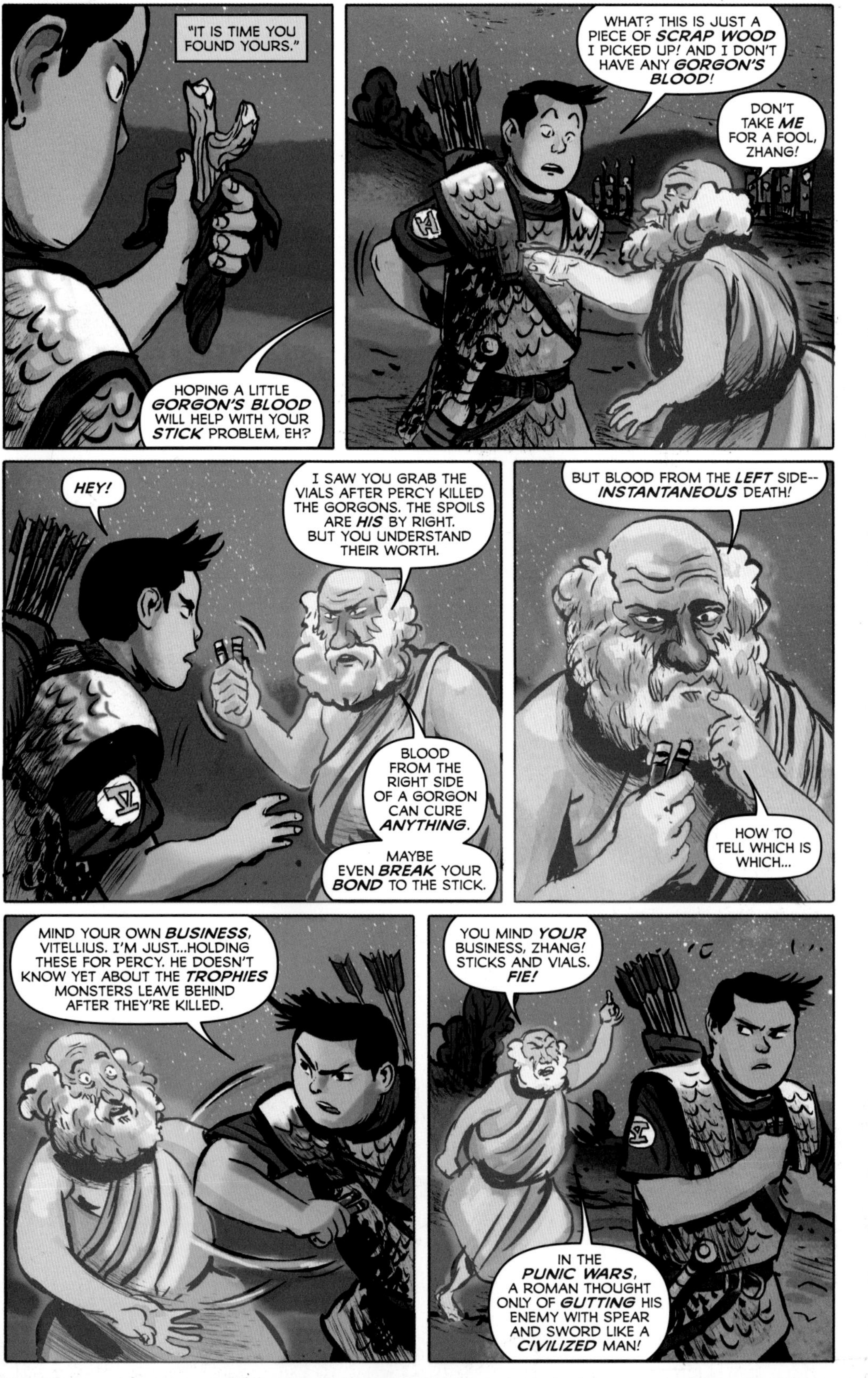

"IT IS TIME YOU FOUND YOURS."
HOPING A LITTLE GORGON'S BLOOD WILL HELP WITH YOUR STICK PROBLEM, EH?
WHAT? THIS IS JUST A PIECE OF SCRAP WOOD I PICKED UP! AND I DON'T HAVE ANY GORGON'S BLOOD!
DON'T TAKE ME FOR A FOOL, ZHANG!
HEY!
I SAW YOU GRAB THE VIALS AFTER PERCY KILLED THE GORGONS. THE SPOILS ARE HIS BY RIGHT. BUT YOU UNDERSTAND THEIR WORTH.
BLOOD FROM THE RIGHT SIDE OF A GORGON CAN CURE ANYTHING.
MAYBE EVEN BREAK YOUR BOND TO THE STICK.
BUT BLOOD FROM THE LEFT SIDE-- INSTANTANEOUS DEATH!
HOW TO TELL WHICH IS WHICH...
MIND YOUR OWN BUSINESS, VITELLIUS. I'M JUST...HOLDING THESE FOR PERCY. HE DOESN'T KNOW YET ABOUT THE TROPHIES MONSTERS LEAVE BEHIND AFTER THEY'RE KILLED.
YOU MIND YOUR BUSINESS, ZHANG! STICKS AND VIALS. FIE!
IN THE PUNIC WARS, A ROMAN THOUGHT ONLY OF GUTTING HIS ENEMY WITH SPEAR AND SWORD LIKE A CIVILIZED MAN!

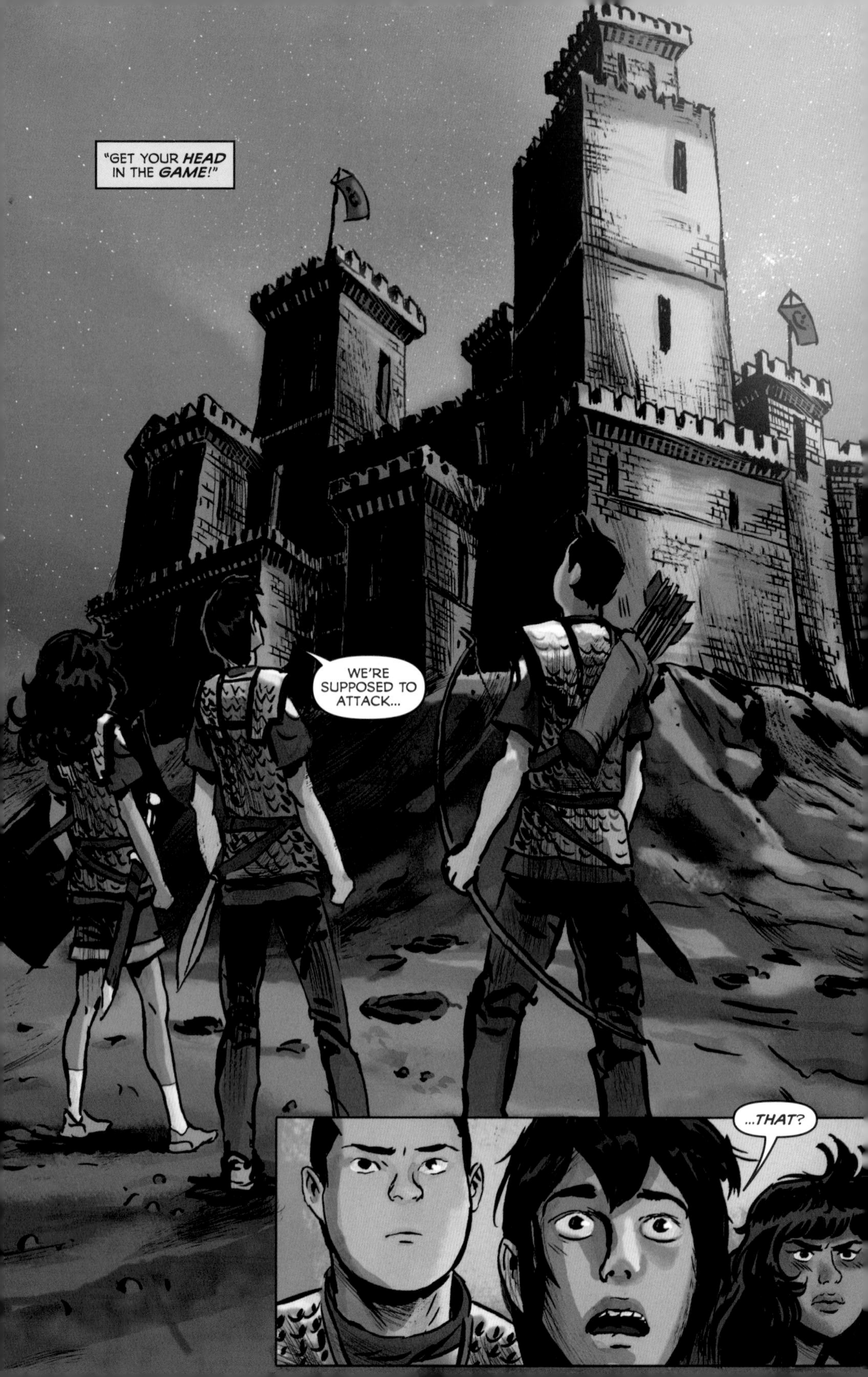
"GET YOUR HEAD IN THE GAME!"
WE'RE SUPPOSED TO ATTACK...
...THAT?

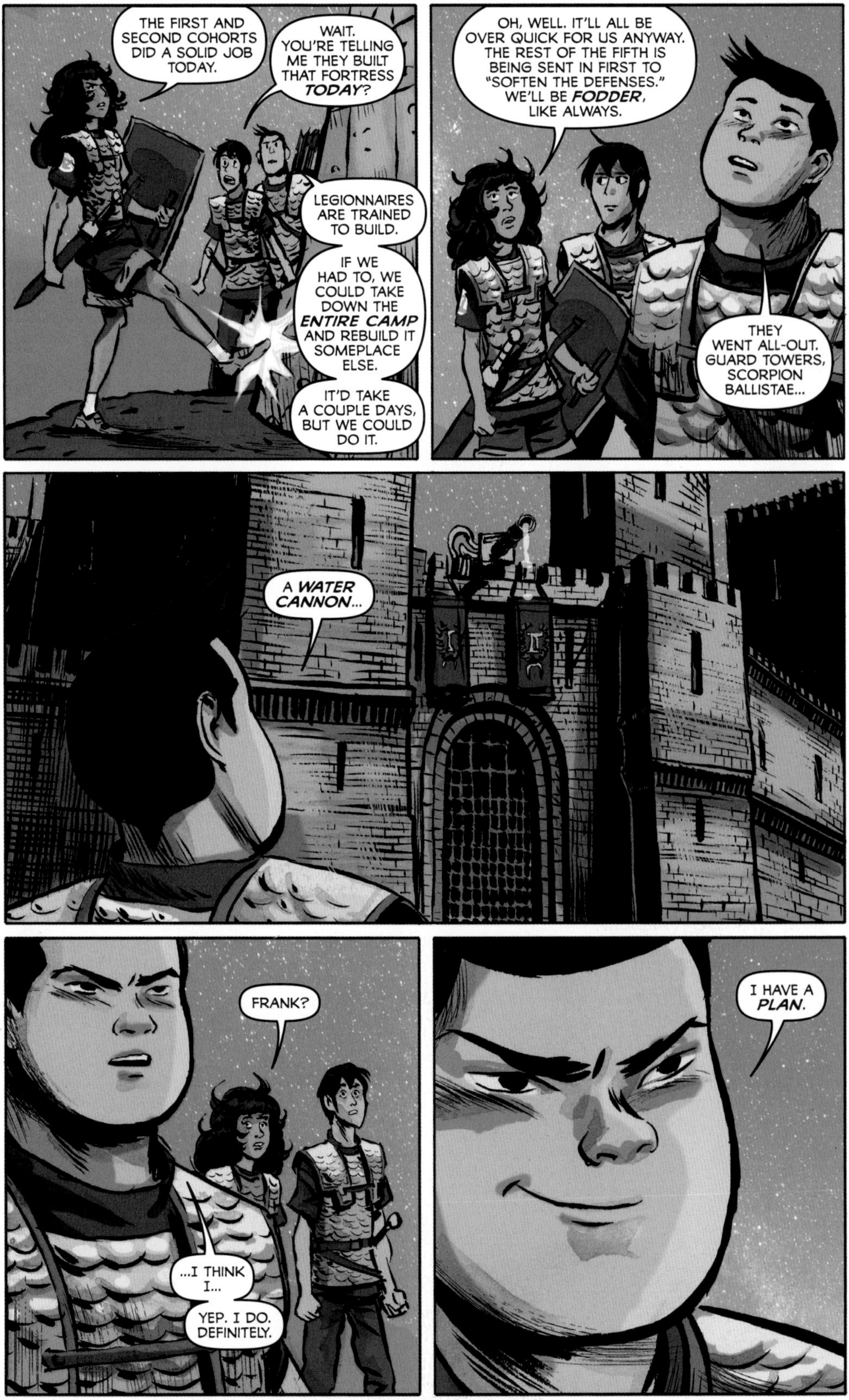
THE FIRST AND SECOND COHORTS DID A SOLID JOB TODAY.
WAIT. YOU'RE TELLING ME THEY BUILT THAT FORTRESS *TODAY*?
LEGIONNAIRES ARE TRAINED TO BUILD.
IF WE HAD TO, WE COULD TAKE DOWN THE *ENTIRE CAMP* AND REBUILD IT SOMEPLACE ELSE.
IT'D TAKE A COUPLE DAYS, BUT WE COULD DO IT.
OH, WELL. IT'LL ALL BE OVER QUICK FOR US ANYWAY. THE REST OF THE FIFTH IS BEING SENT IN FIRST TO "SOFTEN THE DEFENSES." WE'LL BE *FODDER*, LIKE ALWAYS.
THEY WENT ALL-OUT. GUARD TOWERS, SCORPION BALLISTAE...
A *WATER CANNON*...
FRANK?
...I THINK I...
YEP. I DO. DEFINITELY.
I HAVE A *PLAN*.

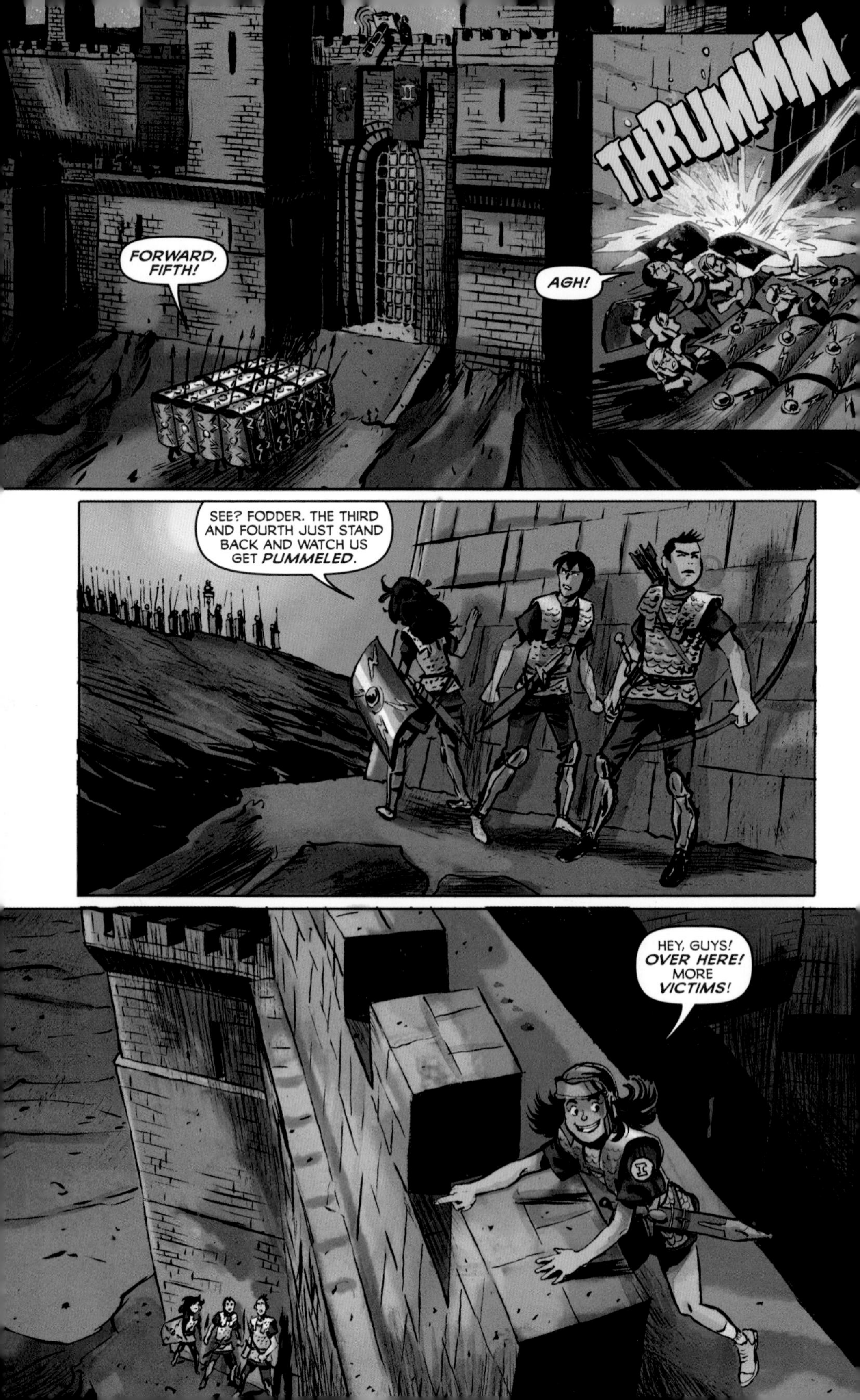

FORWARD, FIFTH!
THRUMMM
AGH!
SEE? FODDER. THE THIRD AND FOURTH JUST STAND BACK AND WATCH US GET *PUMMELED*.
HEY, GUYS! ***OVER HERE!*** MORE ***VICTIMS!***

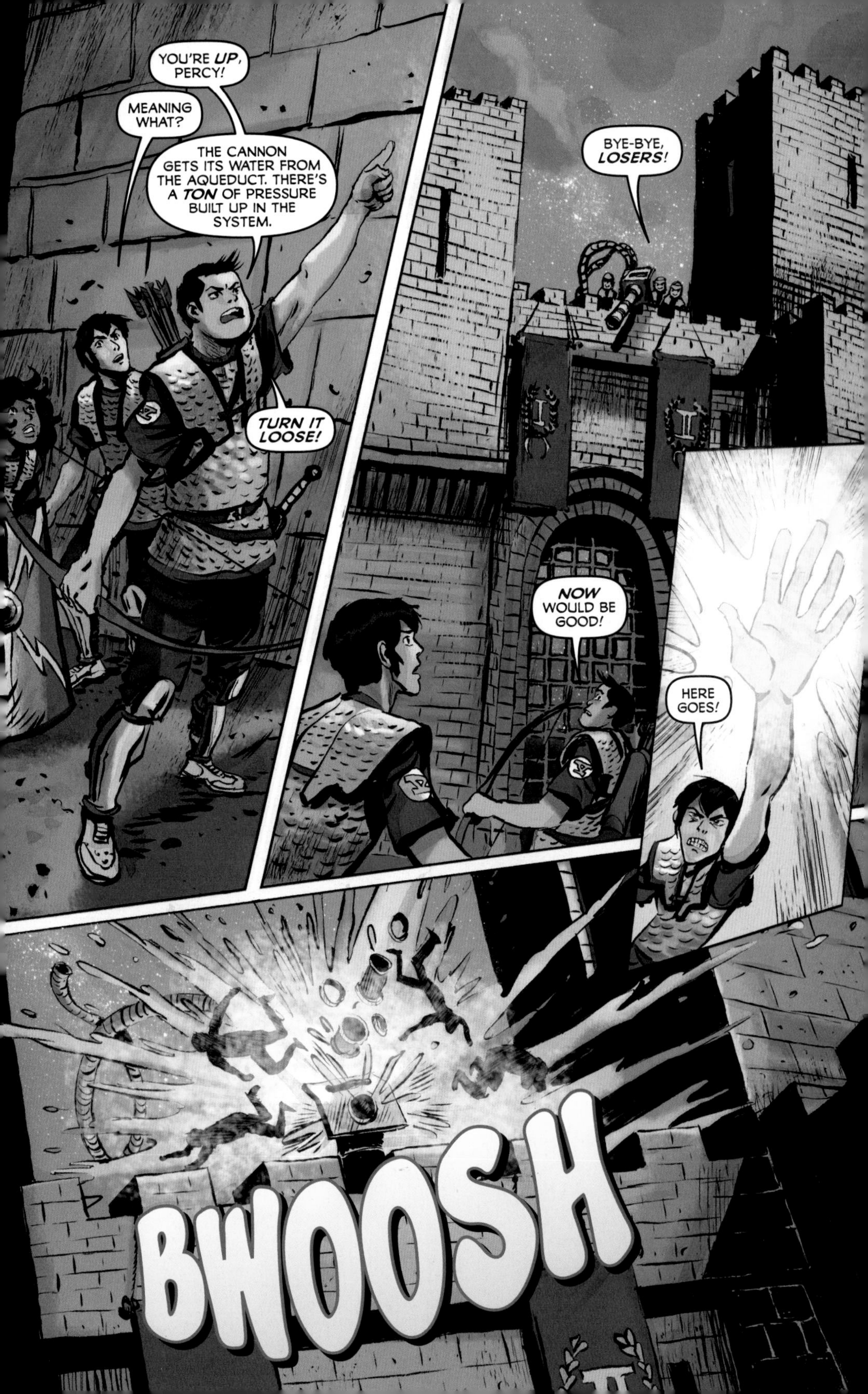

YOU'RE *UP*, PERCY!
MEANING WHAT?
THE CANNON GETS ITS WATER FROM THE AQUEDUCT. THERE'S A *TON* OF PRESSURE BUILT UP IN THE SYSTEM.
TURN IT LOOSE!
BYE-BYE, *LOSERS!*
NOW WOULD BE GOOD!
HERE GOES!
BWOOSH

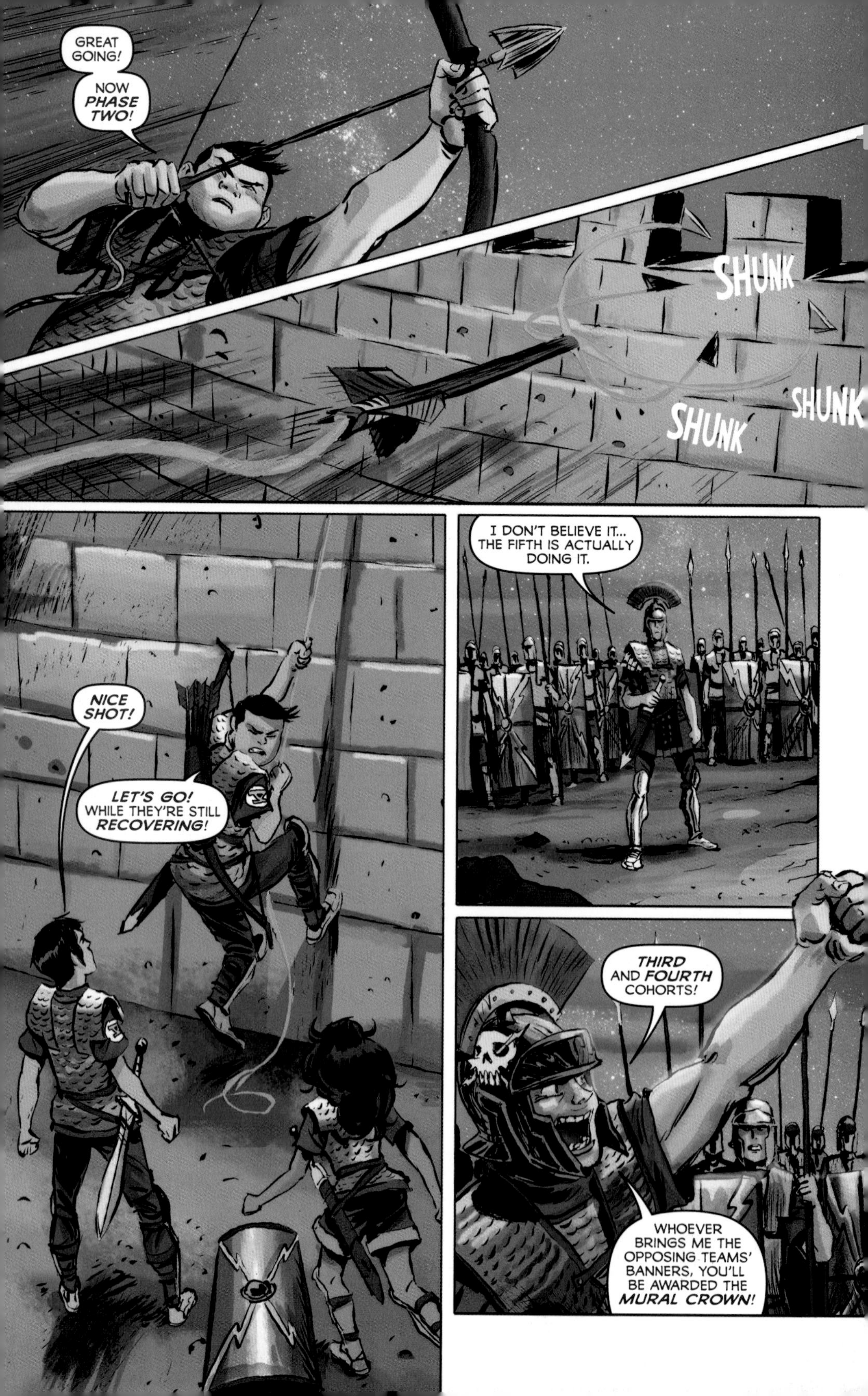
GREAT GOING!
NOW PHASE TWO!
SHUNK
SHUNK
SHUNK
NICE SHOT!
LET'S GO! WHILE THEY'RE STILL RECOVERING!
I DON'T BELIEVE IT... THE FIFTH IS ACTUALLY DOING IT.
THIRD AND FOURTH COHORTS!
WHOEVER BRINGS ME THE OPPOSING TEAMS' BANNERS, YOU'LL BE AWARDED THE MURAL CROWN!

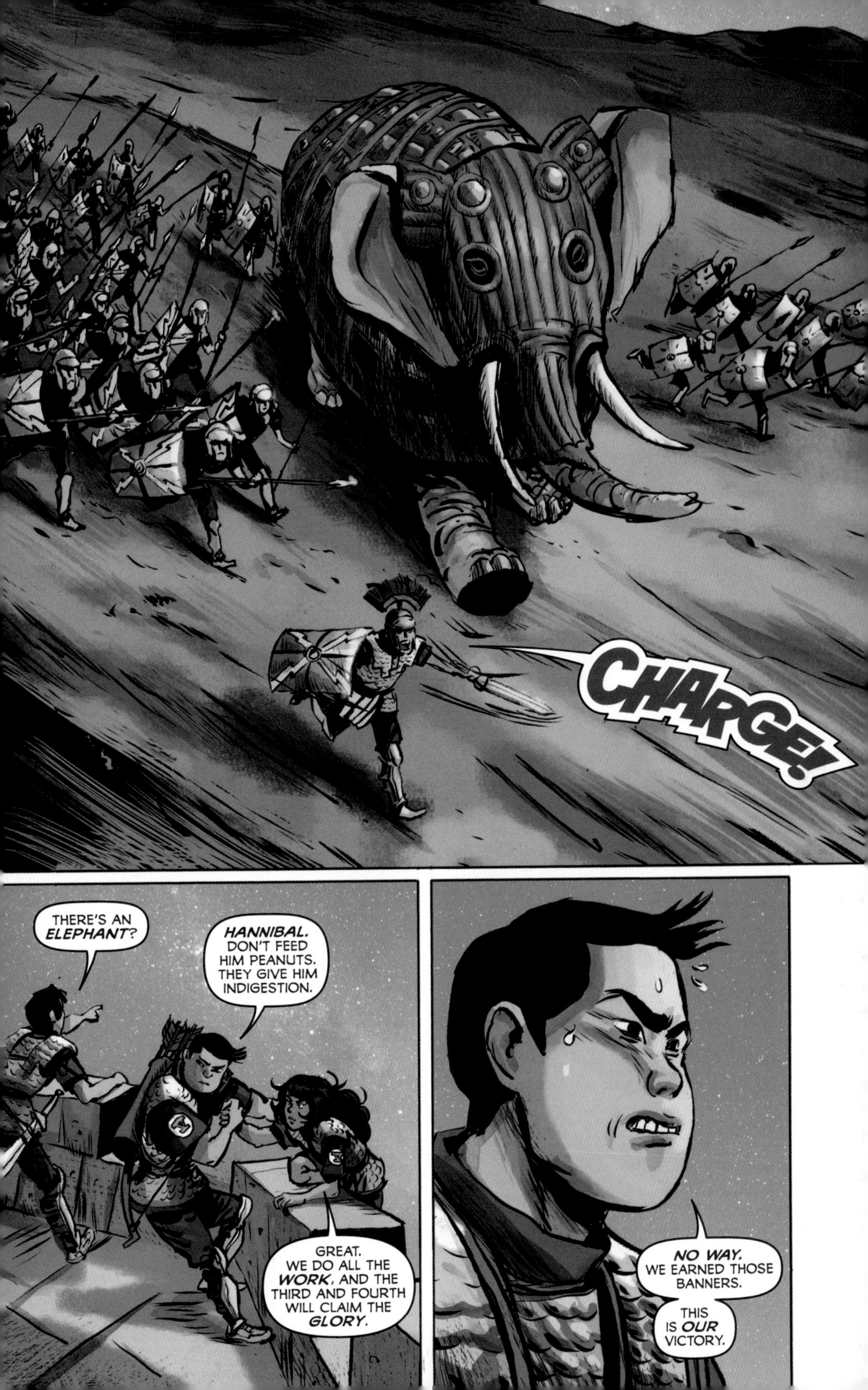
CHARGE!
THERE'S AN *ELEPHANT*?
HANNIBAL. DON'T FEED HIM PEANUTS. THEY GIVE HIM INDIGESTION.
GREAT. WE DO ALL THE ***WORK***, AND THE THIRD AND FOURTH WILL CLAIM THE ***GLORY***.
NO WAY. WE EARNED THOSE BANNERS.
THIS IS ***OUR*** VICTORY.

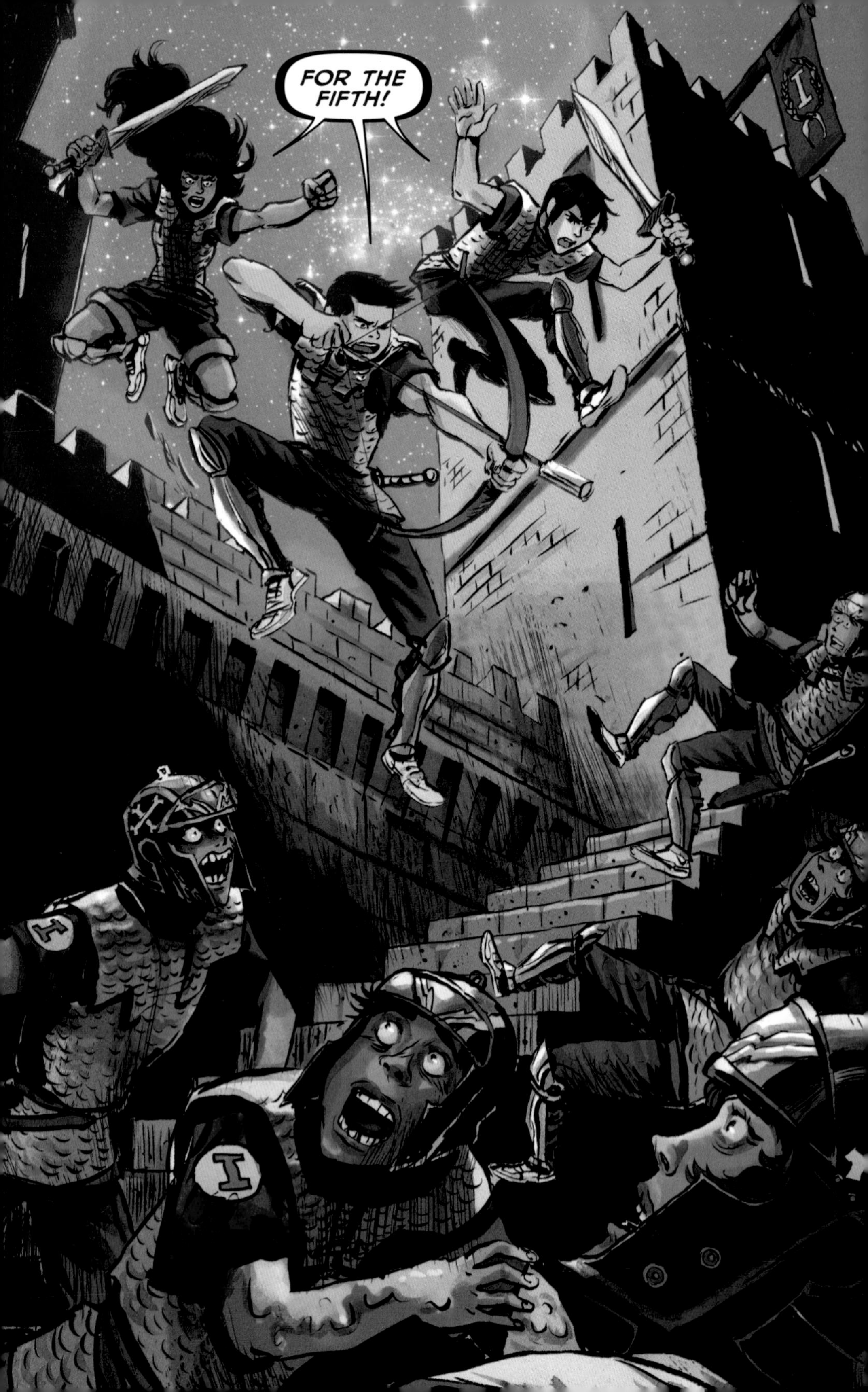
FOR THE FIFTH!

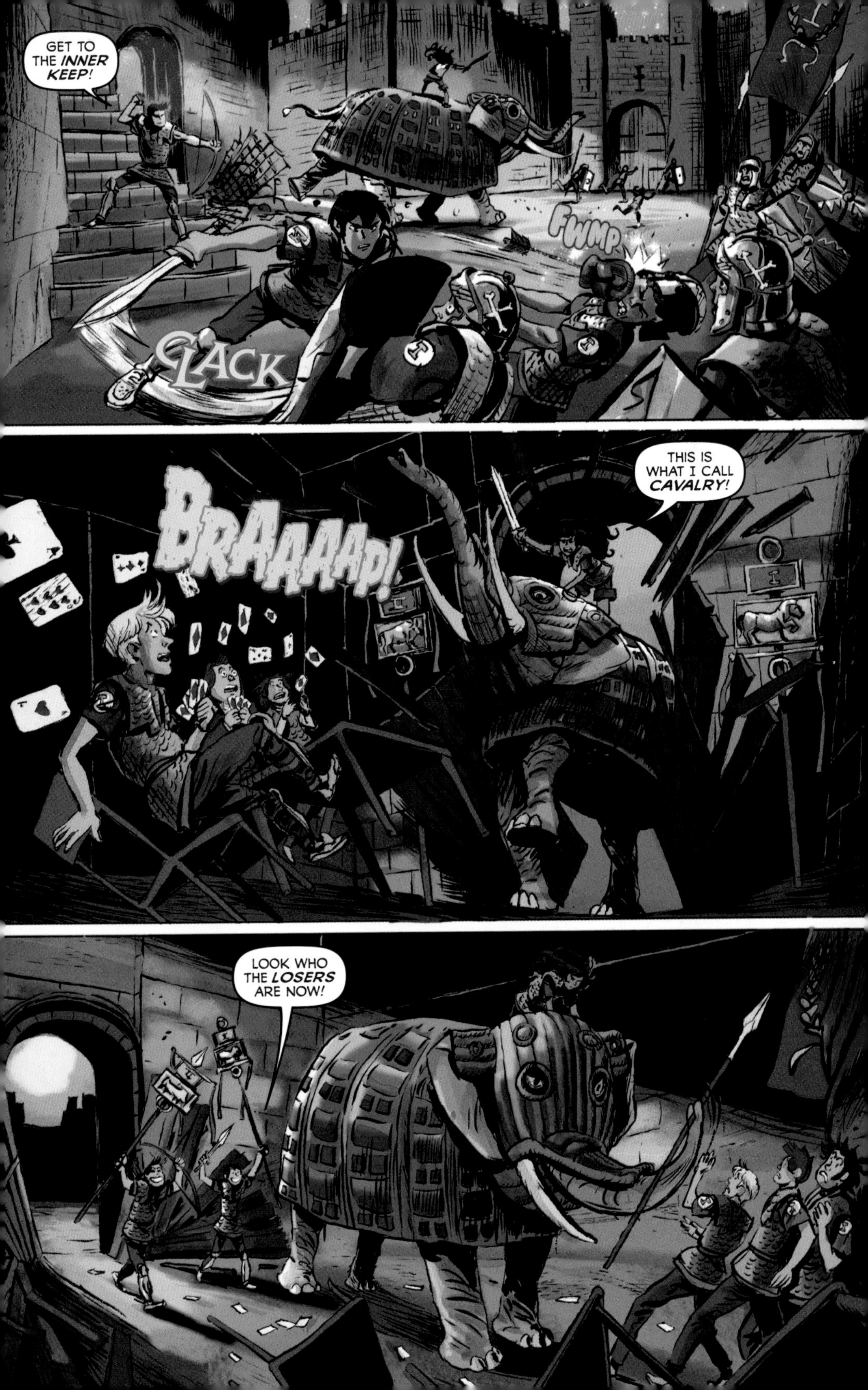
GET TO THE *INNER KEEP*!
FWMP
CLACK
BRAAAAP!
THIS IS WHAT I CALL *CAVALRY*!
LOOK WHO THE *LOSERS* ARE NOW!

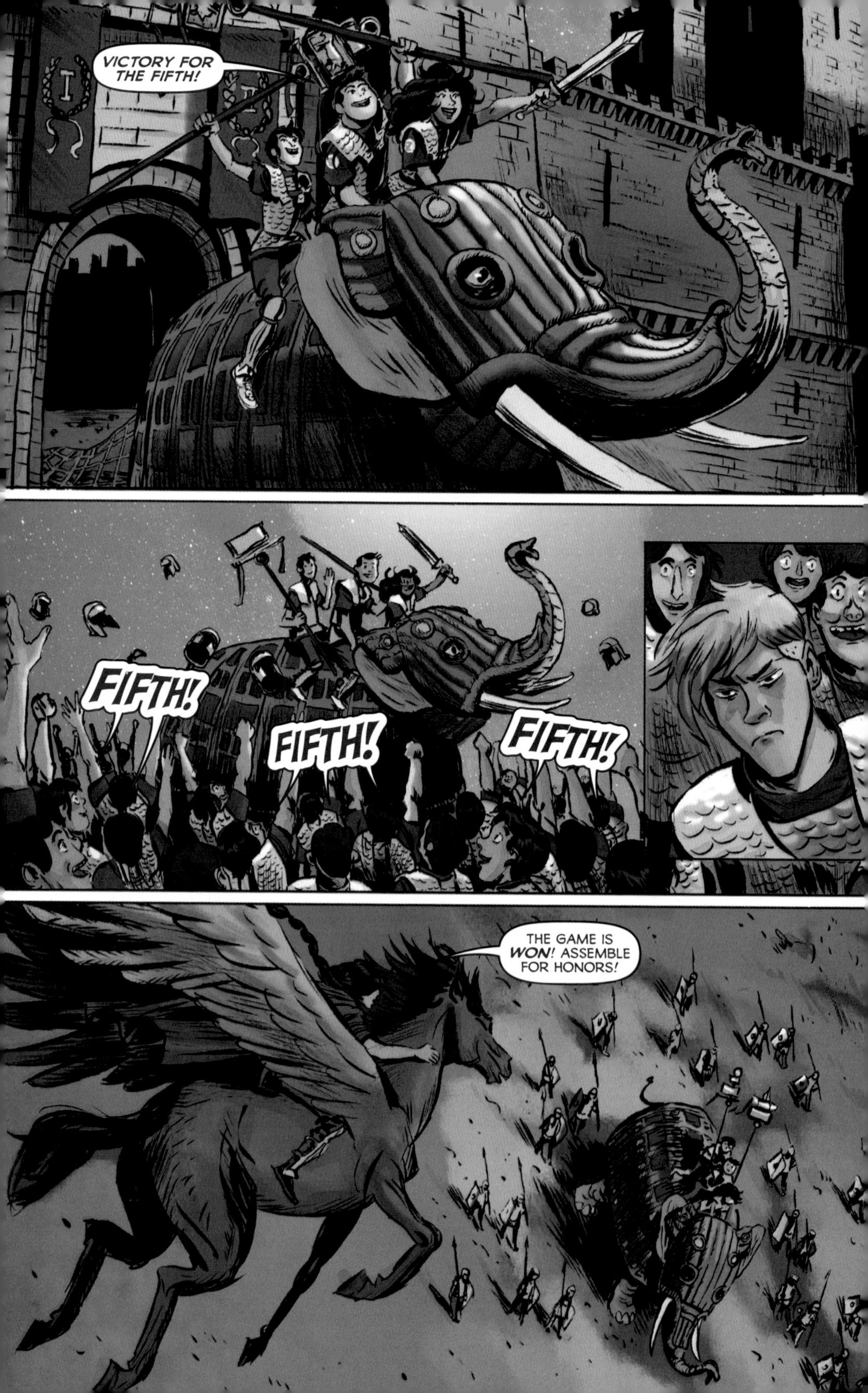
VICTORY FOR THE FIFTH!
FIFTH!
FIFTH!
FIFTH!
THE GAME IS WON! ASSEMBLE FOR HONORS!

CONGRATULATIONS, FRANK. YOU'LL GET THE MURAL CROWN FOR THIS. YOU DID REALLY GREAT.

WE DID GREAT.

NOT BAD FOR *GREEKS* AND *GEEKS*.

SOMEBODY HELP!

GWEN'S HURT BAD!

NO!

SHE'S... GONE.

THIS SWORD...

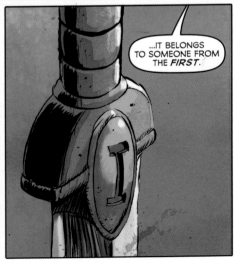

...IT BELONGS TO SOMEONE FROM THE *FIRST*.

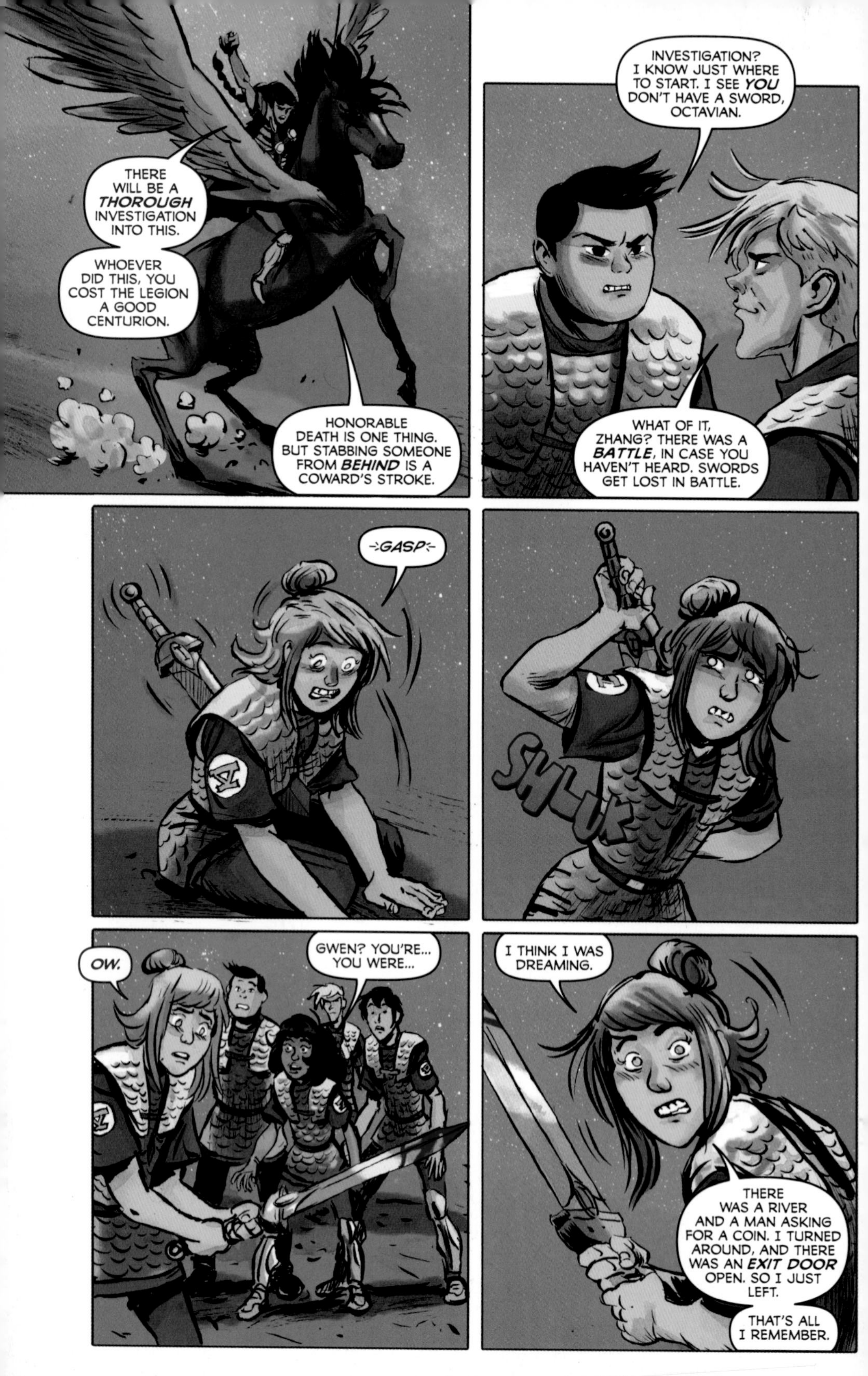
THERE WILL BE A THOROUGH INVESTIGATION INTO THIS.
WHOEVER DID THIS, YOU COST THE LEGION A GOOD CENTURION.
HONORABLE DEATH IS ONE THING. BUT STABBING SOMEONE FROM BEHIND IS A COWARD'S STROKE.
INVESTIGATION? I KNOW JUST WHERE TO START. I SEE YOU DON'T HAVE A SWORD, OCTAVIAN.
WHAT OF IT, ZHANG? THERE WAS A BATTLE, IN CASE YOU HAVEN'T HEARD. SWORDS GET LOST IN BATTLE.
GASP
SHLUK
OW.
GWEN? YOU'RE... YOU WERE...
I THINK I WAS DREAMING.
THERE WAS A RIVER AND A MAN ASKING FOR A COIN. I TURNED AROUND, AND THERE WAS AN EXIT DOOR OPEN. SO I JUST LEFT.
THAT'S ALL I REMEMBER.

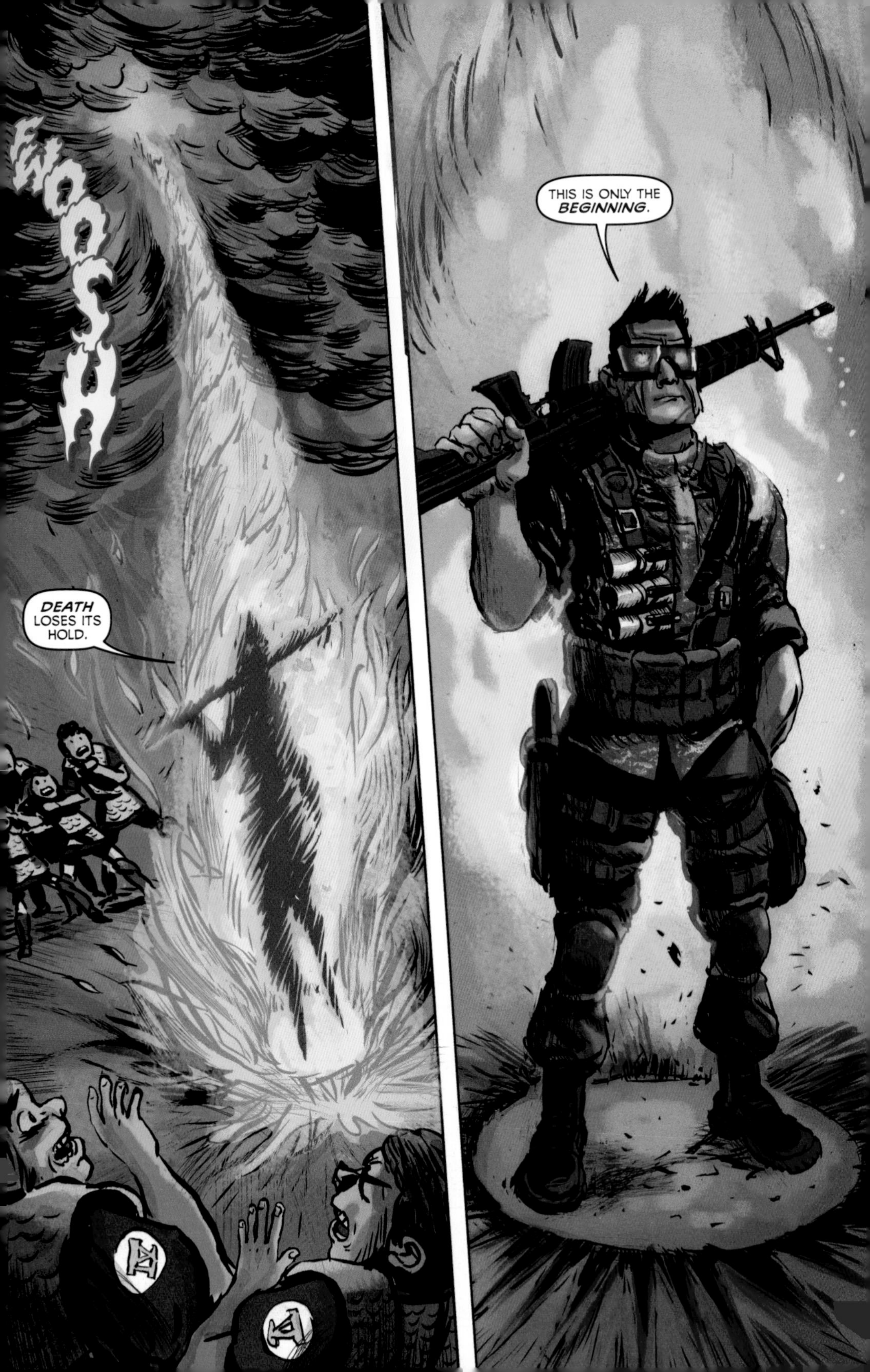
WHOOSH
DEATH LOSES ITS HOLD.
THIS IS ONLY THE BEGINNING.

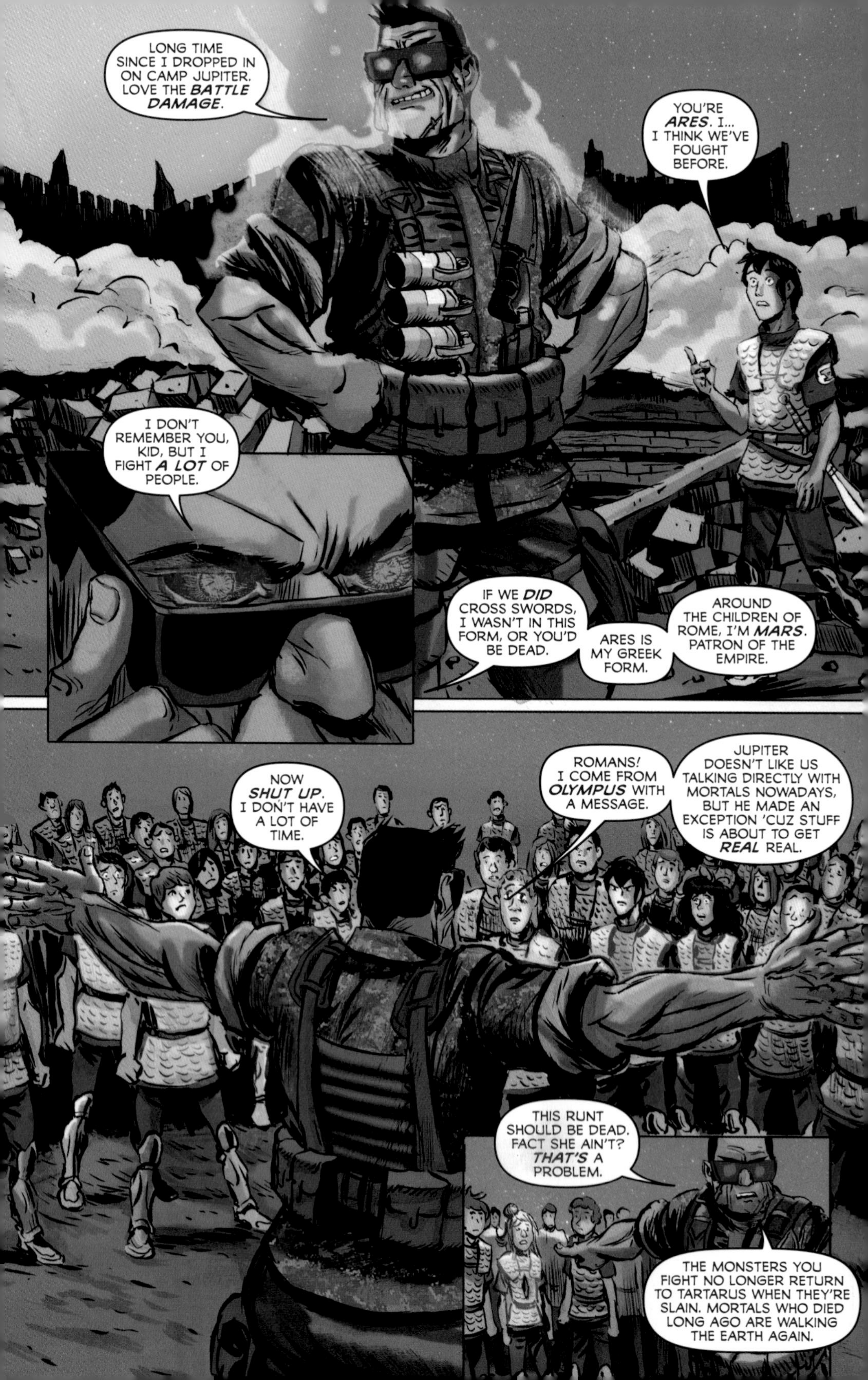
LONG TIME SINCE I DROPPED IN ON CAMP JUPITER. LOVE THE *BATTLE DAMAGE*.
YOU'RE *ARES*. I... I THINK WE'VE FOUGHT BEFORE.
I DON'T REMEMBER YOU, KID, BUT I FIGHT *A LOT* OF PEOPLE.
IF WE *DID* CROSS SWORDS, I WASN'T IN THIS FORM, OR YOU'D BE DEAD.
ARES IS MY GREEK FORM.
AROUND THE CHILDREN OF ROME, I'M *MARS*. PATRON OF THE EMPIRE.
NOW *SHUT UP*. I DON'T HAVE A LOT OF TIME.
ROMANS! I COME FROM *OLYMPUS* WITH A MESSAGE.
JUPITER DOESN'T LIKE US TALKING DIRECTLY WITH MORTALS NOWADAYS, BUT HE MADE AN EXCEPTION 'CUZ STUFF IS ABOUT TO GET *REAL* REAL.
THIS RUNT SHOULD BE DEAD. FACT SHE AIN'T? *THAT'S* A PROBLEM.
THE MONSTERS YOU FIGHT NO LONGER RETURN TO TARTARUS WHEN THEY'RE SLAIN. MORTALS WHO DIED LONG AGO ARE WALKING THE EARTH AGAIN.

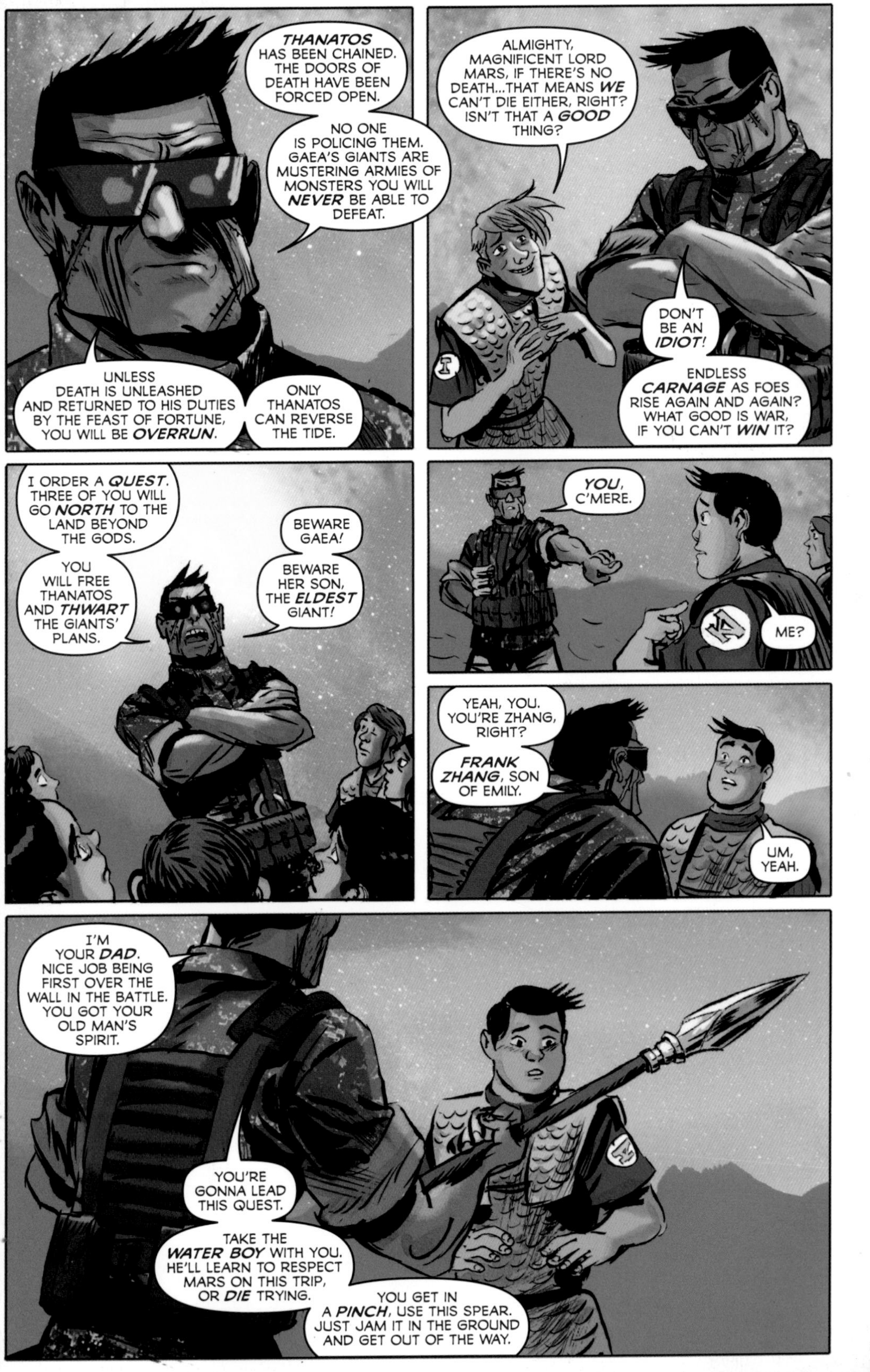
THANATOS HAS BEEN CHAINED. THE DOORS OF DEATH HAVE BEEN FORCED OPEN.
NO ONE IS POLICING THEM. GAEA'S GIANTS ARE MUSTERING ARMIES OF MONSTERS YOU WILL NEVER BE ABLE TO DEFEAT.
UNLESS DEATH IS UNLEASHED AND RETURNED TO HIS DUTIES BY THE FEAST OF FORTUNE, YOU WILL BE OVERRUN.
ONLY THANATOS CAN REVERSE THE TIDE.
ALMIGHTY, MAGNIFICENT LORD MARS, IF THERE'S NO DEATH...THAT MEANS WE CAN'T DIE EITHER, RIGHT? ISN'T THAT A GOOD THING?
DON'T BE AN IDIOT!
ENDLESS CARNAGE AS FOES RISE AGAIN AND AGAIN? WHAT GOOD IS WAR, IF YOU CAN'T WIN IT?
I ORDER A QUEST. THREE OF YOU WILL GO NORTH TO THE LAND BEYOND THE GODS.
YOU WILL FREE THANATOS AND THWART THE GIANTS' PLANS.
BEWARE GAEA!
BEWARE HER SON, THE ELDEST GIANT!
YOU, C'MERE.
ME?
YEAH, YOU. YOU'RE ZHANG, RIGHT?
FRANK ZHANG, SON OF EMILY.
UM, YEAH.
I'M YOUR DAD. NICE JOB BEING FIRST OVER THE WALL IN THE BATTLE. YOU GOT YOUR OLD MAN'S SPIRIT.
YOU'RE GONNA LEAD THIS QUEST.
TAKE THE WATER BOY WITH YOU. HE'LL LEARN TO RESPECT MARS ON THIS TRIP, OR DIE TRYING.
YOU GET IN A PINCH, USE THIS SPEAR. JUST JAM IT IN THE GROUND AND GET OUT OF THE WAY.

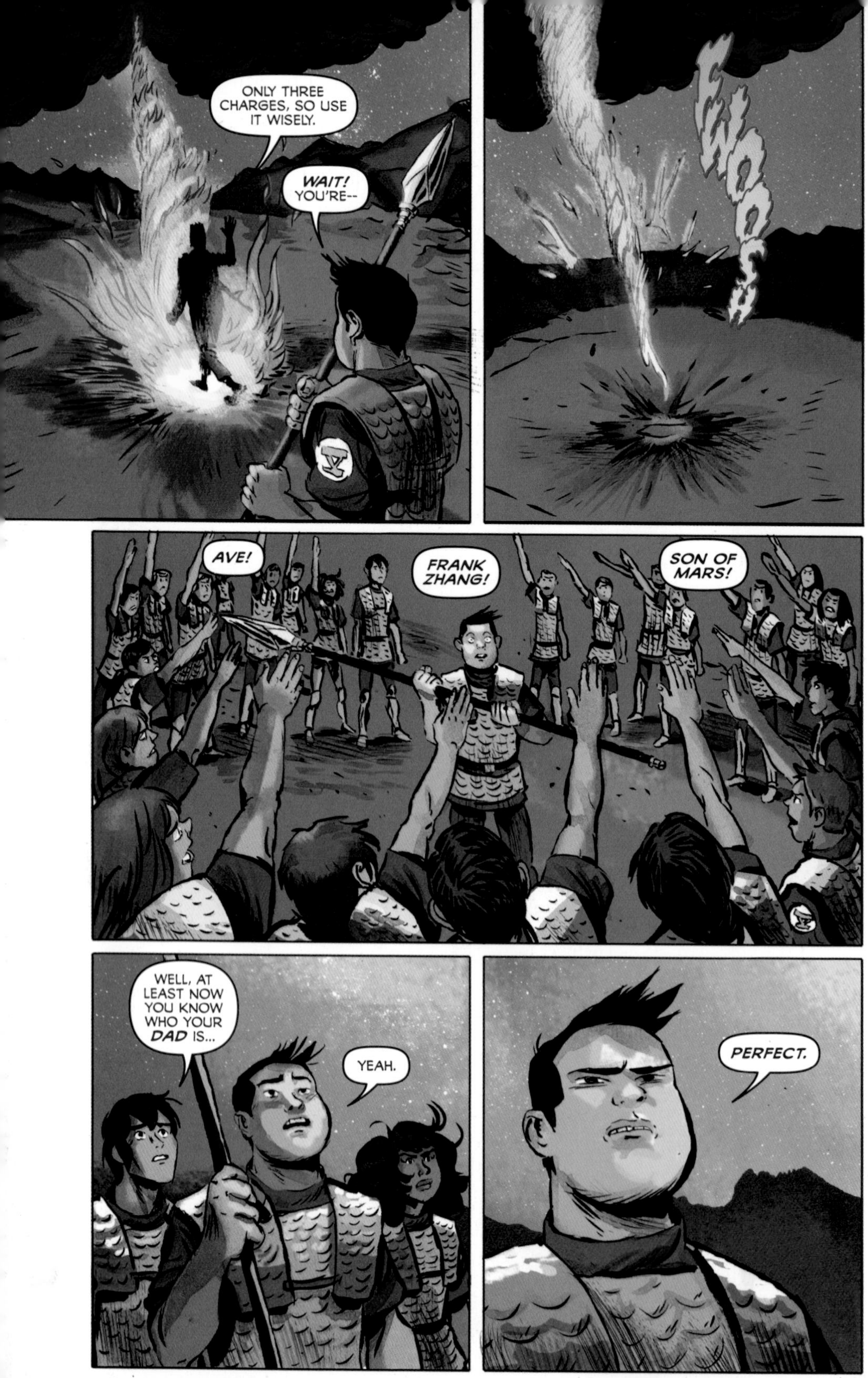
ONLY THREE CHARGES, SO USE IT WISELY.
WAIT! YOU'RE--
WHOOSH
AVE!
FRANK ZHANG!
SON OF MARS!
WELL, AT LEAST NOW YOU KNOW WHO YOUR DAD IS...
YEAH.
PERFECT.

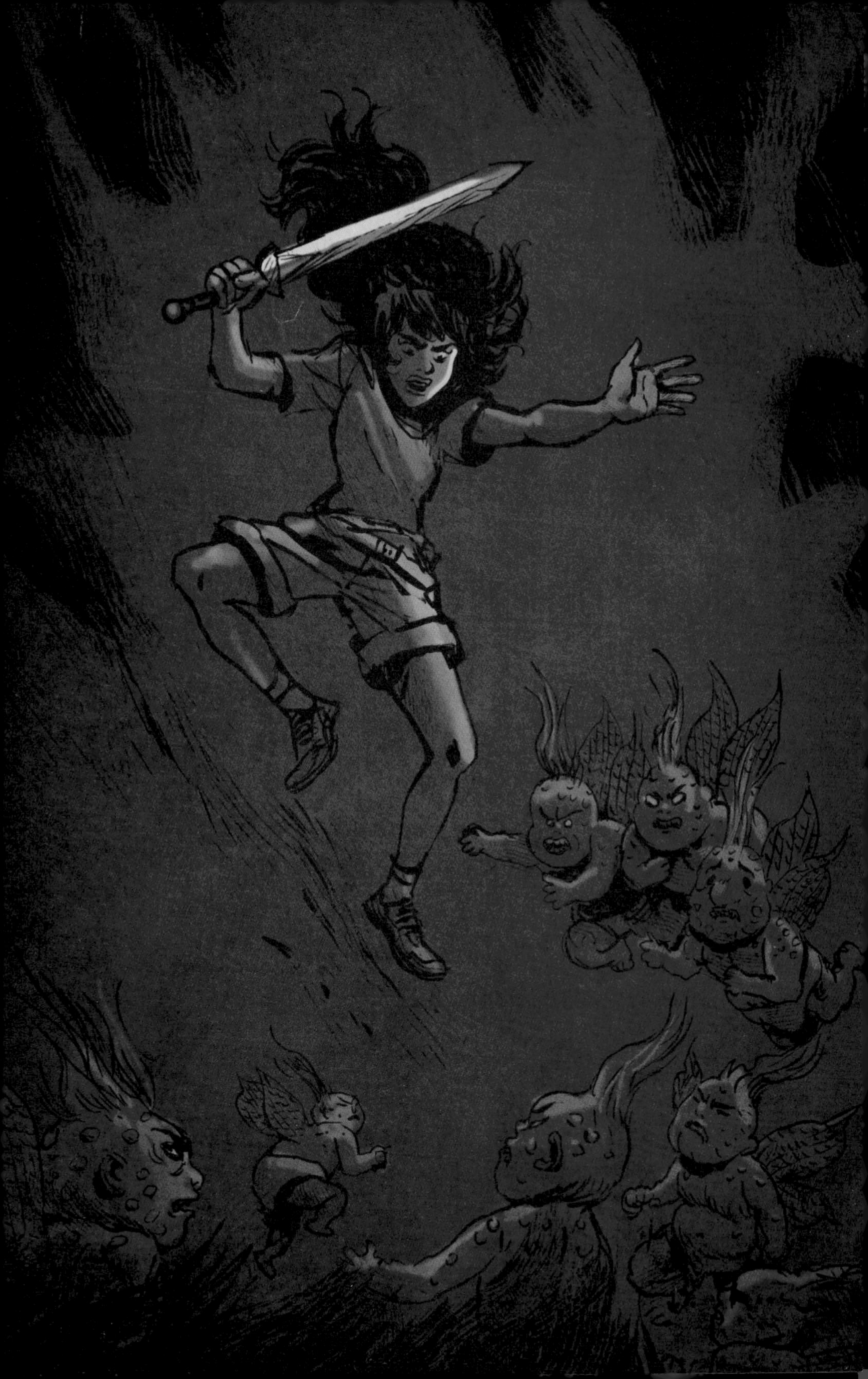

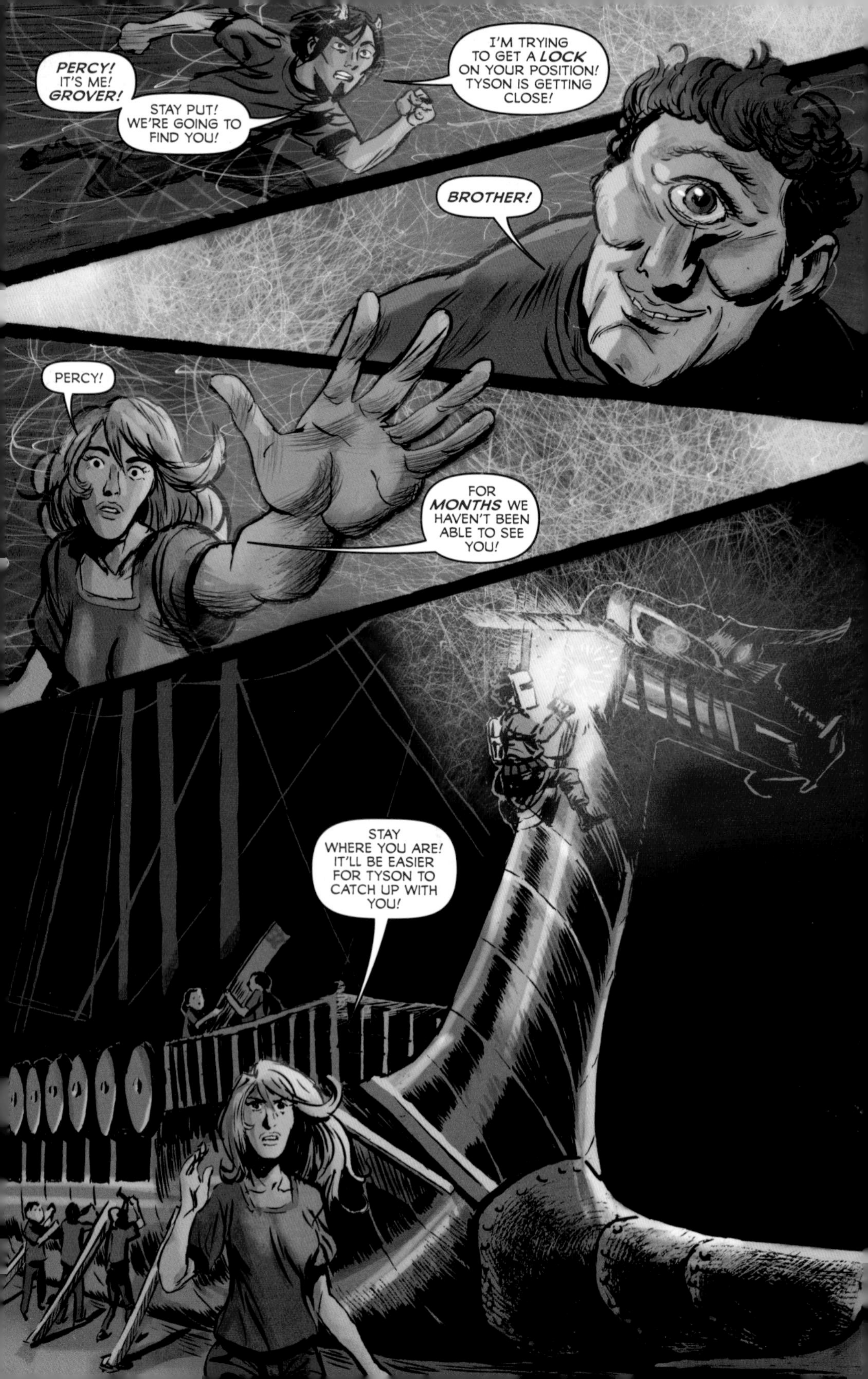
PERCY! IT'S ME! GROVER!
STAY PUT! WE'RE GOING TO FIND YOU!
I'M TRYING TO GET A LOCK ON YOUR POSITION! TYSON IS GETTING CLOSE!
BROTHER!
PERCY!
FOR MONTHS WE HAVEN'T BEEN ABLE TO SEE YOU!
STAY WHERE YOU ARE! IT'LL BE EASIER FOR TYSON TO CATCH UP WITH YOU!

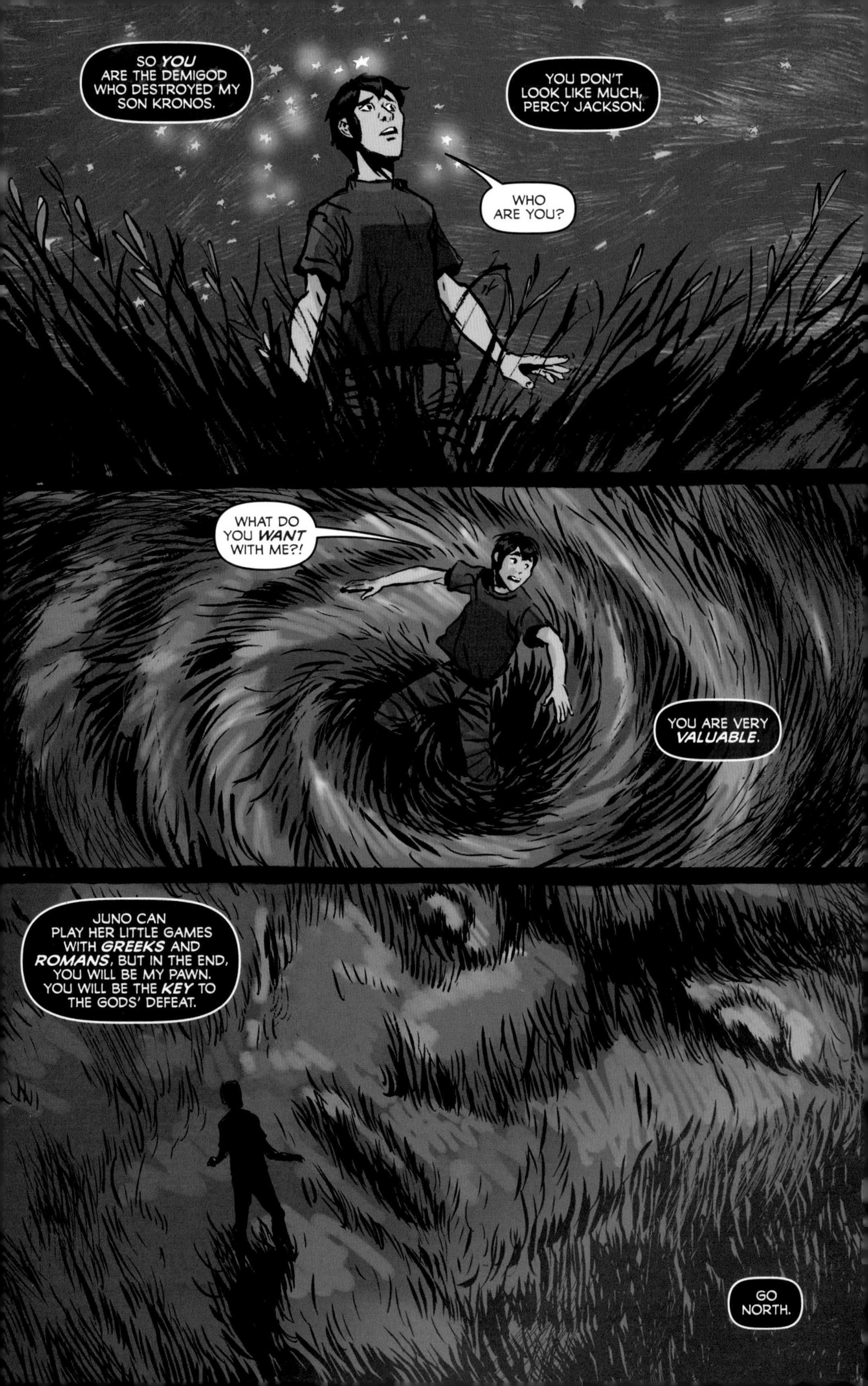
SO *YOU* ARE THE DEMIGOD WHO DESTROYED MY SON KRONOS.
YOU DON'T LOOK LIKE MUCH, PERCY JACKSON.
WHO ARE YOU?
WHAT DO YOU *WANT* WITH ME?!
YOU ARE VERY *VALUABLE*.
JUNO CAN PLAY HER LITTLE GAMES WITH *GREEKS* AND *ROMANS*, BUT IN THE END, YOU WILL BE MY PAWN. YOU WILL BE THE *KEY* TO THE GODS' DEFEAT.
GO NORTH.

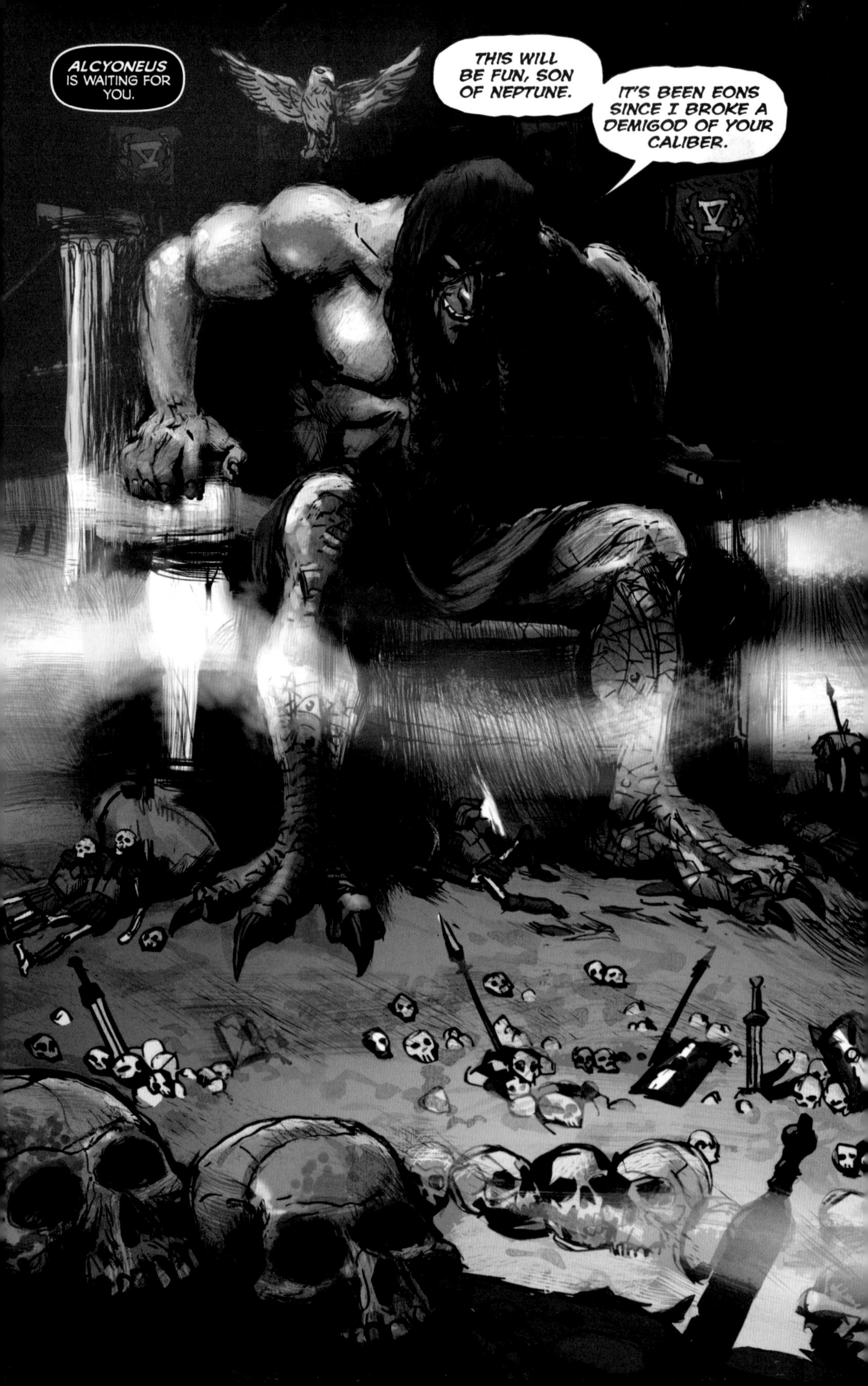
ALCYONEUS IS WAITING FOR YOU.
THIS WILL BE FUN, SON OF NEPTUNE.
IT'S BEEN EONS SINCE I BROKE A DEMIGOD OF YOUR CALIBER.

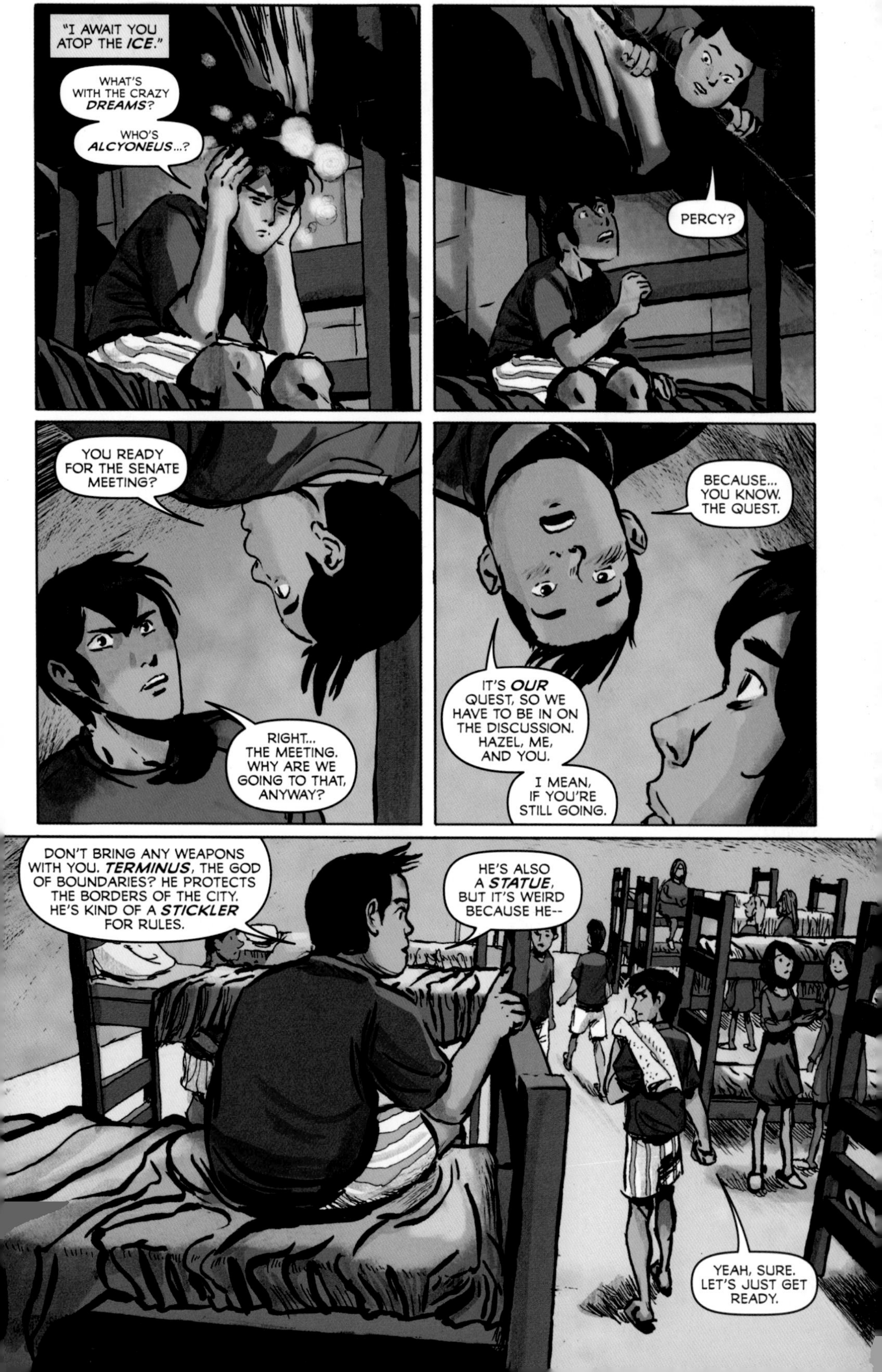
"I AWAIT YOU ATOP THE ICE."
WHAT'S WITH THE CRAZY DREAMS?
WHO'S ALCYONEUS...?
PERCY?
YOU READY FOR THE SENATE MEETING?
RIGHT... THE MEETING. WHY ARE WE GOING TO THAT, ANYWAY?
BECAUSE... YOU KNOW. THE QUEST.
IT'S OUR QUEST, SO WE HAVE TO BE IN ON THE DISCUSSION. HAZEL, ME, AND YOU.
I MEAN, IF YOU'RE STILL GOING.
DON'T BRING ANY WEAPONS WITH YOU. TERMINUS, THE GOD OF BOUNDARIES? HE PROTECTS THE BORDERS OF THE CITY. HE'S KIND OF A STICKLER FOR RULES.
HE'S ALSO A STATUE, BUT IT'S WEIRD BECAUSE HE--
YEAH, SURE. LET'S JUST GET READY.

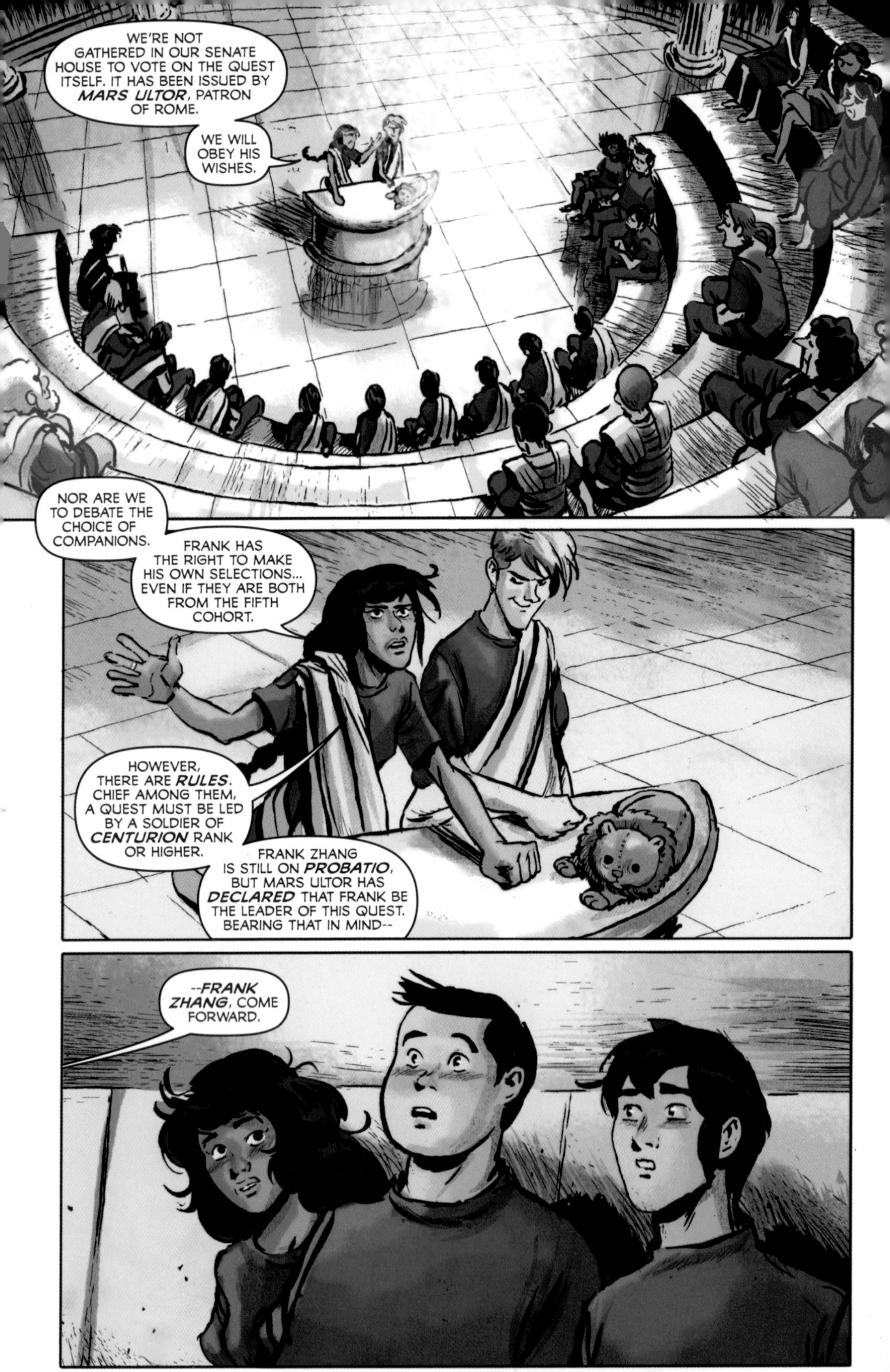

WE'RE NOT GATHERED IN OUR SENATE HOUSE TO VOTE ON THE QUEST ITSELF. IT HAS BEEN ISSUED BY MARS ULTOR, PATRON OF ROME.
WE WILL OBEY HIS WISHES.
NOR ARE WE TO DEBATE THE CHOICE OF COMPANIONS.
FRANK HAS THE RIGHT TO MAKE HIS OWN SELECTIONS... EVEN IF THEY ARE BOTH FROM THE FIFTH COHORT.
HOWEVER, THERE ARE RULES. CHIEF AMONG THEM, A QUEST MUST BE LED BY A SOLDIER OF CENTURION RANK OR HIGHER.
FRANK ZHANG IS STILL ON PROBATIO, BUT MARS ULTOR HAS DECLARED THAT FRANK BE THE LEADER OF THIS QUEST. BEARING THAT IN MIND--
--FRANK ZHANG, COME FORWARD.

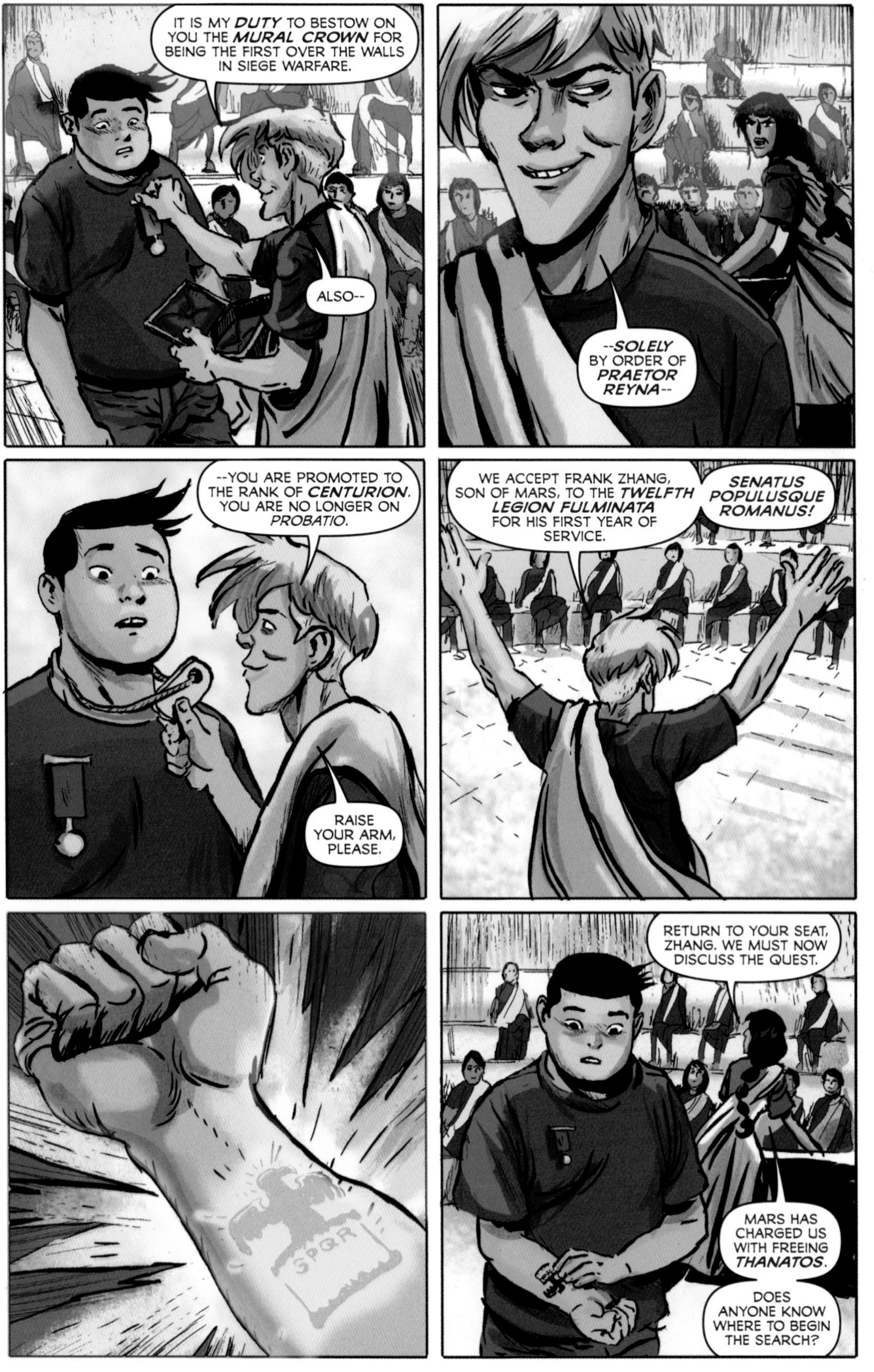
IT IS MY DUTY TO BESTOW ON YOU THE MURAL CROWN FOR BEING THE FIRST OVER THE WALLS IN SIEGE WARFARE.
ALSO--
--SOLELY BY ORDER OF PRAETOR REYNA--
--YOU ARE PROMOTED TO THE RANK OF CENTURION. YOU ARE NO LONGER ON PROBATIO.
RAISE YOUR ARM, PLEASE.
WE ACCEPT FRANK ZHANG, SON OF MARS, TO THE TWELFTH LEGION FULMINATA FOR HIS FIRST YEAR OF SERVICE.
SENATUS POPULUSQUE ROMANUS!
SPQR
RETURN TO YOUR SEAT, ZHANG. WE MUST NOW DISCUSS THE QUEST.
MARS HAS CHARGED US WITH FREEING THANATOS.
DOES ANYONE KNOW WHERE TO BEGIN THE SEARCH?

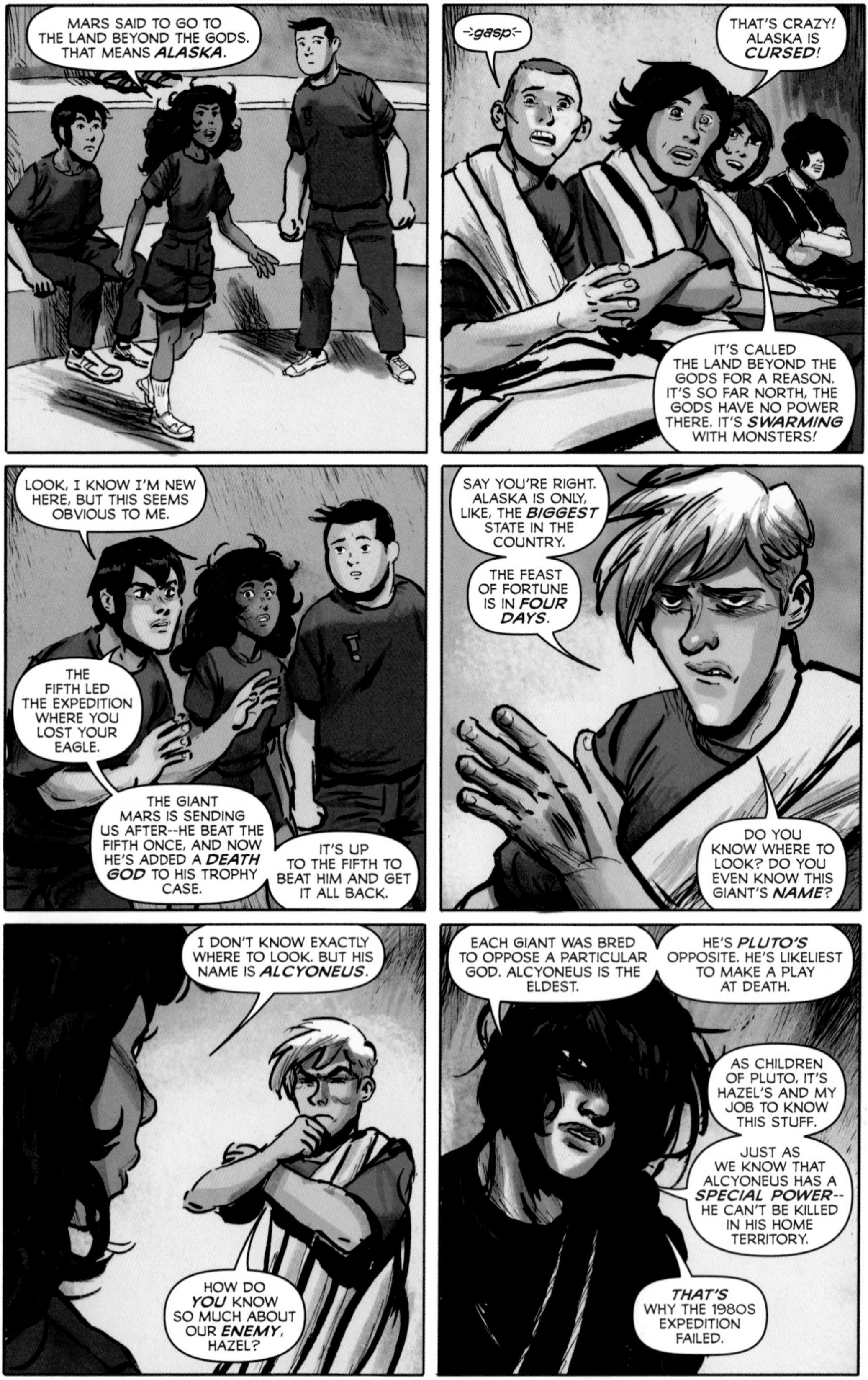
MARS SAID TO GO TO THE LAND BEYOND THE GODS. THAT MEANS ALASKA.
-gasp-
THAT'S CRAZY! ALASKA IS CURSED!
IT'S CALLED THE LAND BEYOND THE GODS FOR A REASON. IT'S SO FAR NORTH, THE GODS HAVE NO POWER THERE. IT'S SWARMING WITH MONSTERS!
LOOK, I KNOW I'M NEW HERE, BUT THIS SEEMS OBVIOUS TO ME.
THE FIFTH LED THE EXPEDITION WHERE YOU LOST YOUR EAGLE.
THE GIANT MARS IS SENDING US AFTER--HE BEAT THE FIFTH ONCE, AND NOW HE'S ADDED A DEATH GOD TO HIS TROPHY CASE.
IT'S UP TO THE FIFTH TO BEAT HIM AND GET IT ALL BACK.
SAY YOU'RE RIGHT. ALASKA IS ONLY, LIKE, THE BIGGEST STATE IN THE COUNTRY.
THE FEAST OF FORTUNE IS IN FOUR DAYS.
DO YOU KNOW WHERE TO LOOK? DO YOU EVEN KNOW THIS GIANT'S NAME?
I DON'T KNOW EXACTLY WHERE TO LOOK. BUT HIS NAME IS ALCYONEUS.
HOW DO YOU KNOW SO MUCH ABOUT OUR ENEMY, HAZEL?
EACH GIANT WAS BRED TO OPPOSE A PARTICULAR GOD. ALCYONEUS IS THE ELDEST.
HE'S PLUTO'S OPPOSITE. HE'S LIKELIEST TO MAKE A PLAY AT DEATH.
AS CHILDREN OF PLUTO, IT'S HAZEL'S AND MY JOB TO KNOW THIS STUFF.
JUST AS WE KNOW THAT ALCYONEUS HAS A SPECIAL POWER--HE CAN'T BE KILLED IN HIS HOME TERRITORY.
THAT'S WHY THE 1980S EXPEDITION FAILED.

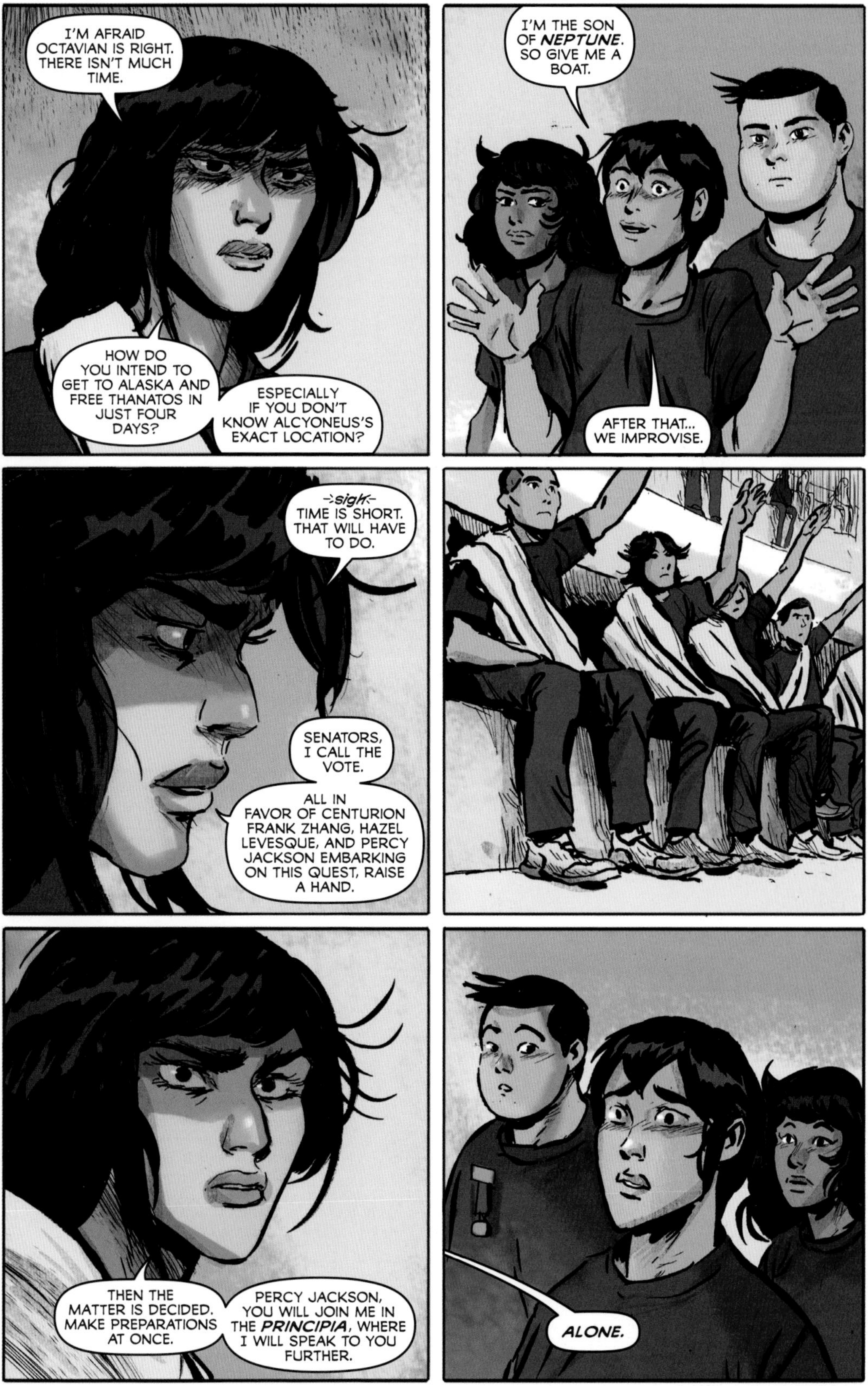
I'M AFRAID OCTAVIAN IS RIGHT. THERE ISN'T MUCH TIME.
HOW DO YOU INTEND TO GET TO ALASKA AND FREE THANATOS IN JUST FOUR DAYS?
ESPECIALLY IF YOU DON'T KNOW ALCYONEUS'S EXACT LOCATION?
I'M THE SON OF ***NEPTUNE***. SO GIVE ME A BOAT.
AFTER THAT... WE IMPROVISE.
-sigh-
TIME IS SHORT. THAT WILL HAVE TO DO.
SENATORS, I CALL THE VOTE.
ALL IN FAVOR OF CENTURION FRANK ZHANG, HAZEL LEVESQUE, AND PERCY JACKSON EMBARKING ON THIS QUEST, RAISE A HAND.
THEN THE MATTER IS DECIDED. MAKE PREPARATIONS AT ONCE.
PERCY JACKSON, YOU WILL JOIN ME IN THE ***PRINCIPIA***, WHERE I WILL SPEAK TO YOU FURTHER.
ALONE.

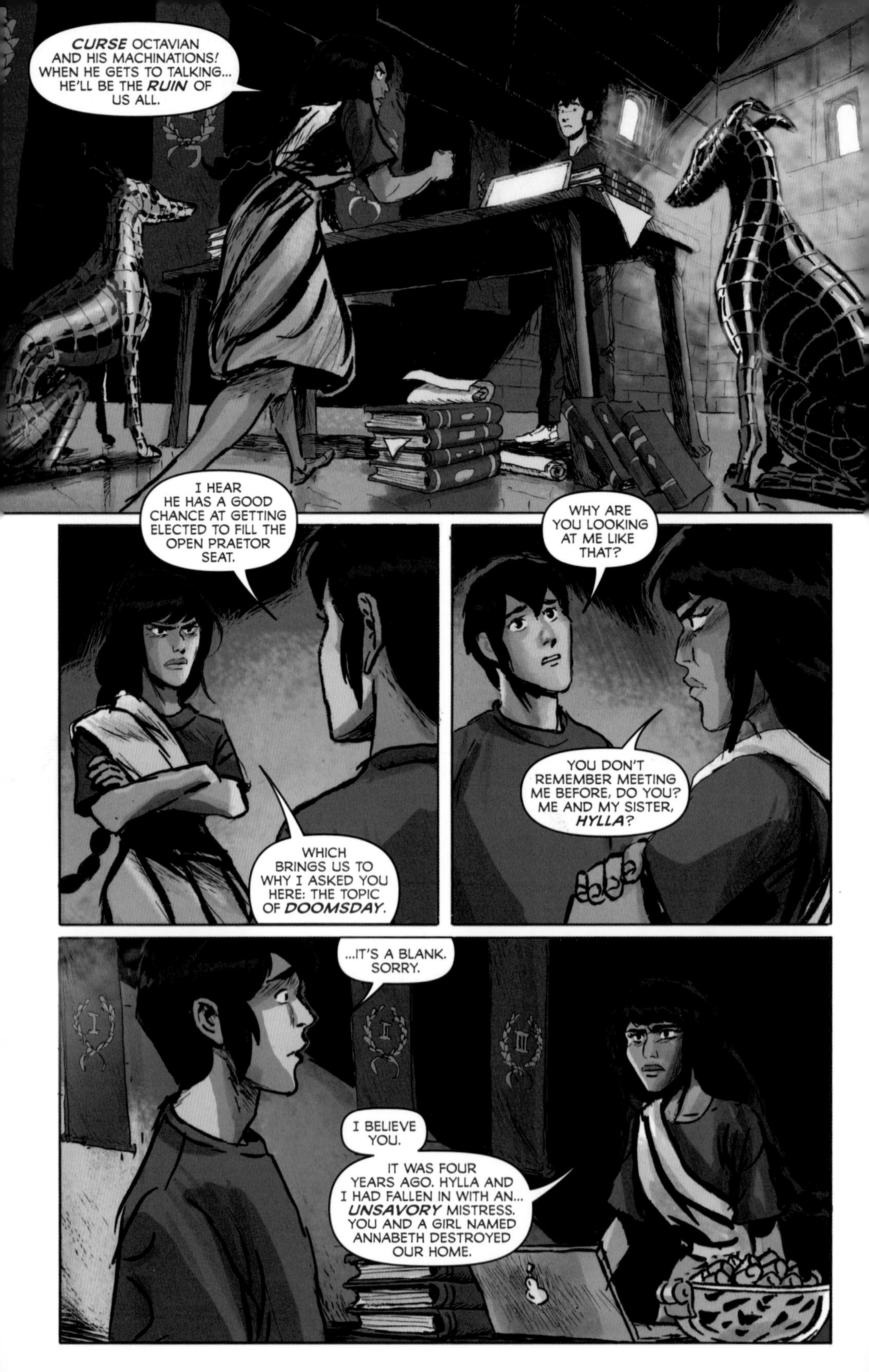
CURSE OCTAVIAN AND HIS MACHINATIONS! WHEN HE GETS TO TALKING... HE'LL BE THE RUIN OF US ALL.
I HEAR HE HAS A GOOD CHANCE AT GETTING ELECTED TO FILL THE OPEN PRAETOR SEAT.
WHICH BRINGS US TO WHY I ASKED YOU HERE: THE TOPIC OF DOOMSDAY.
WHY ARE YOU LOOKING AT ME LIKE THAT?
YOU DON'T REMEMBER MEETING ME BEFORE, DO YOU? ME AND MY SISTER, HYLLA?
...IT'S A BLANK. SORRY.
I BELIEVE YOU.
IT WAS FOUR YEARS AGO. HYLLA AND I HAD FALLEN IN WITH AN... UNSAVORY MISTRESS. YOU AND A GIRL NAMED ANNABETH DESTROYED OUR HOME.

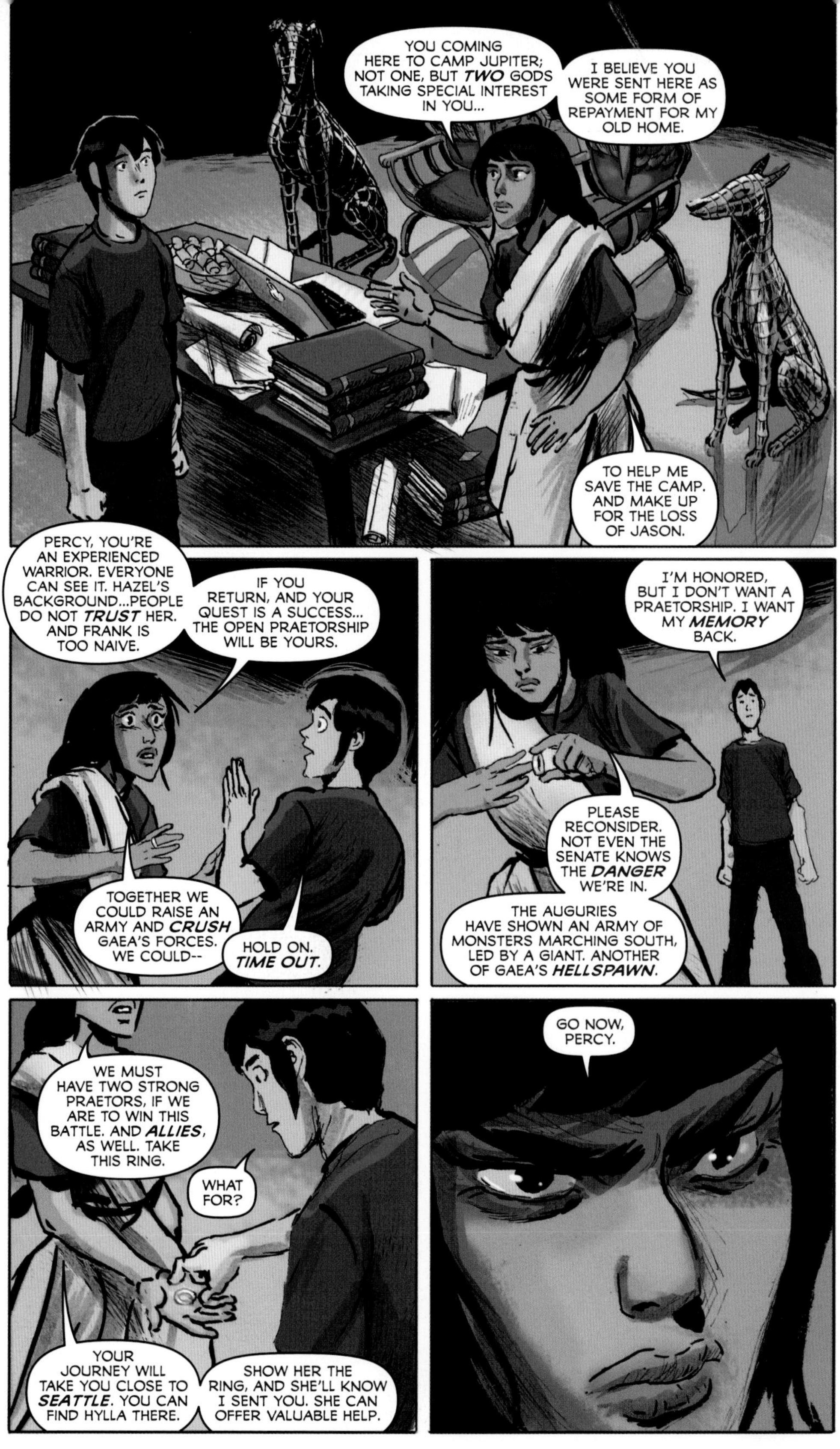
YOU COMING HERE TO CAMP JUPITER; NOT ONE, BUT TWO GODS TAKING SPECIAL INTEREST IN YOU...
I BELIEVE YOU WERE SENT HERE AS SOME FORM OF REPAYMENT FOR MY OLD HOME.
TO HELP ME SAVE THE CAMP. AND MAKE UP FOR THE LOSS OF JASON.
PERCY, YOU'RE AN EXPERIENCED WARRIOR. EVERYONE CAN SEE IT. HAZEL'S BACKGROUND...PEOPLE DO NOT TRUST HER. AND FRANK IS TOO NAIVE.
IF YOU RETURN, AND YOUR QUEST IS A SUCCESS... THE OPEN PRAETORSHIP WILL BE YOURS.
TOGETHER WE COULD RAISE AN ARMY AND CRUSH GAEA'S FORCES. WE COULD--
HOLD ON. TIME OUT.
I'M HONORED, BUT I DON'T WANT A PRAETORSHIP. I WANT MY MEMORY BACK.
PLEASE RECONSIDER. NOT EVEN THE SENATE KNOWS THE DANGER WE'RE IN.
THE AUGURIES HAVE SHOWN AN ARMY OF MONSTERS MARCHING SOUTH, LED BY A GIANT. ANOTHER OF GAEA'S HELLSPAWN.
WE MUST HAVE TWO STRONG PRAETORS, IF WE ARE TO WIN THIS BATTLE. AND ALLIES, AS WELL. TAKE THIS RING.
WHAT FOR?
YOUR JOURNEY WILL TAKE YOU CLOSE TO SEATTLE. YOU CAN FIND HYLLA THERE.
SHOW HER THE RING, AND SHE'LL KNOW I SENT YOU. SHE CAN OFFER VALUABLE HELP.
GO NOW, PERCY.

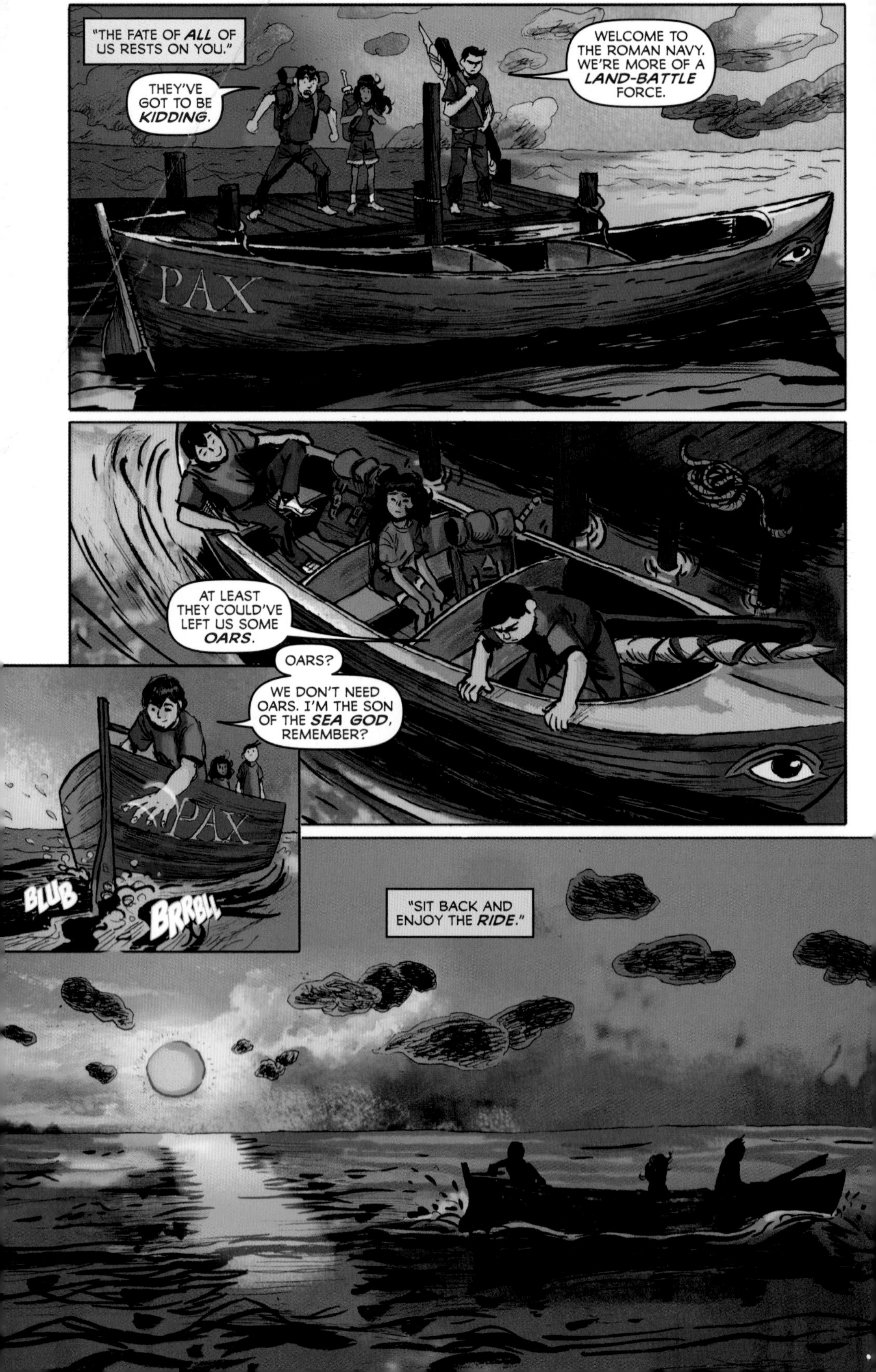
"THE FATE OF ALL OF US RESTS ON YOU."
THEY'VE GOT TO BE KIDDING.
WELCOME TO THE ROMAN NAVY. WE'RE MORE OF A LAND-BATTLE FORCE.
PAX
AT LEAST THEY COULD'VE LEFT US SOME OARS.
OARS?
WE DON'T NEED OARS. I'M THE SON OF THE SEA GOD, REMEMBER?
PAX
BLUB
BRRBLL
"SIT BACK AND ENJOY THE RIDE."

SOMETHING ABOUT THAT PLACE... THE MOUNTAIN LOOKS FAMILIAR.

I THINK I WENT THERE LOOKING FOR MY GIRLFRIEND. YEAH... I REMEMBER. HER NAME IS *ANNABETH*.

MOUNT TAM. KIDS AT CAMP ARE ALWAYS TALKING ABOUT IT. A BIG BATTLE HAPPENED THERE AT THE OLD TITAN BASE.

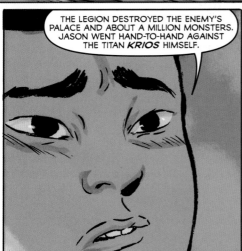

THE LEGION DESTROYED THE ENEMY'S PALACE AND ABOUT A MILLION MONSTERS. JASON WENT HAND-TO-HAND AGAINST THE TITAN *KRIOS* HIMSELF.

THAT WAS BACK IN AUGUST, BEFORE HAZEL AND I GOT TO CAMP.

HAZEL? ARE YOU GETTING SEASICK?

MWUHH

WMMP

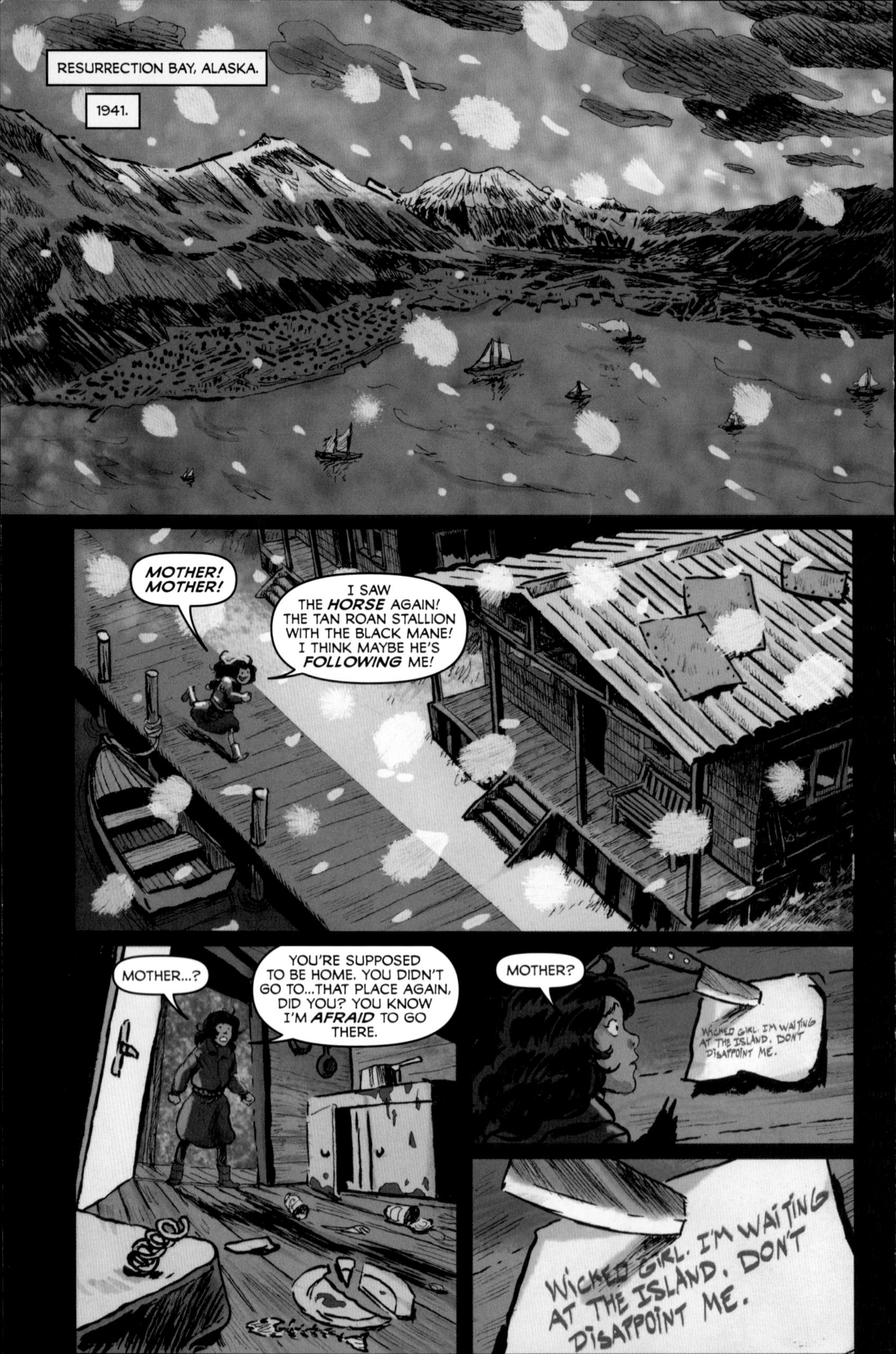
RESURRECTION BAY, ALASKA.
1941.
MOTHER! MOTHER!
I SAW THE HORSE AGAIN! THE TAN ROAN STALLION WITH THE BLACK MANE! I THINK MAYBE HE'S FOLLOWING ME!
MOTHER...?
YOU'RE SUPPOSED TO BE HOME. YOU DIDN'T GO TO...THAT PLACE AGAIN, DID YOU? YOU KNOW I'M AFRAID TO GO THERE.
MOTHER?
WICKED GIRL. I'M WAITING AT THE ISLAND. DON'T DISAPPOINT ME.
WICKED GIRL. I'M WAITING AT THE ISLAND. DON'T DISAPPOINT ME.

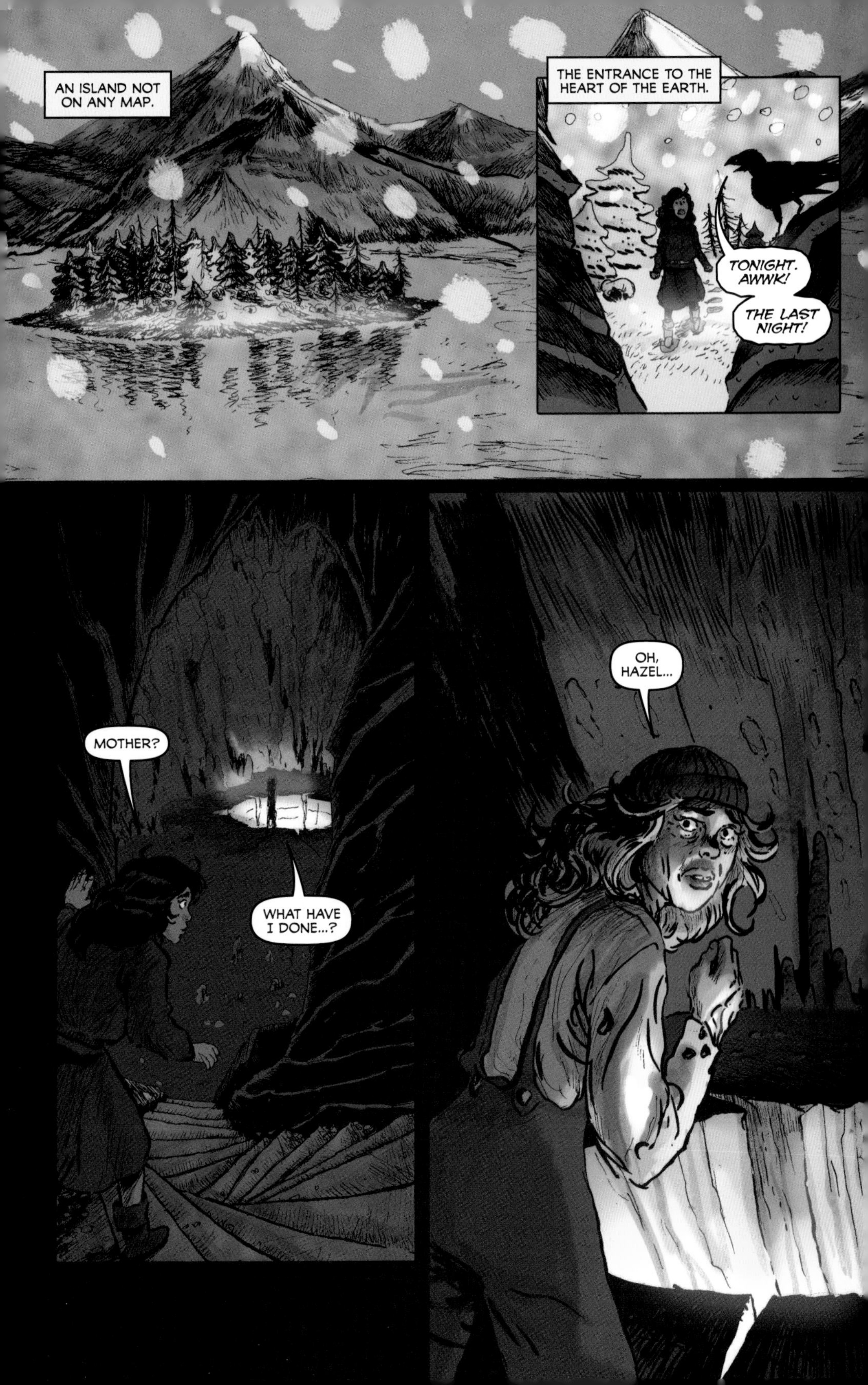
AN ISLAND NOT ON ANY MAP.
THE ENTRANCE TO THE HEART OF THE EARTH.
TONIGHT. AWWK!
THE LAST NIGHT!
MOTHER?
WHAT HAVE I DONE...?
OH, HAZEL...

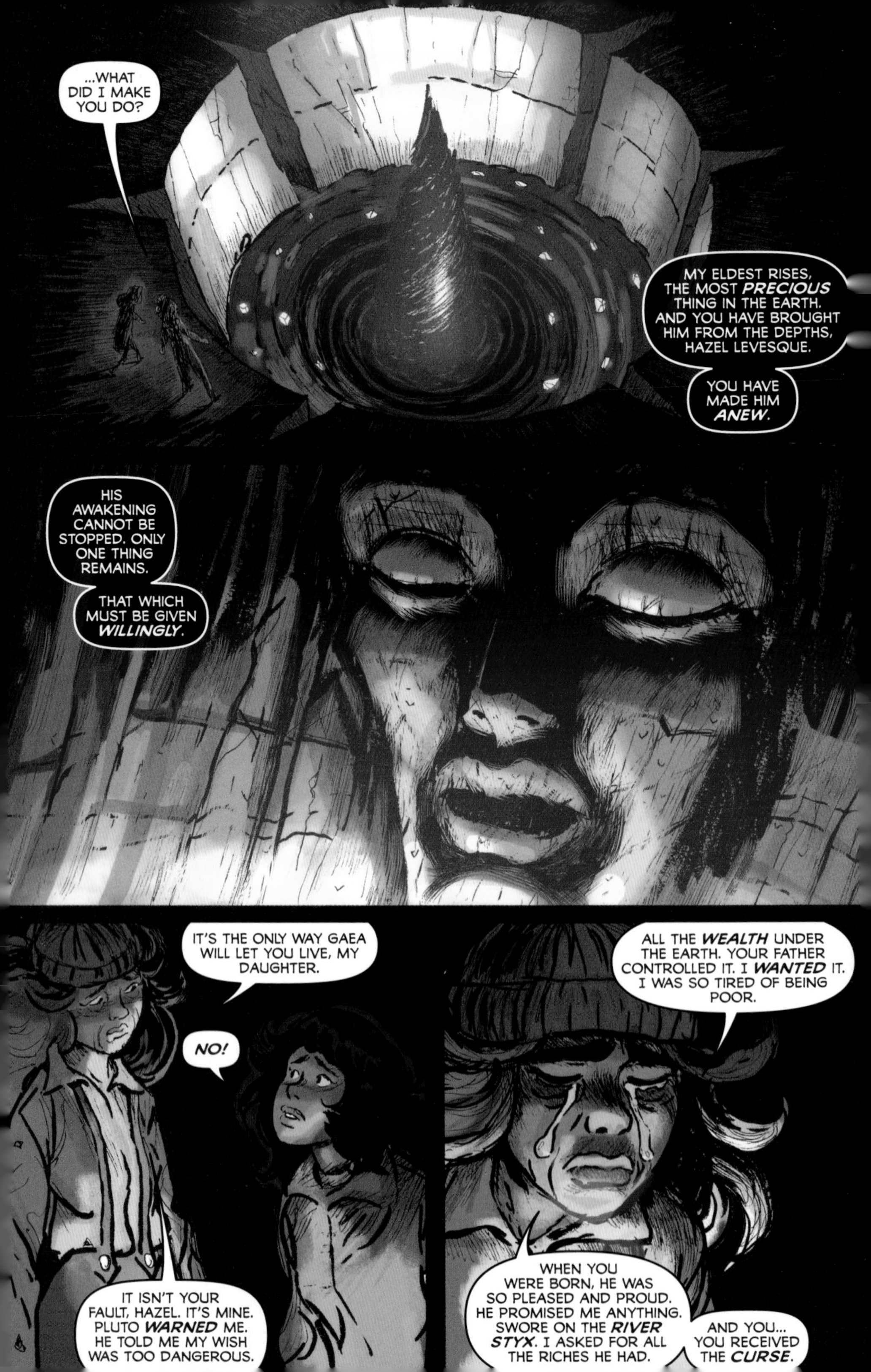

...WHAT DID I MAKE YOU DO?
MY ELDEST RISES, THE MOST PRECIOUS THING IN THE EARTH. AND YOU HAVE BROUGHT HIM FROM THE DEPTHS, HAZEL LEVESQUE.
YOU HAVE MADE HIM ANEW.
HIS AWAKENING CANNOT BE STOPPED. ONLY ONE THING REMAINS.
THAT WHICH MUST BE GIVEN WILLINGLY.
IT'S THE ONLY WAY GAEA WILL LET YOU LIVE, MY DAUGHTER.
NO!
IT ISN'T YOUR FAULT, HAZEL. IT'S MINE. PLUTO WARNED ME. HE TOLD ME MY WISH WAS TOO DANGEROUS.
ALL THE WEALTH UNDER THE EARTH. YOUR FATHER CONTROLLED IT. I WANTED IT. I WAS SO TIRED OF BEING POOR.
WHEN YOU WERE BORN, HE WAS SO PLEASED AND PROUD. HE PROMISED ME ANYTHING. SWORE ON THE RIVER STYX. I ASKED FOR ALL THE RICHES HE HAD.
AND YOU... YOU RECEIVED THE CURSE.

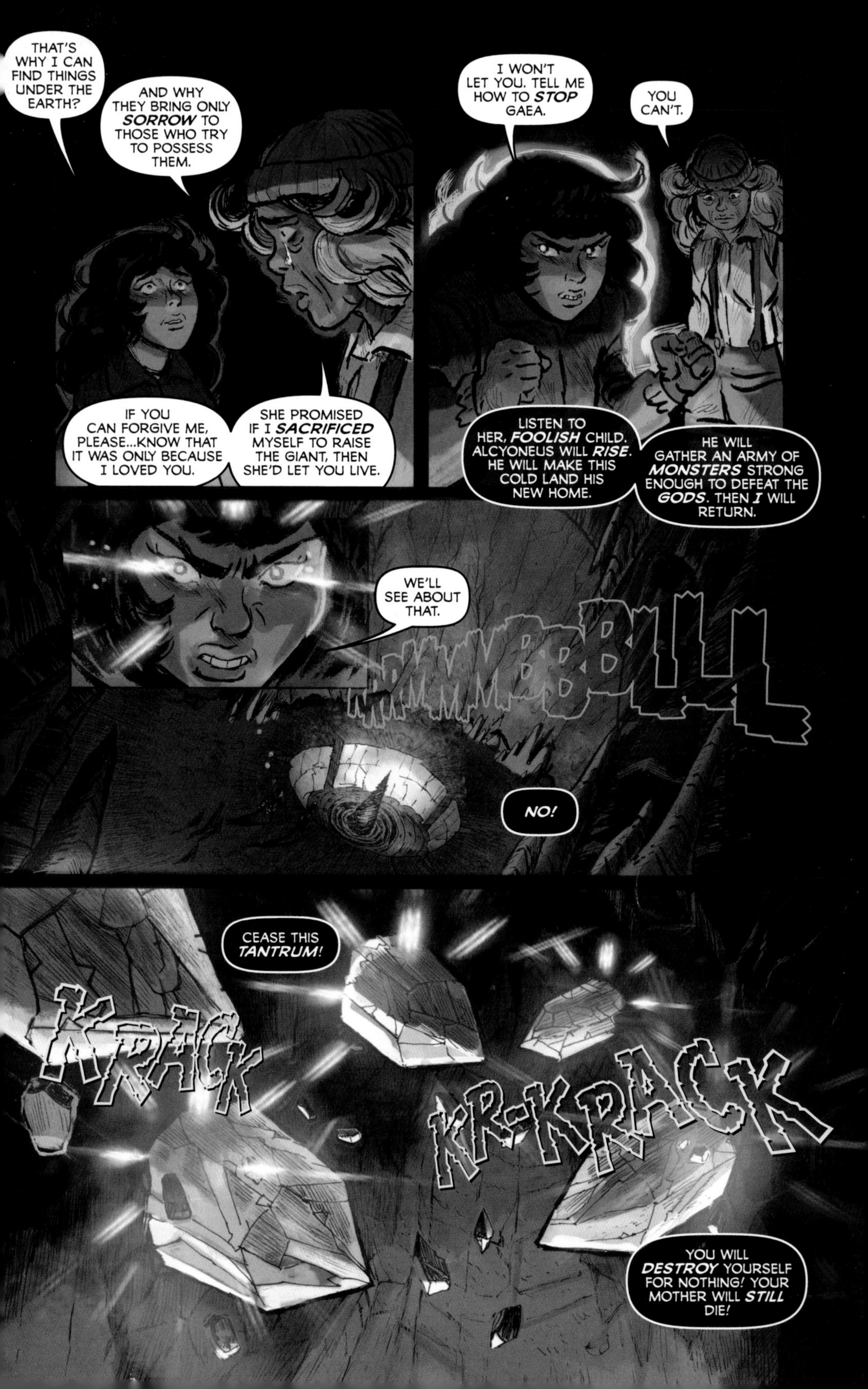
THAT'S WHY I CAN FIND THINGS UNDER THE EARTH?
AND WHY THEY BRING ONLY SORROW TO THOSE WHO TRY TO POSSESS THEM.
SHE PROMISED IF I SACRIFICED MYSELF TO RAISE THE GIANT, THEN SHE'D LET YOU LIVE.
IF YOU CAN FORGIVE ME, PLEASE...KNOW THAT IT WAS ONLY BECAUSE I LOVED YOU.
I WON'T LET YOU. TELL ME HOW TO STOP GAEA.
YOU CAN'T.
LISTEN TO HER, FOOLISH CHILD. ALCYONEUS WILL RISE. HE WILL MAKE THIS COLD LAND HIS NEW HOME.
HE WILL GATHER AN ARMY OF MONSTERS STRONG ENOUGH TO DEFEAT THE GODS. THEN I WILL RETURN.
WE'LL SEE ABOUT THAT.
RRMMMBBBLLL
NO!
CEASE THIS TANTRUM!
KRACK
KR-KRACK
YOU WILL DESTROY YOURSELF FOR NOTHING! YOUR MOTHER WILL STILL DIE!

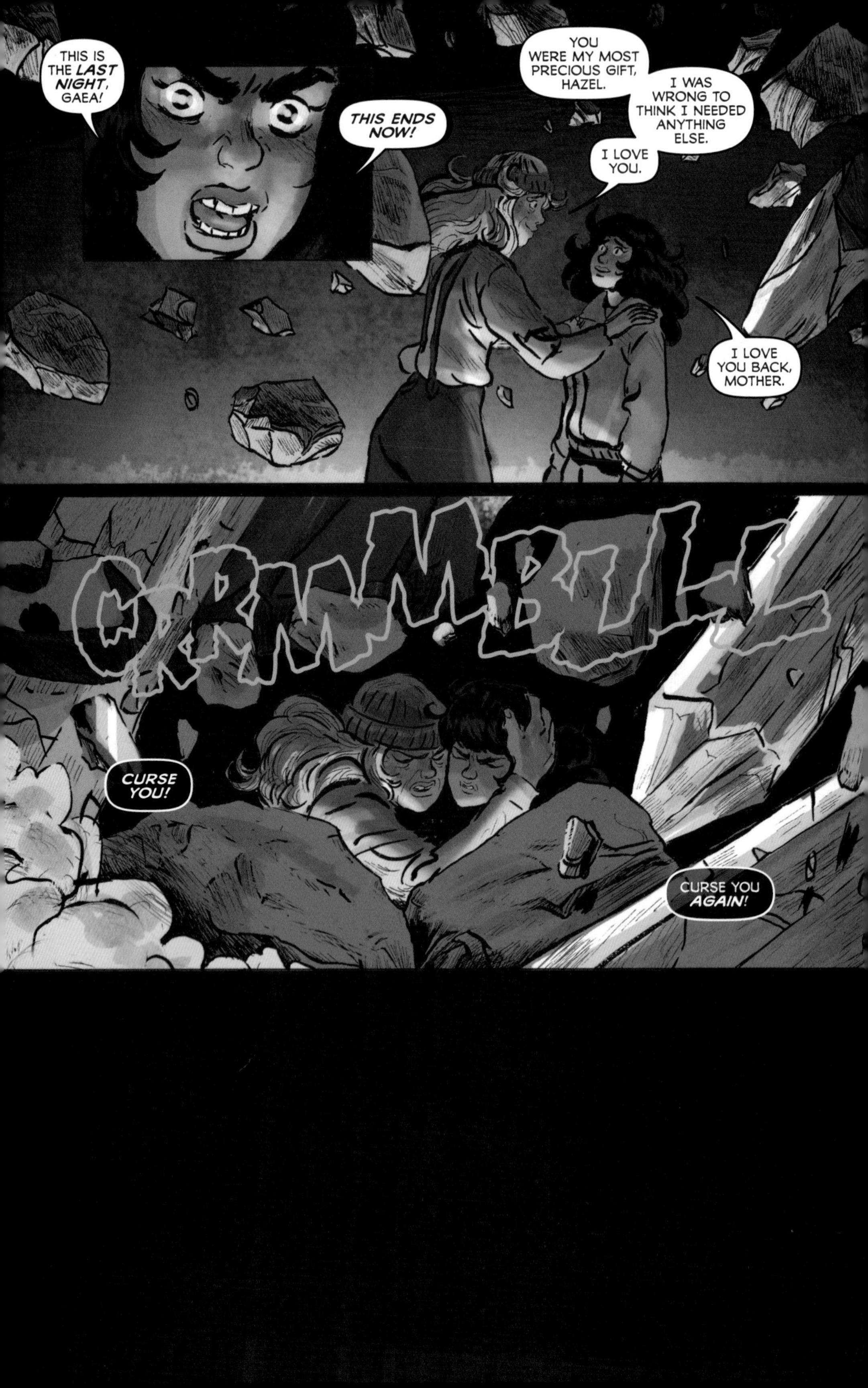
THIS IS THE *LAST NIGHT*, GAEA!
THIS ENDS NOW!
YOU WERE MY MOST PRECIOUS GIFT, HAZEL.
I WAS WRONG TO THINK I NEEDED ANYTHING ELSE.
I LOVE YOU.
I LOVE YOU BACK, MOTHER.
CRMMBLL
CURSE YOU!
CURSE YOU *AGAIN!*

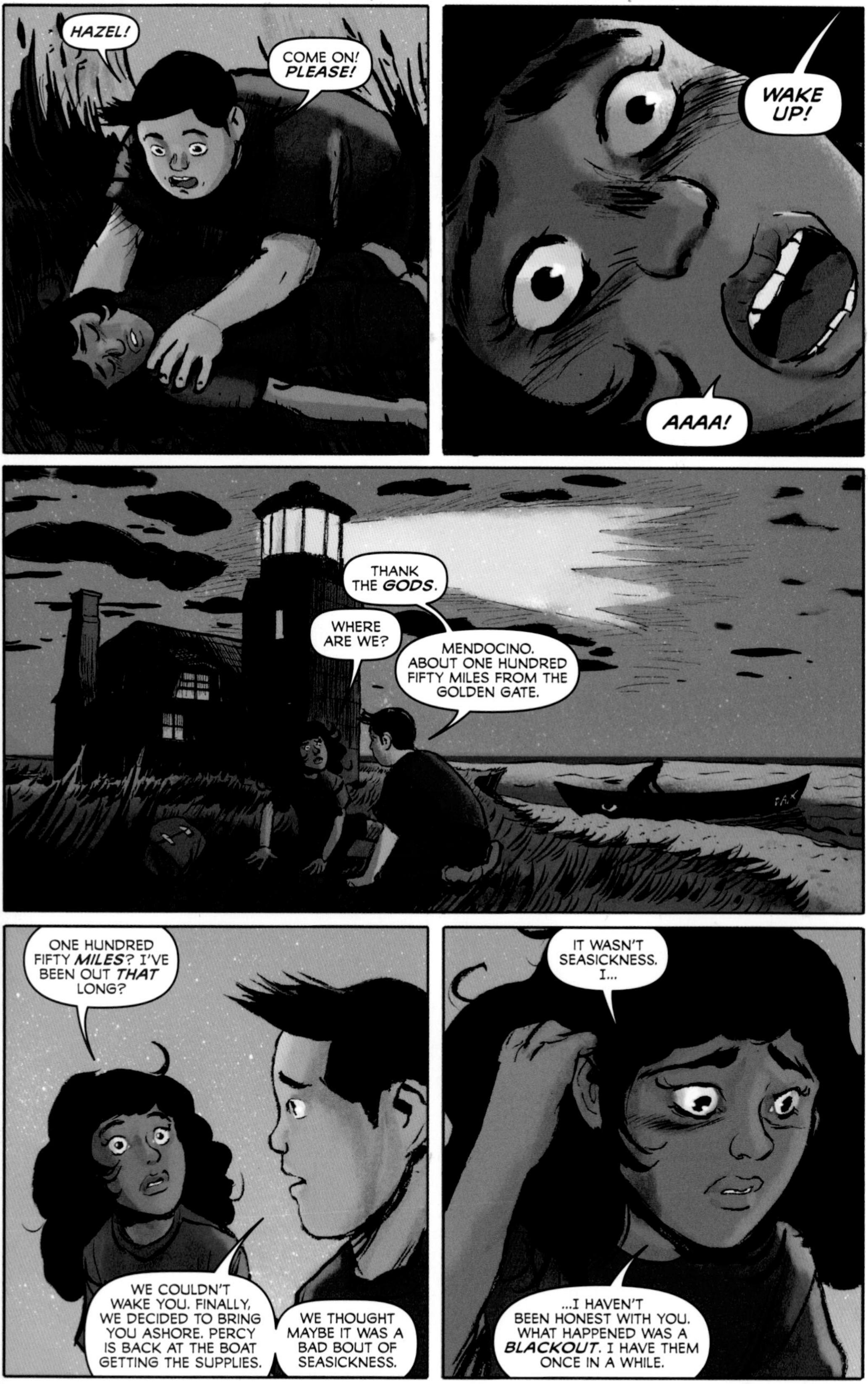
HAZEL!
COME ON! PLEASE!
WAKE UP!
AAAA!
THANK THE GODS.
WHERE ARE WE?
MENDOCINO. ABOUT ONE HUNDRED FIFTY MILES FROM THE GOLDEN GATE.
ONE HUNDRED FIFTY MILES? I'VE BEEN OUT THAT LONG?
WE COULDN'T WAKE YOU. FINALLY, WE DECIDED TO BRING YOU ASHORE. PERCY IS BACK AT THE BOAT GETTING THE SUPPLIES.
WE THOUGHT MAYBE IT WAS A BAD BOUT OF SEASICKNESS.
IT WASN'T SEASICKNESS. I...
...I HAVEN'T BEEN HONEST WITH YOU. WHAT HAPPENED WAS A BLACKOUT. I HAVE THEM ONCE IN A WHILE.

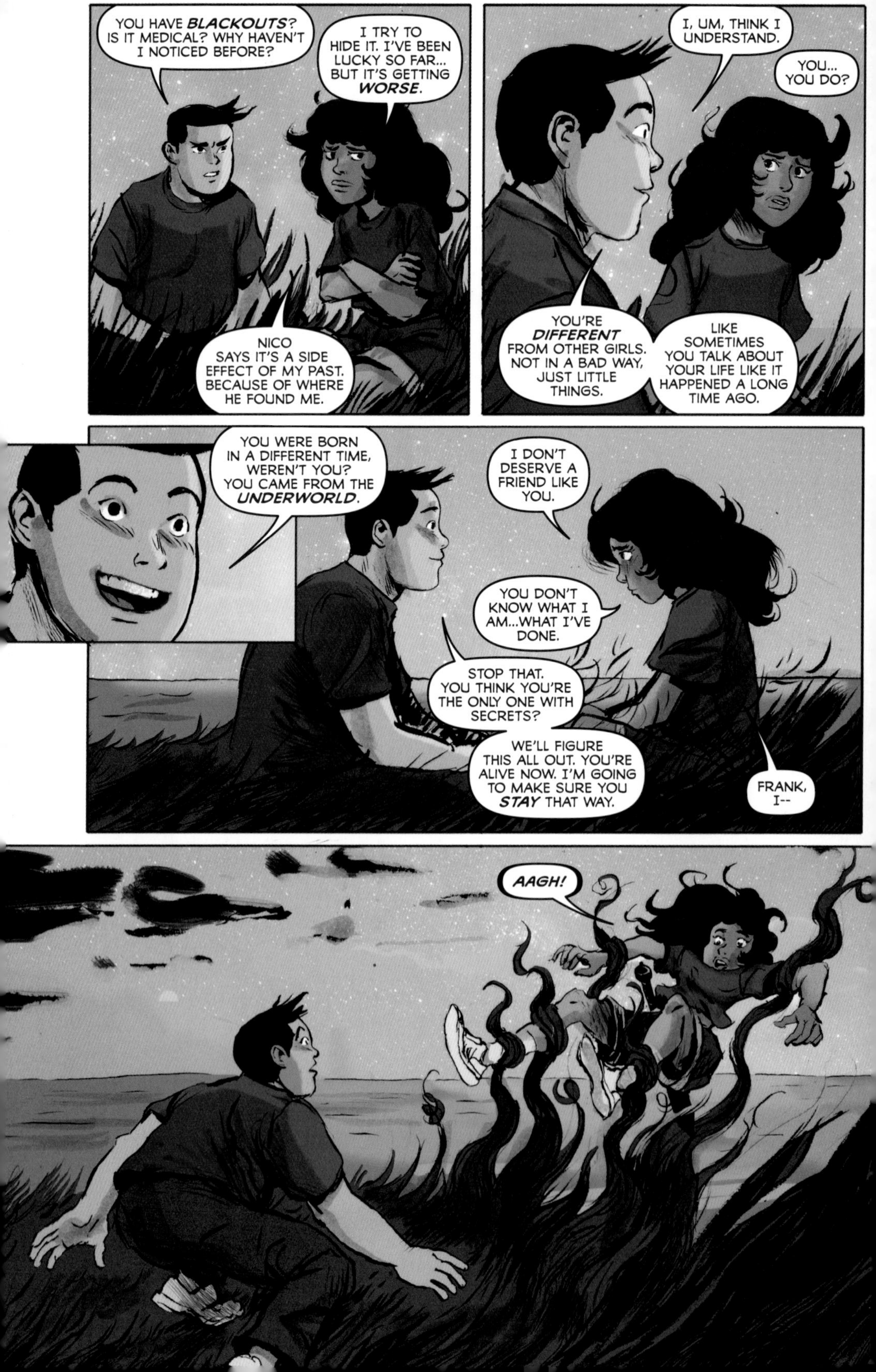
YOU HAVE BLACKOUTS? IS IT MEDICAL? WHY HAVEN'T I NOTICED BEFORE?
I TRY TO HIDE IT. I'VE BEEN LUCKY SO FAR... BUT IT'S GETTING WORSE.
NICO SAYS IT'S A SIDE EFFECT OF MY PAST. BECAUSE OF WHERE HE FOUND ME.
I, UM, THINK I UNDERSTAND.
YOU... YOU DO?
YOU'RE DIFFERENT FROM OTHER GIRLS. NOT IN A BAD WAY, JUST LITTLE THINGS.
LIKE SOMETIMES YOU TALK ABOUT YOUR LIFE LIKE IT HAPPENED A LONG TIME AGO.
YOU WERE BORN IN A DIFFERENT TIME, WEREN'T YOU? YOU CAME FROM THE UNDERWORLD.
I DON'T DESERVE A FRIEND LIKE YOU.
YOU DON'T KNOW WHAT I AM...WHAT I'VE DONE.
STOP THAT. YOU THINK YOU'RE THE ONLY ONE WITH SECRETS?
WE'LL FIGURE THIS ALL OUT. YOU'RE ALIVE NOW. I'M GOING TO MAKE SURE YOU STAY THAT WAY.
FRANK, I--
AAGH!

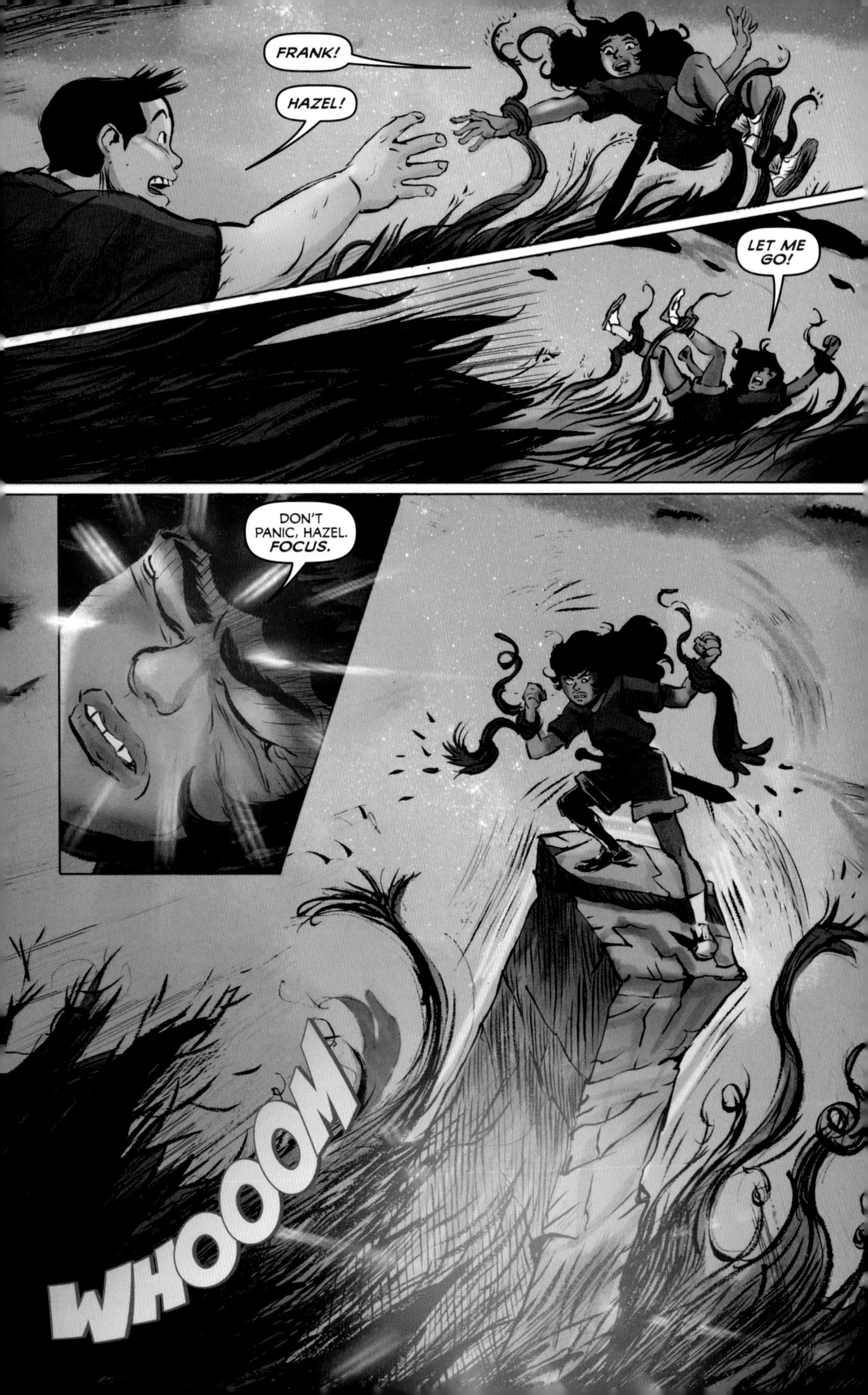
FRANK!
HAZEL!
LET ME GO!
DON'T PANIC, HAZEL. FOCUS.
WHOOOM

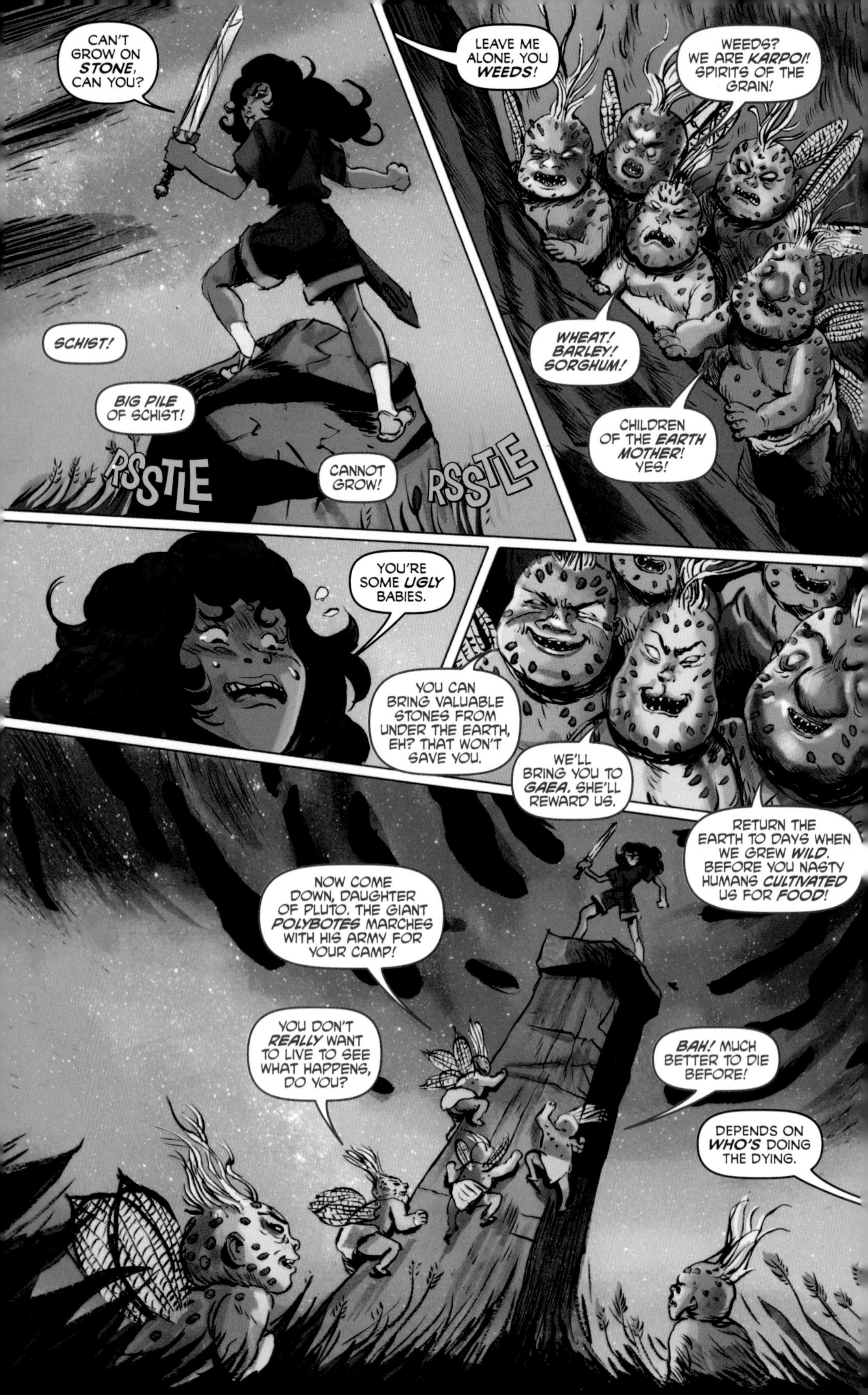
CAN'T GROW ON STONE, CAN YOU?
SCHIST!
BIG PILE OF SCHIST!
RSSTLE
CANNOT GROW!
RSSTLE
LEAVE ME ALONE, YOU WEEDS!
WEEDS? WE ARE KARPOI! SPIRITS OF THE GRAIN!
WHEAT! BARLEY! SORGHUM!
CHILDREN OF THE EARTH MOTHER! YES!
YOU'RE SOME UGLY BABIES.
YOU CAN BRING VALUABLE STONES FROM UNDER THE EARTH, EH? THAT WON'T SAVE YOU.
WE'LL BRING YOU TO GAEA. SHE'LL REWARD US.
RETURN THE EARTH TO DAYS WHEN WE GREW WILD. BEFORE YOU NASTY HUMANS CULTIVATED US FOR FOOD!
NOW COME DOWN, DAUGHTER OF PLUTO. THE GIANT POLYBOTES MARCHES WITH HIS ARMY FOR YOUR CAMP!
YOU DON'T REALLY WANT TO LIVE TO SEE WHAT HAPPENS, DO YOU?
BAH! MUCH BETTER TO DIE BEFORE!
DEPENDS ON WHO'S DOING THE DYING.

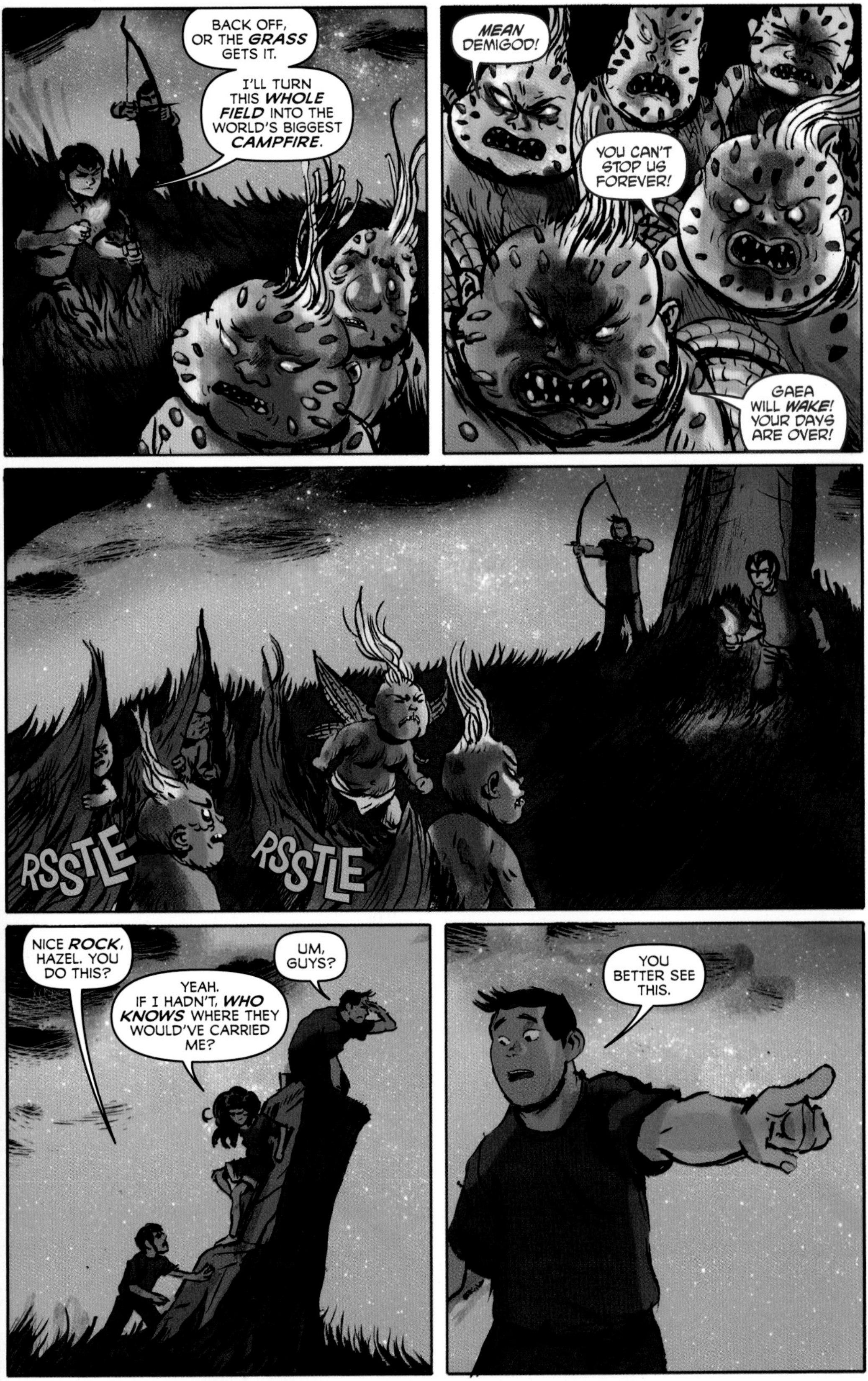
BACK OFF, OR THE *GRASS* GETS IT.
I'LL TURN THIS *WHOLE FIELD* INTO THE WORLD'S BIGGEST *CAMPFIRE*.
MEAN DEMIGOD!
YOU CAN'T STOP US FOREVER!
GAEA WILL *WAKE*! YOUR DAYS ARE OVER!
RSSTLE
RSSTLE
NICE *ROCK*, HAZEL. YOU DO THIS?
YEAH. IF I HADN'T, *WHO KNOWS* WHERE THEY WOULD'VE CARRIED ME?
UM, GUYS?
YOU BETTER SEE THIS.

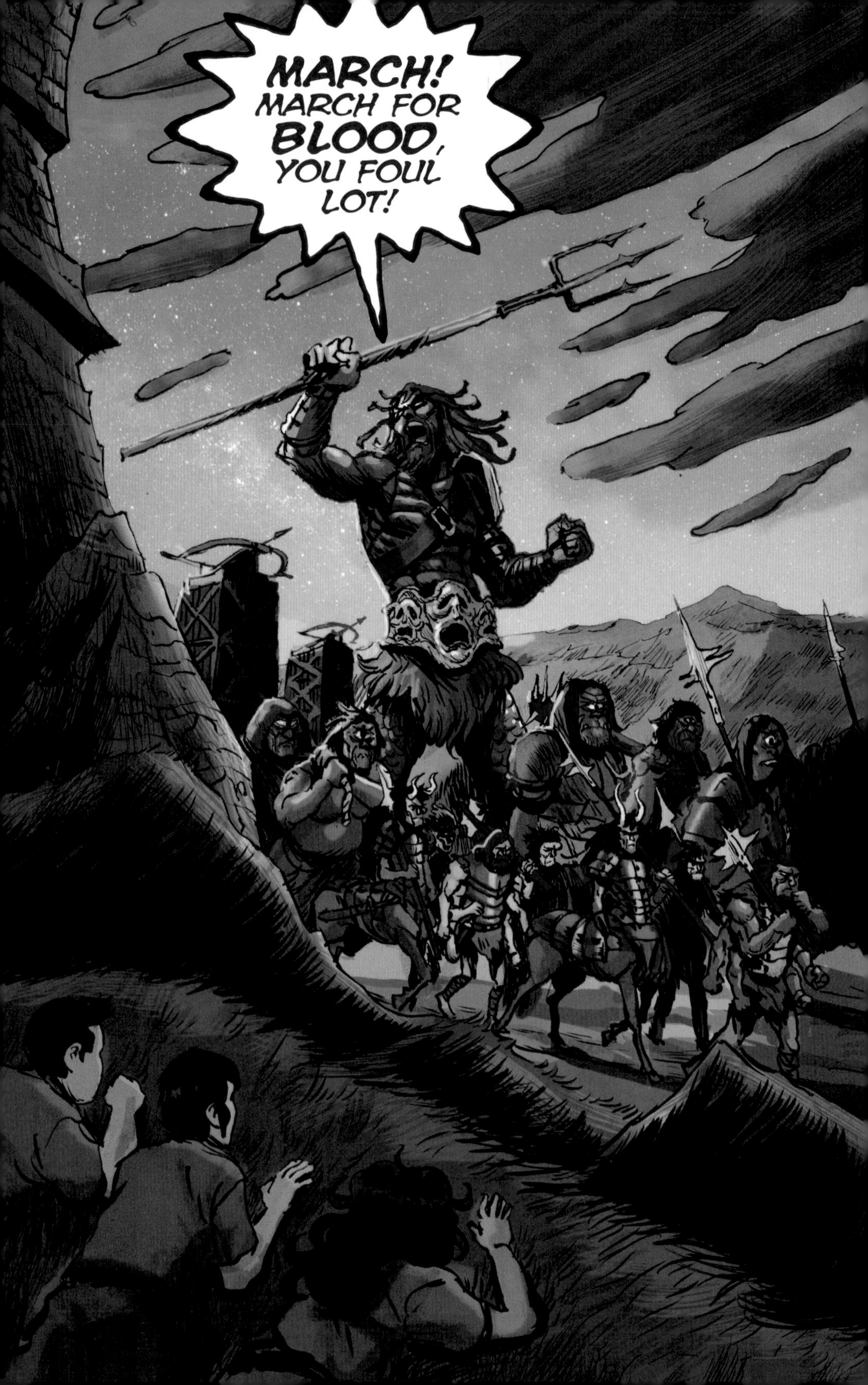
MARCH! MARCH FOR BLOOD, YOU FOUL LOT!

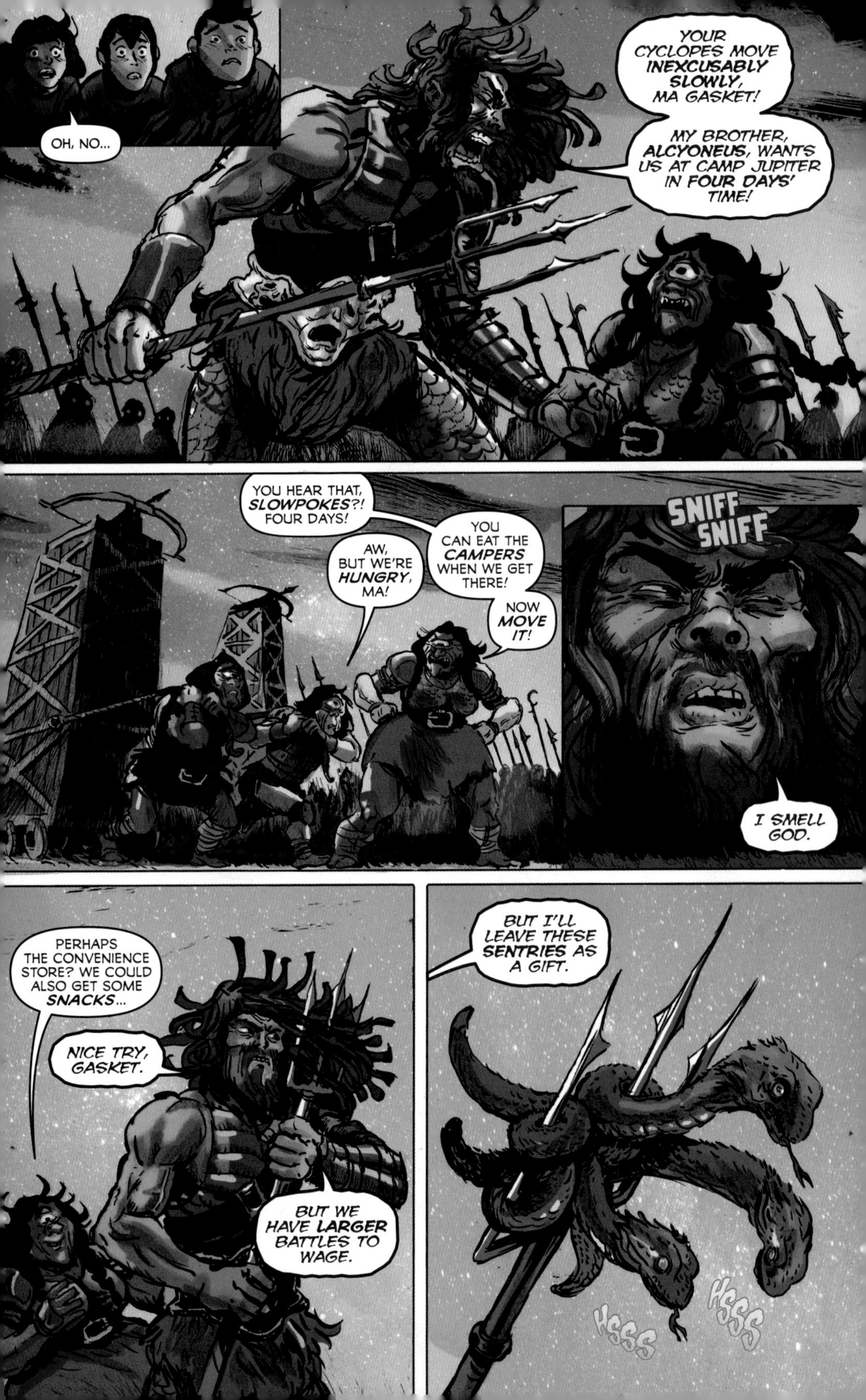
OH, NO...
YOUR CYCLOPES MOVE INEXCUSABLY SLOWLY, MA GASKET!
MY BROTHER, ALCYONEUS, WANTS US AT CAMP JUPITER IN FOUR DAYS' TIME!
YOU HEAR THAT, SLOWPOKES?! FOUR DAYS!
AW, BUT WE'RE HUNGRY, MA!
YOU CAN EAT THE CAMPERS WHEN WE GET THERE!
NOW MOVE IT!
SNIFF SNIFF
I SMELL GOD.
PERHAPS THE CONVENIENCE STORE? WE COULD ALSO GET SOME SNACKS...
NICE TRY, GASKET.
BUT WE HAVE LARGER BATTLES TO WAGE.
BUT I'LL LEAVE THESE SENTRIES AS A GIFT.
HSSS
HSSS

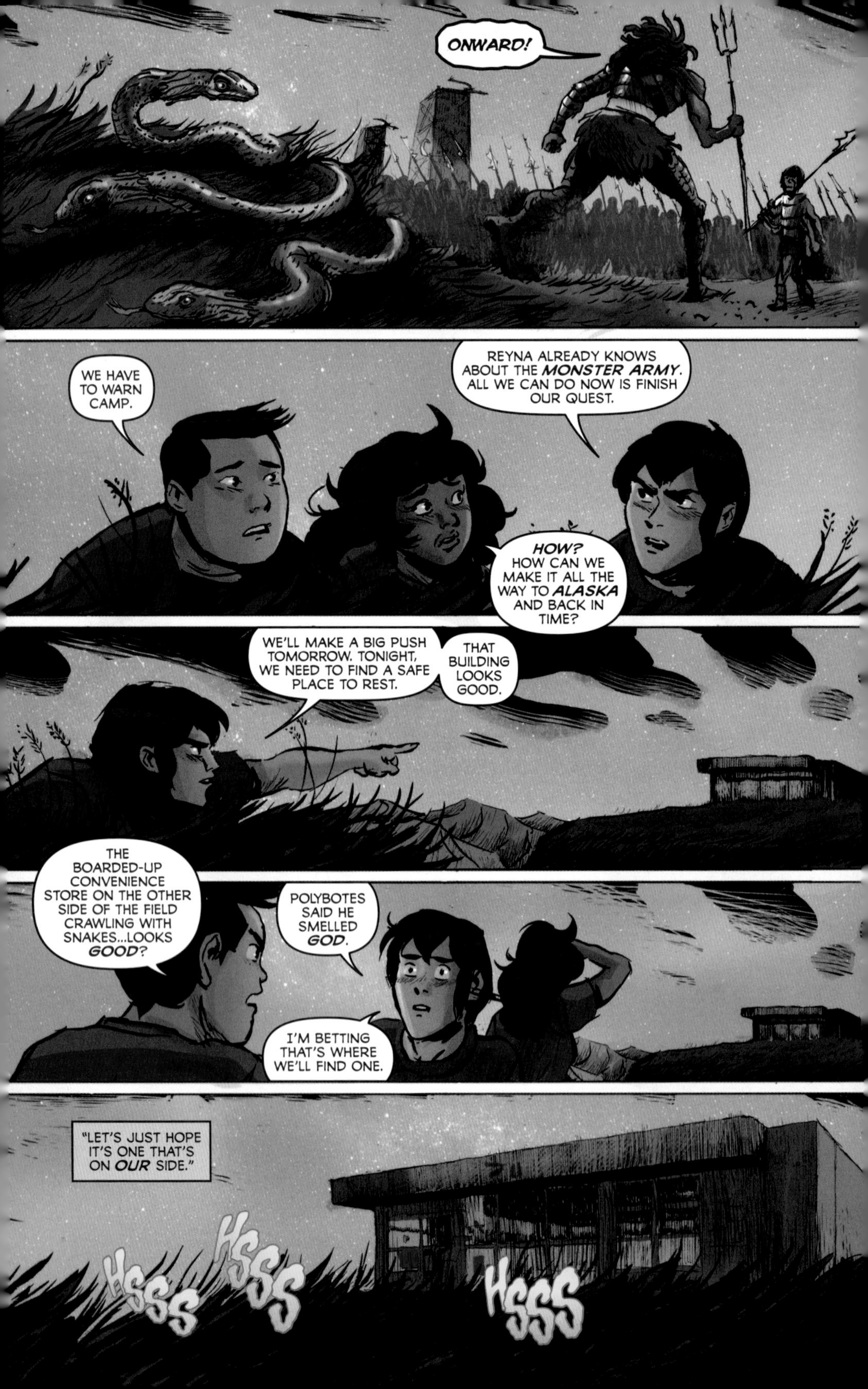
ONWARD!
WE HAVE TO WARN CAMP.
REYNA ALREADY KNOWS ABOUT THE MONSTER ARMY. ALL WE CAN DO NOW IS FINISH OUR QUEST.
HOW? HOW CAN WE MAKE IT ALL THE WAY TO ALASKA AND BACK IN TIME?
WE'LL MAKE A BIG PUSH TOMORROW. TONIGHT, WE NEED TO FIND A SAFE PLACE TO REST.
THAT BUILDING LOOKS GOOD.
THE BOARDED-UP CONVENIENCE STORE ON THE OTHER SIDE OF THE FIELD CRAWLING WITH SNAKES...LOOKS GOOD?
POLYBOTES SAID HE SMELLED GOD.
I'M BETTING THAT'S WHERE WE'LL FIND ONE.
"LET'S JUST HOPE IT'S ONE THAT'S ON OUR SIDE."
HSSS
HSSS
HSSS

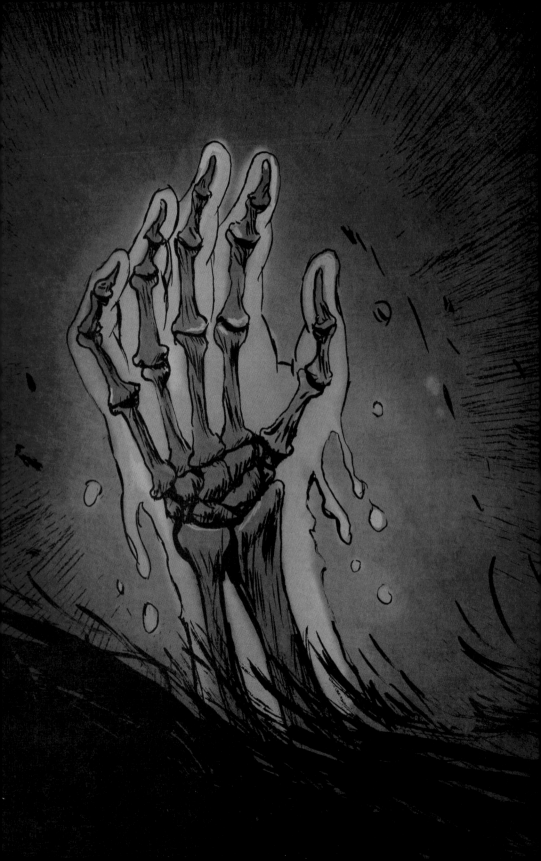

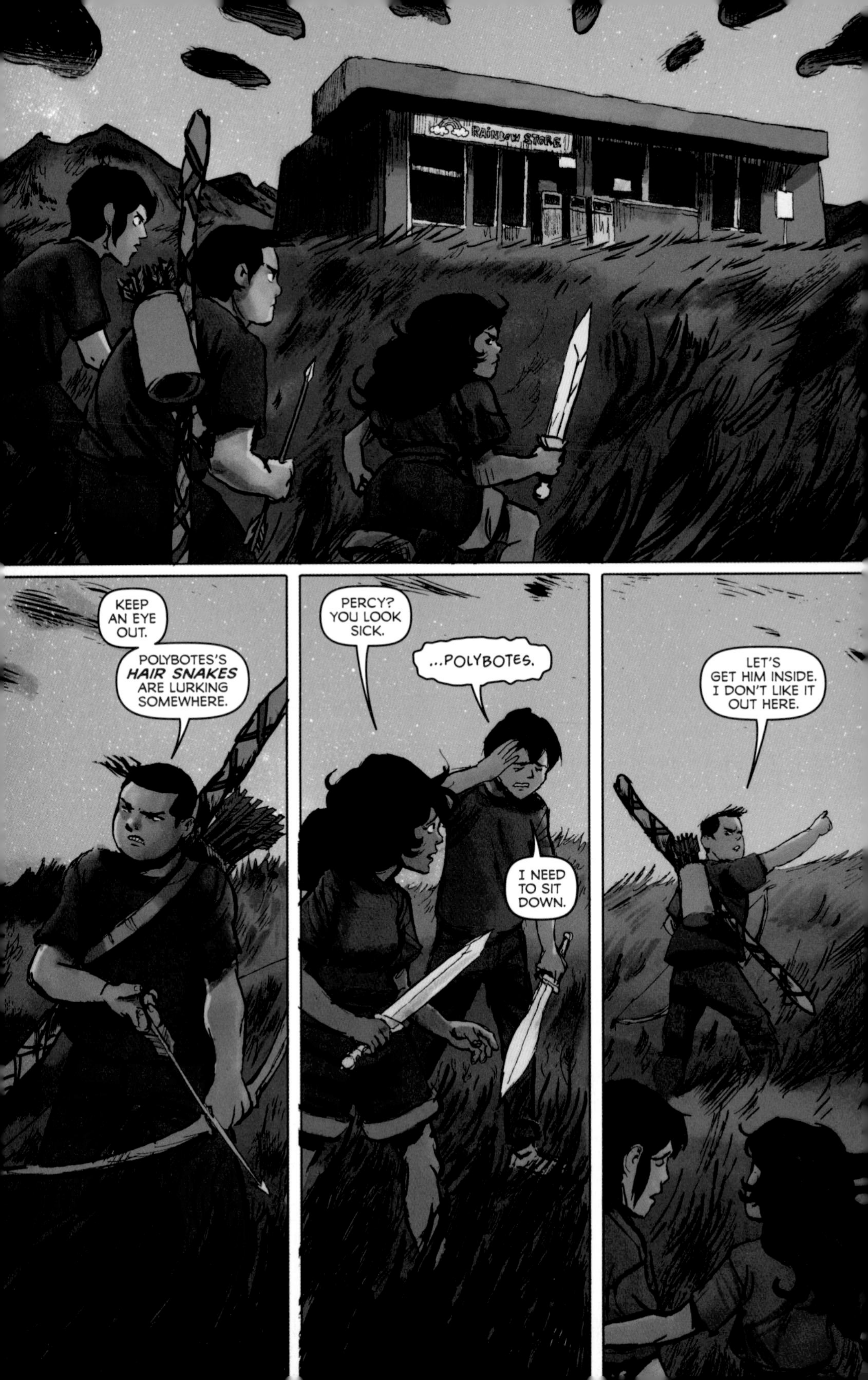
RAINBOW STORE
KEEP AN EYE OUT.
POLYBOTES'S *HAIR SNAKES* ARE LURKING SOMEWHERE.
PERCY? YOU LOOK SICK.
...POLYBOTES.
I NEED TO SIT DOWN.
LET'S GET HIM INSIDE. I DON'T LIKE IT OUT HERE.

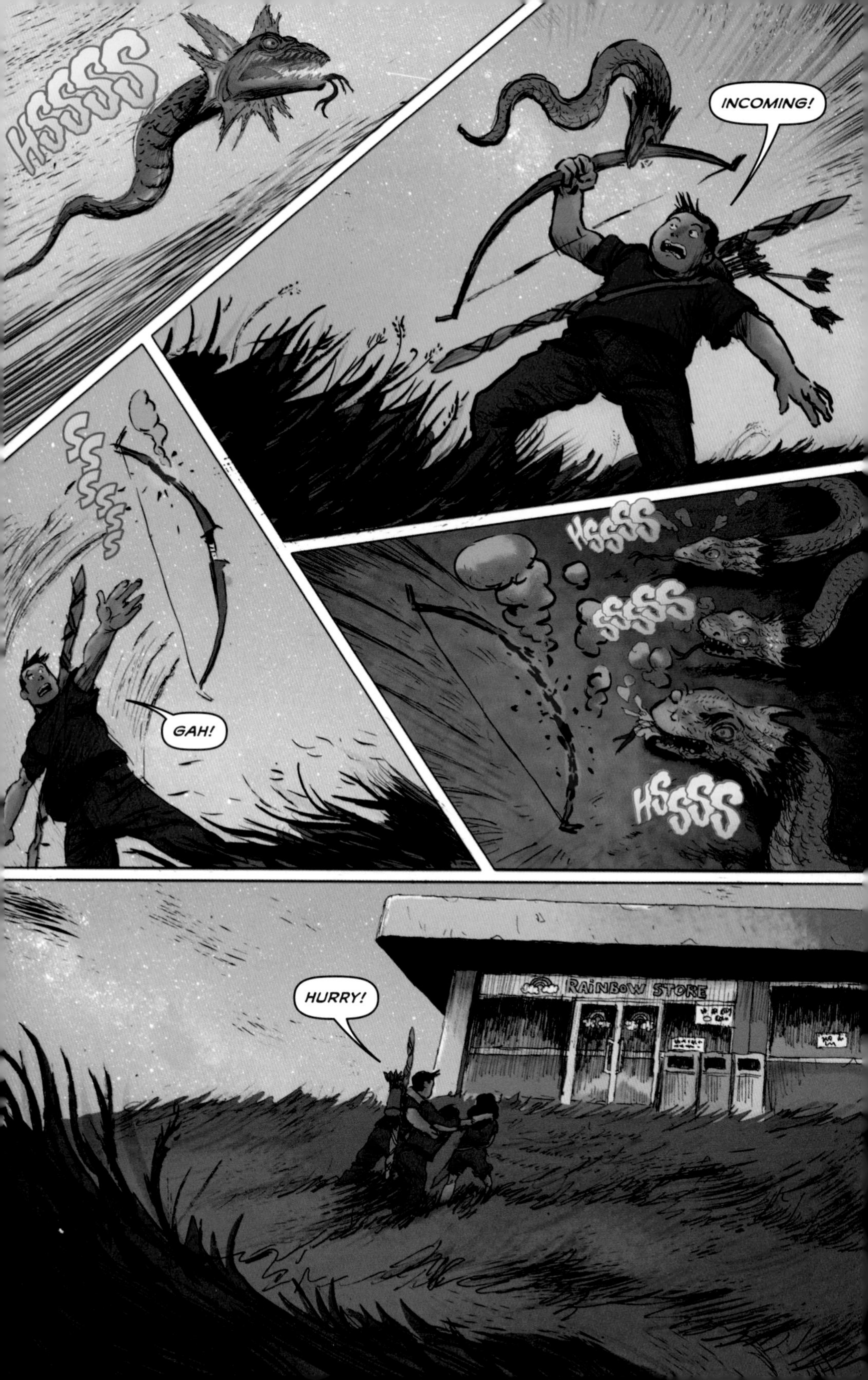
HSSSS
INCOMING!
SSSSS
GAH!
HSSSS
SSSSS
HSSSS
RAINBOW STORE
HURRY!

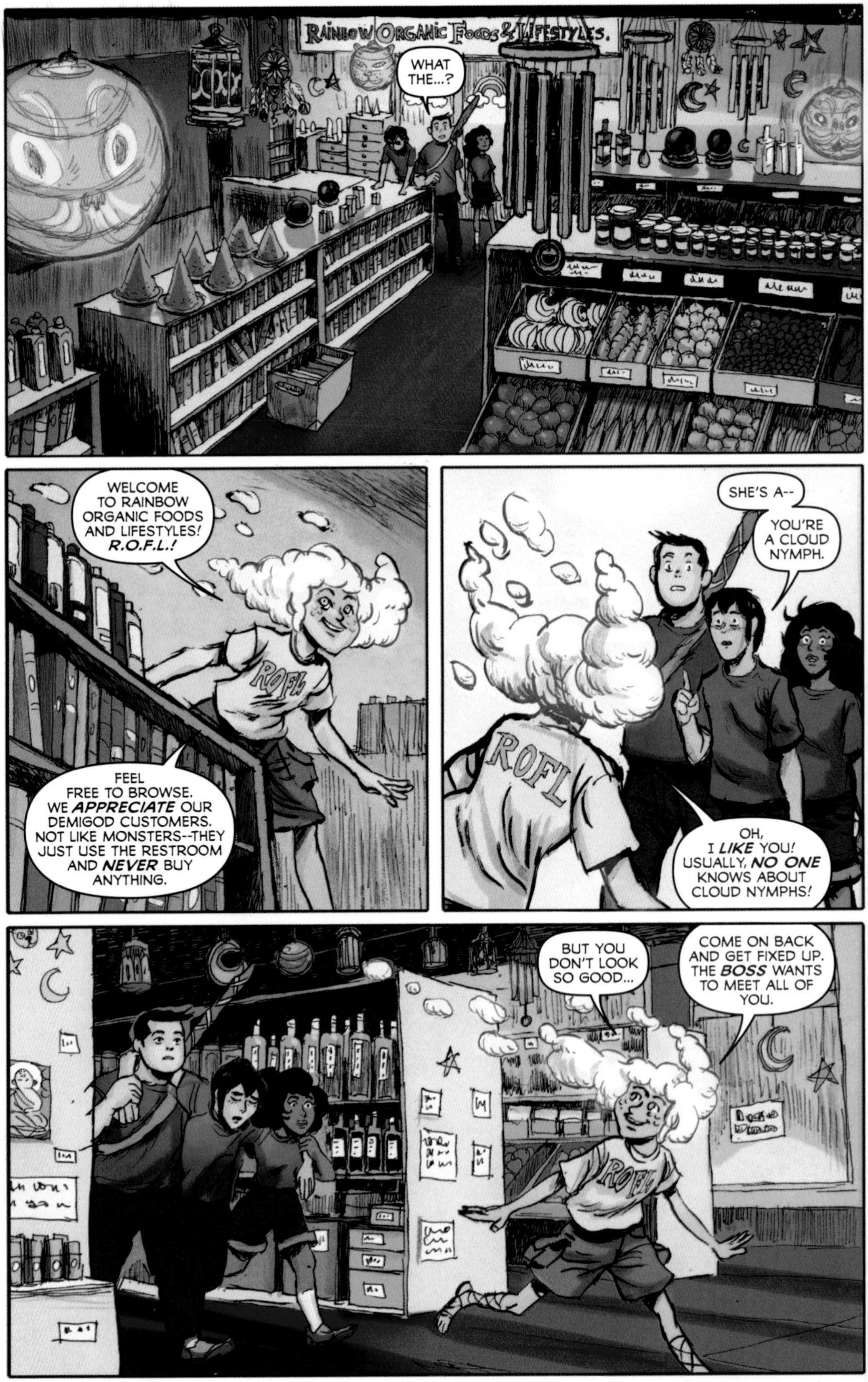
RAINBOW ORGANIC FOODS & LIFESTYLES.
WHAT THE...?
WELCOME TO RAINBOW ORGANIC FOODS AND LIFESTYLES! R.O.F.L.!
FEEL FREE TO BROWSE. WE APPRECIATE OUR DEMIGOD CUSTOMERS. NOT LIKE MONSTERS--THEY JUST USE THE RESTROOM AND NEVER BUY ANYTHING.
SHE'S A--
YOU'RE A CLOUD NYMPH.
OH, I LIKE YOU! USUALLY, NO ONE KNOWS ABOUT CLOUD NYMPHS!
BUT YOU DON'T LOOK SO GOOD...
COME ON BACK AND GET FIXED UP. THE BOSS WANTS TO MEET ALL OF YOU.

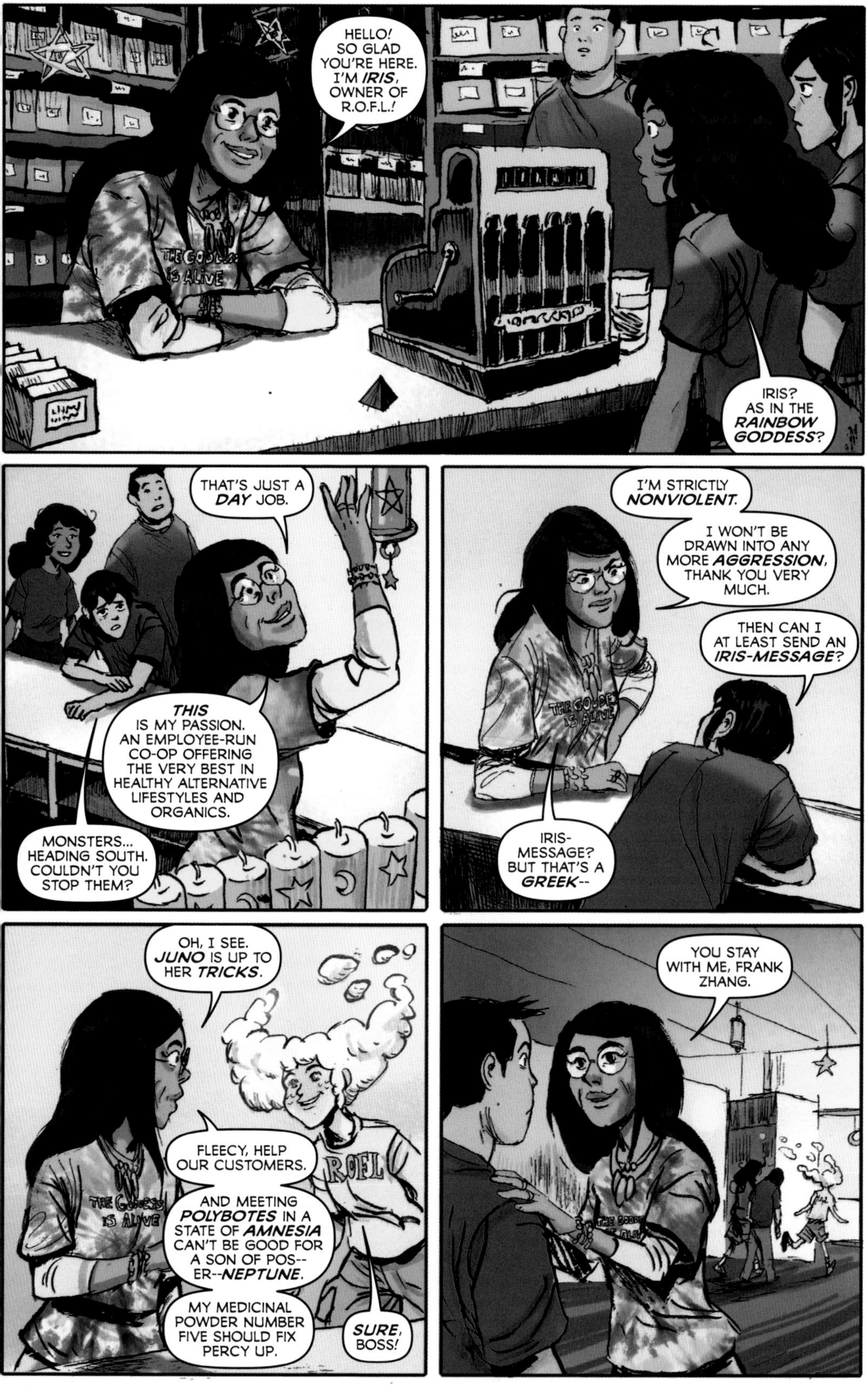
HELLO! SO GLAD YOU'RE HERE. I'M *IRIS*, OWNER OF R.O.F.L.!
IRIS? AS IN THE *RAINBOW GODDESS*?
THAT'S JUST A *DAY* JOB.
THIS IS MY PASSION. AN EMPLOYEE-RUN CO-OP OFFERING THE VERY BEST IN HEALTHY ALTERNATIVE LIFESTYLES AND ORGANICS.
MONSTERS... HEADING SOUTH. COULDN'T YOU STOP THEM?
I'M STRICTLY *NONVIOLENT*.
I WON'T BE DRAWN INTO ANY MORE *AGGRESSION*, THANK YOU VERY MUCH.
THEN CAN I AT LEAST SEND AN *IRIS-MESSAGE*?
IRIS-MESSAGE? BUT THAT'S A *GREEK*--
OH, I SEE. *JUNO* IS UP TO HER *TRICKS*.
FLEECY, HELP OUR CUSTOMERS.
AND MEETING *POLYBOTES* IN A STATE OF *AMNESIA* CAN'T BE GOOD FOR A SON OF POS-- ER--*NEPTUNE*.
MY MEDICINAL POWDER NUMBER FIVE SHOULD FIX PERCY UP.
SURE, BOSS!
ROFL
YOU STAY WITH ME, FRANK ZHANG.

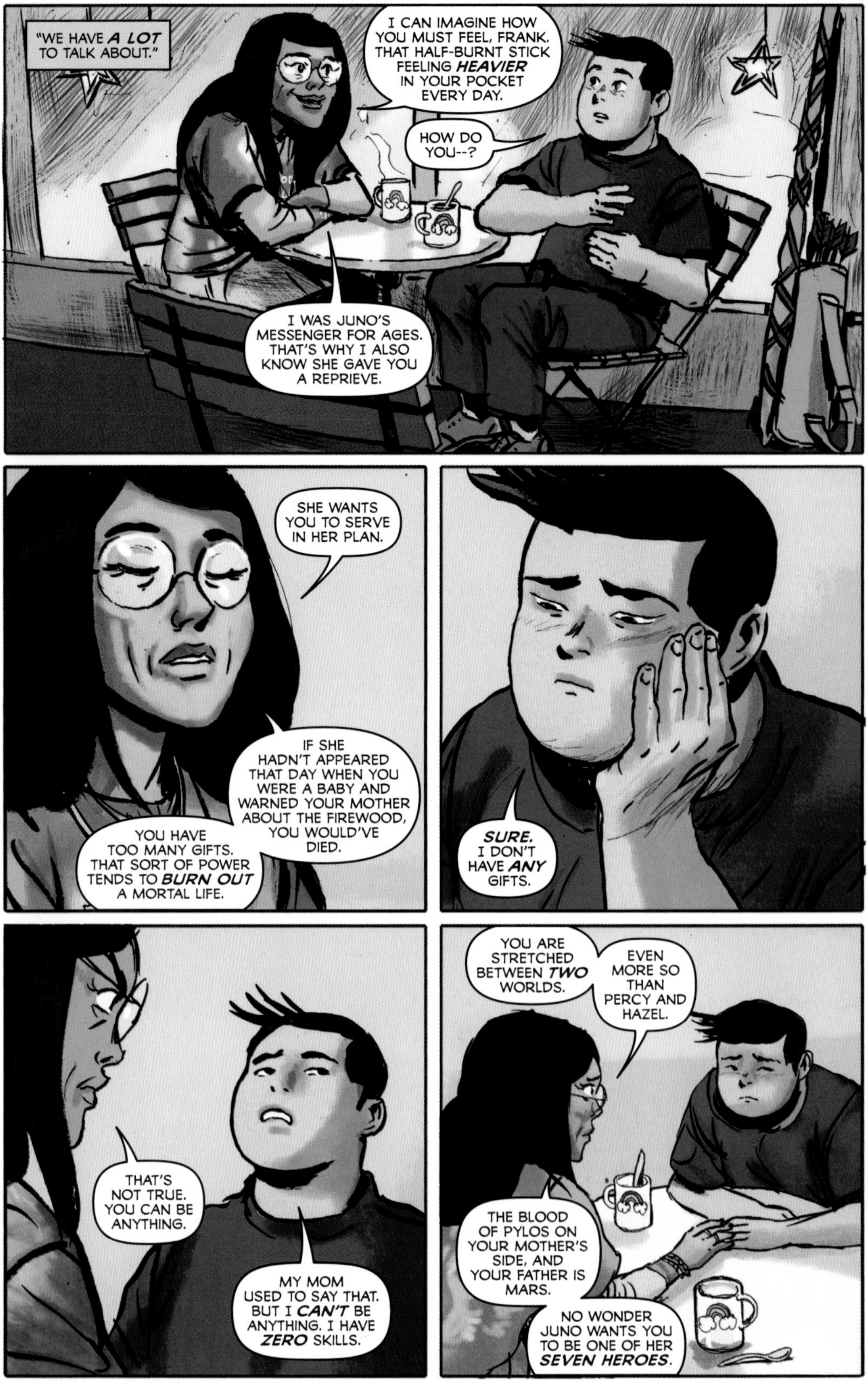
"WE HAVE *A LOT* TO TALK ABOUT."
I CAN IMAGINE HOW YOU MUST FEEL, FRANK. THAT HALF-BURNT STICK FEELING *HEAVIER* IN YOUR POCKET EVERY DAY.
HOW DO YOU--?
I WAS JUNO'S MESSENGER FOR AGES. THAT'S WHY I ALSO KNOW SHE GAVE YOU A REPRIEVE.
SHE WANTS YOU TO SERVE IN HER PLAN.
IF SHE HADN'T APPEARED THAT DAY WHEN YOU WERE A BABY AND WARNED YOUR MOTHER ABOUT THE FIREWOOD, YOU WOULD'VE DIED.
YOU HAVE TOO MANY GIFTS. THAT SORT OF POWER TENDS TO *BURN OUT* A MORTAL LIFE.
SURE. I DON'T HAVE *ANY* GIFTS.
THAT'S NOT TRUE. YOU CAN BE ANYTHING.
MY MOM USED TO SAY THAT. BUT I *CAN'T* BE ANYTHING. I HAVE *ZERO* SKILLS.
YOU ARE STRETCHED BETWEEN *TWO* WORLDS.
EVEN MORE SO THAN PERCY AND HAZEL.
THE BLOOD OF PYLOS ON YOUR MOTHER'S SIDE, AND YOUR FATHER IS MARS.
NO WONDER JUNO WANTS YOU TO BE ONE OF HER *SEVEN HEROES*.

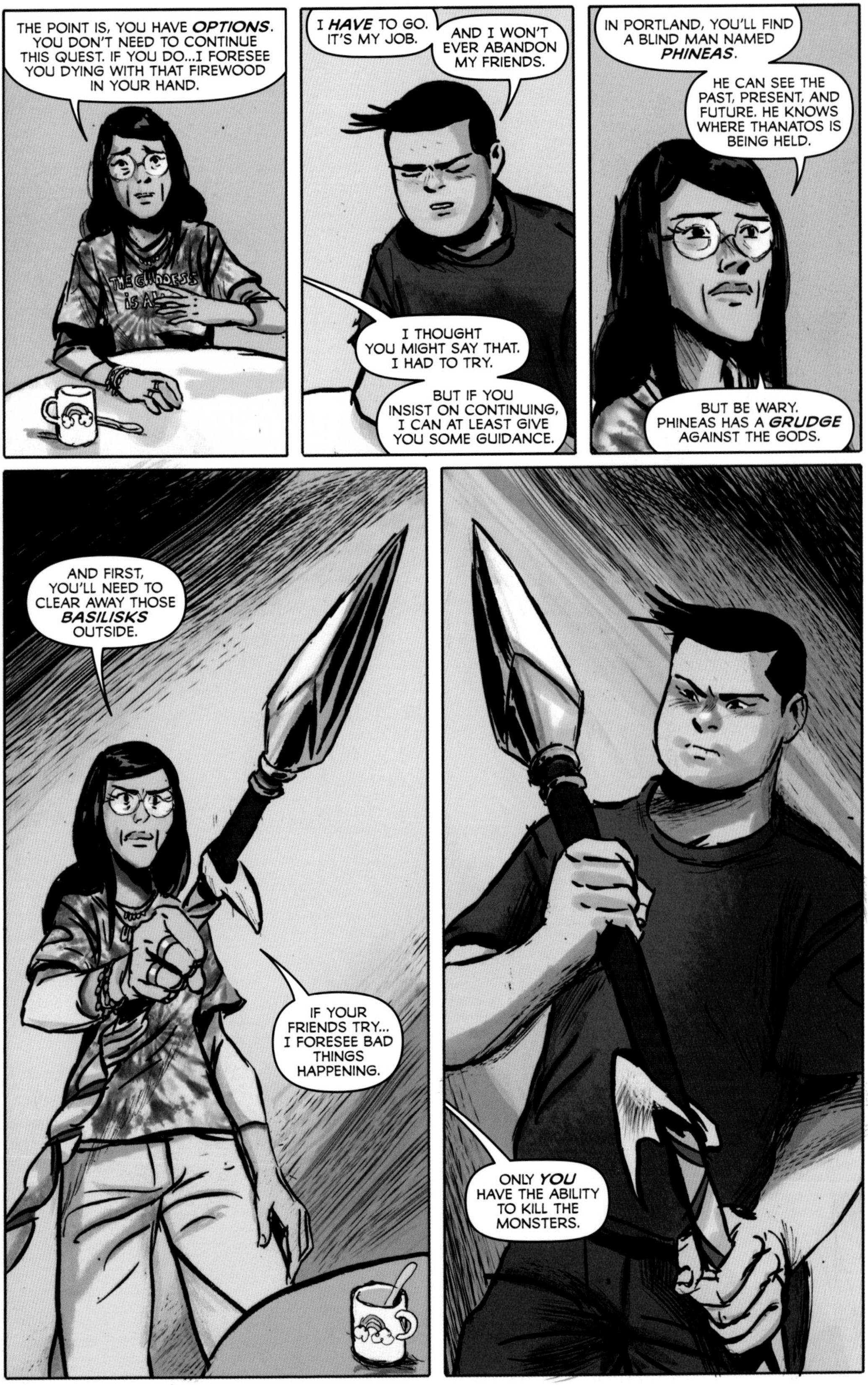
THE POINT IS, YOU HAVE *OPTIONS*. YOU DON'T NEED TO CONTINUE THIS QUEST. IF YOU DO...I FORESEE YOU DYING WITH THAT FIREWOOD IN YOUR HAND.
I *HAVE* TO GO. IT'S MY JOB.
AND I WON'T EVER ABANDON MY FRIENDS.
I THOUGHT YOU MIGHT SAY THAT. I HAD TO TRY.
BUT IF YOU INSIST ON CONTINUING, I CAN AT LEAST GIVE YOU SOME GUIDANCE.
IN PORTLAND, YOU'LL FIND A BLIND MAN NAMED *PHINEAS*.
HE CAN SEE THE PAST, PRESENT, AND FUTURE. HE KNOWS WHERE THANATOS IS BEING HELD.
BUT BE WARY. PHINEAS HAS A *GRUDGE* AGAINST THE GODS.
AND FIRST, YOU'LL NEED TO CLEAR AWAY THOSE *BASILISKS* OUTSIDE.
IF YOUR FRIENDS TRY... I FORESEE BAD THINGS HAPPENING.
ONLY *YOU* HAVE THE ABILITY TO KILL THE MONSTERS.

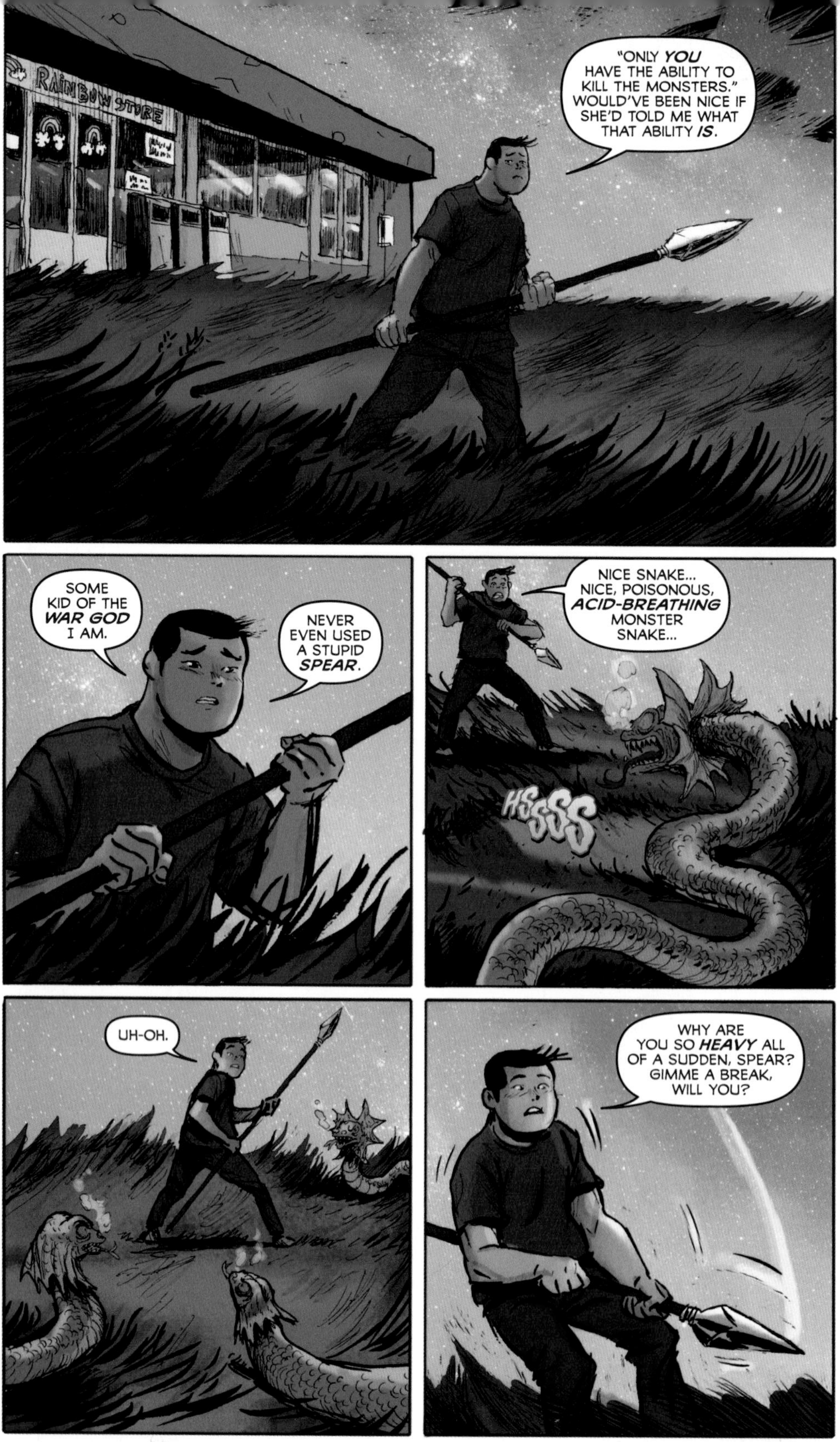
RAINBOW STORE
"ONLY YOU HAVE THE ABILITY TO KILL THE MONSTERS." WOULD'VE BEEN NICE IF SHE'D TOLD ME WHAT THAT ABILITY IS.
SOME KID OF THE WAR GOD I AM.
NEVER EVEN USED A STUPID SPEAR.
NICE SNAKE... NICE, POISONOUS, ACID-BREATHING MONSTER SNAKE...
HSSSS
UH-OH.
WHY ARE YOU SO HEAVY ALL OF A SUDDEN, SPEAR? GIMME A BREAK, WILL YOU?

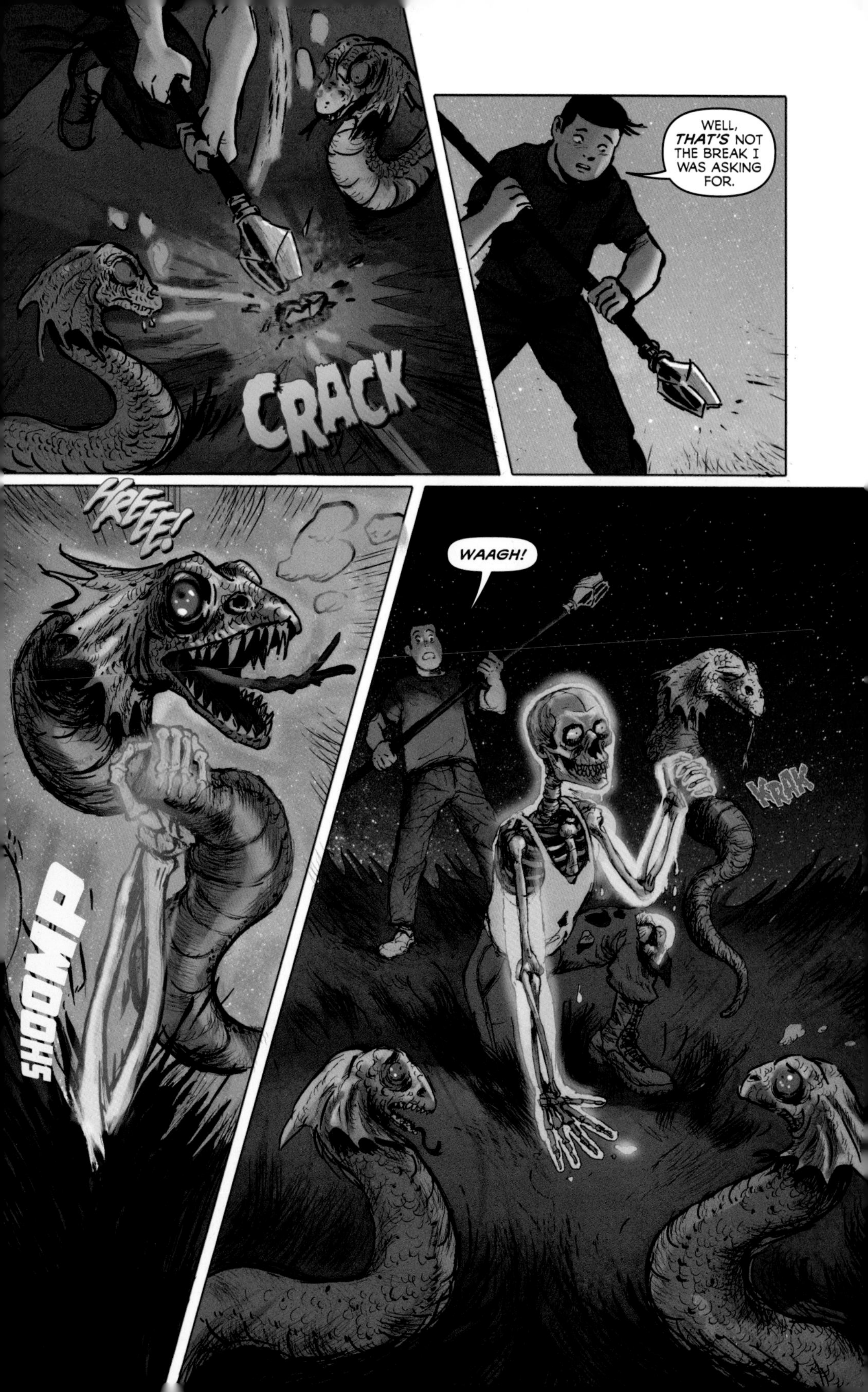
CRACK
WELL, THAT'S NOT THE BREAK I WAS ASKING FOR.
HREEE!
SHOOMP
WAAGH!
KRAK

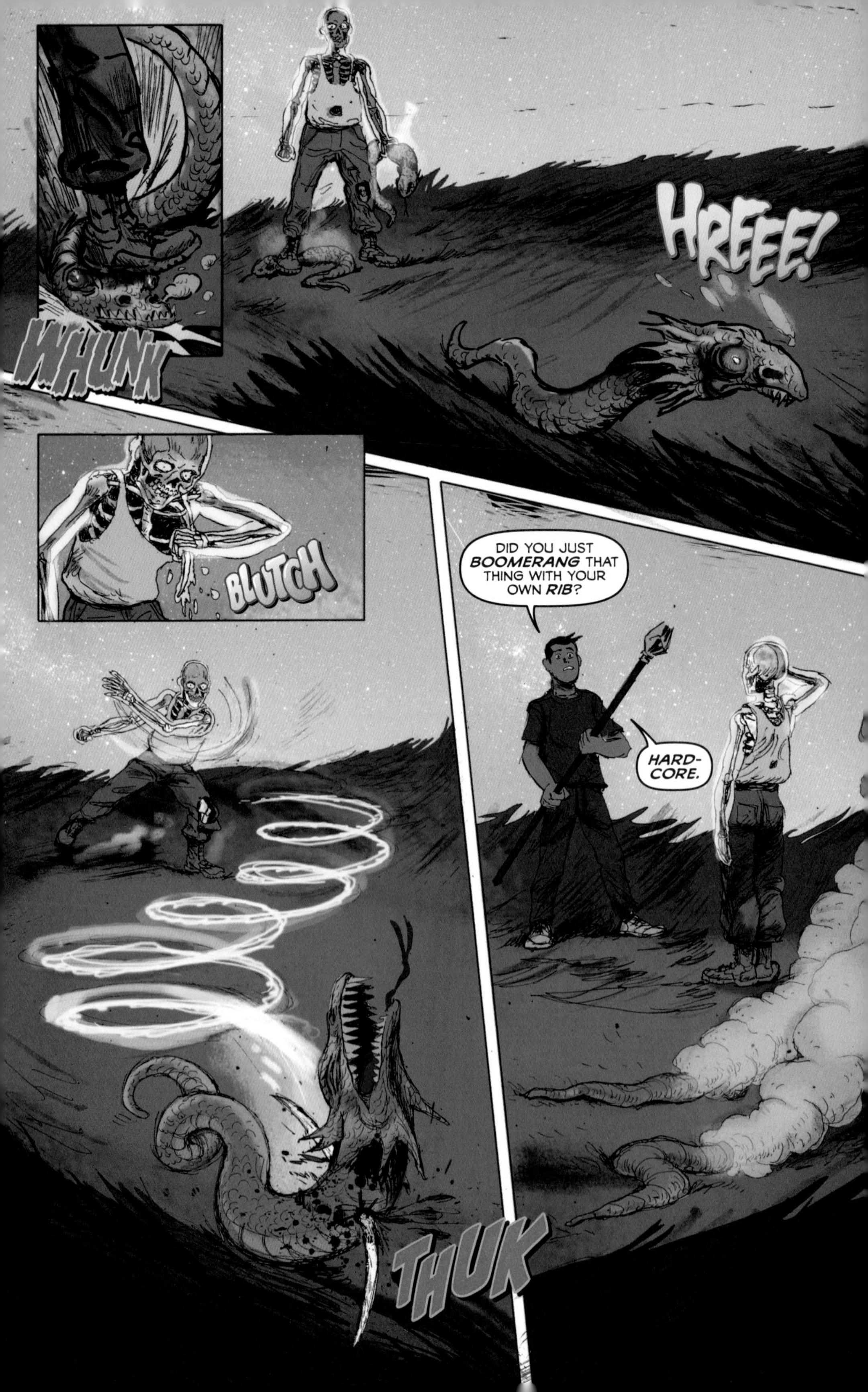
WHUNK
HREEE!
BLUTCH
THUK
DID YOU JUST BOOMERANG THAT THING WITH YOUR OWN RIB?
HARD-CORE.

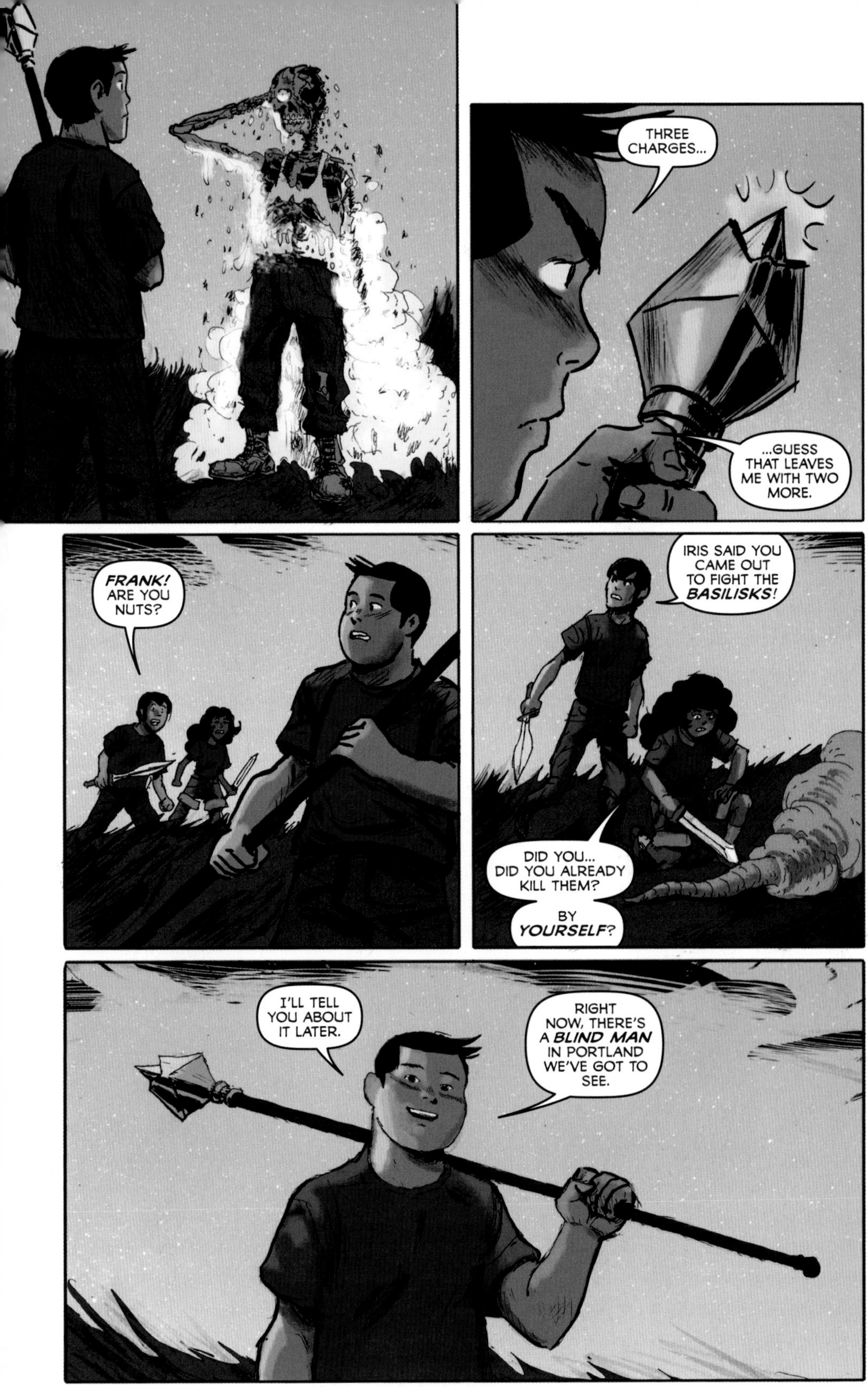
THREE CHARGES...
...GUESS THAT LEAVES ME WITH TWO MORE.
FRANK! ARE YOU NUTS?
IRIS SAID YOU CAME OUT TO FIGHT THE BASILISKS!
DID YOU... DID YOU ALREADY KILL THEM?
BY YOURSELF?
I'LL TELL YOU ABOUT IT LATER.
RIGHT NOW, THERE'S A BLIND MAN IN PORTLAND WE'VE GOT TO SEE.

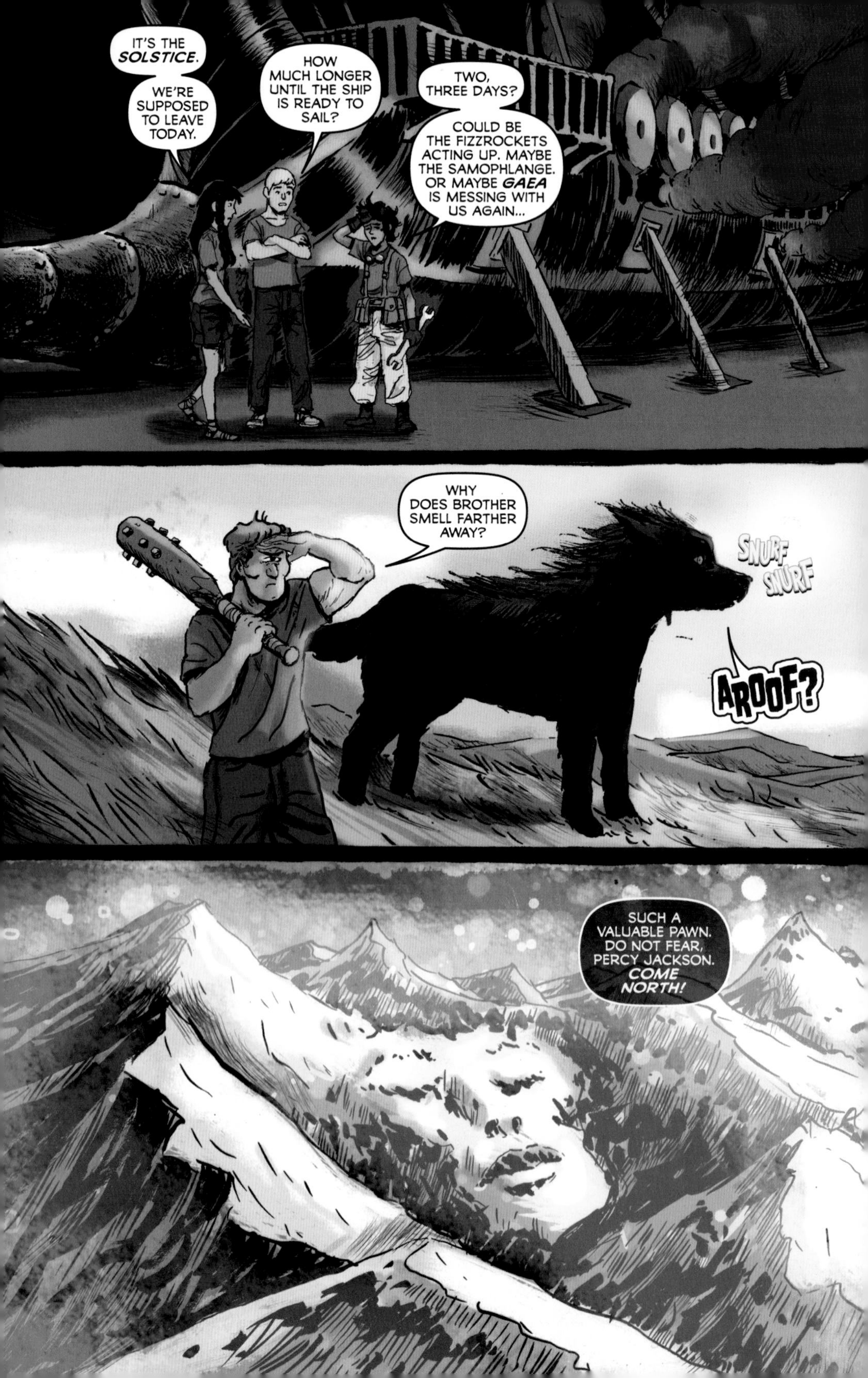
IT'S THE *SOLSTICE*.
WE'RE SUPPOSED TO LEAVE TODAY.
HOW MUCH LONGER UNTIL THE SHIP IS READY TO SAIL?
TWO, THREE DAYS?
COULD BE THE FIZZROCKETS ACTING UP. MAYBE THE SAMOPHLANGE. OR MAYBE *GAEA* IS MESSING WITH US AGAIN...
WHY DOES BROTHER SMELL FARTHER AWAY?
SNURF SNURF
AROOF?
SUCH A VALUABLE PAWN. DO NOT FEAR, PERCY JACKSON. *COME NORTH!*

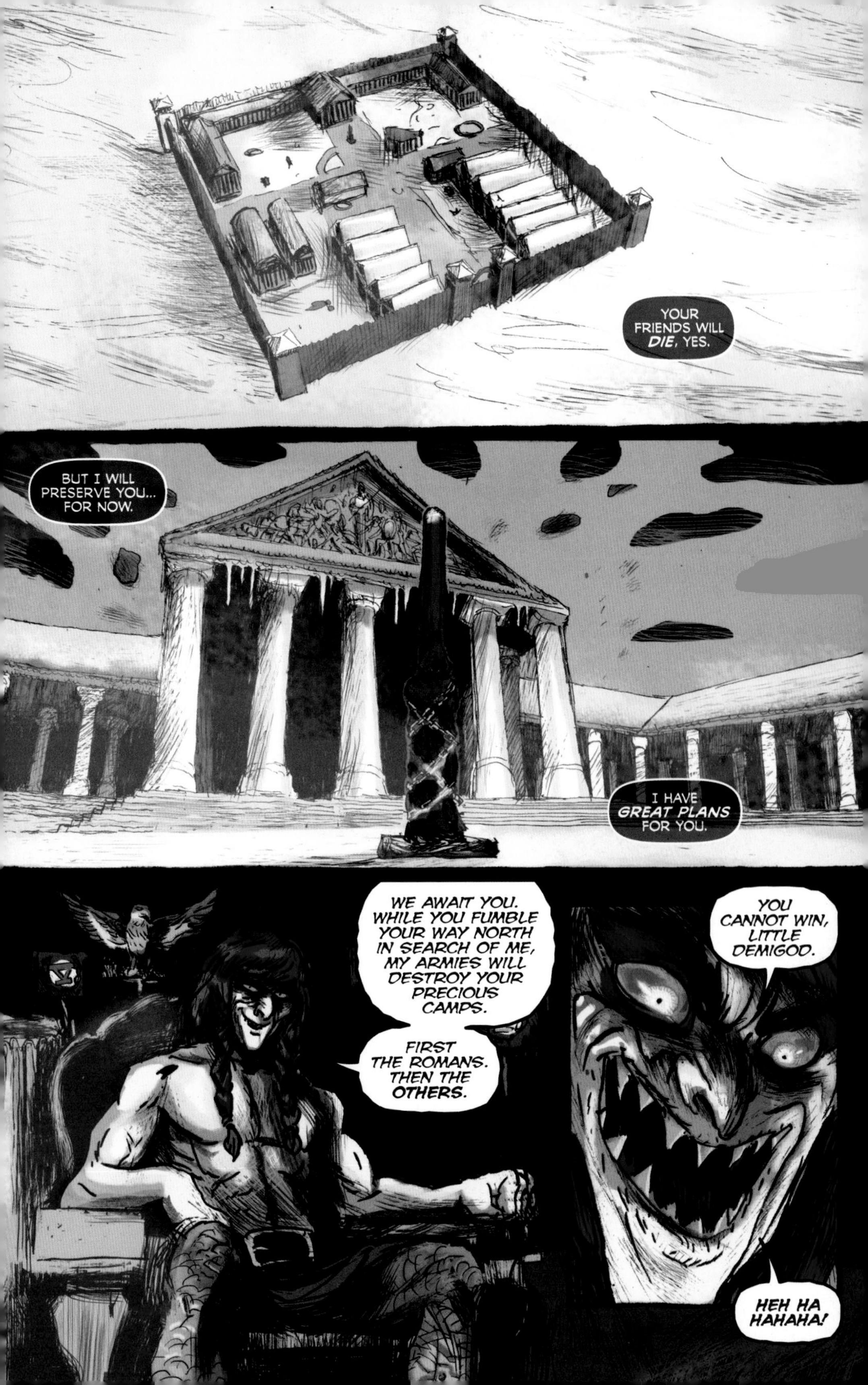
YOUR FRIENDS WILL DIE, YES.
BUT I WILL PRESERVE YOU... FOR NOW.
I HAVE GREAT PLANS FOR YOU.
WE AWAIT YOU. WHILE YOU FUMBLE YOUR WAY NORTH IN SEARCH OF ME, MY ARMIES WILL DESTROY YOUR PRECIOUS CAMPS.
FIRST THE ROMANS. THEN THE OTHERS.
YOU CANNOT WIN, LITTLE DEMIGOD.
HEH HA HAHAHA!

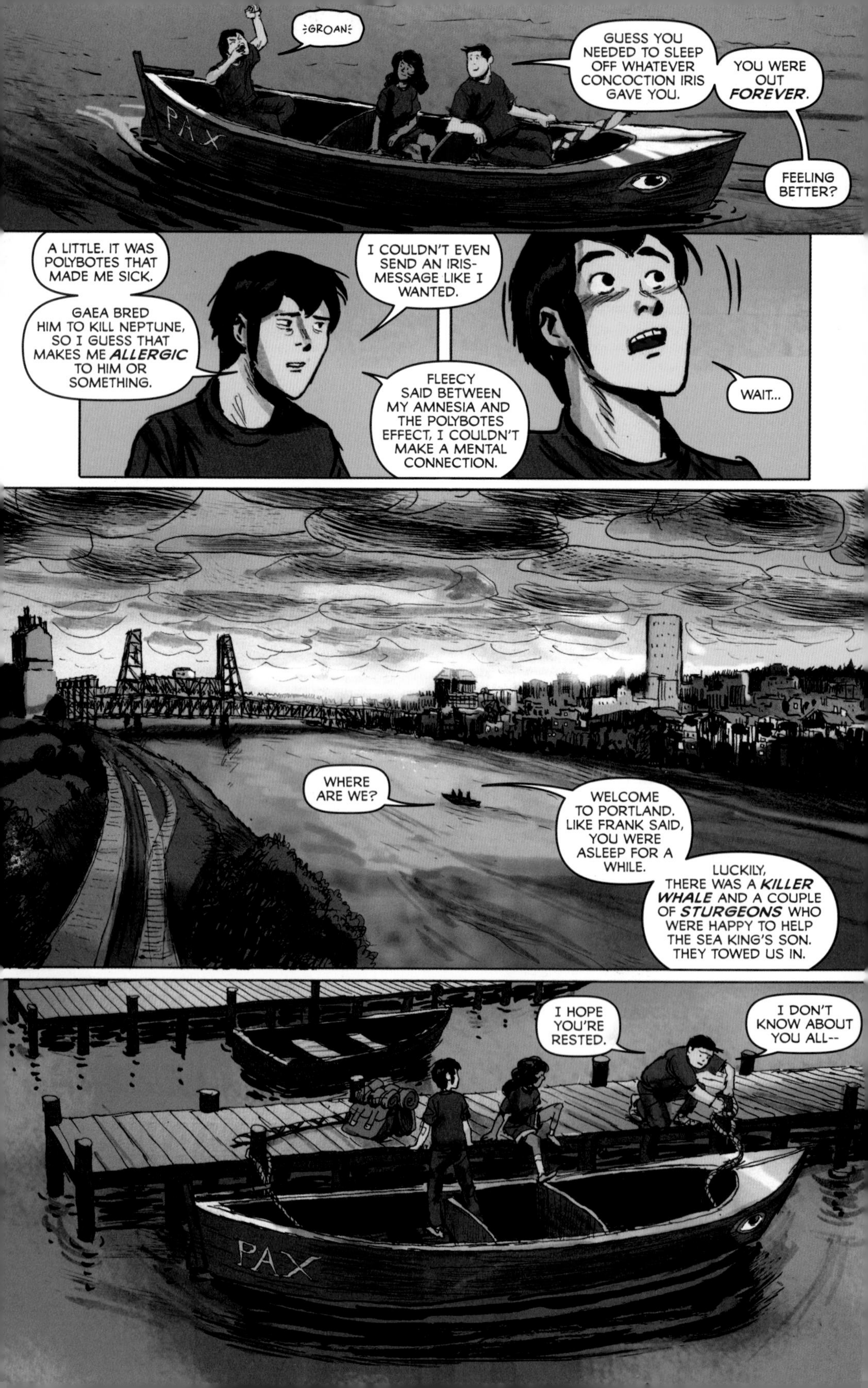

GROAN
GUESS YOU NEEDED TO SLEEP OFF WHATEVER CONCOCTION IRIS GAVE YOU.
YOU WERE OUT FOREVER.
FEELING BETTER?
A LITTLE. IT WAS POLYBOTES THAT MADE ME SICK.
GAEA BRED HIM TO KILL NEPTUNE, SO I GUESS THAT MAKES ME ALLERGIC TO HIM OR SOMETHING.
I COULDN'T EVEN SEND AN IRIS-MESSAGE LIKE I WANTED.
FLEECY SAID BETWEEN MY AMNESIA AND THE POLYBOTES EFFECT, I COULDN'T MAKE A MENTAL CONNECTION.
WAIT...
WHERE ARE WE?
WELCOME TO PORTLAND. LIKE FRANK SAID, YOU WERE ASLEEP FOR A WHILE.
LUCKILY, THERE WAS A KILLER WHALE AND A COUPLE OF STURGEONS WHO WERE HAPPY TO HELP THE SEA KING'S SON. THEY TOWED US IN.
I HOPE YOU'RE RESTED.
I DON'T KNOW ABOUT YOU ALL--

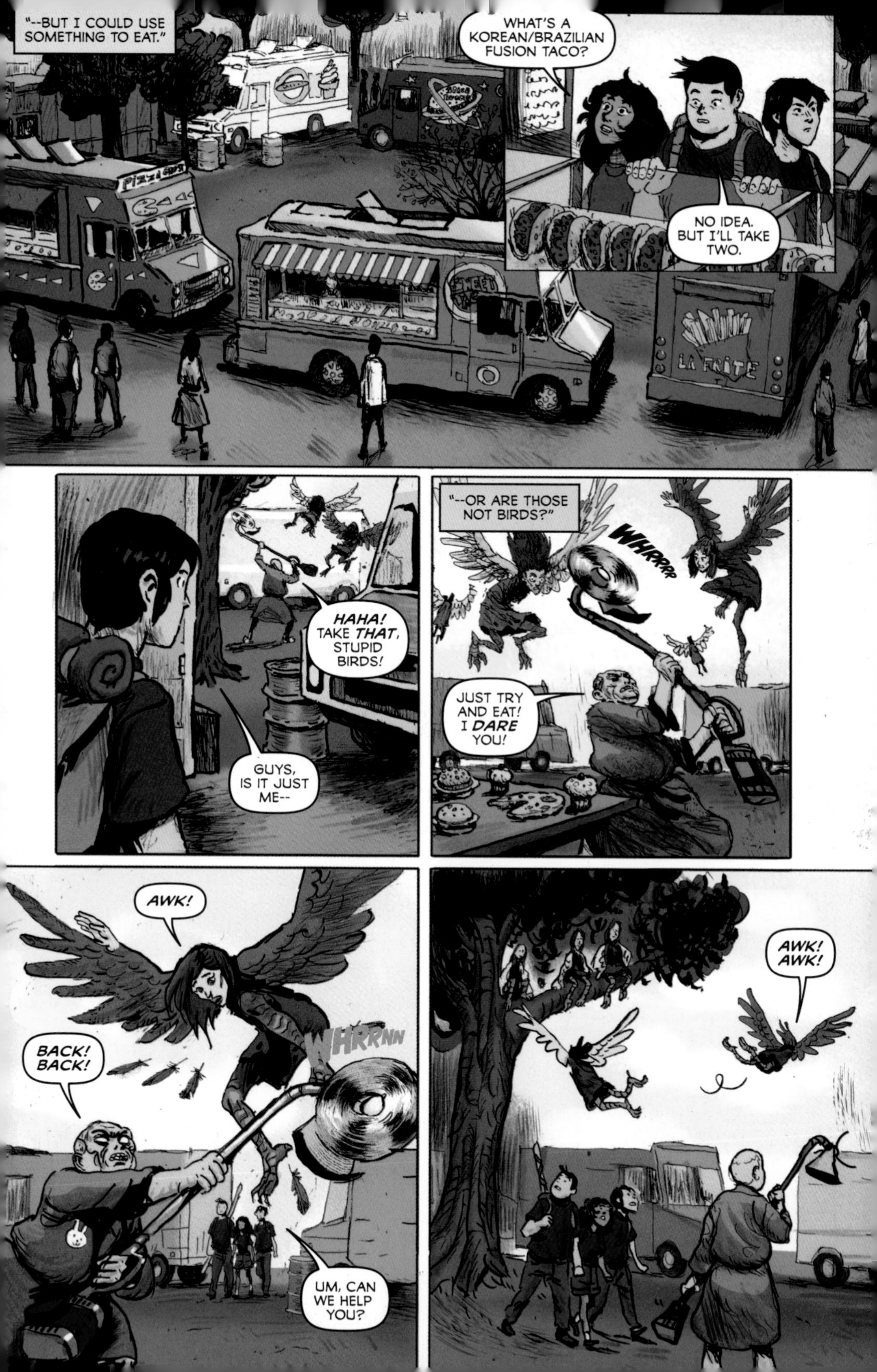
"--BUT I COULD USE SOMETHING TO EAT."
WHAT'S A KOREAN/BRAZILIAN FUSION TACO?
NO IDEA. BUT I'LL TAKE TWO.
PIZZA
LA FRITE
HAHA! TAKE THAT, STUPID BIRDS!
GUYS, IS IT JUST ME--
"--OR ARE THOSE NOT BIRDS?"
WHRRRR
JUST TRY AND EAT! I DARE YOU!
AWK!
BACK! BACK!
WHRRNN
UM, CAN WE HELP YOU?
AWK! AWK!

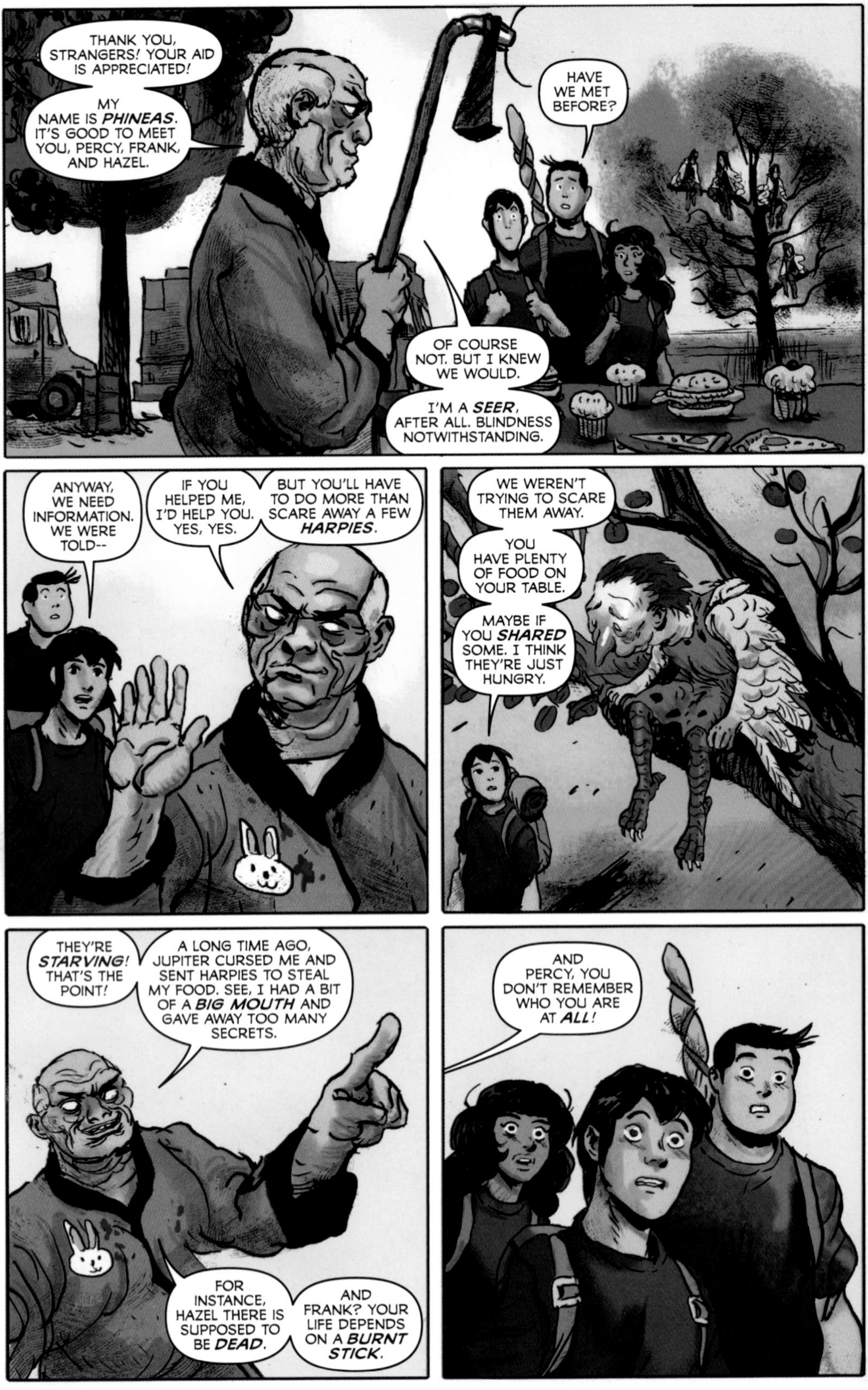
THANK YOU, STRANGERS! YOUR AID IS APPRECIATED!
MY NAME IS ***PHINEAS***. IT'S GOOD TO MEET YOU, PERCY, FRANK, AND HAZEL.
HAVE WE MET BEFORE?
OF COURSE NOT. BUT I KNEW WE WOULD.
I'M A ***SEER***, AFTER ALL. BLINDNESS NOTWITHSTANDING.
ANYWAY, WE NEED INFORMATION. WE WERE TOLD--
IF YOU HELPED ME, I'D HELP YOU. YES, YES.
BUT YOU'LL HAVE TO DO MORE THAN SCARE AWAY A FEW ***HARPIES***.
WE WEREN'T TRYING TO SCARE THEM AWAY.
YOU HAVE PLENTY OF FOOD ON YOUR TABLE.
MAYBE IF YOU ***SHARED*** SOME. I THINK THEY'RE JUST HUNGRY.
THEY'RE ***STARVING***! THAT'S THE POINT!
A LONG TIME AGO, JUPITER CURSED ME AND SENT HARPIES TO STEAL MY FOOD. SEE, I HAD A BIT OF A ***BIG MOUTH*** AND GAVE AWAY TOO MANY SECRETS.
FOR INSTANCE, HAZEL THERE IS SUPPOSED TO BE ***DEAD***.
AND FRANK? YOUR LIFE DEPENDS ON A ***BURNT STICK***.
AND PERCY, YOU DON'T REMEMBER WHO YOU ARE AT ***ALL***!

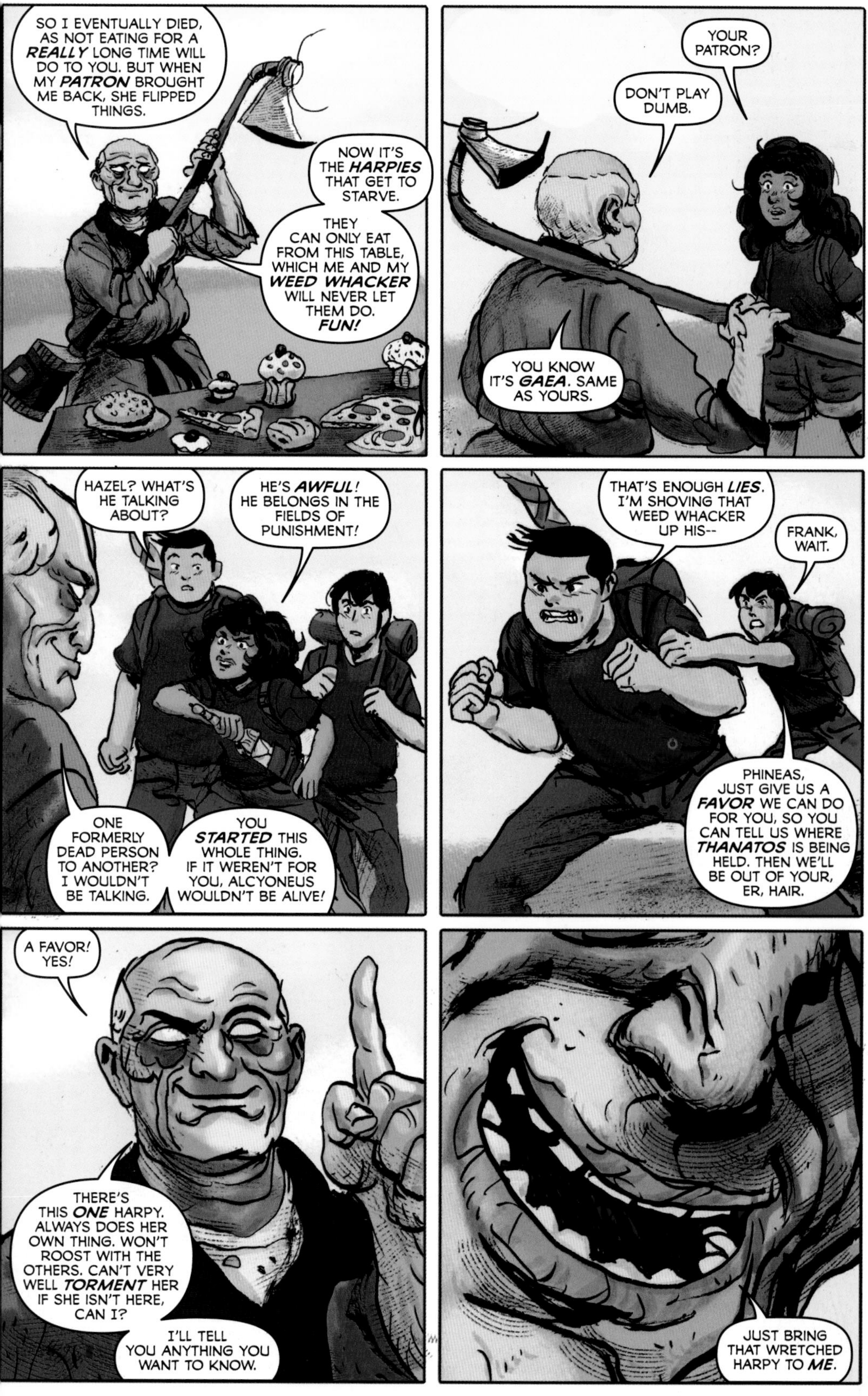
SO I EVENTUALLY DIED, AS NOT EATING FOR A *REALLY* LONG TIME WILL DO TO YOU. BUT WHEN MY *PATRON* BROUGHT ME BACK, SHE FLIPPED THINGS.
NOW IT'S THE *HARPIES* THAT GET TO STARVE.
THEY CAN ONLY EAT FROM THIS TABLE, WHICH ME AND MY *WEED WHACKER* WILL NEVER LET THEM DO. *FUN!*
YOUR PATRON?
DON'T PLAY DUMB.
YOU KNOW IT'S *GAEA*. SAME AS YOURS.
HAZEL? WHAT'S HE TALKING ABOUT?
HE'S *AWFUL!* HE BELONGS IN THE FIELDS OF PUNISHMENT!
ONE FORMERLY DEAD PERSON TO ANOTHER? I WOULDN'T BE TALKING.
YOU *STARTED* THIS WHOLE THING. IF IT WEREN'T FOR YOU, ALCYONEUS WOULDN'T BE ALIVE!
THAT'S ENOUGH *LIES*. I'M SHOVING THAT WEED WHACKER UP HIS--
FRANK, WAIT.
PHINEAS, JUST GIVE US A *FAVOR* WE CAN DO FOR YOU, SO YOU CAN TELL US WHERE *THANATOS* IS BEING HELD. THEN WE'LL BE OUT OF YOUR, ER, HAIR.
A FAVOR! YES!
THERE'S THIS *ONE* HARPY. ALWAYS DOES HER OWN THING. WON'T ROOST WITH THE OTHERS. CAN'T VERY WELL *TORMENT* HER IF SHE ISN'T HERE, CAN I?
I'LL TELL YOU ANYTHING YOU WANT TO KNOW.
JUST BRING THAT WRETCHED HARPY TO *ME*.

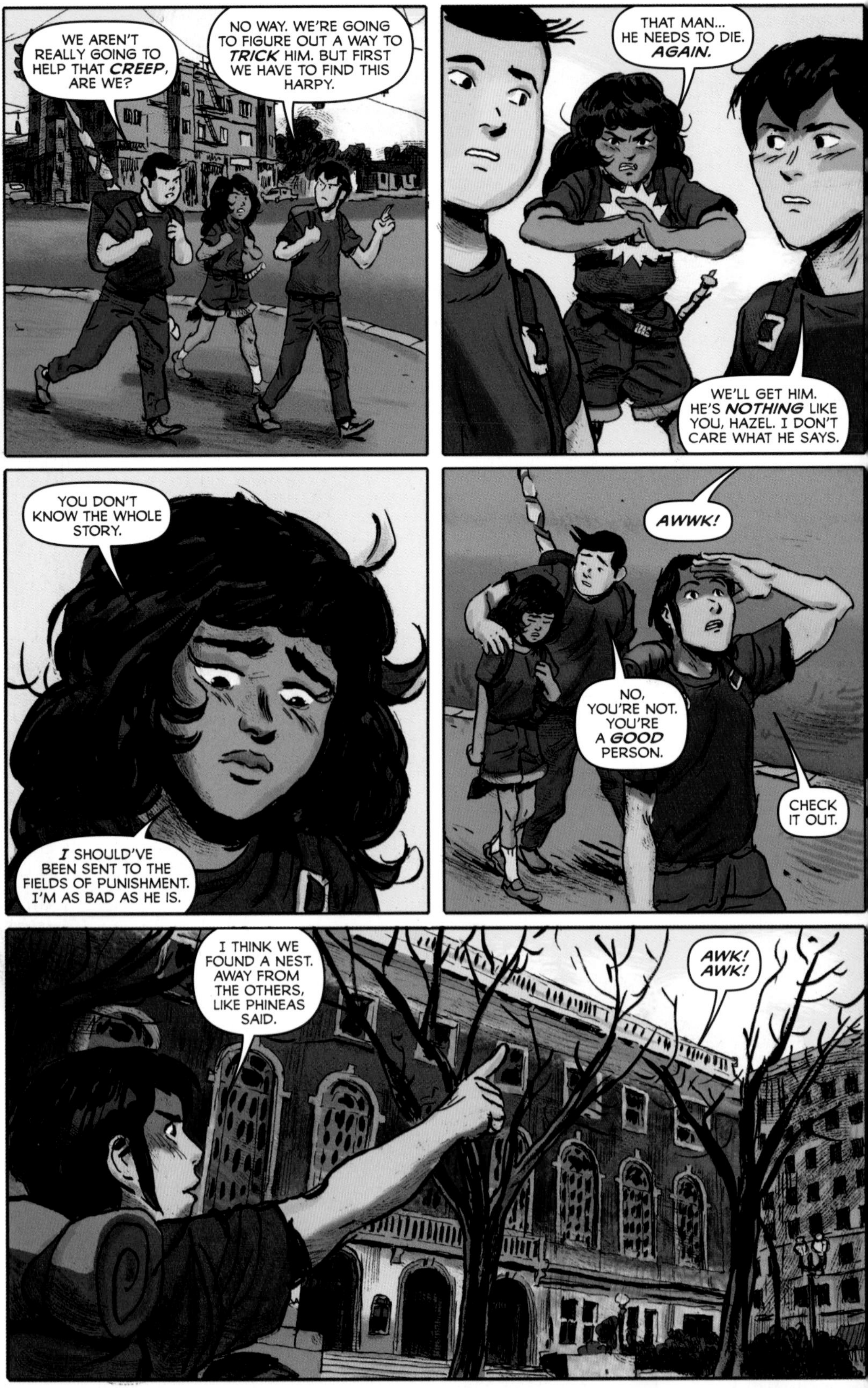
WE AREN'T REALLY GOING TO HELP THAT CREEP, ARE WE?
NO WAY. WE'RE GOING TO FIGURE OUT A WAY TO TRICK HIM. BUT FIRST WE HAVE TO FIND THIS HARPY.
THAT MAN... HE NEEDS TO DIE. AGAIN.
WE'LL GET HIM. HE'S NOTHING LIKE YOU, HAZEL. I DON'T CARE WHAT HE SAYS.
YOU DON'T KNOW THE WHOLE STORY.
I SHOULD'VE BEEN SENT TO THE FIELDS OF PUNISHMENT. I'M AS BAD AS HE IS.
AWWK!
NO, YOU'RE NOT. YOU'RE A GOOD PERSON.
CHECK IT OUT.
I THINK WE FOUND A NEST. AWAY FROM THE OTHERS, LIKE PHINEAS SAID.
AWK! AWK!

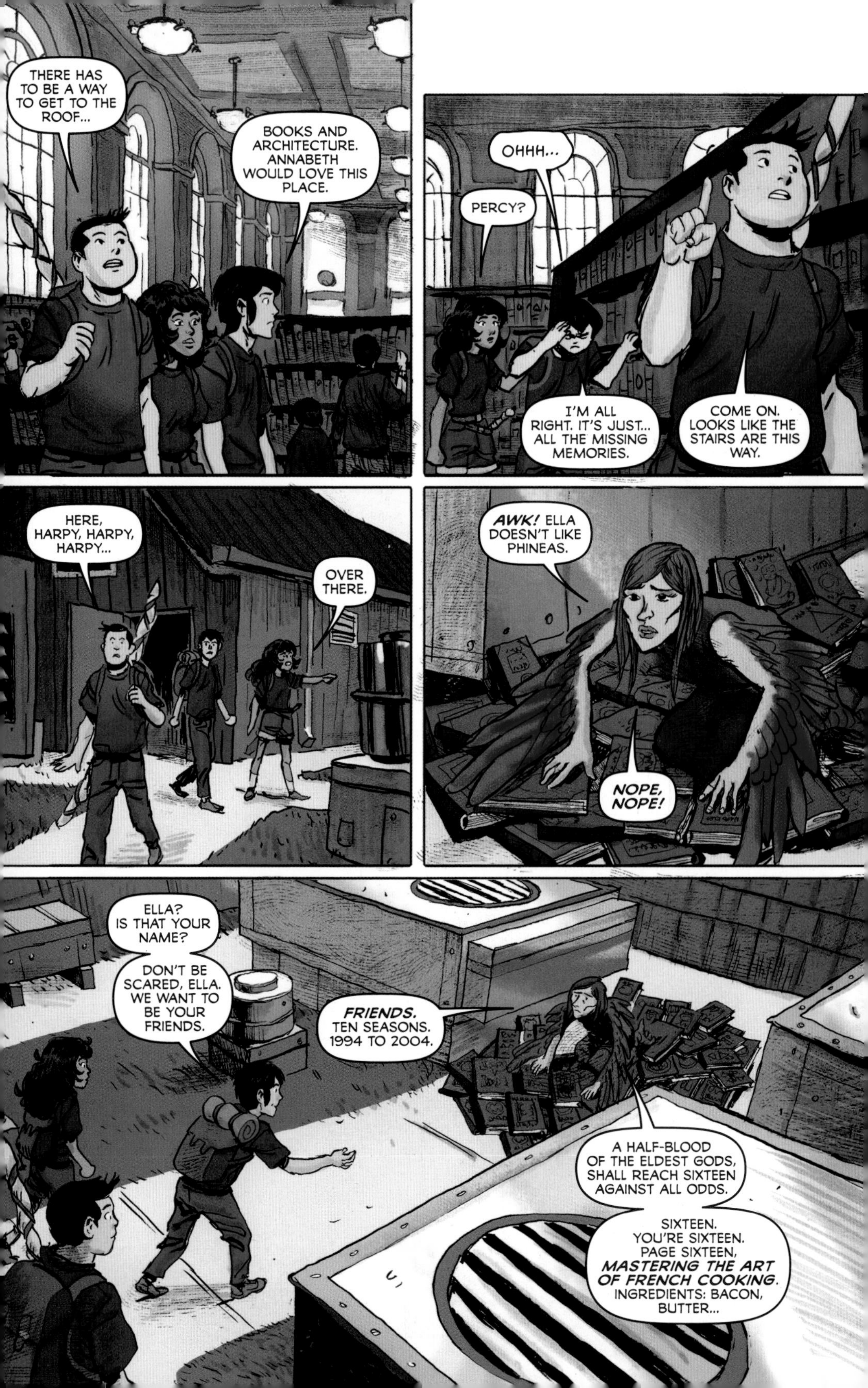
THERE HAS TO BE A WAY TO GET TO THE ROOF...
BOOKS AND ARCHITECTURE. ANNABETH WOULD LOVE THIS PLACE.
OHHH...
PERCY?
I'M ALL RIGHT. IT'S JUST... ALL THE MISSING MEMORIES.
COME ON. LOOKS LIKE THE STAIRS ARE THIS WAY.
HERE, HARPY, HARPY, HARPY...
OVER THERE.
AWK! ELLA DOESN'T LIKE PHINEAS.
NOPE, NOPE!
ELLA? IS THAT YOUR NAME?
DON'T BE SCARED, ELLA. WE WANT TO BE YOUR FRIENDS.
FRIENDS. TEN SEASONS. 1994 TO 2004.
A HALF-BLOOD OF THE ELDEST GODS, SHALL REACH SIXTEEN AGAINST ALL ODDS.
SIXTEEN. YOU'RE SIXTEEN. PAGE SIXTEEN, MASTERING THE ART OF FRENCH COOKING. INGREDIENTS: BACON, BUTTER...

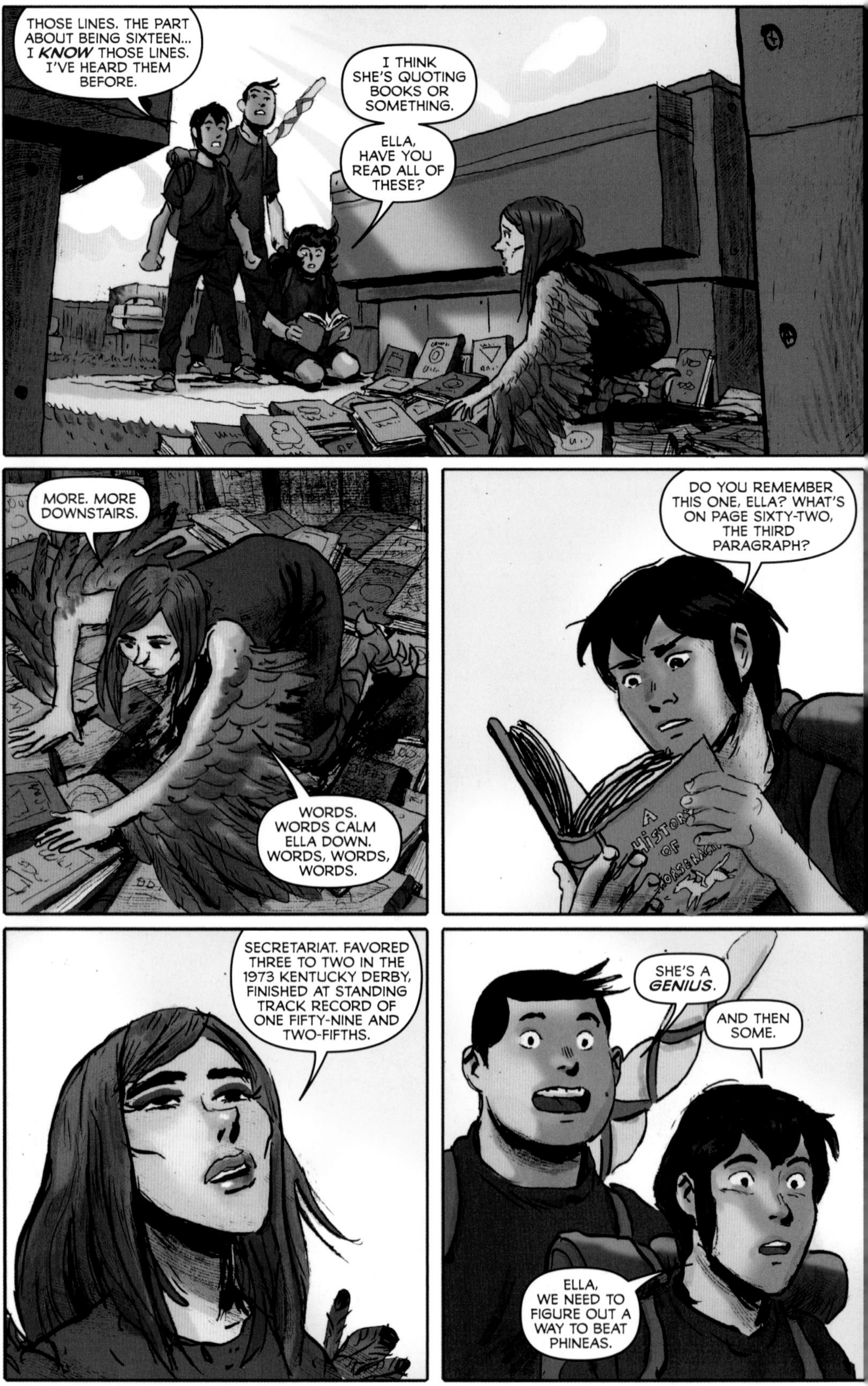
THOSE LINES. THE PART ABOUT BEING SIXTEEN... I **KNOW** THOSE LINES. I'VE HEARD THEM BEFORE.
I THINK SHE'S QUOTING BOOKS OR SOMETHING.
ELLA, HAVE YOU READ ALL OF THESE?
MORE. MORE DOWNSTAIRS.
WORDS. WORDS CALM ELLA DOWN. WORDS, WORDS, WORDS.
DO YOU REMEMBER THIS ONE, ELLA? WHAT'S ON PAGE SIXTY-TWO, THE THIRD PARAGRAPH?
SECRETARIAT. FAVORED THREE TO TWO IN THE 1973 KENTUCKY DERBY, FINISHED AT STANDING TRACK RECORD OF ONE FIFTY-NINE AND TWO-FIFTHS.
SHE'S A **GENIUS**.
AND THEN SOME.
ELLA, WE NEED TO FIGURE OUT A WAY TO BEAT PHINEAS.

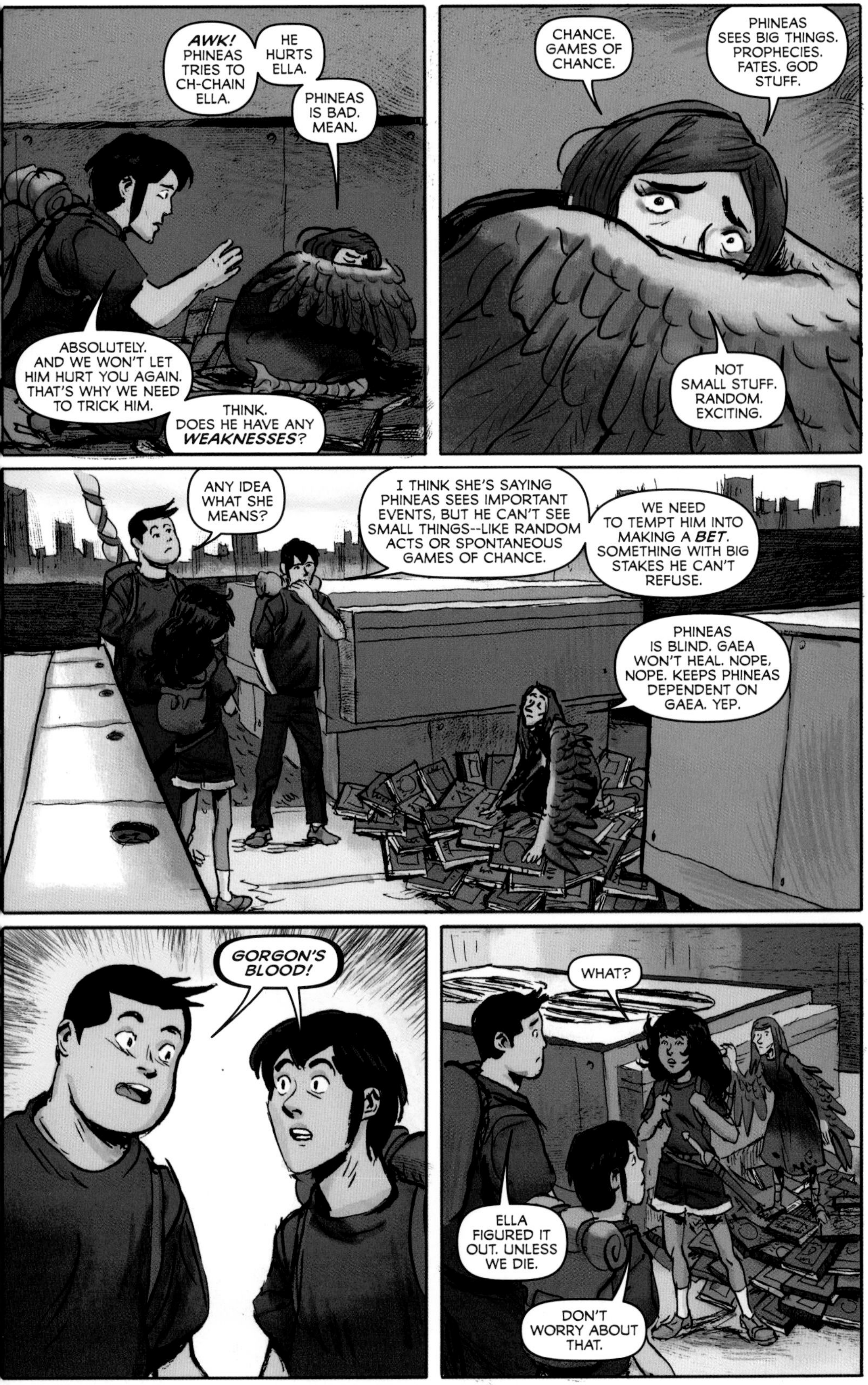
AWK! PHINEAS TRIES TO CH-CHAIN ELLA.
HE HURTS ELLA.
PHINEAS IS BAD. MEAN.
ABSOLUTELY. AND WE WON'T LET HIM HURT YOU AGAIN. THAT'S WHY WE NEED TO TRICK HIM.
THINK. DOES HE HAVE ANY WEAKNESSES?
CHANCE. GAMES OF CHANCE.
PHINEAS SEES BIG THINGS. PROPHECIES. FATES. GOD STUFF.
NOT SMALL STUFF. RANDOM. EXCITING.
ANY IDEA WHAT SHE MEANS?
I THINK SHE'S SAYING PHINEAS SEES IMPORTANT EVENTS, BUT HE CAN'T SEE SMALL THINGS--LIKE RANDOM ACTS OR SPONTANEOUS GAMES OF CHANCE.
WE NEED TO TEMPT HIM INTO MAKING A BET. SOMETHING WITH BIG STAKES HE CAN'T REFUSE.
PHINEAS IS BLIND. GAEA WON'T HEAL. NOPE, NOPE. KEEPS PHINEAS DEPENDENT ON GAEA. YEP.
GORGON'S BLOOD!
WHAT?
ELLA FIGURED IT OUT. UNLESS WE DIE.
DON'T WORRY ABOUT THAT.

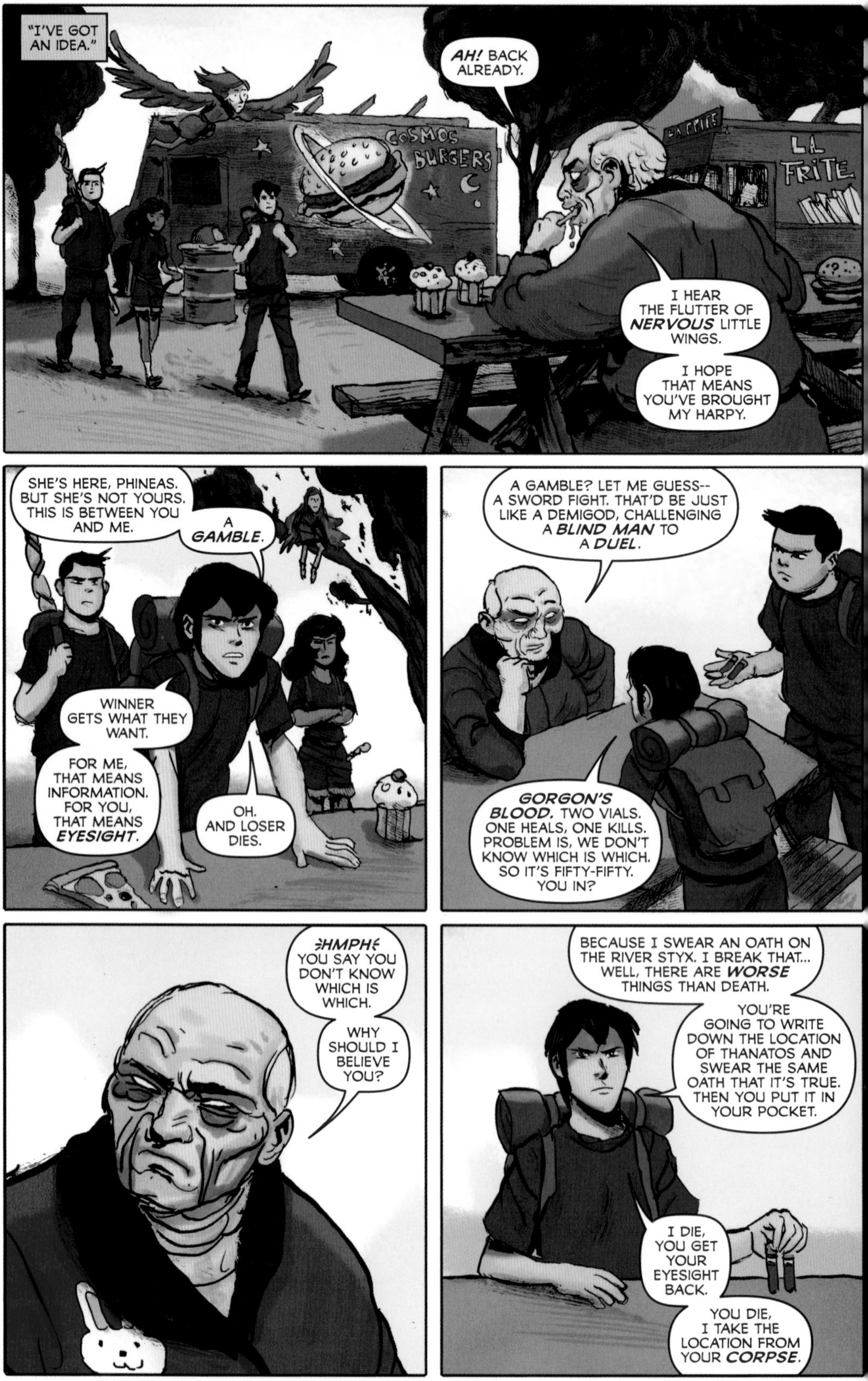

"I'VE GOT AN IDEA."
COSMOS BURGERS
LA FRITE
AH! BACK ALREADY.
I HEAR THE FLUTTER OF NERVOUS LITTLE WINGS.
I HOPE THAT MEANS YOU'VE BROUGHT MY HARPY.
SHE'S HERE, PHINEAS. BUT SHE'S NOT YOURS. THIS IS BETWEEN YOU AND ME.
A GAMBLE.
WINNER GETS WHAT THEY WANT.
FOR ME, THAT MEANS INFORMATION. FOR YOU, THAT MEANS EYESIGHT.
OH. AND LOSER DIES.
A GAMBLE? LET ME GUESS-- A SWORD FIGHT. THAT'D BE JUST LIKE A DEMIGOD, CHALLENGING A BLIND MAN TO A DUEL.
GORGON'S BLOOD. TWO VIALS. ONE HEALS, ONE KILLS. PROBLEM IS, WE DON'T KNOW WHICH IS WHICH. SO IT'S FIFTY-FIFTY. YOU IN?
HMPH
YOU SAY YOU DON'T KNOW WHICH IS WHICH.
WHY SHOULD I BELIEVE YOU?
BECAUSE I SWEAR AN OATH ON THE RIVER STYX. I BREAK THAT... WELL, THERE ARE WORSE THINGS THAN DEATH.
YOU'RE GOING TO WRITE DOWN THE LOCATION OF THANATOS AND SWEAR THE SAME OATH THAT IT'S TRUE. THEN YOU PUT IT IN YOUR POCKET.
I DIE, YOU GET YOUR EYESIGHT BACK.
YOU DIE, I TAKE THE LOCATION FROM YOUR CORPSE.

TEMPTING...WITH MY SIGHT RESTORED, I WOULDN'T NEED GAEA ANYMORE.
I COULD CATCH THAT BLASTED HARPY MYSELF.
IF ONLY YOU KNEW HOW VALUABLE SHE WAS.
I WAS A KING ONCE. I COULD BE AGAIN!
MR. JACKSON, YOU HAVE A DEAL.
I SWEAR ON THE RIVER STYX THAT THIS IS INDEED THE LOCATION OF ALCYONEUS'S LAIR.
NOT THAT YOU'LL LIVE LONG ENOUGH TO READ IT.
CHOOSE.
NOT SO HASTY, BOY. GIVE AN OLD, BLIND MAN A MOMENT...
TINK

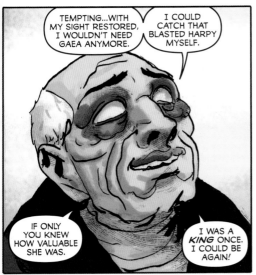

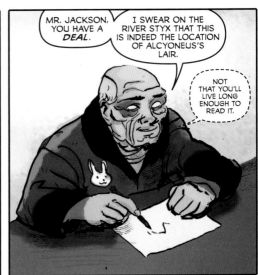

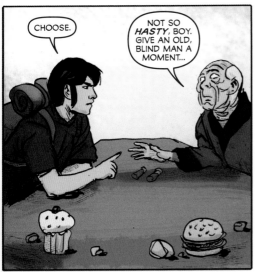

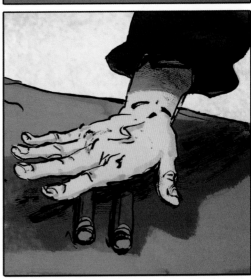

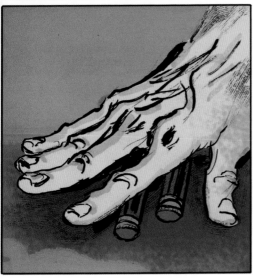

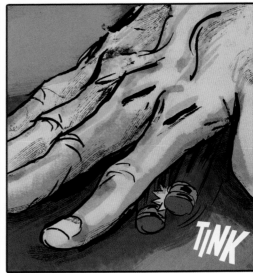

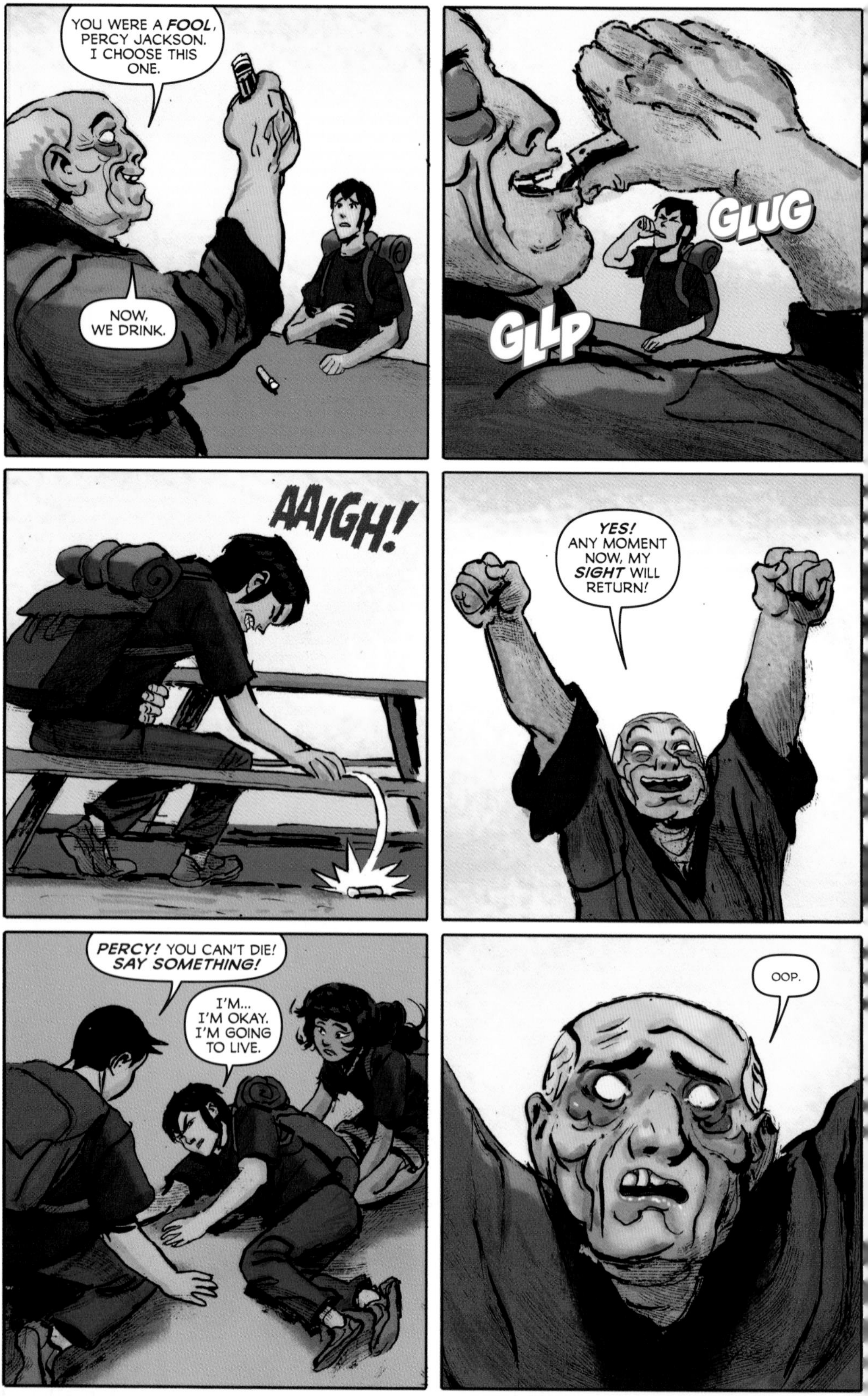
YOU WERE A *FOOL*, PERCY JACKSON. I CHOOSE THIS ONE.
NOW, WE DRINK.
GLUG
GLLP
AAIGH!
YES! ANY MOMENT NOW, MY *SIGHT* WILL RETURN!
PERCY! YOU CAN'T DIE! *SAY SOMETHING!*
I'M... I'M OKAY. I'M GOING TO LIVE.
OOP.

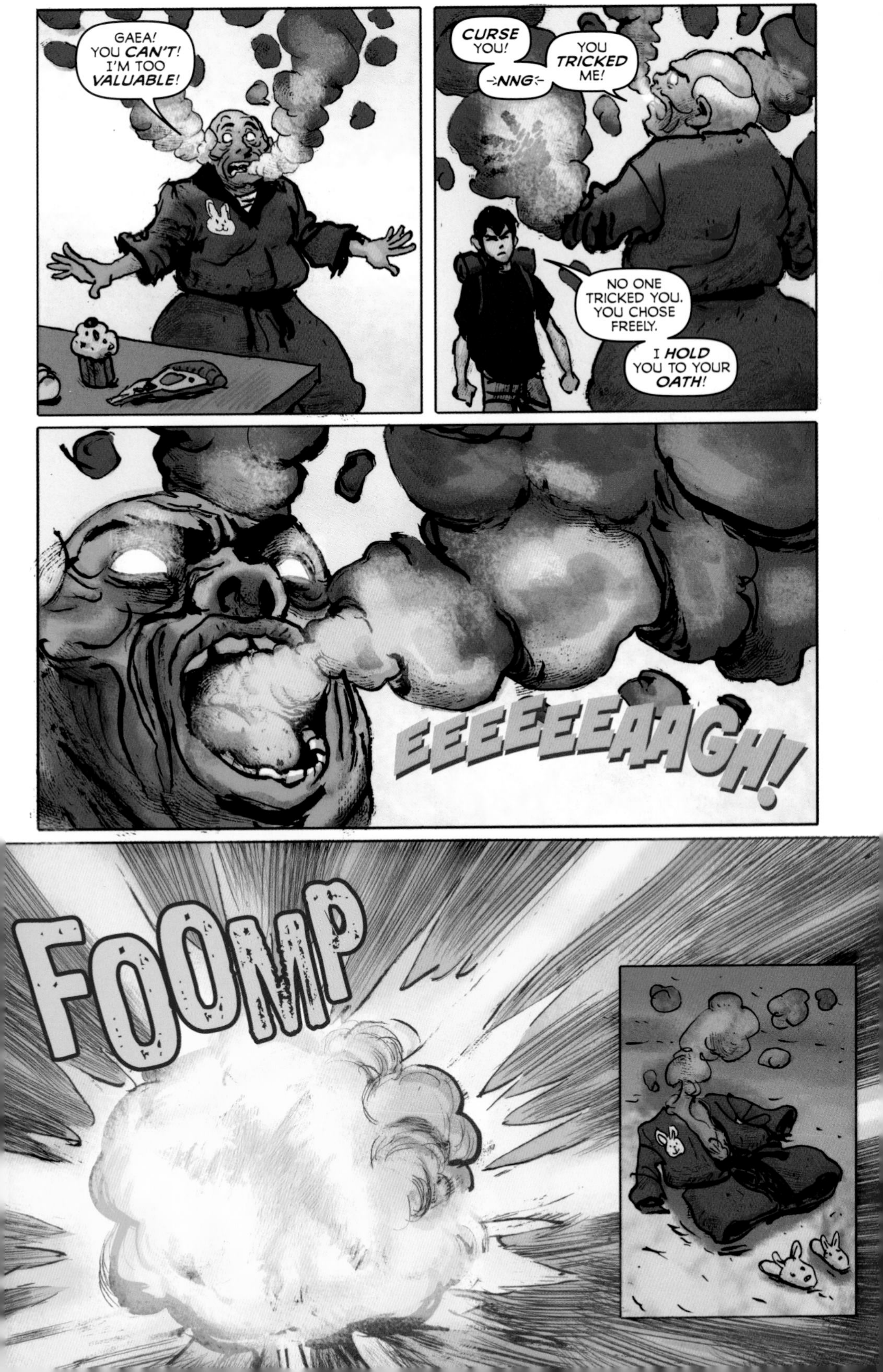
GAEA! YOU CAN'T! I'M TOO VALUABLE!
CURSE YOU!
-NNG-
YOU TRICKED ME!
NO ONE TRICKED YOU. YOU CHOSE FREELY.
I HOLD YOU TO YOUR OATH!
EEEEEEAAGH!
FOOMP

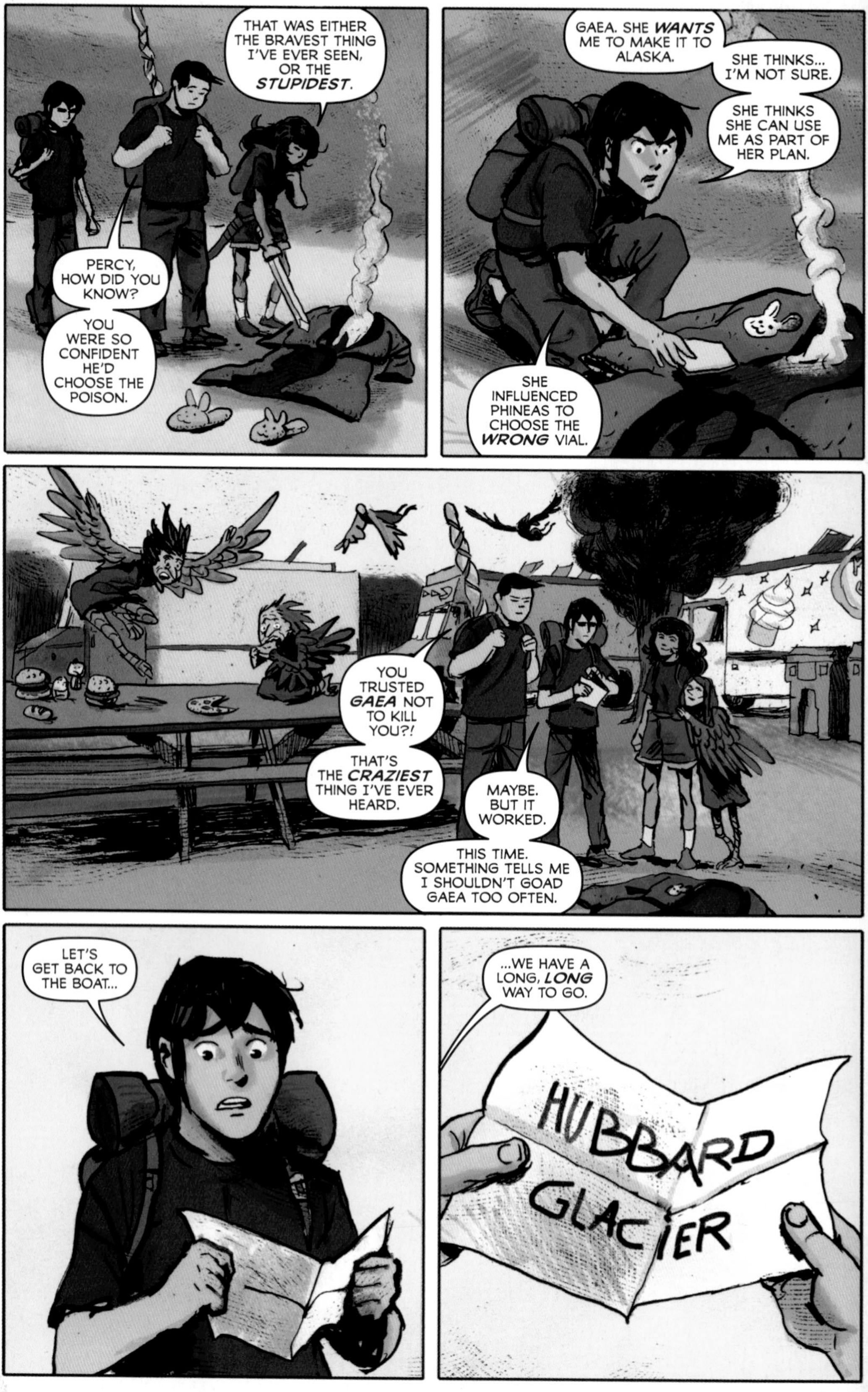
THAT WAS EITHER THE BRAVEST THING I'VE EVER SEEN, OR THE *STUPIDEST*.
PERCY, HOW DID YOU KNOW?
YOU WERE SO CONFIDENT HE'D CHOOSE THE POISON.
GAEA. SHE *WANTS* ME TO MAKE IT TO ALASKA.
SHE THINKS... I'M NOT SURE.
SHE THINKS SHE CAN USE ME AS PART OF HER PLAN.
SHE INFLUENCED PHINEAS TO CHOOSE THE *WRONG* VIAL.
YOU TRUSTED *GAEA* NOT TO KILL YOU?!
THAT'S THE *CRAZIEST* THING I'VE EVER HEARD.
MAYBE. BUT IT WORKED.
THIS TIME. SOMETHING TELLS ME I SHOULDN'T GOAD GAEA TOO OFTEN.
LET'S GET BACK TO THE BOAT...
...WE HAVE A LONG, *LONG* WAY TO GO.
HUBBARD
GLACIER

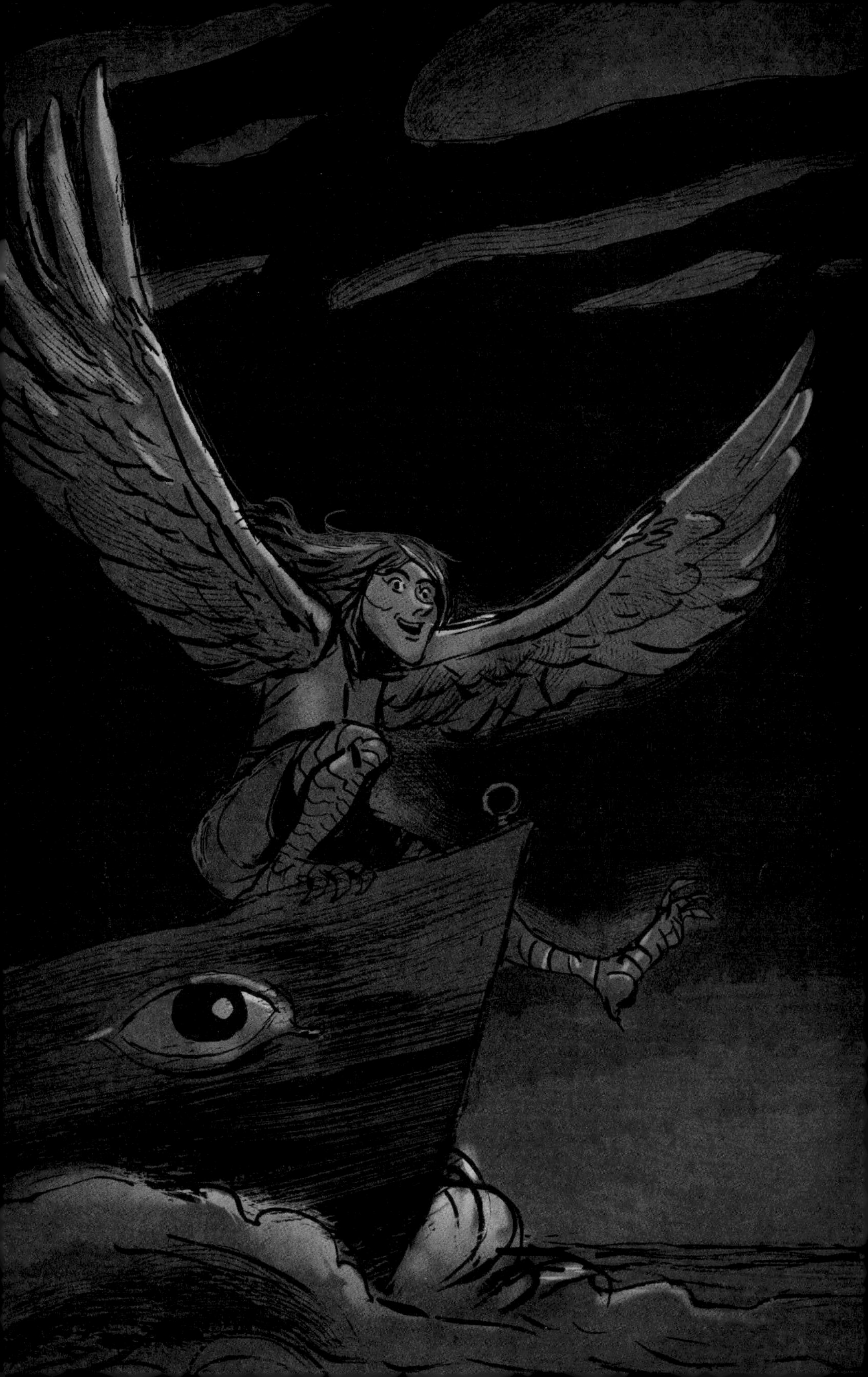

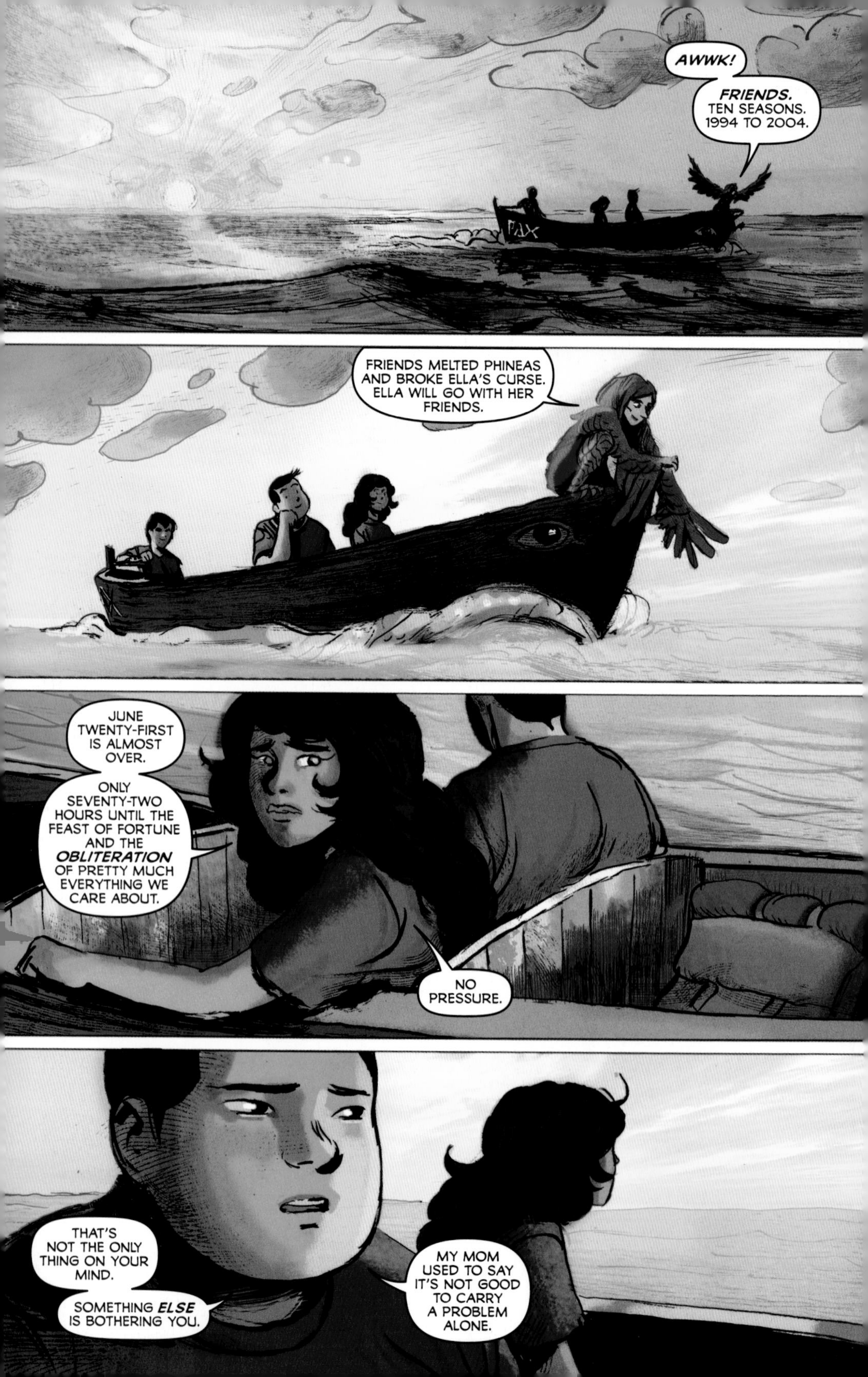
AWWK!
FRIENDS. TEN SEASONS. 1994 TO 2004.
FRIENDS MELTED PHINEAS AND BROKE ELLA'S CURSE. ELLA WILL GO WITH HER FRIENDS.
JUNE TWENTY-FIRST IS ALMOST OVER.
ONLY SEVENTY-TWO HOURS UNTIL THE FEAST OF FORTUNE AND THE OBLITERATION OF PRETTY MUCH EVERYTHING WE CARE ABOUT.
NO PRESSURE.
THAT'S NOT THE ONLY THING ON YOUR MIND.
SOMETHING ELSE IS BOTHERING YOU.
MY MOM USED TO SAY IT'S NOT GOOD TO CARRY A PROBLEM ALONE.

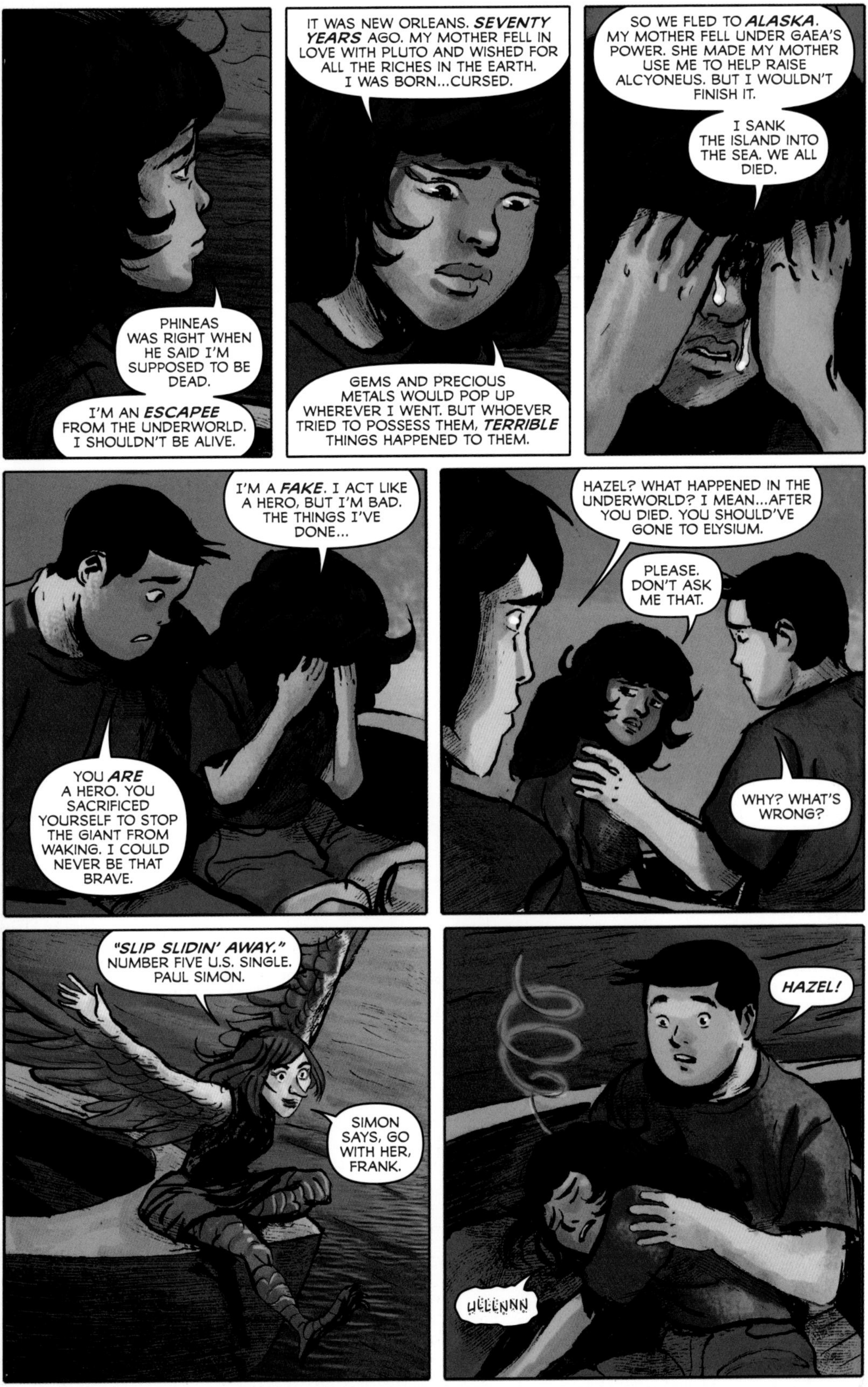

PHINEAS WAS RIGHT WHEN HE SAID I'M SUPPOSED TO BE DEAD.
I'M AN ESCAPEE FROM THE UNDERWORLD. I SHOULDN'T BE ALIVE.
IT WAS NEW ORLEANS. SEVENTY YEARS AGO. MY MOTHER FELL IN LOVE WITH PLUTO AND WISHED FOR ALL THE RICHES IN THE EARTH. I WAS BORN...CURSED.
GEMS AND PRECIOUS METALS WOULD POP UP WHEREVER I WENT. BUT WHOEVER TRIED TO POSSESS THEM, TERRIBLE THINGS HAPPENED TO THEM.
SO WE FLED TO ALASKA. MY MOTHER FELL UNDER GAEA'S POWER. SHE MADE MY MOTHER USE ME TO HELP RAISE ALCYONEUS. BUT I WOULDN'T FINISH IT.
I SANK THE ISLAND INTO THE SEA. WE ALL DIED.
I'M A FAKE. I ACT LIKE A HERO, BUT I'M BAD. THE THINGS I'VE DONE...
YOU ARE A HERO. YOU SACRIFICED YOURSELF TO STOP THE GIANT FROM WAKING. I COULD NEVER BE THAT BRAVE.
HAZEL? WHAT HAPPENED IN THE UNDERWORLD? I MEAN...AFTER YOU DIED. YOU SHOULD'VE GONE TO ELYSIUM.
PLEASE. DON'T ASK ME THAT.
WHY? WHAT'S WRONG?
"SLIP SLIDIN' AWAY." NUMBER FIVE U.S. SINGLE. PAUL SIMON.
SIMON SAYS, GO WITH HER, FRANK.
HAZEL!
ULLLNNN

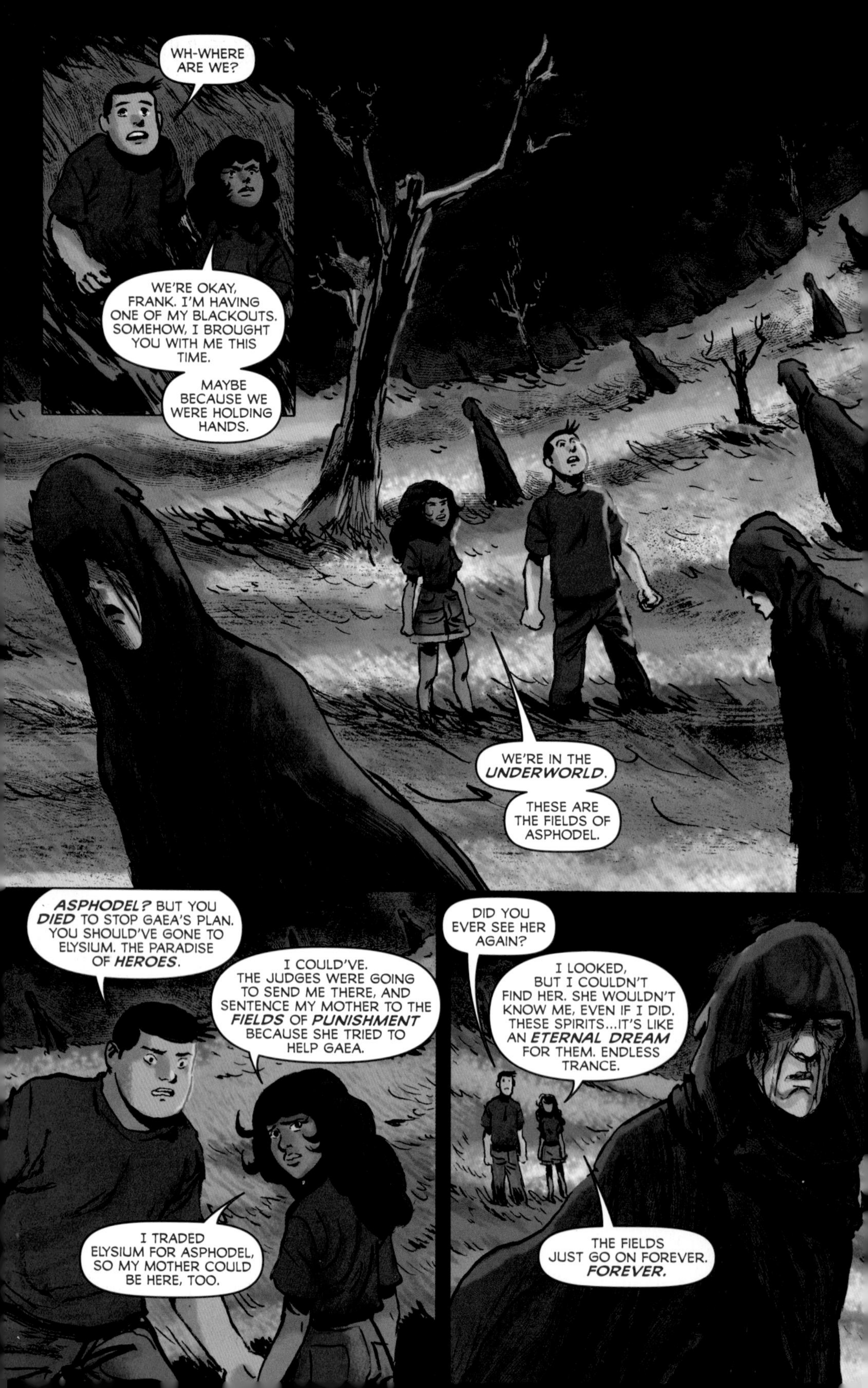
WH-WHERE ARE WE?
WE'RE OKAY, FRANK. I'M HAVING ONE OF MY BLACKOUTS. SOMEHOW, I BROUGHT YOU WITH ME THIS TIME.
MAYBE BECAUSE WE WERE HOLDING HANDS.
WE'RE IN THE UNDERWORLD.
THESE ARE THE FIELDS OF ASPHODEL.
ASPHODEL? BUT YOU DIED TO STOP GAEA'S PLAN. YOU SHOULD'VE GONE TO ELYSIUM. THE PARADISE OF HEROES.
I COULD'VE. THE JUDGES WERE GOING TO SEND ME THERE, AND SENTENCE MY MOTHER TO THE FIELDS OF PUNISHMENT BECAUSE SHE TRIED TO HELP GAEA.
I TRADED ELYSIUM FOR ASPHODEL, SO MY MOTHER COULD BE HERE, TOO.
DID YOU EVER SEE HER AGAIN?
I LOOKED, BUT I COULDN'T FIND HER. SHE WOULDN'T KNOW ME, EVEN IF I DID. THESE SPIRITS...IT'S LIKE AN ETERNAL DREAM FOR THEM. ENDLESS TRANCE.
THE FIELDS JUST GO ON FOREVER. FOREVER.

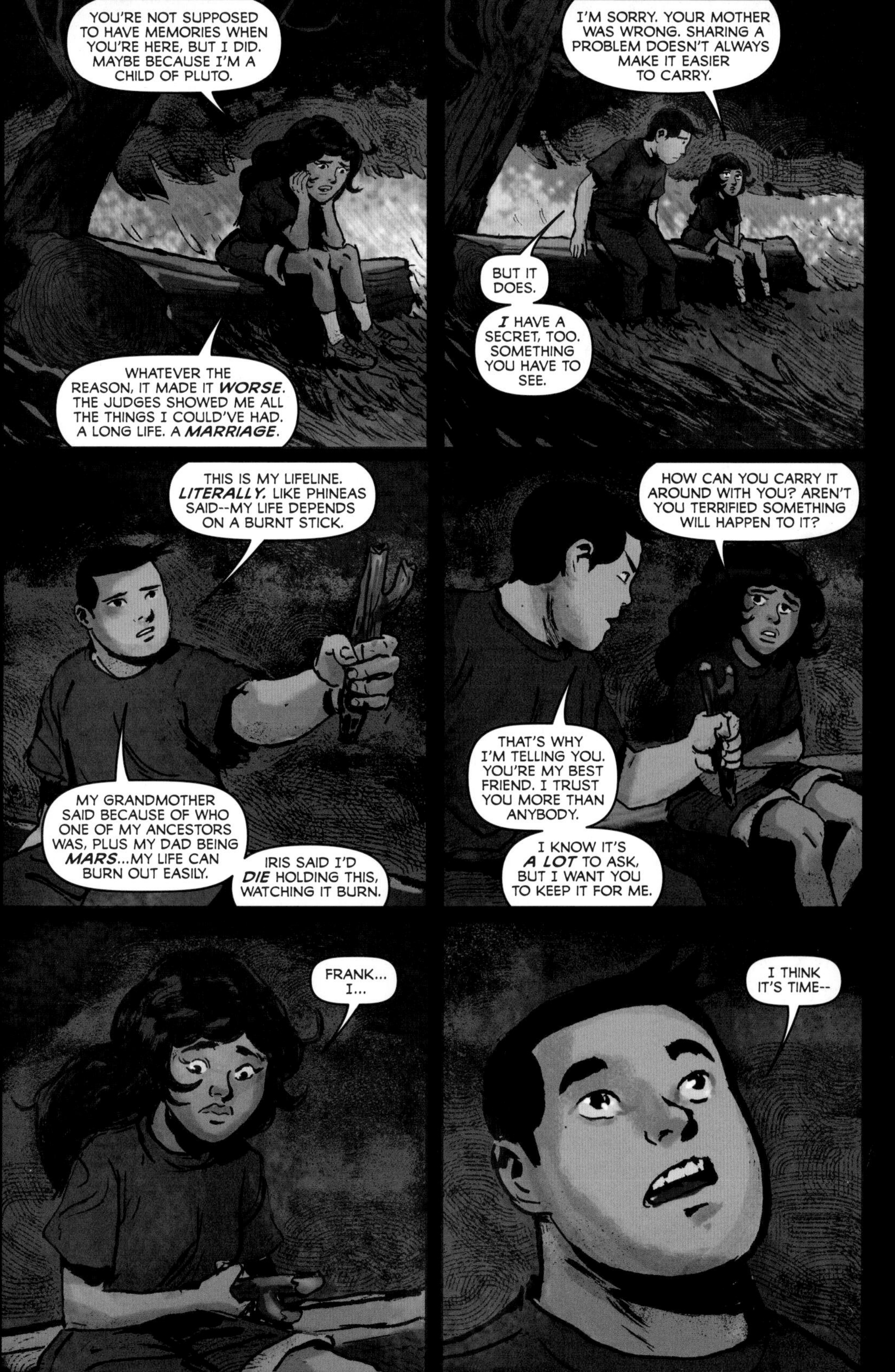
YOU'RE NOT SUPPOSED TO HAVE MEMORIES WHEN YOU'RE HERE, BUT I DID. MAYBE BECAUSE I'M A CHILD OF PLUTO.
WHATEVER THE REASON, IT MADE IT *WORSE*. THE JUDGES SHOWED ME ALL THE THINGS I COULD'VE HAD. A LONG LIFE. A *MARRIAGE*.
I'M SORRY. YOUR MOTHER WAS WRONG. SHARING A PROBLEM DOESN'T ALWAYS MAKE IT EASIER TO CARRY.
BUT IT DOES.
I HAVE A SECRET, TOO. SOMETHING YOU HAVE TO SEE.
THIS IS MY LIFELINE. *LITERALLY.* LIKE PHINEAS SAID--MY LIFE DEPENDS ON A BURNT STICK.
MY GRANDMOTHER SAID BECAUSE OF WHO ONE OF MY ANCESTORS WAS, PLUS MY DAD BEING *MARS*...MY LIFE CAN BURN OUT EASILY.
IRIS SAID I'D *DIE* HOLDING THIS, WATCHING IT BURN.
HOW CAN YOU CARRY IT AROUND WITH YOU? AREN'T YOU TERRIFIED SOMETHING WILL HAPPEN TO IT?
THAT'S WHY I'M TELLING YOU. YOU'RE MY BEST FRIEND. I TRUST YOU MORE THAN ANYBODY.
I KNOW IT'S *A LOT* TO ASK, BUT I WANT YOU TO KEEP IT FOR ME.
FRANK... I...
I THINK IT'S TIME--

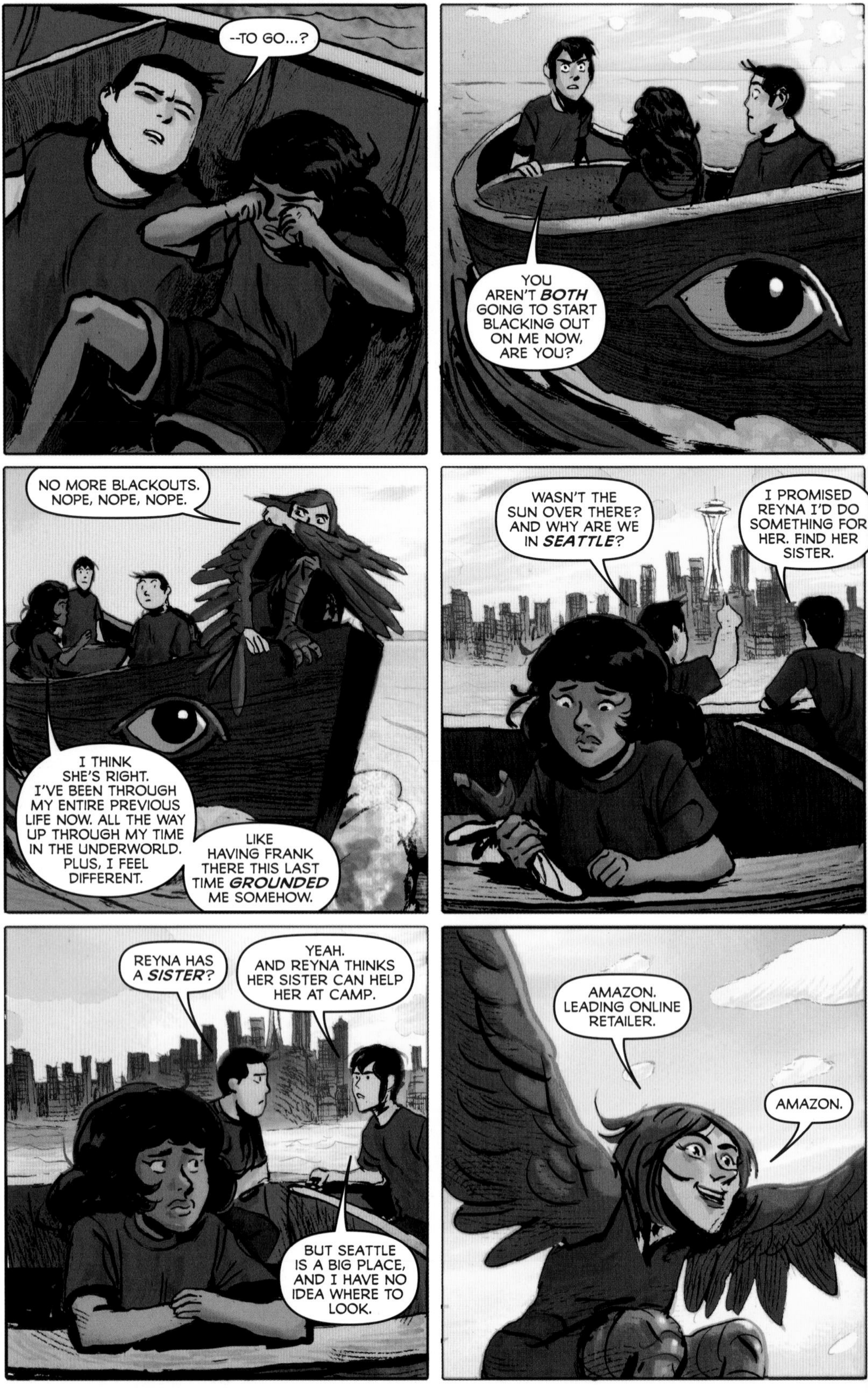
--TO GO...?
YOU AREN'T *BOTH* GOING TO START BLACKING OUT ON ME NOW, ARE YOU?
NO MORE BLACKOUTS. NOPE, NOPE, NOPE.
I THINK SHE'S RIGHT. I'VE BEEN THROUGH MY ENTIRE PREVIOUS LIFE NOW. ALL THE WAY UP THROUGH MY TIME IN THE UNDERWORLD. PLUS, I FEEL DIFFERENT.
LIKE HAVING FRANK THERE THIS LAST TIME *GROUNDED* ME SOMEHOW.
WASN'T THE SUN OVER THERE? AND WHY ARE WE IN *SEATTLE*?
I PROMISED REYNA I'D DO SOMETHING FOR HER. FIND HER SISTER.
REYNA HAS A *SISTER*?
YEAH. AND REYNA THINKS HER SISTER CAN HELP HER AT CAMP.
BUT SEATTLE IS A BIG PLACE, AND I HAVE NO IDEA WHERE TO LOOK.
AMAZON. LEADING ONLINE RETAILER.
AMAZON.

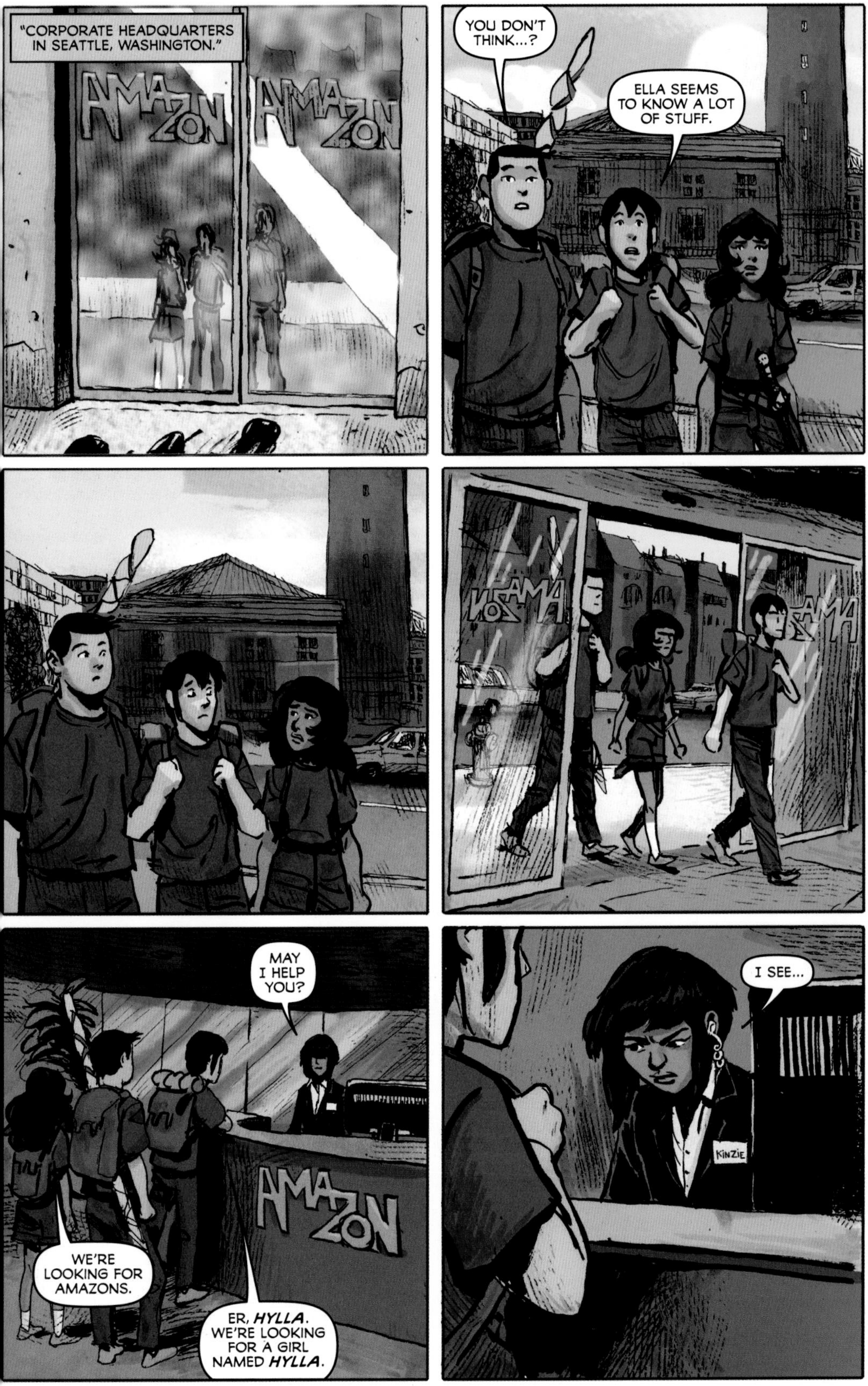
"CORPORATE HEADQUARTERS IN SEATTLE, WASHINGTON."
AMAZON
AMAZON
YOU DON'T THINK...?
ELLA SEEMS TO KNOW A LOT OF STUFF.
MAY I HELP YOU?
AMAZON
WE'RE LOOKING FOR AMAZONS.
ER, *HYLLA*. WE'RE LOOKING FOR A GIRL NAMED *HYLLA*.
I SEE...
KINZIE

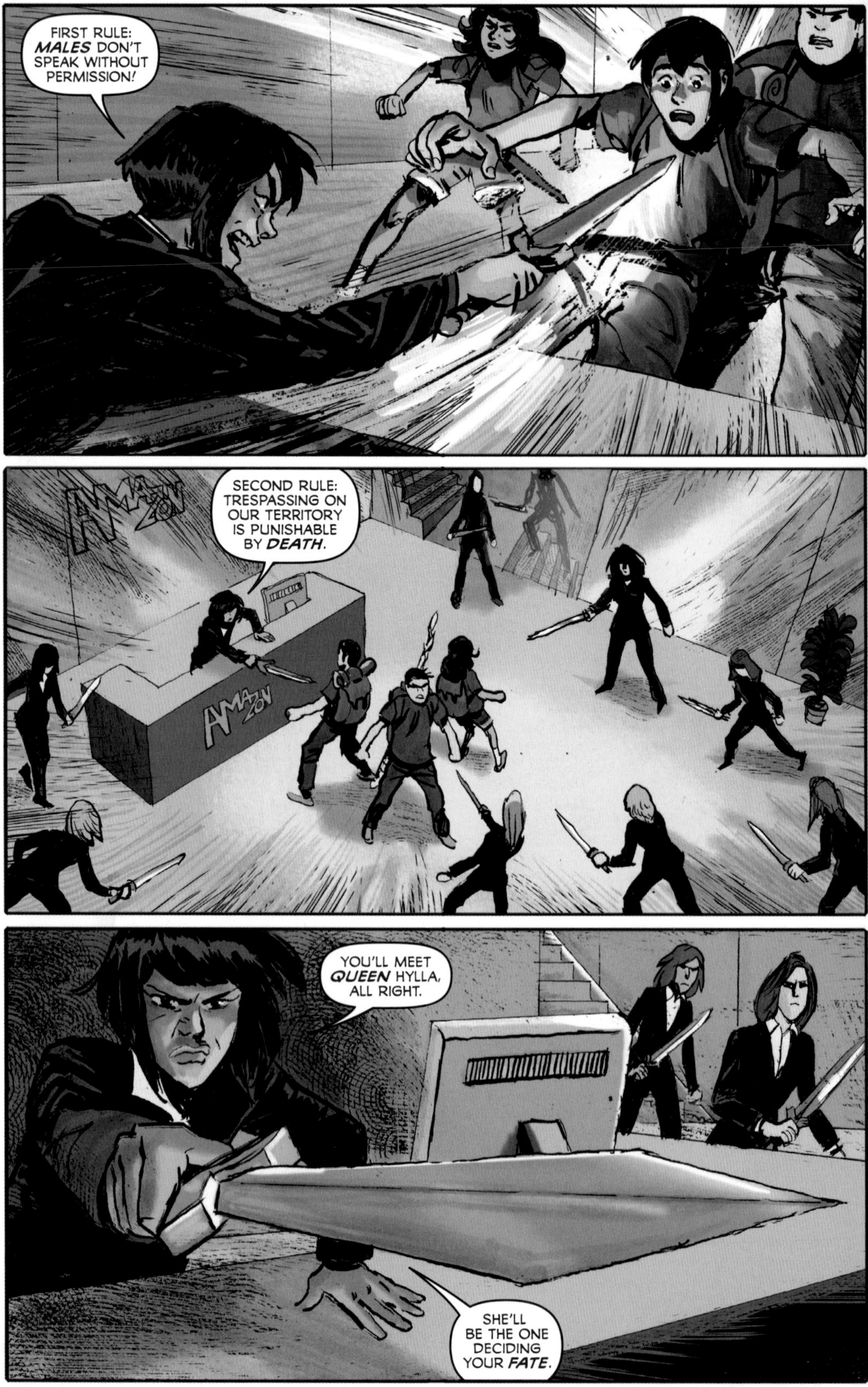
FIRST RULE: ***MALES*** DON'T SPEAK WITHOUT PERMISSION!
SECOND RULE: TRESPASSING ON OUR TERRITORY IS PUNISHABLE BY ***DEATH***.
AMAZON
AMAZON
YOU'LL MEET ***QUEEN*** HYLLA, ALL RIGHT.
SHE'LL BE THE ONE DECIDING YOUR ***FATE***.

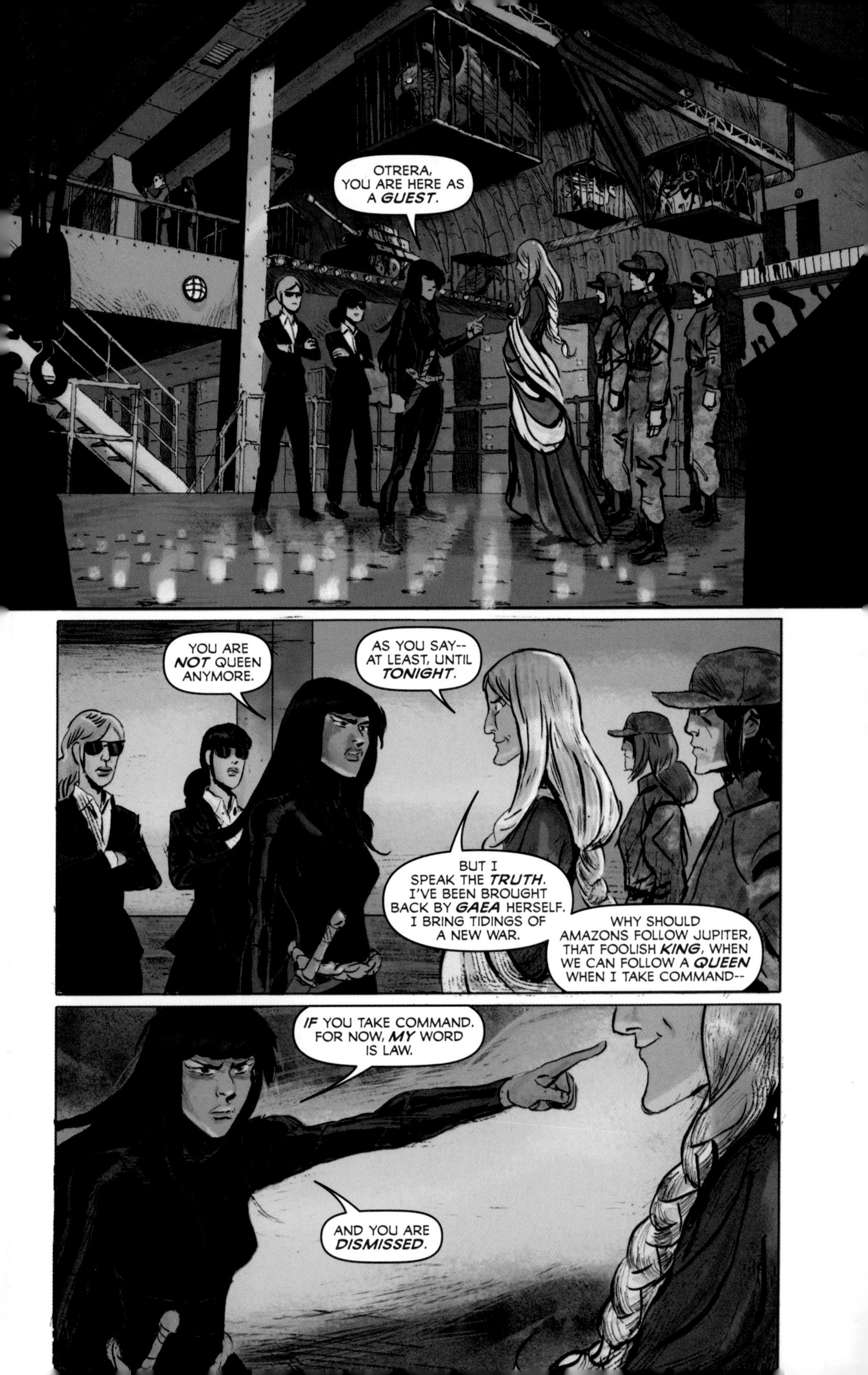
OTRERA, YOU ARE HERE AS A *GUEST*.
YOU ARE *NOT* QUEEN ANYMORE.
AS YOU SAY-- AT LEAST, UNTIL *TONIGHT*.
BUT I SPEAK THE *TRUTH*. I'VE BEEN BROUGHT BACK BY *GAEA* HERSELF. I BRING TIDINGS OF A NEW WAR.
WHY SHOULD AMAZONS FOLLOW JUPITER, THAT FOOLISH *KING*, WHEN WE CAN FOLLOW A *QUEEN* WHEN I TAKE COMMAND--
IF YOU TAKE COMMAND. FOR NOW, *MY* WORD IS LAW.
AND YOU ARE *DISMISSED*.

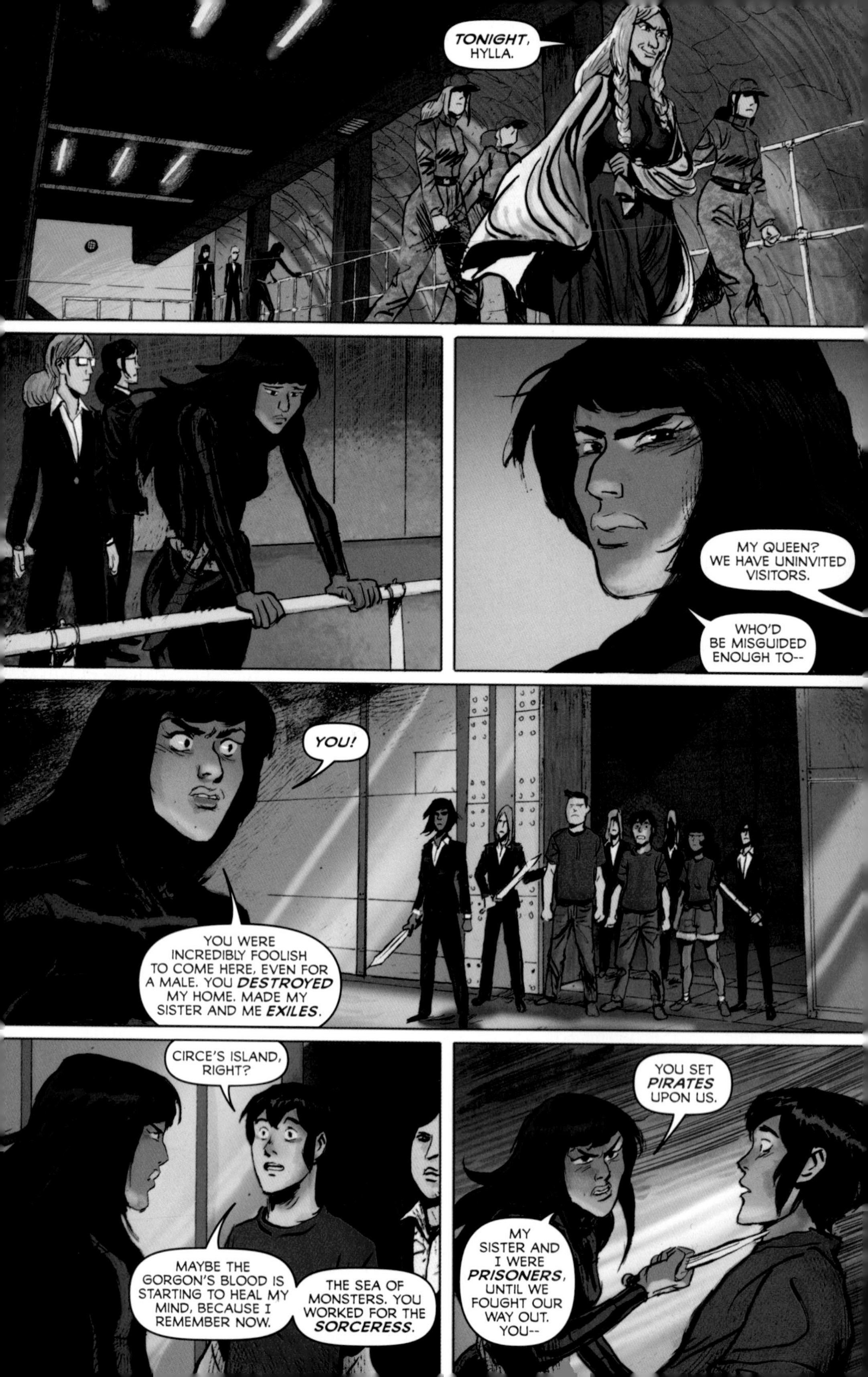
TONIGHT, HYLLA.
MY QUEEN? WE HAVE UNINVITED VISITORS.
WHO'D BE MISGUIDED ENOUGH TO--
YOU!
YOU WERE INCREDIBLY FOOLISH TO COME HERE, EVEN FOR A MALE. YOU DESTROYED MY HOME. MADE MY SISTER AND ME EXILES.
CIRCE'S ISLAND, RIGHT?
MAYBE THE GORGON'S BLOOD IS STARTING TO HEAL MY MIND, BECAUSE I REMEMBER NOW.
THE SEA OF MONSTERS. YOU WORKED FOR THE SORCERESS.
YOU SET PIRATES UPON US.
MY SISTER AND I WERE PRISONERS, UNTIL WE FOUGHT OUR WAY OUT. YOU--

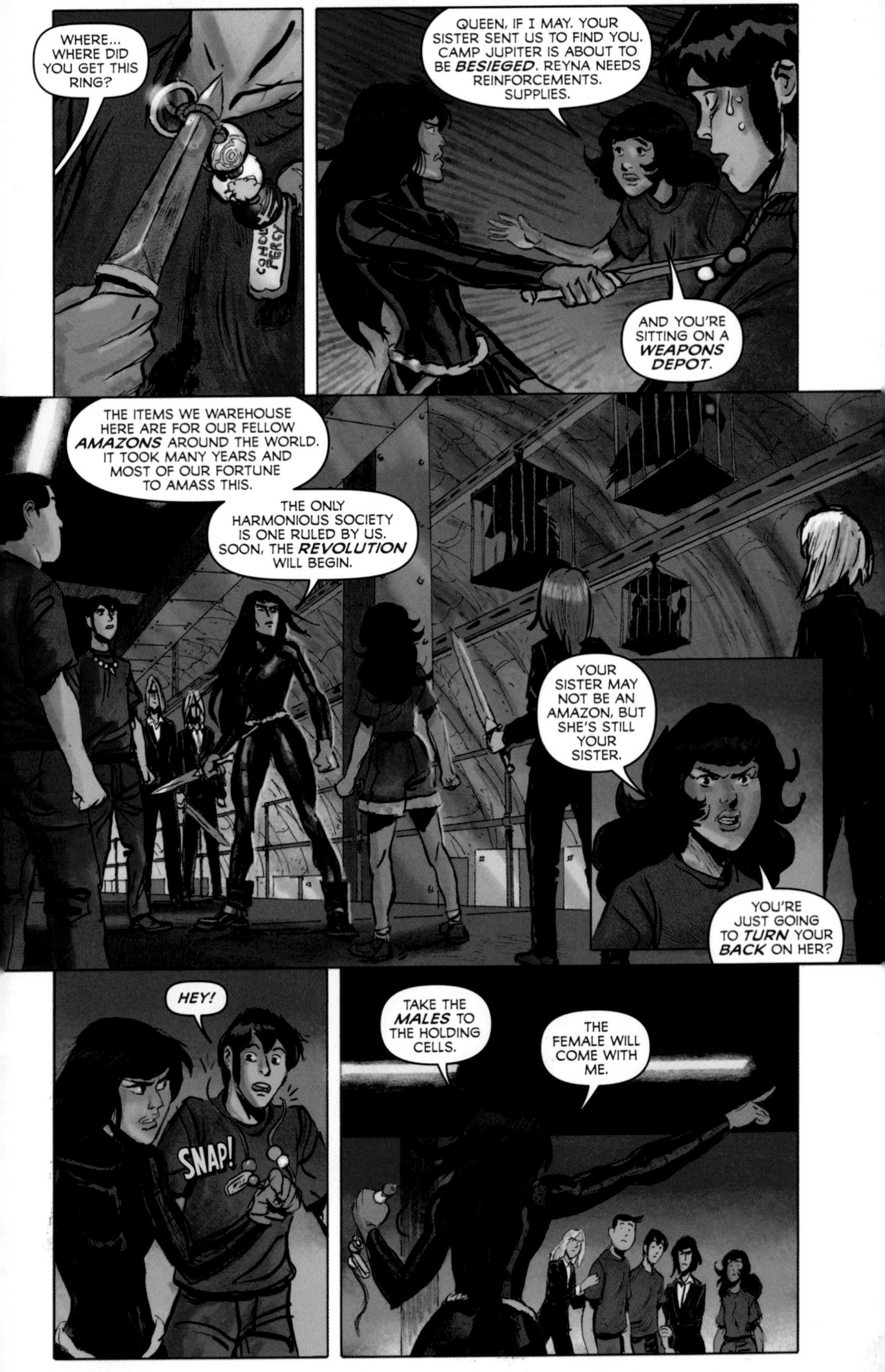
WHERE... WHERE DID YOU GET THIS RING?
QUEEN, IF I MAY. YOUR SISTER SENT US TO FIND YOU. CAMP JUPITER IS ABOUT TO BE BESIEGED. REYNA NEEDS REINFORCEMENTS. SUPPLIES.
AND YOU'RE SITTING ON A WEAPONS DEPOT.
THE ITEMS WE WAREHOUSE HERE ARE FOR OUR FELLOW AMAZONS AROUND THE WORLD. IT TOOK MANY YEARS AND MOST OF OUR FORTUNE TO AMASS THIS.
THE ONLY HARMONIOUS SOCIETY IS ONE RULED BY US. SOON, THE REVOLUTION WILL BEGIN.
YOUR SISTER MAY NOT BE AN AMAZON, BUT SHE'S STILL YOUR SISTER.
YOU'RE JUST GOING TO TURN YOUR BACK ON HER?
HEY!
SNAP!
TAKE THE MALES TO THE HOLDING CELLS.
THE FEMALE WILL COME WITH ME.

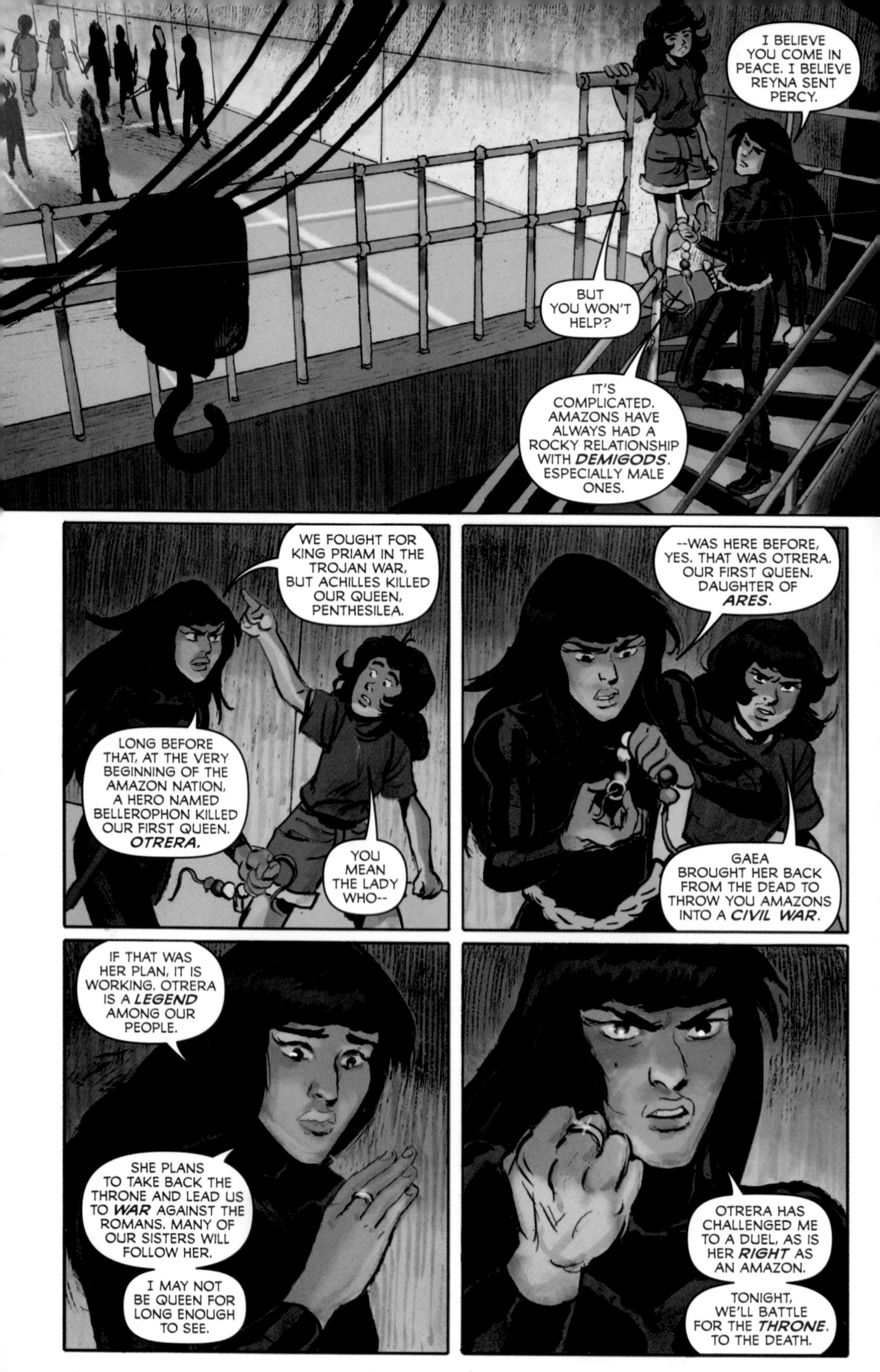
I BELIEVE YOU COME IN PEACE. I BELIEVE REYNA SENT PERCY.
BUT YOU WON'T HELP?
IT'S COMPLICATED. AMAZONS HAVE ALWAYS HAD A ROCKY RELATIONSHIP WITH *DEMIGODS*. ESPECIALLY MALE ONES.
WE FOUGHT FOR KING PRIAM IN THE TROJAN WAR, BUT ACHILLES KILLED OUR QUEEN, PENTHESILEA.
LONG BEFORE THAT, AT THE VERY BEGINNING OF THE AMAZON NATION, A HERO NAMED BELLEROPHON KILLED OUR FIRST QUEEN. ***OTRERA.***
YOU MEAN THE LADY WHO--
--WAS HERE BEFORE, YES. THAT WAS OTRERA. OUR FIRST QUEEN. DAUGHTER OF ***ARES***.
GAEA BROUGHT HER BACK FROM THE DEAD TO THROW YOU AMAZONS INTO A ***CIVIL WAR***.
IF THAT WAS HER PLAN, IT IS WORKING. OTRERA IS A ***LEGEND*** AMONG OUR PEOPLE.
SHE PLANS TO TAKE BACK THE THRONE AND LEAD US TO ***WAR*** AGAINST THE ROMANS. MANY OF OUR SISTERS WILL FOLLOW HER.
I MAY NOT BE QUEEN FOR LONG ENOUGH TO SEE.
OTRERA HAS CHALLENGED ME TO A DUEL, AS IS HER ***RIGHT*** AS AN AMAZON.
TONIGHT, WE'LL BATTLE FOR THE ***THRONE***. TO THE DEATH.

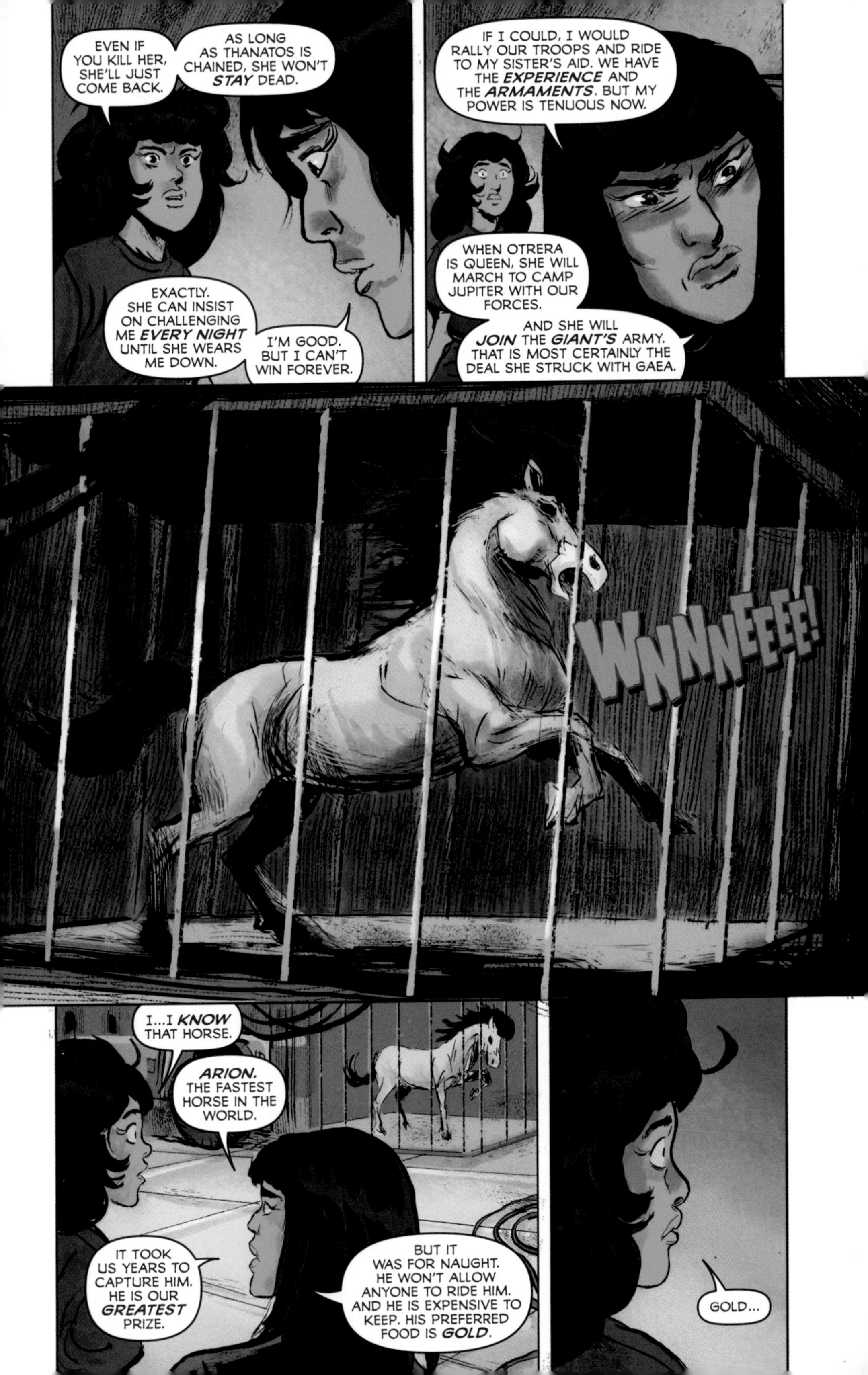
EVEN IF YOU KILL HER, SHE'LL JUST COME BACK.
AS LONG AS THANATOS IS CHAINED, SHE WON'T STAY DEAD.
EXACTLY. SHE CAN INSIST ON CHALLENGING ME EVERY NIGHT UNTIL SHE WEARS ME DOWN.
I'M GOOD. BUT I CAN'T WIN FOREVER.
IF I COULD, I WOULD RALLY OUR TROOPS AND RIDE TO MY SISTER'S AID. WE HAVE THE EXPERIENCE AND THE ARMAMENTS. BUT MY POWER IS TENUOUS NOW.
WHEN OTRERA IS QUEEN, SHE WILL MARCH TO CAMP JUPITER WITH OUR FORCES.
AND SHE WILL JOIN THE GIANT'S ARMY. THAT IS MOST CERTAINLY THE DEAL SHE STRUCK WITH GAEA.
WNNNEEEE!
I...I KNOW THAT HORSE.
ARION. THE FASTEST HORSE IN THE WORLD.
IT TOOK US YEARS TO CAPTURE HIM. HE IS OUR GREATEST PRIZE.
BUT IT WAS FOR NAUGHT. HE WON'T ALLOW ANYONE TO RIDE HIM. AND HE IS EXPENSIVE TO KEEP. HIS PREFERRED FOOD IS GOLD.
GOLD...

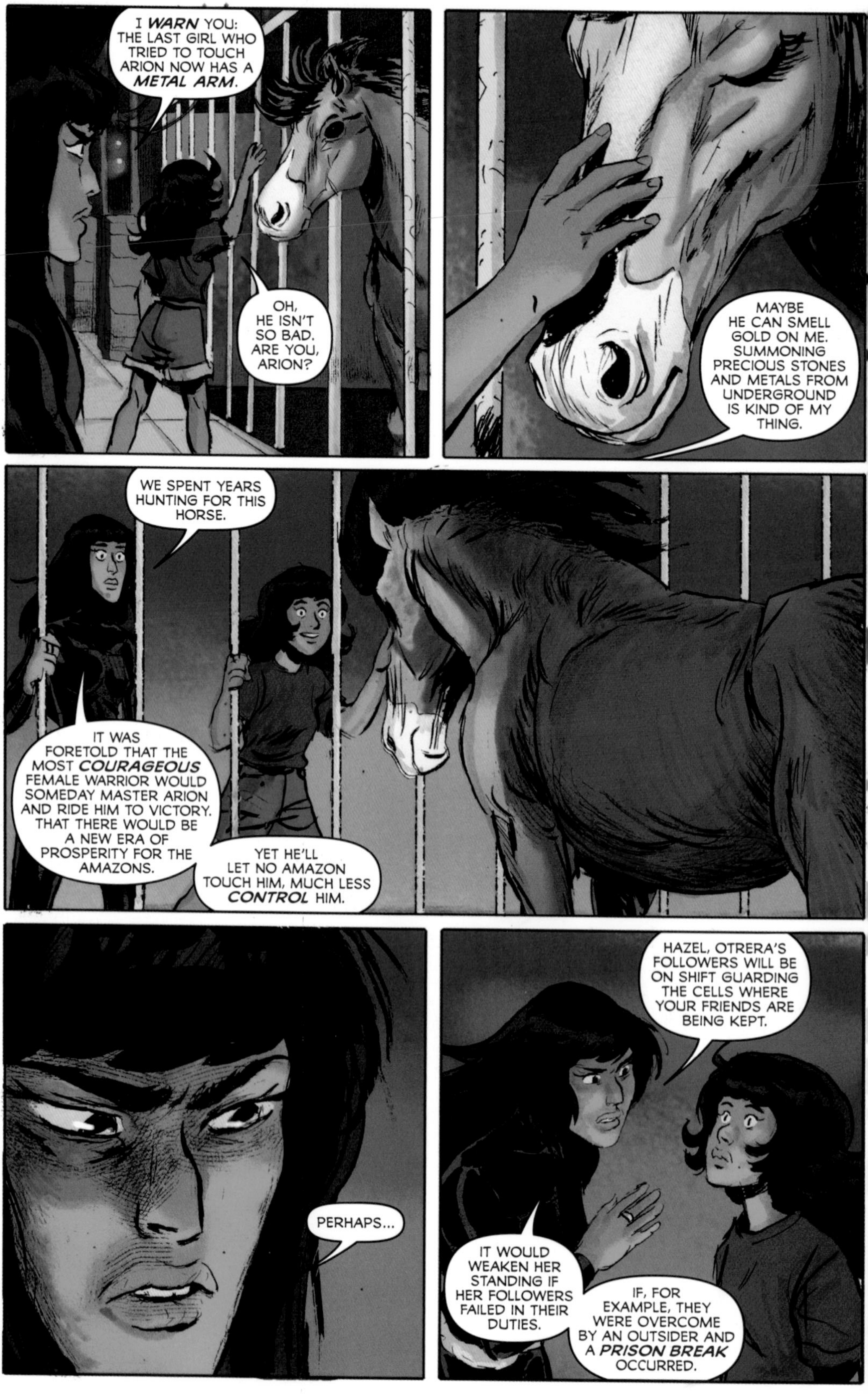
I WARN YOU: THE LAST GIRL WHO TRIED TO TOUCH ARION NOW HAS A METAL ARM.
OH, HE ISN'T SO BAD. ARE YOU, ARION?
MAYBE HE CAN SMELL GOLD ON ME. SUMMONING PRECIOUS STONES AND METALS FROM UNDERGROUND IS KIND OF MY THING.
WE SPENT YEARS HUNTING FOR THIS HORSE.
IT WAS FORETOLD THAT THE MOST COURAGEOUS FEMALE WARRIOR WOULD SOMEDAY MASTER ARION AND RIDE HIM TO VICTORY. THAT THERE WOULD BE A NEW ERA OF PROSPERITY FOR THE AMAZONS.
YET HE'LL LET NO AMAZON TOUCH HIM, MUCH LESS CONTROL HIM.
PERHAPS...
HAZEL, OTRERA'S FOLLOWERS WILL BE ON SHIFT GUARDING THE CELLS WHERE YOUR FRIENDS ARE BEING KEPT.
IT WOULD WEAKEN HER STANDING IF HER FOLLOWERS FAILED IN THEIR DUTIES.
IF, FOR EXAMPLE, THEY WERE OVERCOME BY AN OUTSIDER AND A PRISON BREAK OCCURRED.

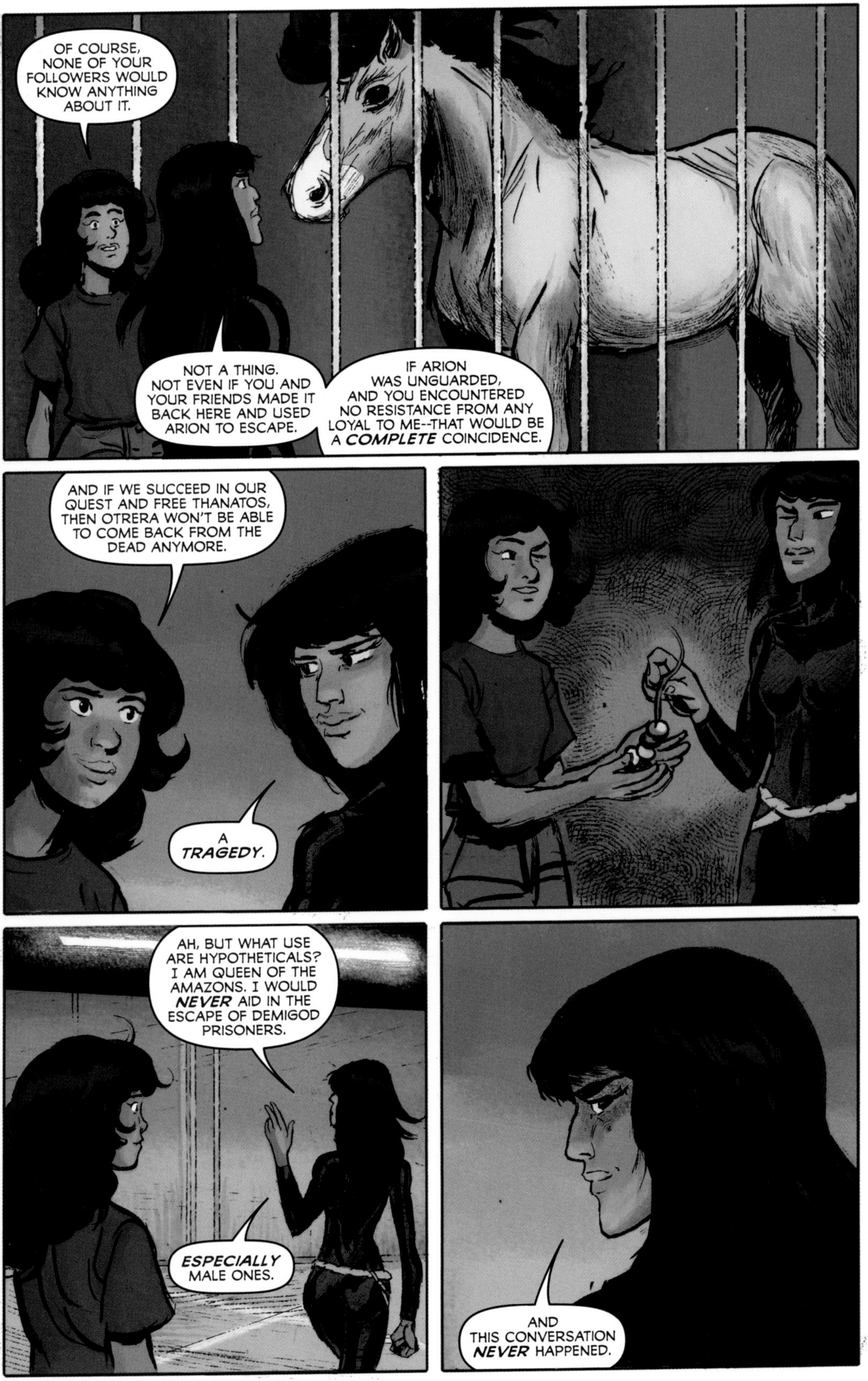
OF COURSE, NONE OF YOUR FOLLOWERS WOULD KNOW ANYTHING ABOUT IT.
NOT A THING. NOT EVEN IF YOU AND YOUR FRIENDS MADE IT BACK HERE AND USED ARION TO ESCAPE.
IF ARION WAS UNGUARDED, AND YOU ENCOUNTERED NO RESISTANCE FROM ANY LOYAL TO ME--THAT WOULD BE A ***COMPLETE*** COINCIDENCE.
AND IF WE SUCCEED IN OUR QUEST AND FREE THANATOS, THEN OTRERA WON'T BE ABLE TO COME BACK FROM THE DEAD ANYMORE.
A ***TRAGEDY***.
AH, BUT WHAT USE ARE HYPOTHETICALS? I AM QUEEN OF THE AMAZONS. I WOULD ***NEVER*** AID IN THE ESCAPE OF DEMIGOD PRISONERS.
ESPECIALLY MALE ONES.
AND THIS CONVERSATION ***NEVER*** HAPPENED.

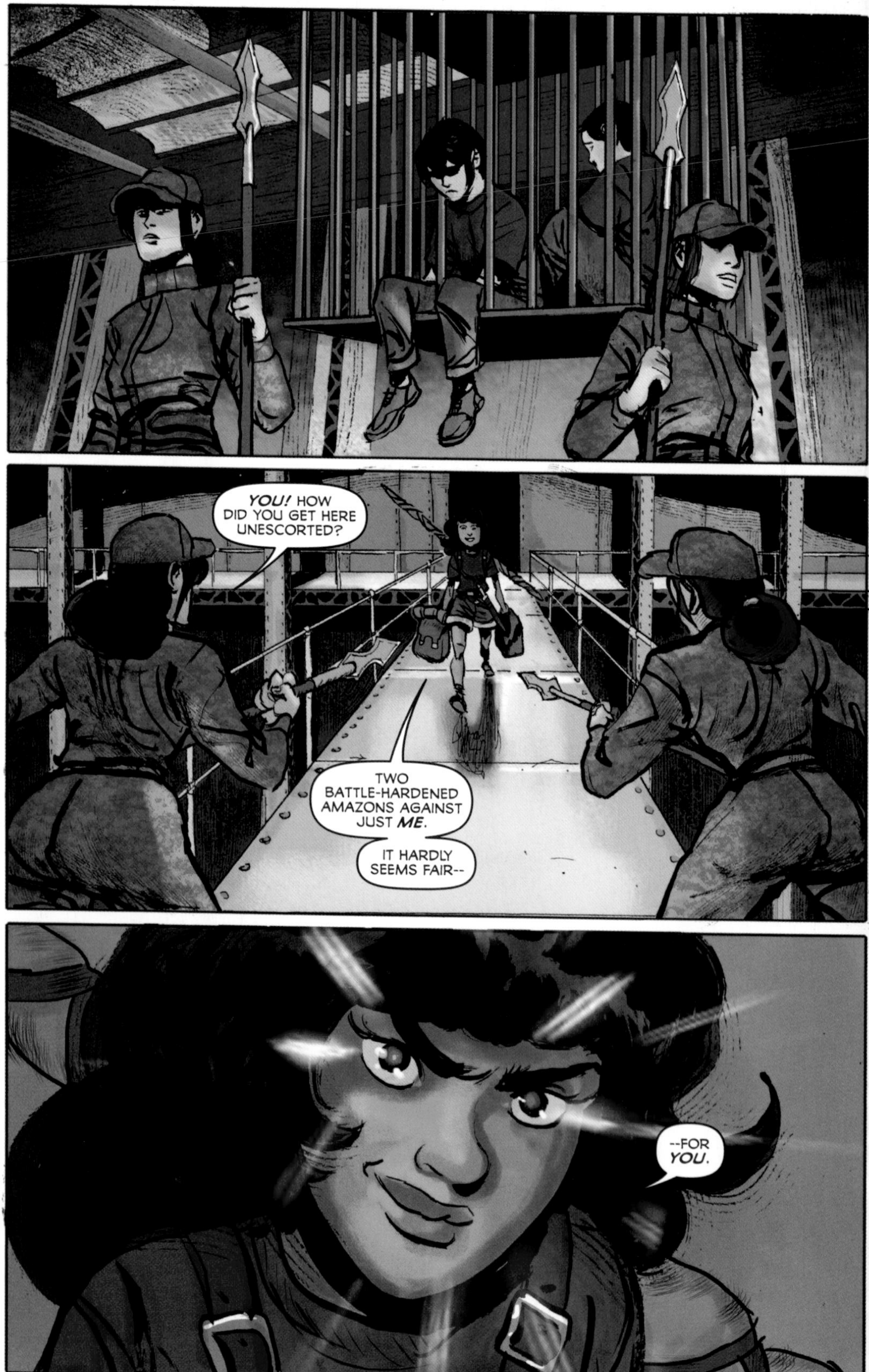
YOU! HOW DID YOU GET HERE UNESCORTED?
TWO BATTLE-HARDENED AMAZONS AGAINST JUST ME.
IT HARDLY SEEMS FAIR--
--FOR YOU.

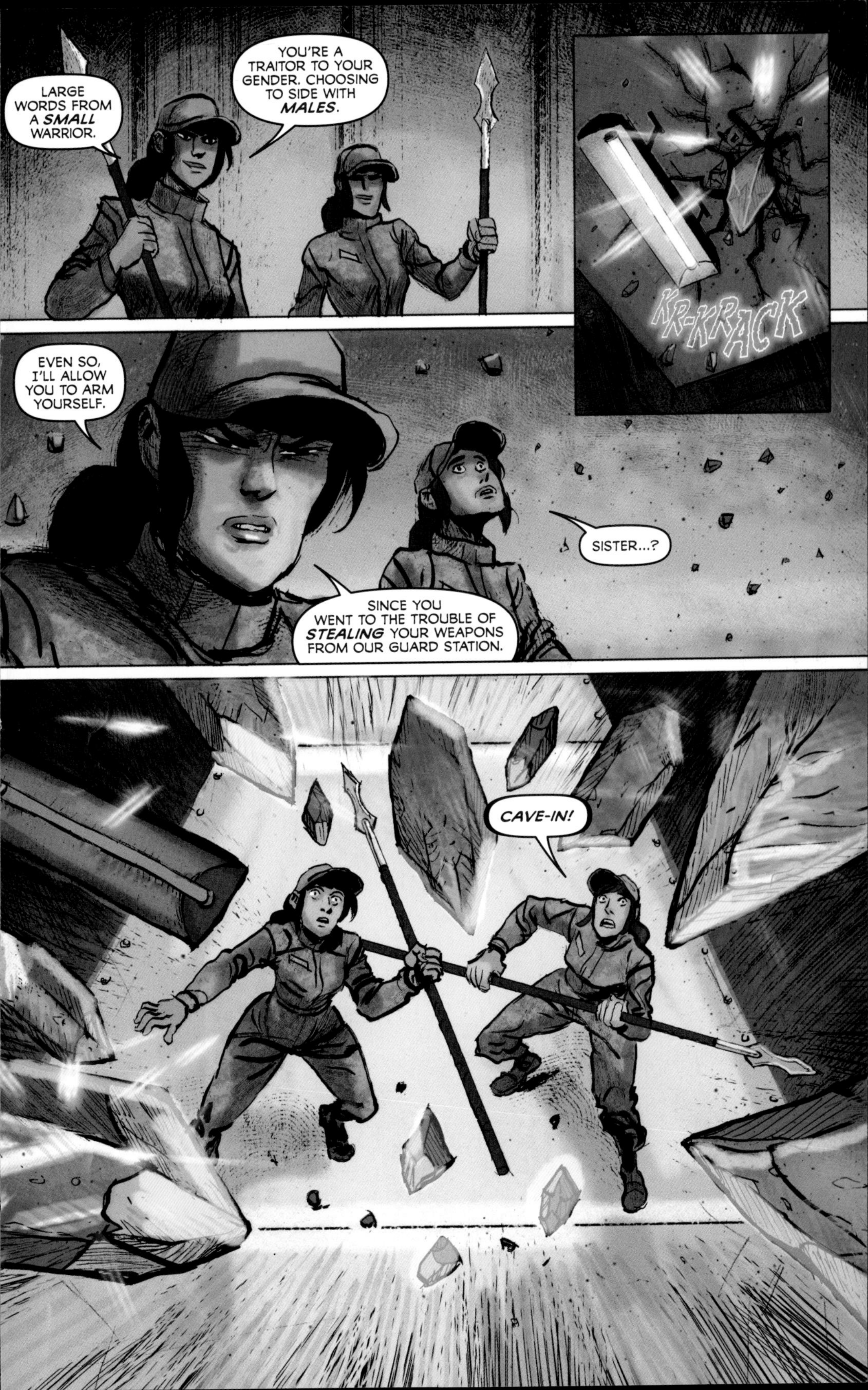
LARGE WORDS FROM A SMALL WARRIOR.
YOU'RE A TRAITOR TO YOUR GENDER. CHOOSING TO SIDE WITH MALES.
KR-KRACK
EVEN SO, I'LL ALLOW YOU TO ARM YOURSELF.
SISTER...?
SINCE YOU WENT TO THE TROUBLE OF STEALING YOUR WEAPONS FROM OUR GUARD STATION.
CAVE-IN!

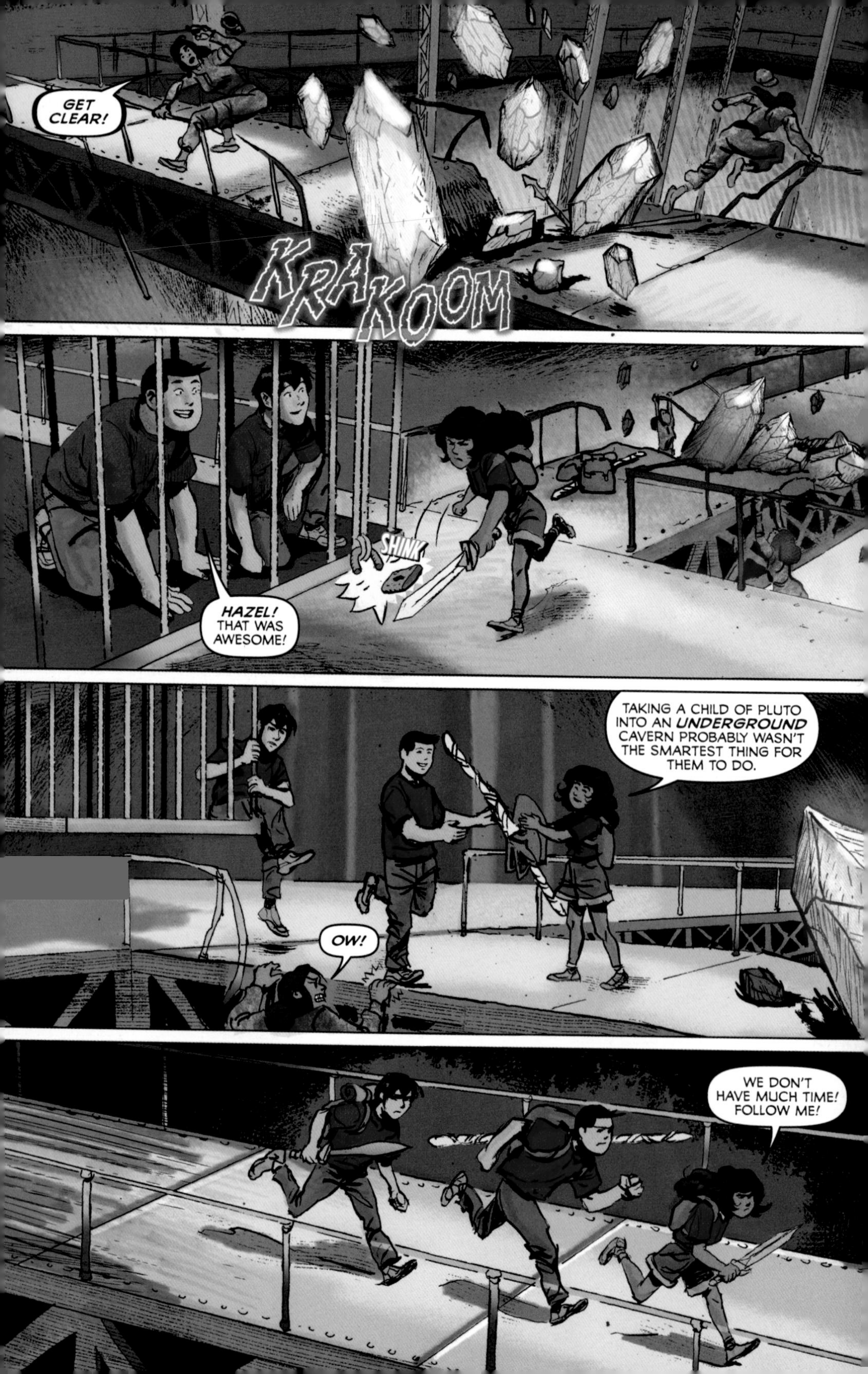
GET CLEAR!
KRAKOOM
SHINK
HAZEL! THAT WAS AWESOME!
TAKING A CHILD OF PLUTO INTO AN UNDERGROUND CAVERN PROBABLY WASN'T THE SMARTEST THING FOR THEM TO DO.
OW!
WE DON'T HAVE MUCH TIME! FOLLOW ME!

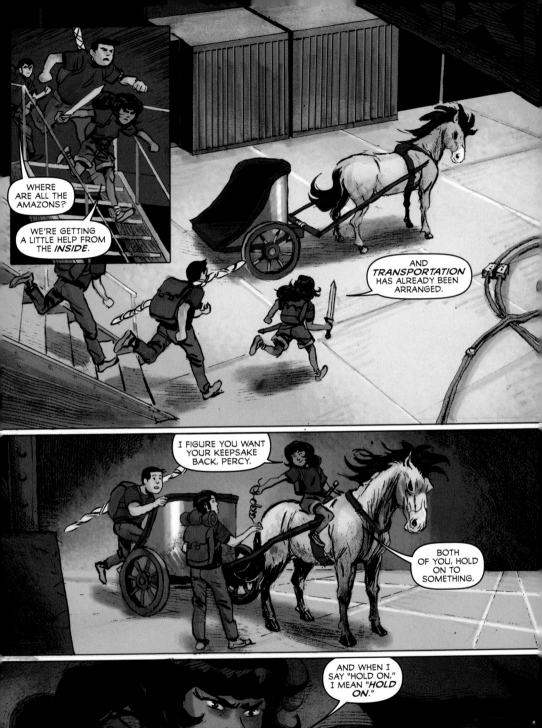

WHERE ARE ALL THE AMAZONS?

WE'RE GETTING A LITTLE HELP FROM THE *INSIDE*.

AND *TRANSPORTATION* HAS ALREADY BEEN ARRANGED.

I FIGURE YOU WANT YOUR KEEPSAKE BACK, PERCY.

BOTH OF YOU, HOLD ON TO SOMETHING.

AND WHEN I SAY "HOLD ON," I MEAN "*HOLD ON*."

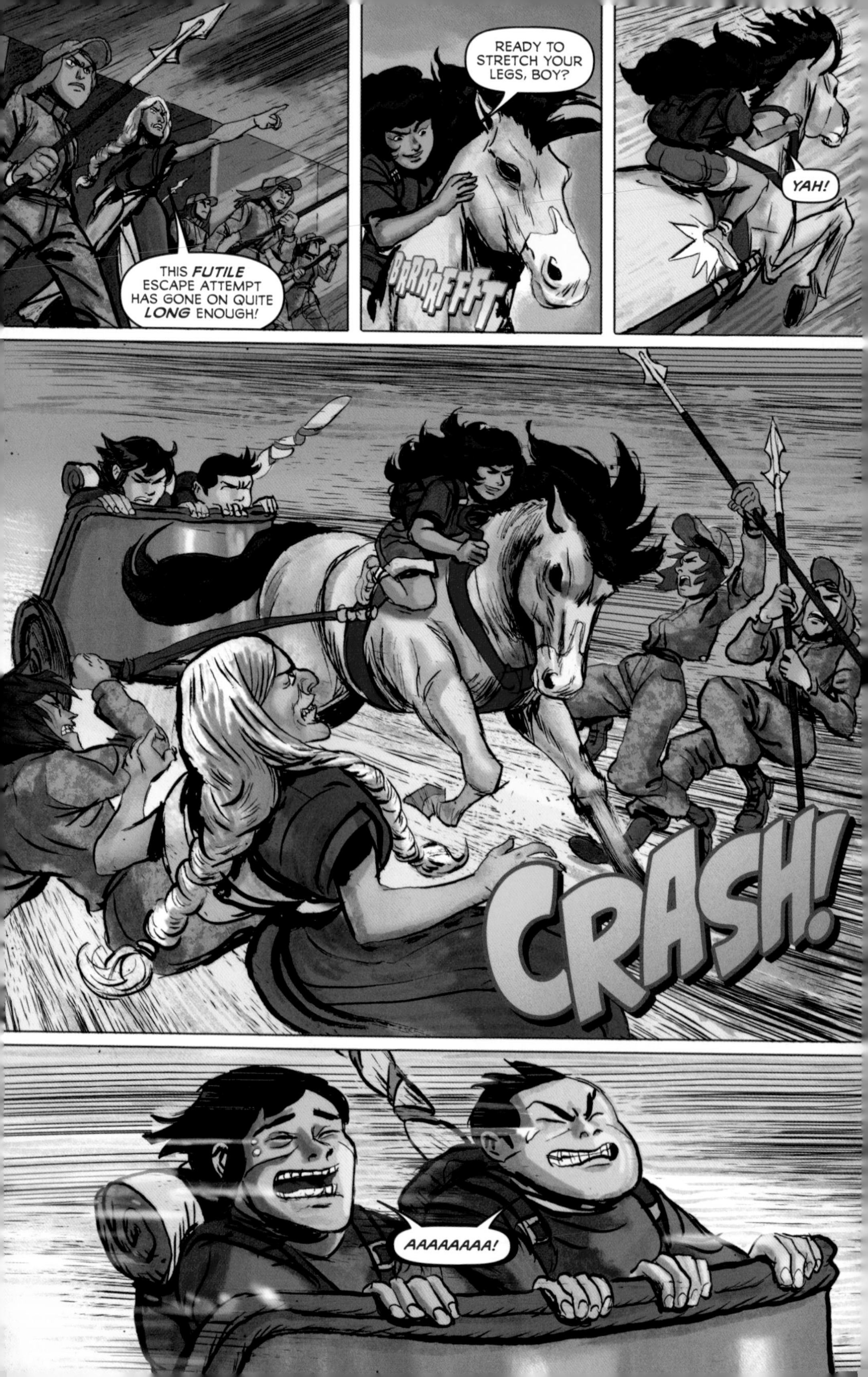
THIS *FUTILE* ESCAPE ATTEMPT HAS GONE ON QUITE *LONG* ENOUGH!
READY TO STRETCH YOUR LEGS, BOY?
BRRRRFFFT
YAH!
CRASH!
AAAAAAAA!

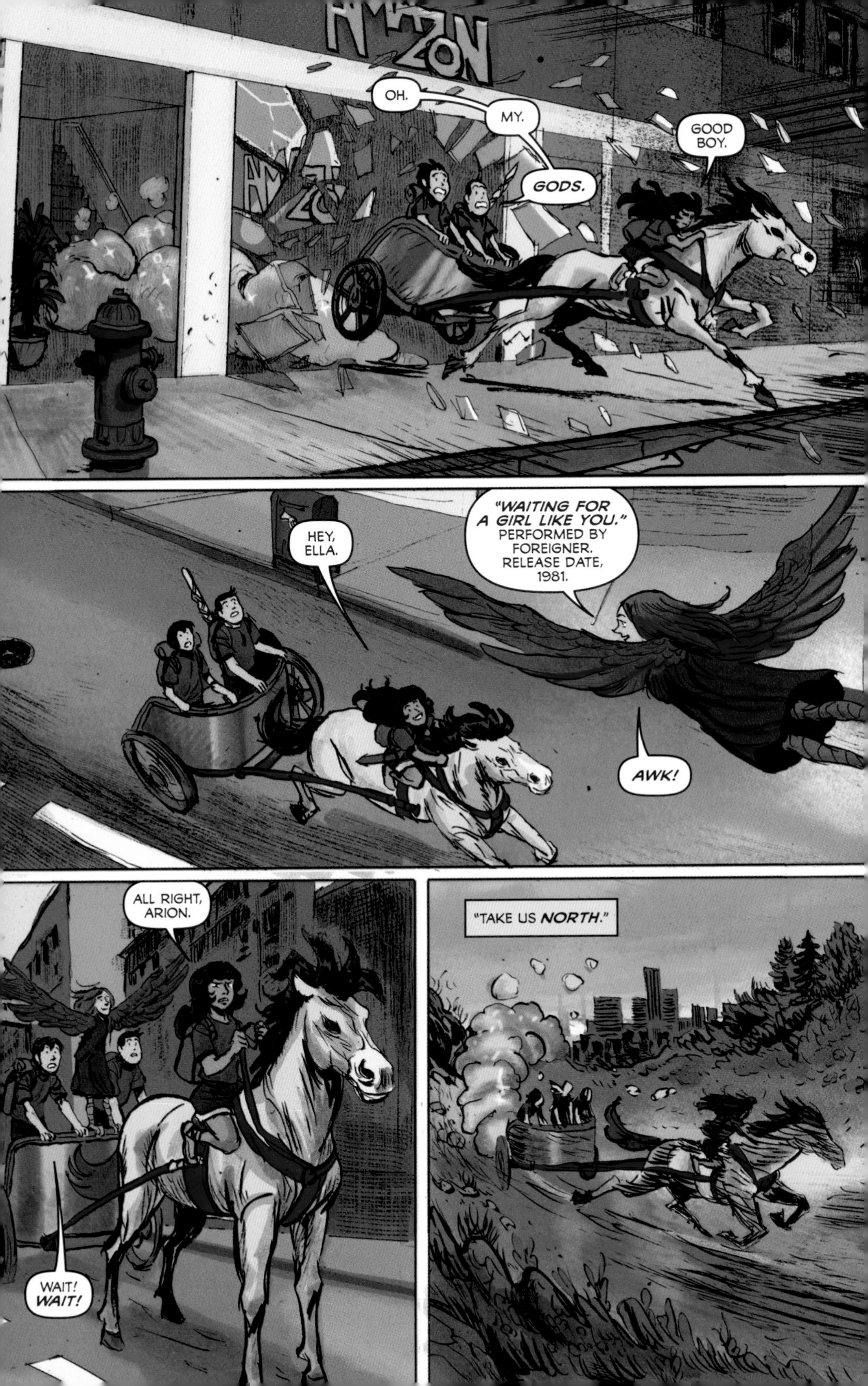
AMAZON
AMAZON
OH.
MY.
GODS.
GOOD BOY.
HEY, ELLA.
"WAITING FOR A GIRL LIKE YOU." PERFORMED BY FOREIGNER. RELEASE DATE, 1981.
AWK!
ALL RIGHT, ARION.
WAIT! WAIT!
"TAKE US NORTH."

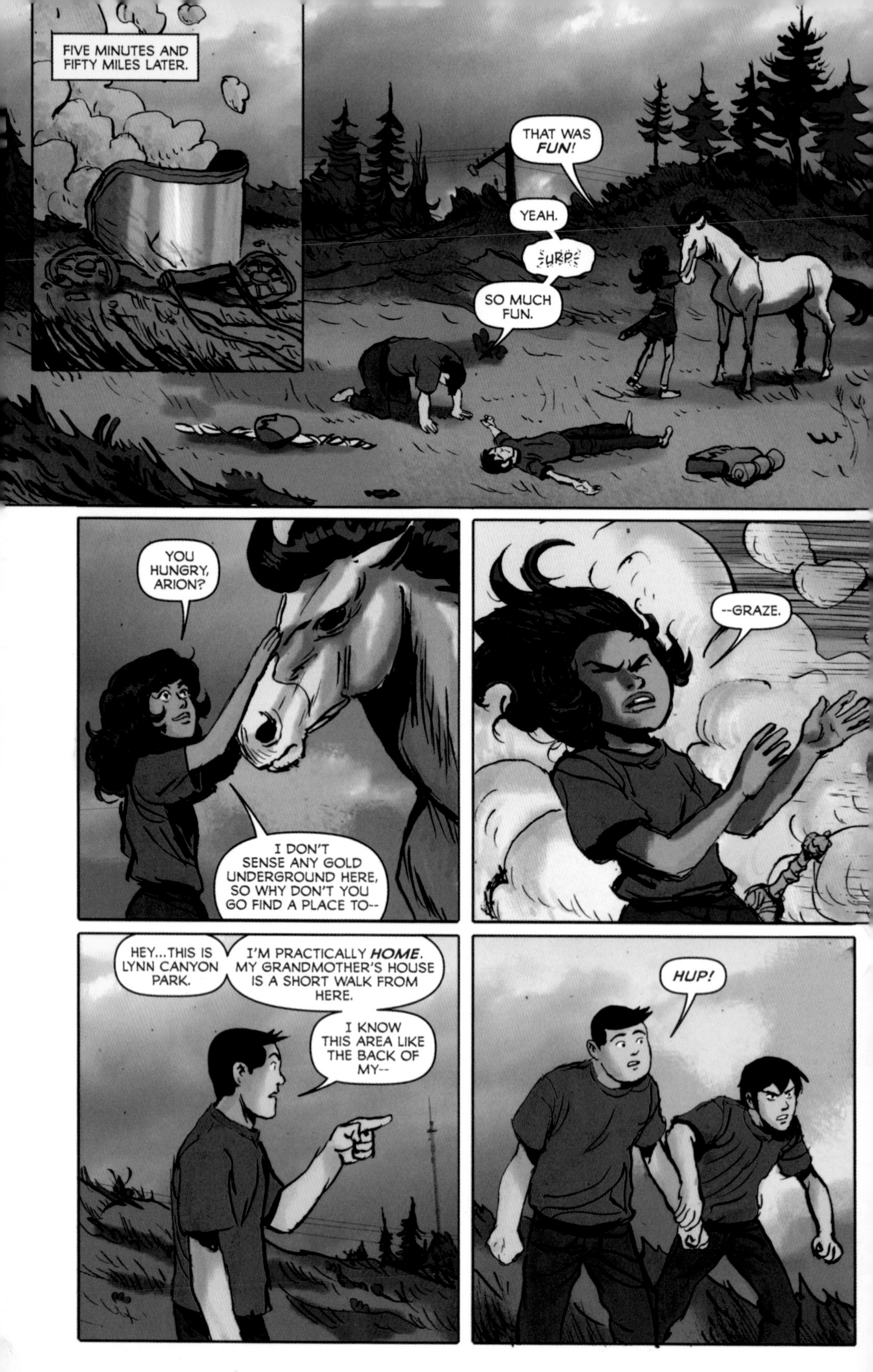
FIVE MINUTES AND FIFTY MILES LATER.
THAT WAS FUN!
YEAH.
URP
SO MUCH FUN.
YOU HUNGRY, ARION?
I DON'T SENSE ANY GOLD UNDERGROUND HERE, SO WHY DON'T YOU GO FIND A PLACE TO--
--GRAZE.
HEY...THIS IS LYNN CANYON PARK.
I'M PRACTICALLY HOME. MY GRANDMOTHER'S HOUSE IS A SHORT WALK FROM HERE.
I KNOW THIS AREA LIKE THE BACK OF MY--
HUP!

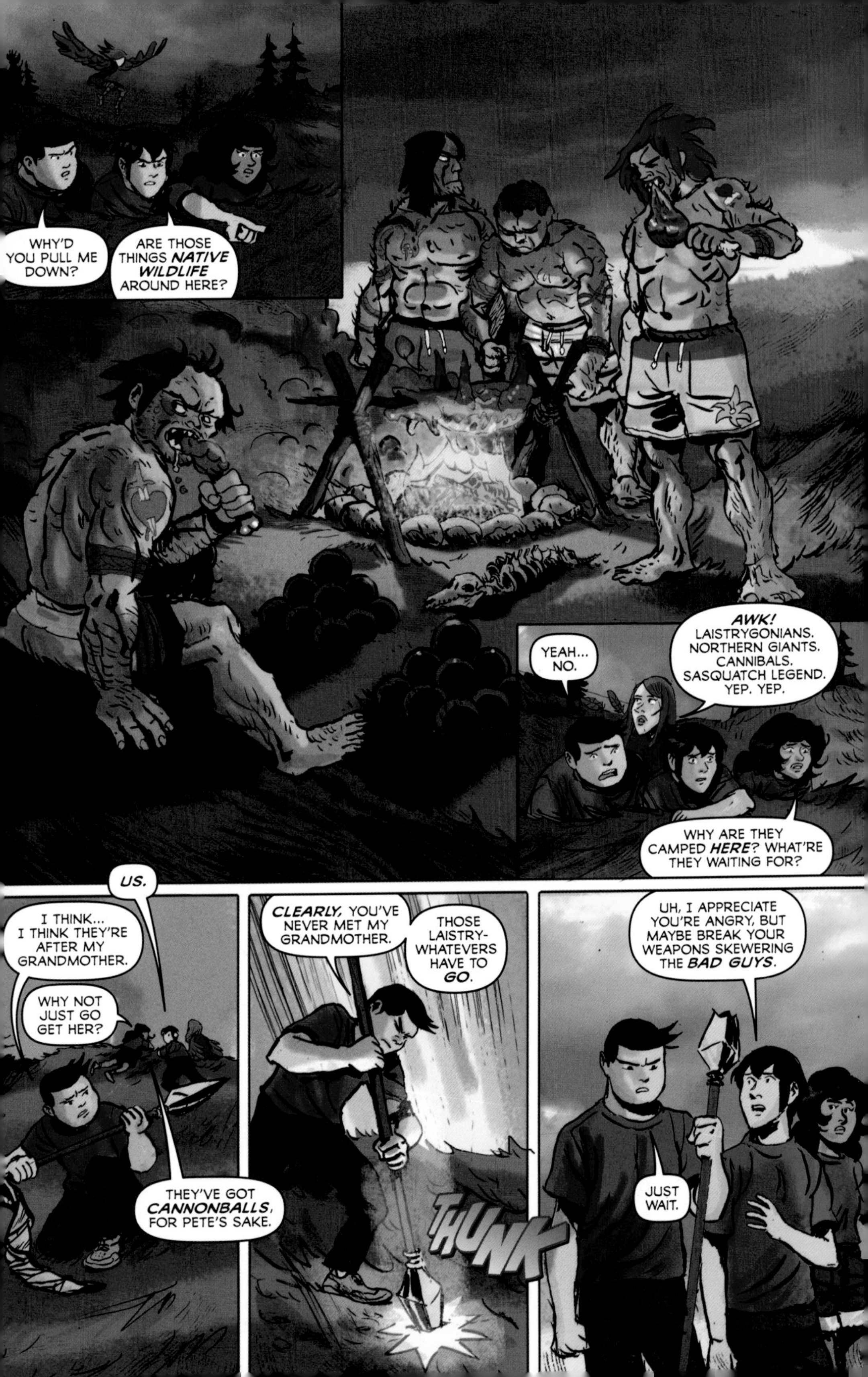
WHY'D YOU PULL ME DOWN?
ARE THOSE THINGS NATIVE WILDLIFE AROUND HERE?
YEAH... NO.
AWK! LAISTRYGONIANS. NORTHERN GIANTS. CANNIBALS. SASQUATCH LEGEND. YEP. YEP.
WHY ARE THEY CAMPED HERE? WHAT'RE THEY WAITING FOR?
US.
I THINK... I THINK THEY'RE AFTER MY GRANDMOTHER.
WHY NOT JUST GO GET HER?
THEY'VE GOT CANNONBALLS, FOR PETE'S SAKE.
CLEARLY, YOU'VE NEVER MET MY GRANDMOTHER.
THOSE LAISTRY-WHATEVERS HAVE TO GO.
THUNK
UH, I APPRECIATE YOU'RE ANGRY, BUT MAYBE BREAK YOUR WEAPONS SKEWERING THE BAD GUYS.
JUST WAIT.

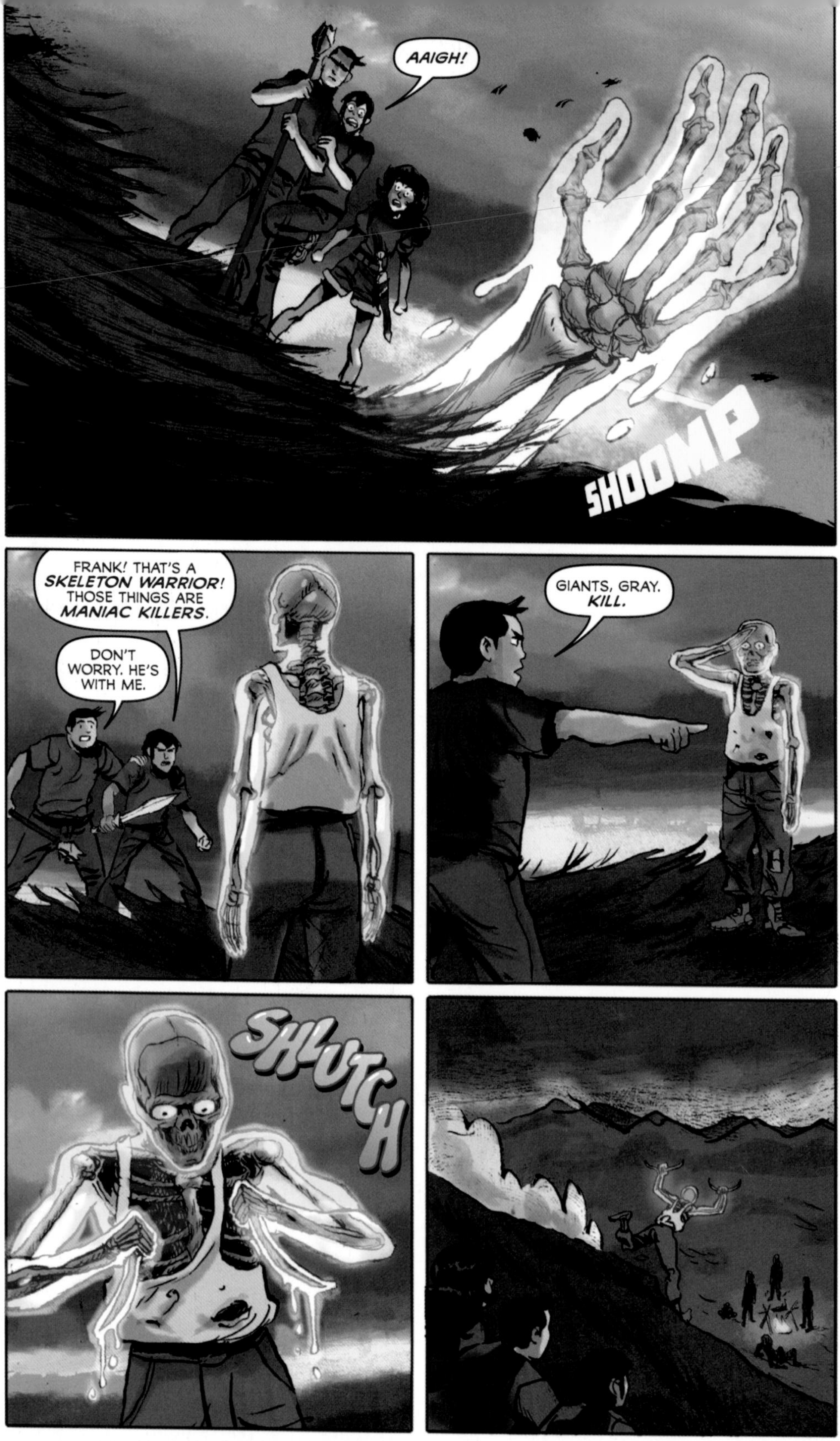
AAIGH!
SHOOMP
FRANK! THAT'S A SKELETON WARRIOR! THOSE THINGS ARE MANIAC KILLERS.
DON'T WORRY. HE'S WITH ME.
GIANTS, GRAY. KILL.
SHLUTCH

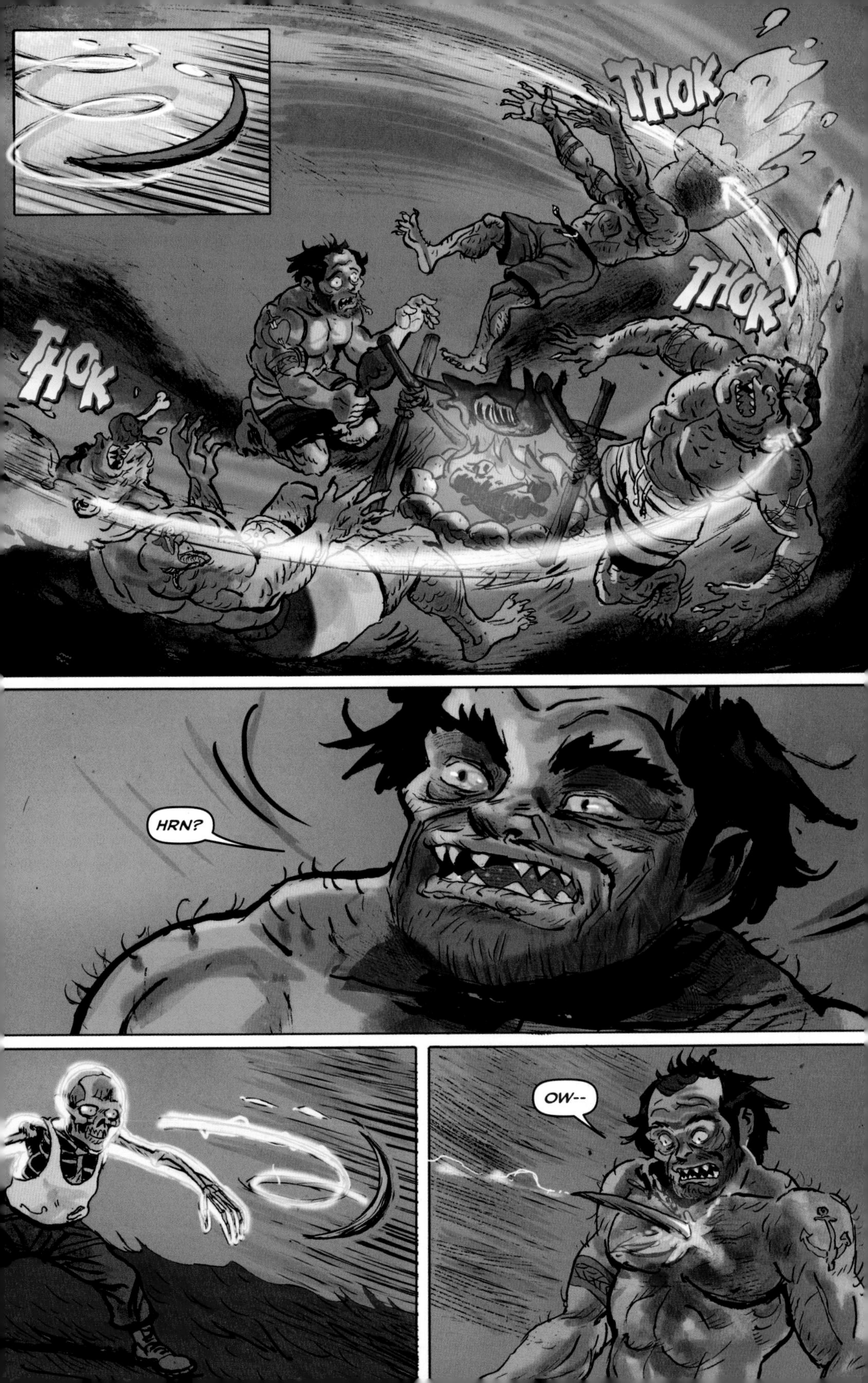
THOK
THOK
THOK
HRN?
OW--

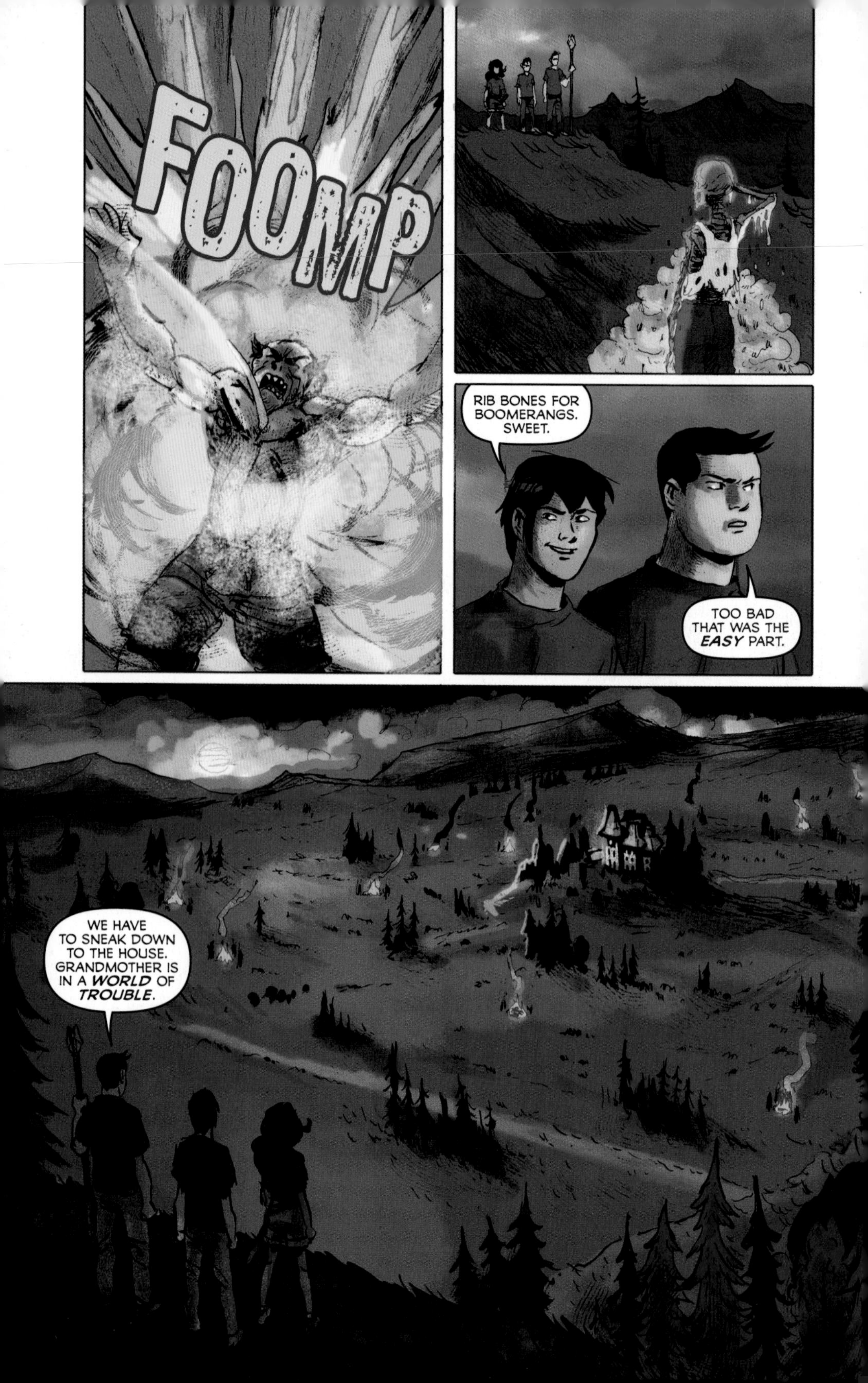
FOOMP
RIB BONES FOR BOOMERANGS. SWEET.
TOO BAD THAT WAS THE *EASY* PART.
WE HAVE TO SNEAK DOWN TO THE HOUSE. GRANDMOTHER IS IN A *WORLD* OF *TROUBLE*.

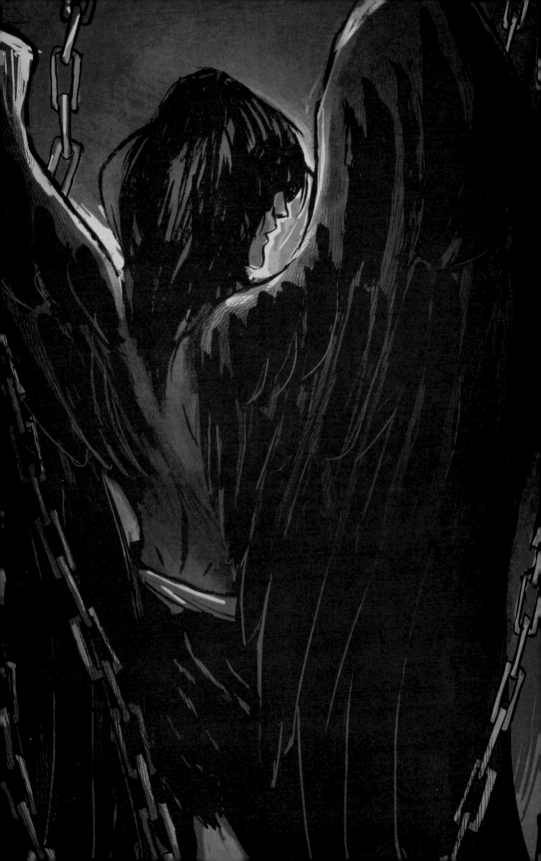

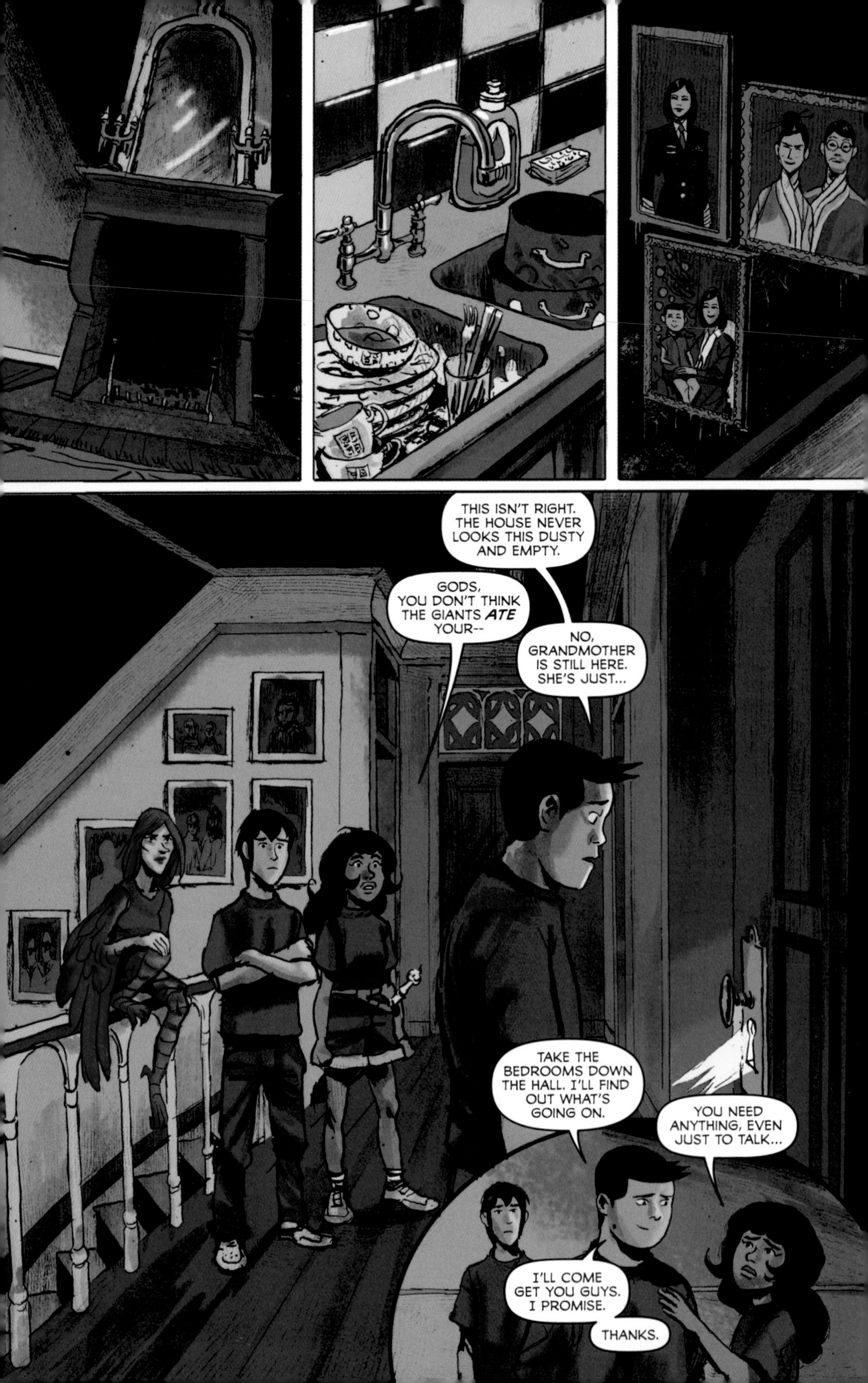
THIS ISN'T RIGHT. THE HOUSE NEVER LOOKS THIS DUSTY AND EMPTY.
GODS, YOU DON'T THINK THE GIANTS *ATE* YOUR--
NO, GRANDMOTHER IS STILL HERE. SHE'S JUST...
TAKE THE BEDROOMS DOWN THE HALL. I'LL FIND OUT WHAT'S GOING ON.
YOU NEED ANYTHING, EVEN JUST TO TALK...
I'LL COME GET YOU GUYS. I PROMISE.
THANKS.

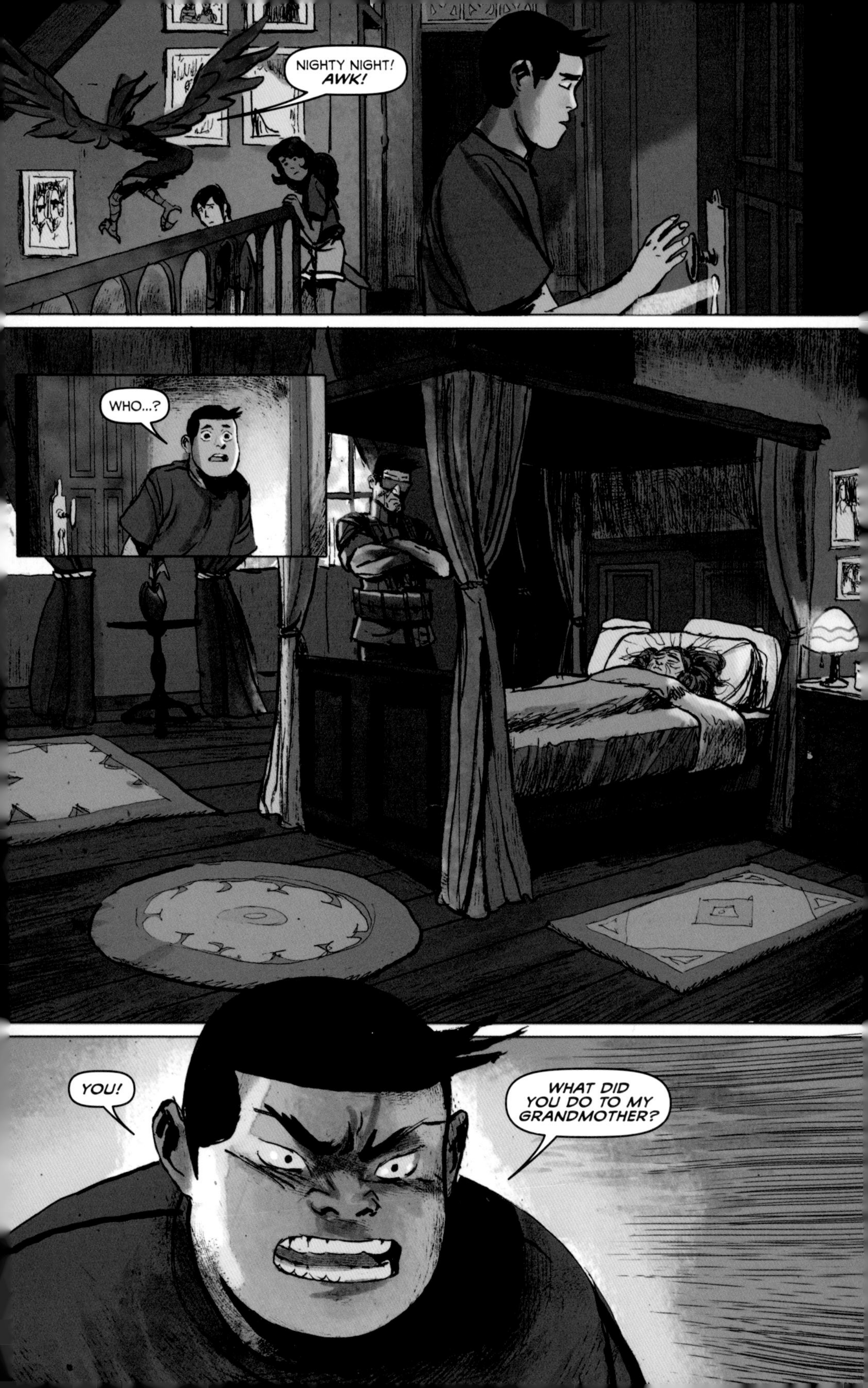
NIGHTY NIGHT! AWK!
WHO...?
YOU!
WHAT DID YOU DO TO MY GRANDMOTHER?

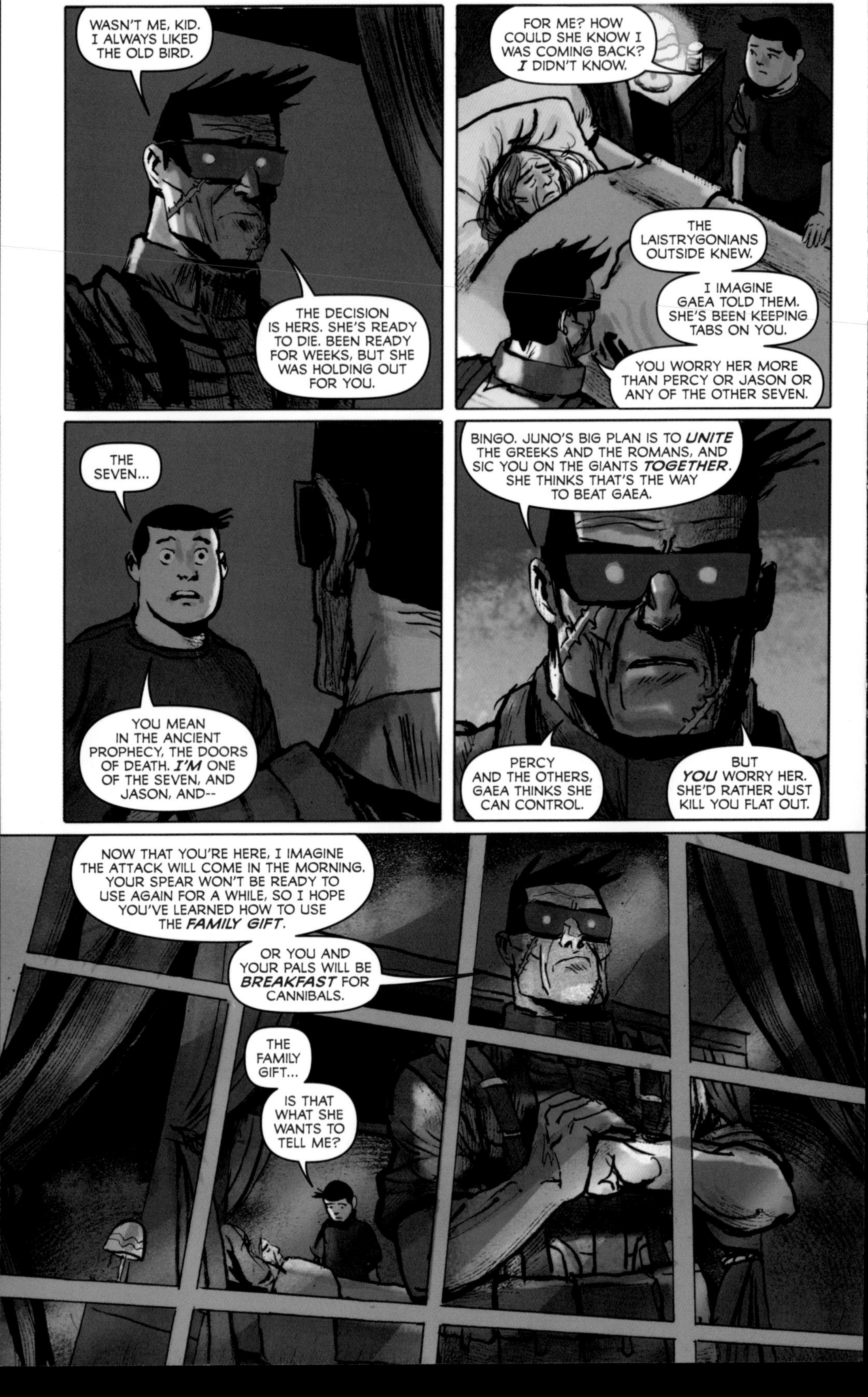

WASN'T ME, KID. I ALWAYS LIKED THE OLD BIRD.
THE DECISION IS HERS. SHE'S READY TO DIE. BEEN READY FOR WEEKS, BUT SHE WAS HOLDING OUT FOR YOU.
FOR ME? HOW COULD SHE KNOW I WAS COMING BACK? *I* DIDN'T KNOW.
THE LAISTRYGONIANS OUTSIDE KNEW.
I IMAGINE GAEA TOLD THEM. SHE'S BEEN KEEPING TABS ON YOU.
YOU WORRY HER MORE THAN PERCY OR JASON OR ANY OF THE OTHER SEVEN.
THE SEVEN...
YOU MEAN IN THE ANCIENT PROPHECY, THE DOORS OF DEATH. *I'M* ONE OF THE SEVEN, AND JASON, AND--
BINGO. JUNO'S BIG PLAN IS TO ***UNITE*** THE GREEKS AND THE ROMANS, AND SIC YOU ON THE GIANTS ***TOGETHER***. SHE THINKS THAT'S THE WAY TO BEAT GAEA.
PERCY AND THE OTHERS, GAEA THINKS SHE CAN CONTROL.
BUT ***YOU*** WORRY HER. SHE'D RATHER JUST KILL YOU FLAT OUT.
NOW THAT YOU'RE HERE, I IMAGINE THE ATTACK WILL COME IN THE MORNING. YOUR SPEAR WON'T BE READY TO USE AGAIN FOR A WHILE, SO I HOPE YOU'VE LEARNED HOW TO USE THE ***FAMILY GIFT***.
OR YOU AND YOUR PALS WILL BE ***BREAKFAST*** FOR CANNIBALS.
THE FAMILY GIFT...
IS THAT WHAT SHE WANTS TO TELL ME?

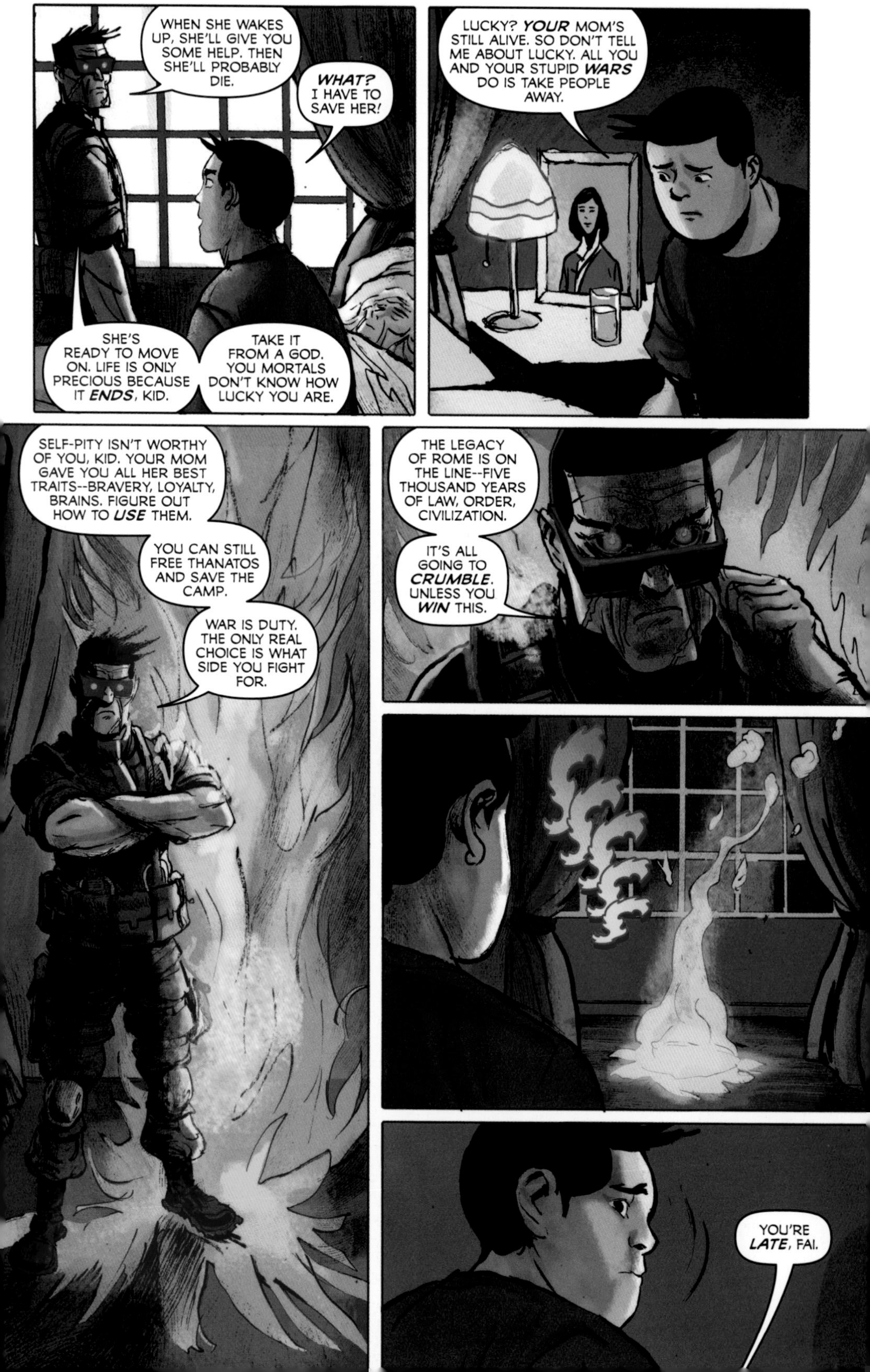

WHEN SHE WAKES UP, SHE'LL GIVE YOU SOME HELP. THEN SHE'LL PROBABLY DIE.
WHAT? I HAVE TO SAVE HER!
SHE'S READY TO MOVE ON. LIFE IS ONLY PRECIOUS BECAUSE IT ENDS, KID.
TAKE IT FROM A GOD. YOU MORTALS DON'T KNOW HOW LUCKY YOU ARE.
LUCKY? YOUR MOM'S STILL ALIVE. SO DON'T TELL ME ABOUT LUCKY. ALL YOU AND YOUR STUPID WARS DO IS TAKE PEOPLE AWAY.
SELF-PITY ISN'T WORTHY OF YOU, KID. YOUR MOM GAVE YOU ALL HER BEST TRAITS--BRAVERY, LOYALTY, BRAINS. FIGURE OUT HOW TO USE THEM.
YOU CAN STILL FREE THANATOS AND SAVE THE CAMP.
WAR IS DUTY. THE ONLY REAL CHOICE IS WHAT SIDE YOU FIGHT FOR.
THE LEGACY OF ROME IS ON THE LINE--FIVE THOUSAND YEARS OF LAW, ORDER, CIVILIZATION.
IT'S ALL GOING TO CRUMBLE. UNLESS YOU WIN THIS.
YOU'RE LATE, FAI.

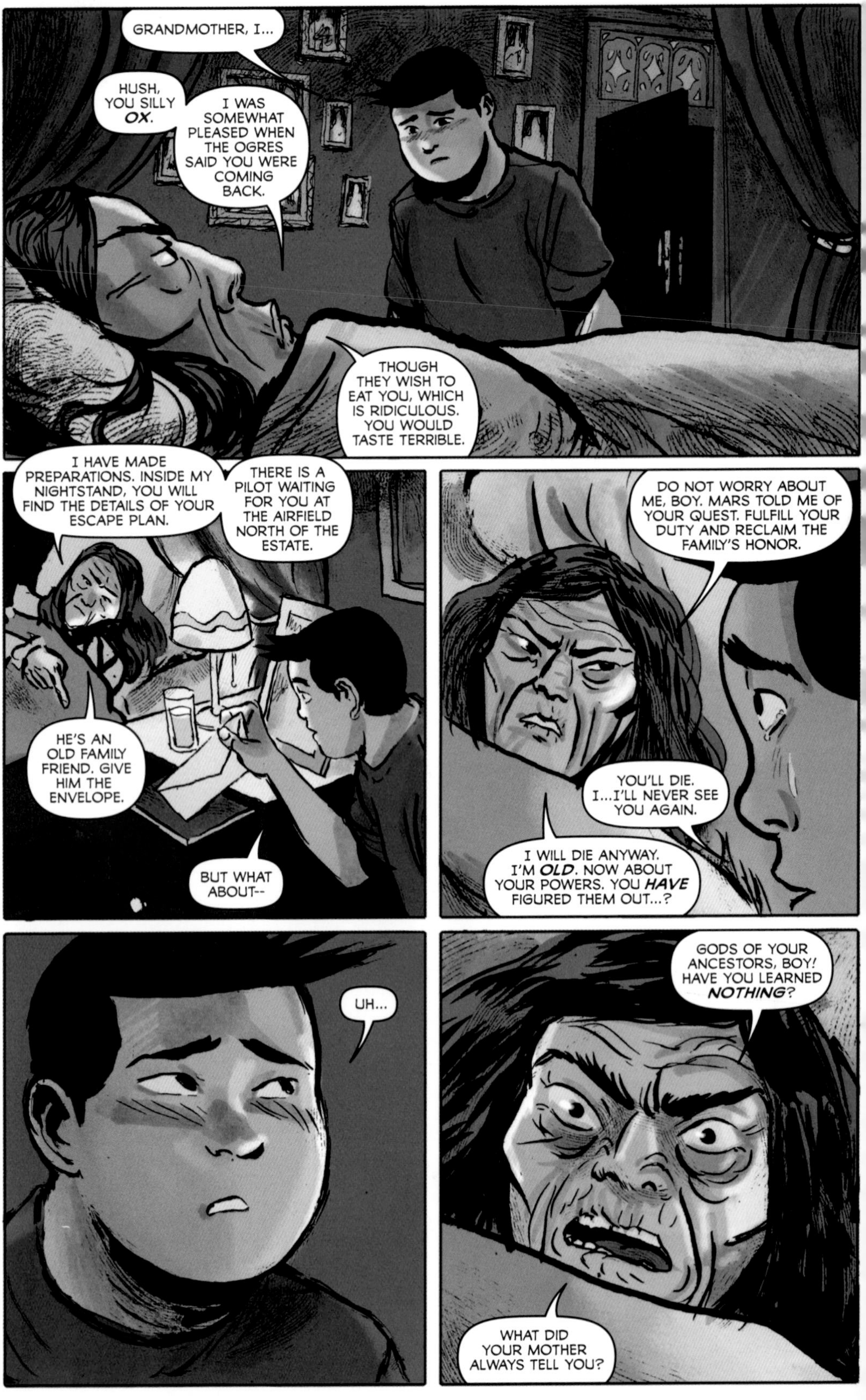
GRANDMOTHER, I...
HUSH, YOU SILLY ***OX***.
I WAS SOMEWHAT PLEASED WHEN THE OGRES SAID YOU WERE COMING BACK.
THOUGH THEY WISH TO EAT YOU, WHICH IS RIDICULOUS. YOU WOULD TASTE TERRIBLE.
I HAVE MADE PREPARATIONS. INSIDE MY NIGHTSTAND, YOU WILL FIND THE DETAILS OF YOUR ESCAPE PLAN.
THERE IS A PILOT WAITING FOR YOU AT THE AIRFIELD NORTH OF THE ESTATE.
HE'S AN OLD FAMILY FRIEND. GIVE HIM THE ENVELOPE.
BUT WHAT ABOUT--
DO NOT WORRY ABOUT ME, BOY. MARS TOLD ME OF YOUR QUEST. FULFILL YOUR DUTY AND RECLAIM THE FAMILY'S HONOR.
YOU'LL DIE. I...I'LL NEVER SEE YOU AGAIN.
I WILL DIE ANYWAY. I'M ***OLD***. NOW ABOUT YOUR POWERS. YOU ***HAVE*** FIGURED THEM OUT...?
UH...
GODS OF YOUR ANCESTORS, BOY! HAVE YOU LEARNED ***NOTHING***?
WHAT DID YOUR MOTHER ALWAYS TELL YOU?

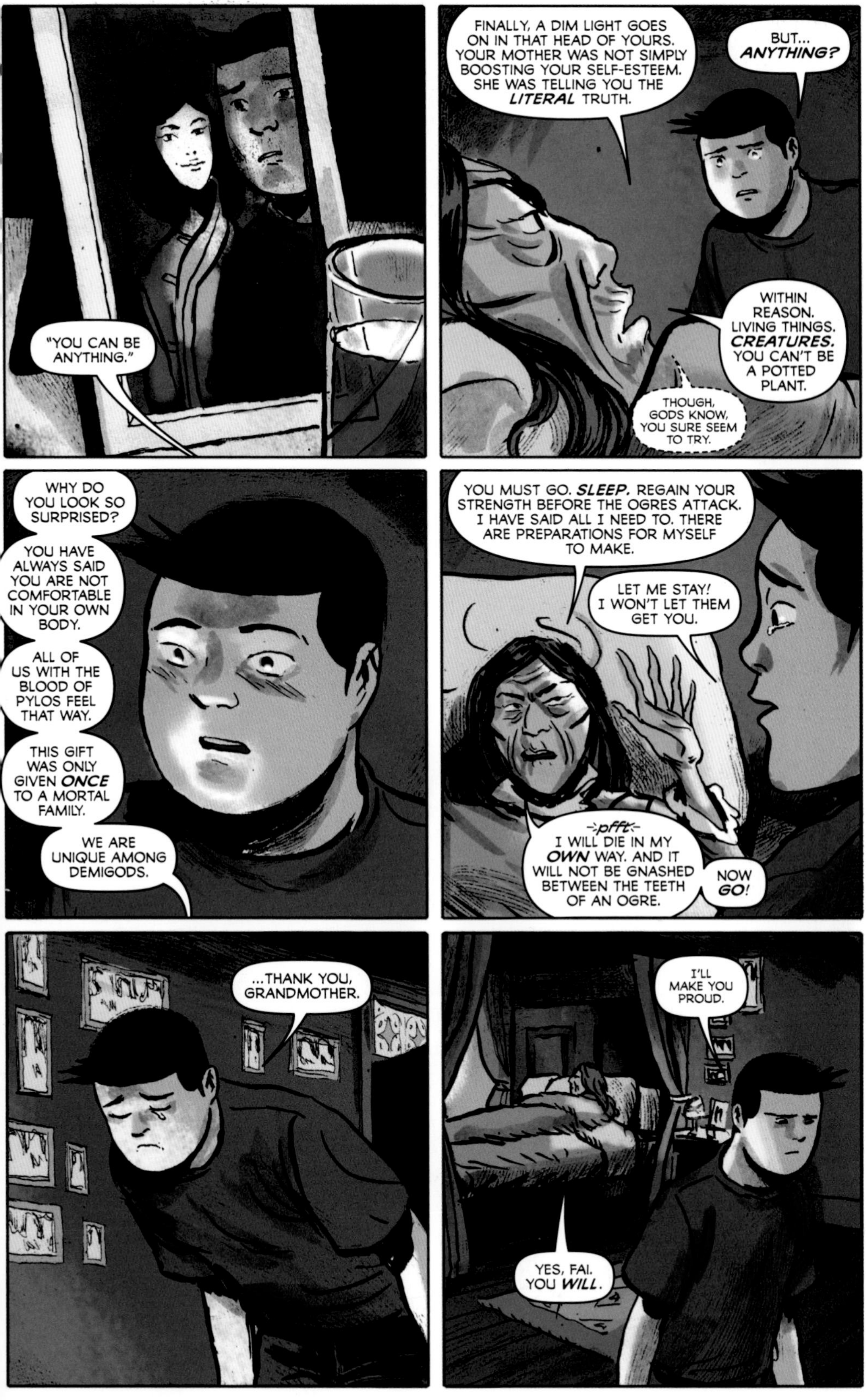
"YOU CAN BE ANYTHING."
FINALLY, A DIM LIGHT GOES ON IN THAT HEAD OF YOURS. YOUR MOTHER WAS NOT SIMPLY BOOSTING YOUR SELF-ESTEEM. SHE WAS TELLING YOU THE *LITERAL* TRUTH.
BUT... ***ANYTHING?***
WITHIN REASON. LIVING THINGS. ***CREATURES.*** YOU CAN'T BE A POTTED PLANT.
THOUGH, GODS KNOW, YOU SURE SEEM TO TRY.
WHY DO YOU LOOK SO SURPRISED?
YOU HAVE ALWAYS SAID YOU ARE NOT COMFORTABLE IN YOUR OWN BODY.
ALL OF US WITH THE BLOOD OF PYLOS FEEL THAT WAY.
THIS GIFT WAS ONLY GIVEN ***ONCE*** TO A MORTAL FAMILY.
WE ARE UNIQUE AMONG DEMIGODS.
YOU MUST GO. ***SLEEP.*** REGAIN YOUR STRENGTH BEFORE THE OGRES ATTACK. I HAVE SAID ALL I NEED TO. THERE ARE PREPARATIONS FOR MYSELF TO MAKE.
LET ME STAY! I WON'T LET THEM GET YOU.
pfft
I WILL DIE IN MY ***OWN*** WAY. AND IT WILL NOT BE GNASHED BETWEEN THE TEETH OF AN OGRE.
NOW ***GO!***
...THANK YOU, GRANDMOTHER.
I'LL MAKE YOU PROUD.
YES, FAI. YOU ***WILL***.

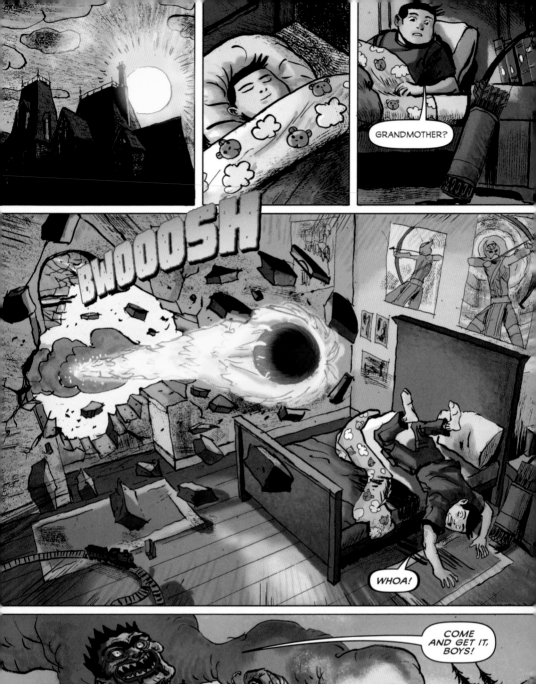

GRANDMOTHER?

BWOOOSH

WHOA!

COME AND GET IT, BOYS!

KISS THE COOK

KLNG KLNG KLNG

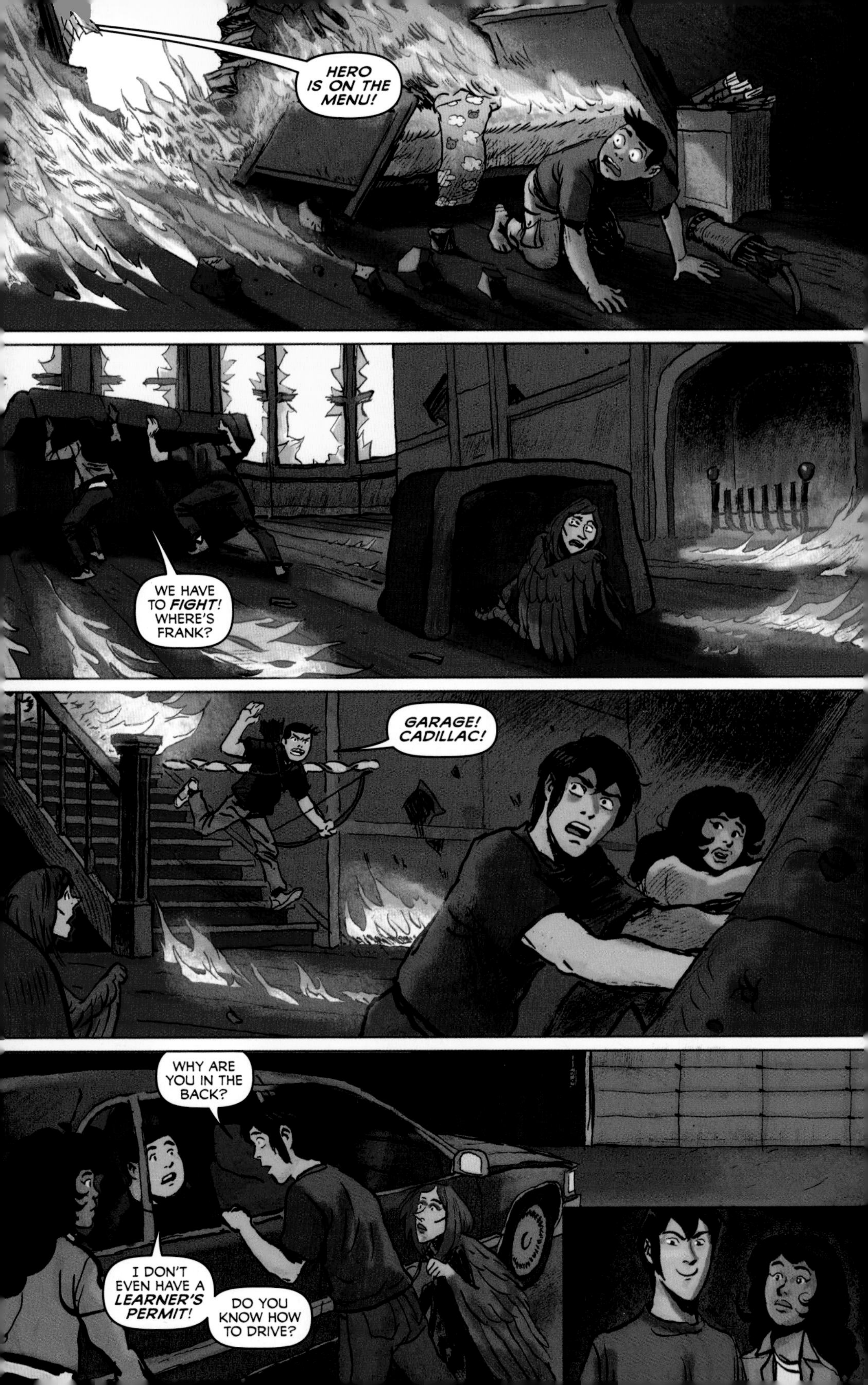
HERO IS ON THE MENU!
WE HAVE TO FIGHT! WHERE'S FRANK?
GARAGE! CADILLAC!
WHY ARE YOU IN THE BACK?
I DON'T EVEN HAVE A LEARNER'S PERMIT!
DO YOU KNOW HOW TO DRIVE?

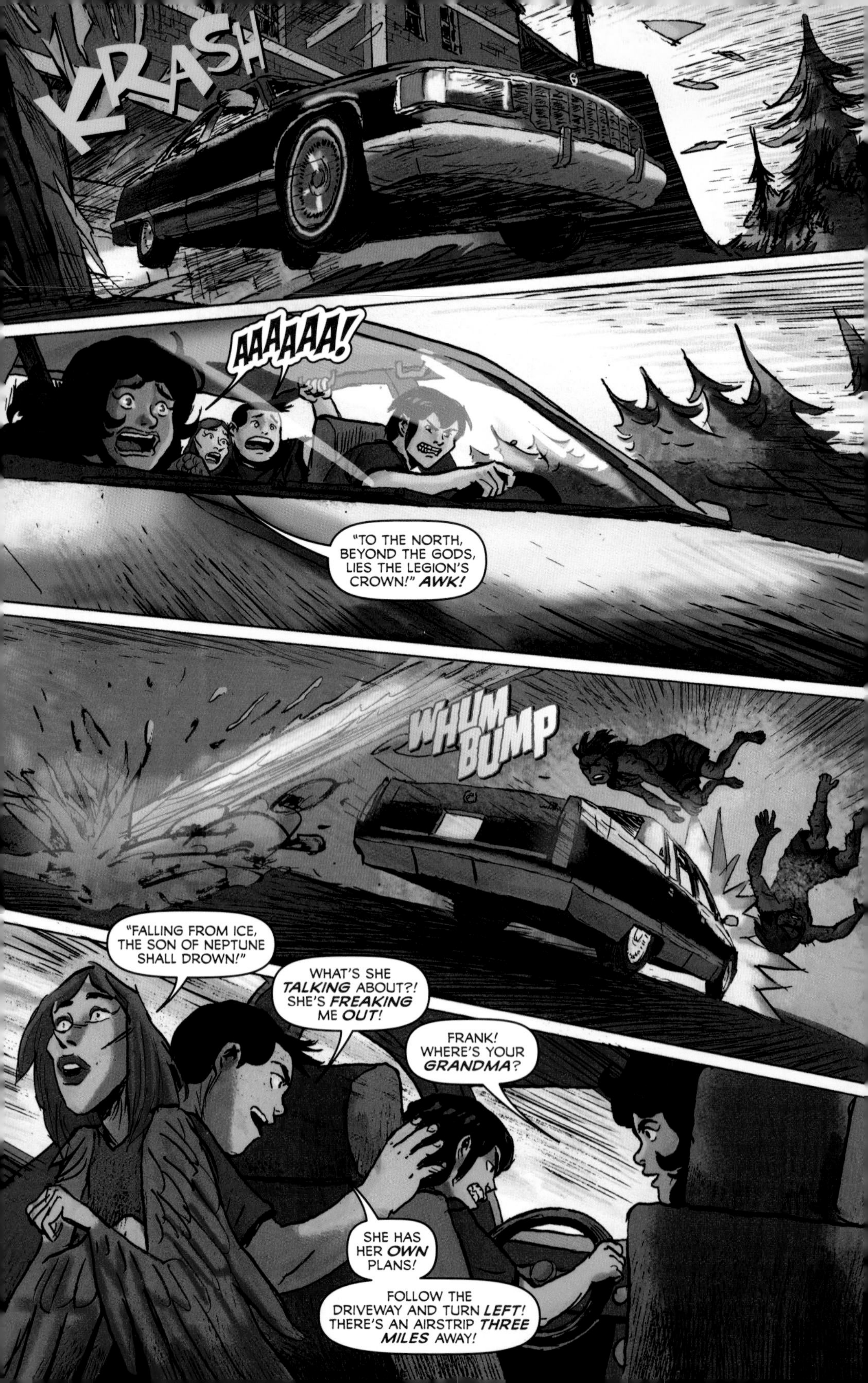
KRASH
AAAAAA!
"TO THE NORTH, BEYOND THE GODS, LIES THE LEGION'S CROWN!" AWK!
WHUM BUMP
"FALLING FROM ICE, THE SON OF NEPTUNE SHALL DROWN!"
WHAT'S SHE TALKING ABOUT?! SHE'S FREAKING ME OUT!
FRANK! WHERE'S YOUR GRANDMA?
SHE HAS HER OWN PLANS!
FOLLOW THE DRIVEWAY AND TURN LEFT! THERE'S AN AIRSTRIP THREE MILES AWAY!

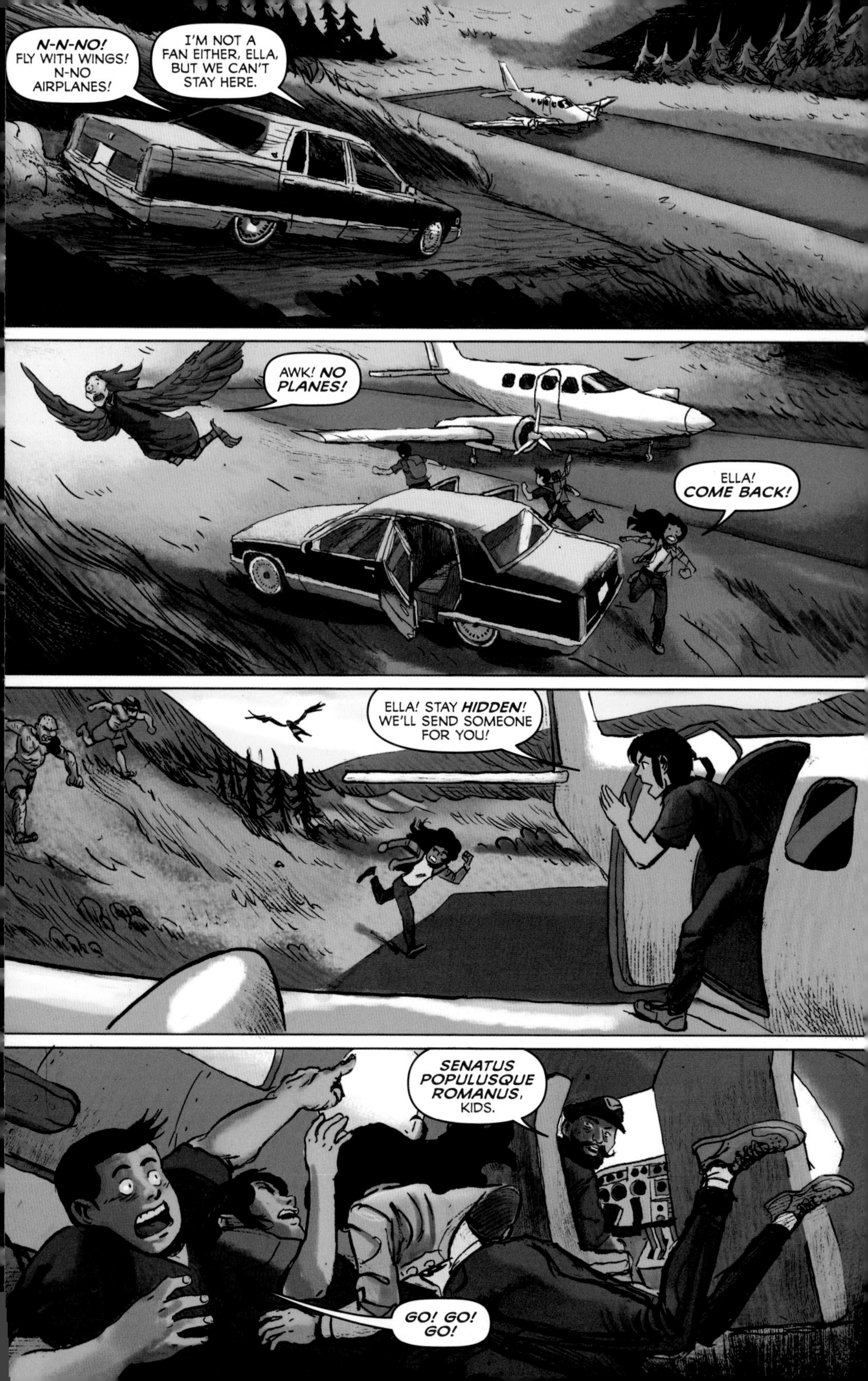
N-N-NO! FLY WITH WINGS! N-NO AIRPLANES!
I'M NOT A FAN EITHER, ELLA, BUT WE CAN'T STAY HERE.
AWK! NO PLANES!
ELLA! COME BACK!
ELLA! STAY HIDDEN! WE'LL SEND SOMEONE FOR YOU!
SENATUS POPULUSQUE ROMANUS, KIDS.
GO! GO! GO!

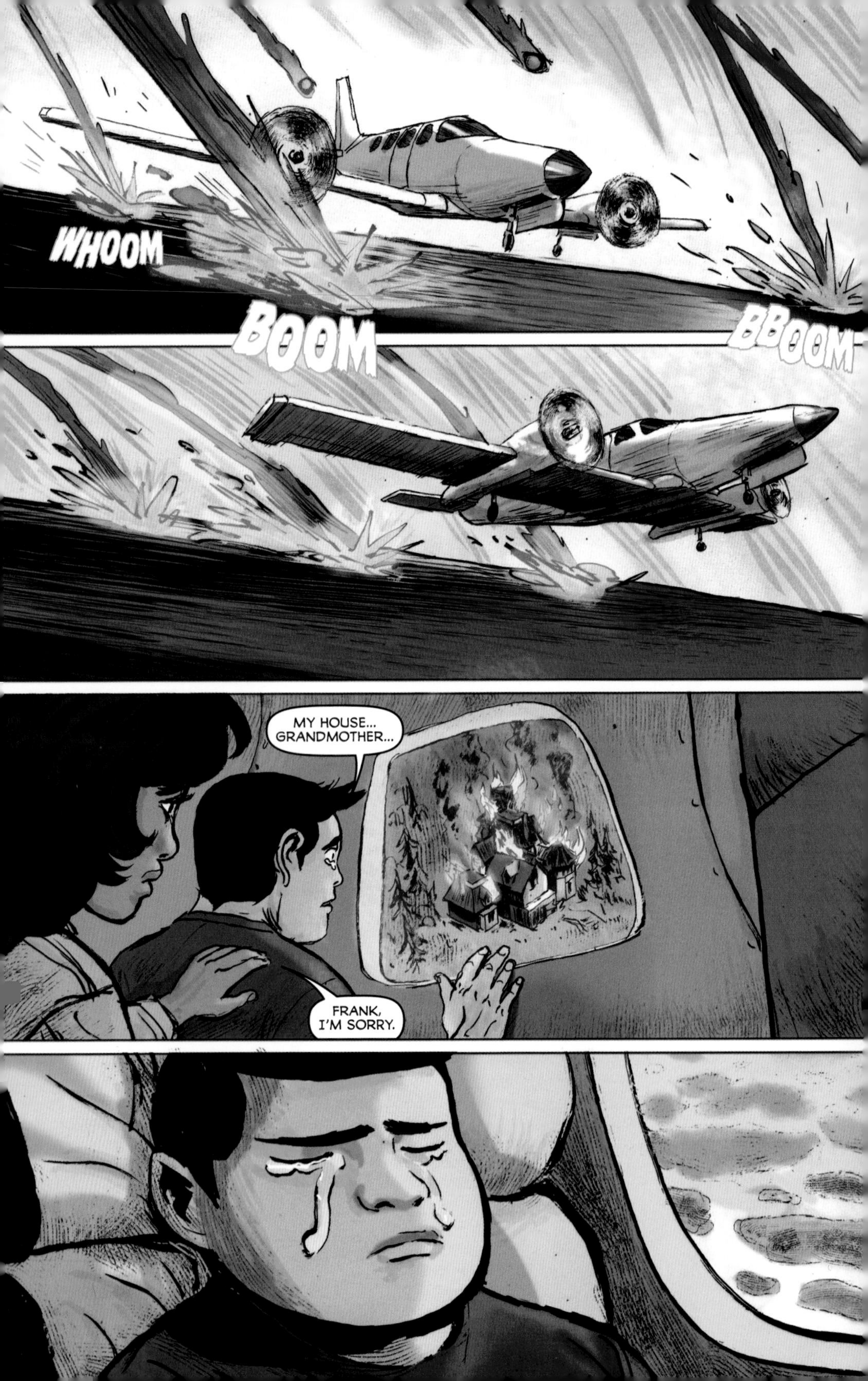
WHOOM
BOOM
BBOOM
MY HOUSE... GRANDMOTHER...
FRANK, I'M SORRY.

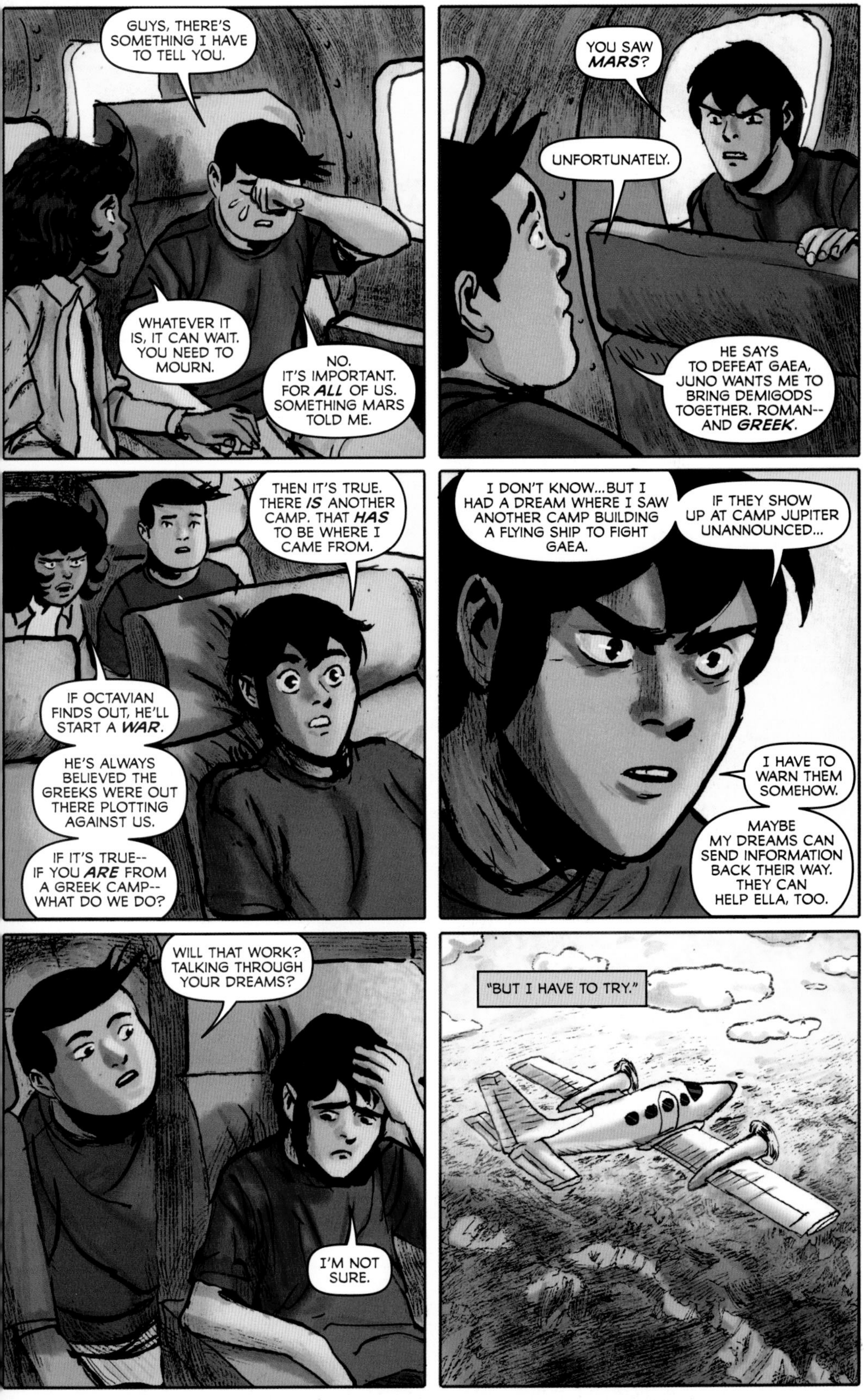
GUYS, THERE'S SOMETHING I HAVE TO TELL YOU.
WHATEVER IT IS, IT CAN WAIT. YOU NEED TO MOURN.
NO. IT'S IMPORTANT. FOR ALL OF US. SOMETHING MARS TOLD ME.
YOU SAW MARS?
UNFORTUNATELY.
HE SAYS TO DEFEAT GAEA, JUNO WANTS ME TO BRING DEMIGODS TOGETHER. ROMAN-- AND GREEK.
THEN IT'S TRUE. THERE IS ANOTHER CAMP. THAT HAS TO BE WHERE I CAME FROM.
IF OCTAVIAN FINDS OUT, HE'LL START A WAR.
HE'S ALWAYS BELIEVED THE GREEKS WERE OUT THERE PLOTTING AGAINST US.
IF IT'S TRUE-- IF YOU ARE FROM A GREEK CAMP-- WHAT DO WE DO?
I DON'T KNOW...BUT I HAD A DREAM WHERE I SAW ANOTHER CAMP BUILDING A FLYING SHIP TO FIGHT GAEA.
IF THEY SHOW UP AT CAMP JUPITER UNANNOUNCED...
I HAVE TO WARN THEM SOMEHOW.
MAYBE MY DREAMS CAN SEND INFORMATION BACK THEIR WAY. THEY CAN HELP ELLA, TOO.
WILL THAT WORK? TALKING THROUGH YOUR DREAMS?
I'M NOT SURE.
"BUT I HAVE TO TRY."

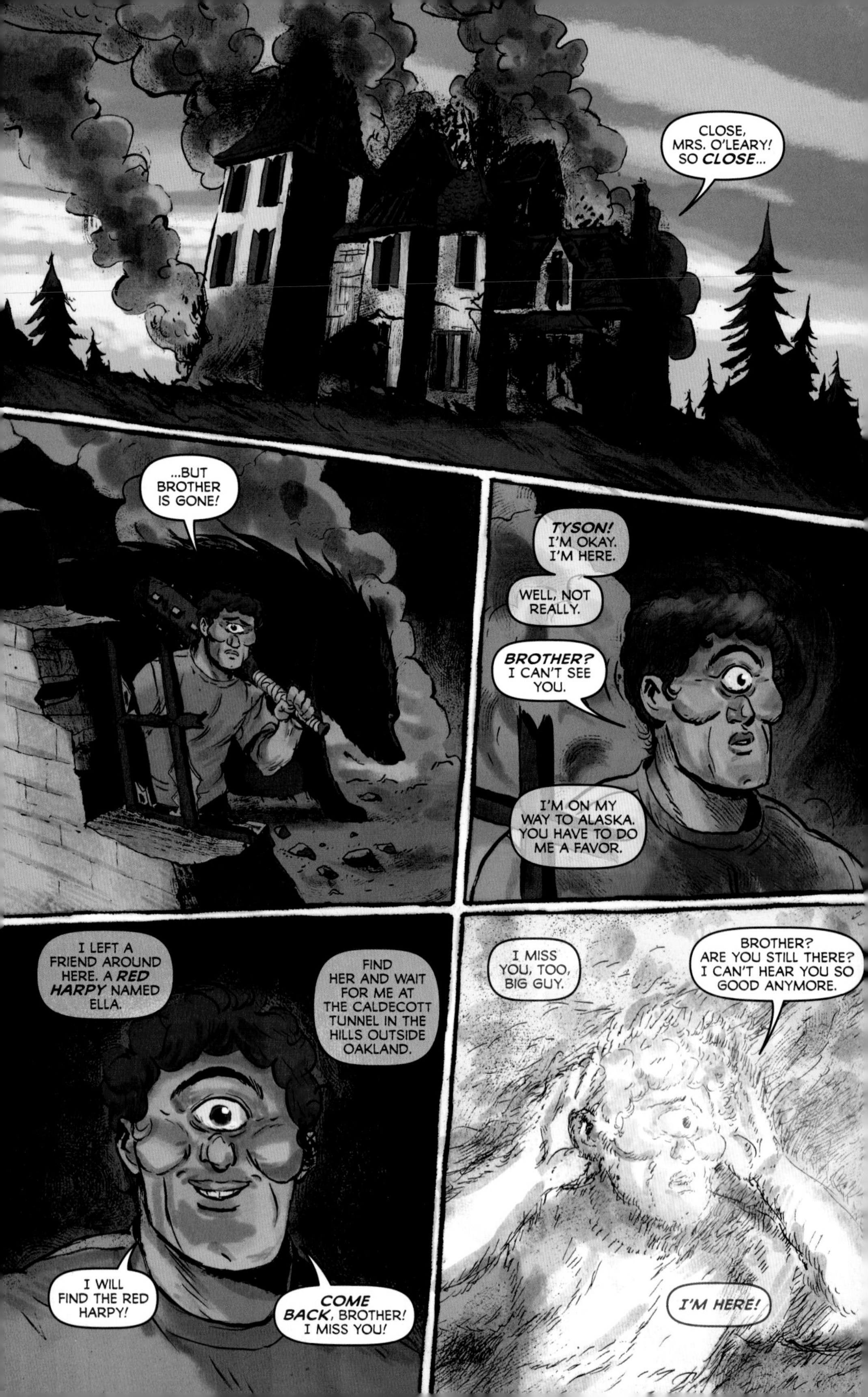

CLOSE, MRS. O'LEARY! SO *CLOSE*...
...BUT BROTHER IS GONE!
TYSON! I'M OKAY. I'M HERE.
WELL, NOT REALLY.
BROTHER? I CAN'T SEE YOU.
I'M ON MY WAY TO ALASKA. YOU HAVE TO DO ME A FAVOR.
I LEFT A FRIEND AROUND HERE. A *RED HARPY* NAMED ELLA.
FIND HER AND WAIT FOR ME AT THE CALDECOTT TUNNEL IN THE HILLS OUTSIDE OAKLAND.
I WILL FIND THE RED HARPY!
COME BACK, BROTHER! I MISS YOU!
I MISS YOU, TOO, BIG GUY.
BROTHER? ARE YOU STILL THERE? I CAN'T HEAR YOU SO GOOD ANYMORE.
I'M HERE!

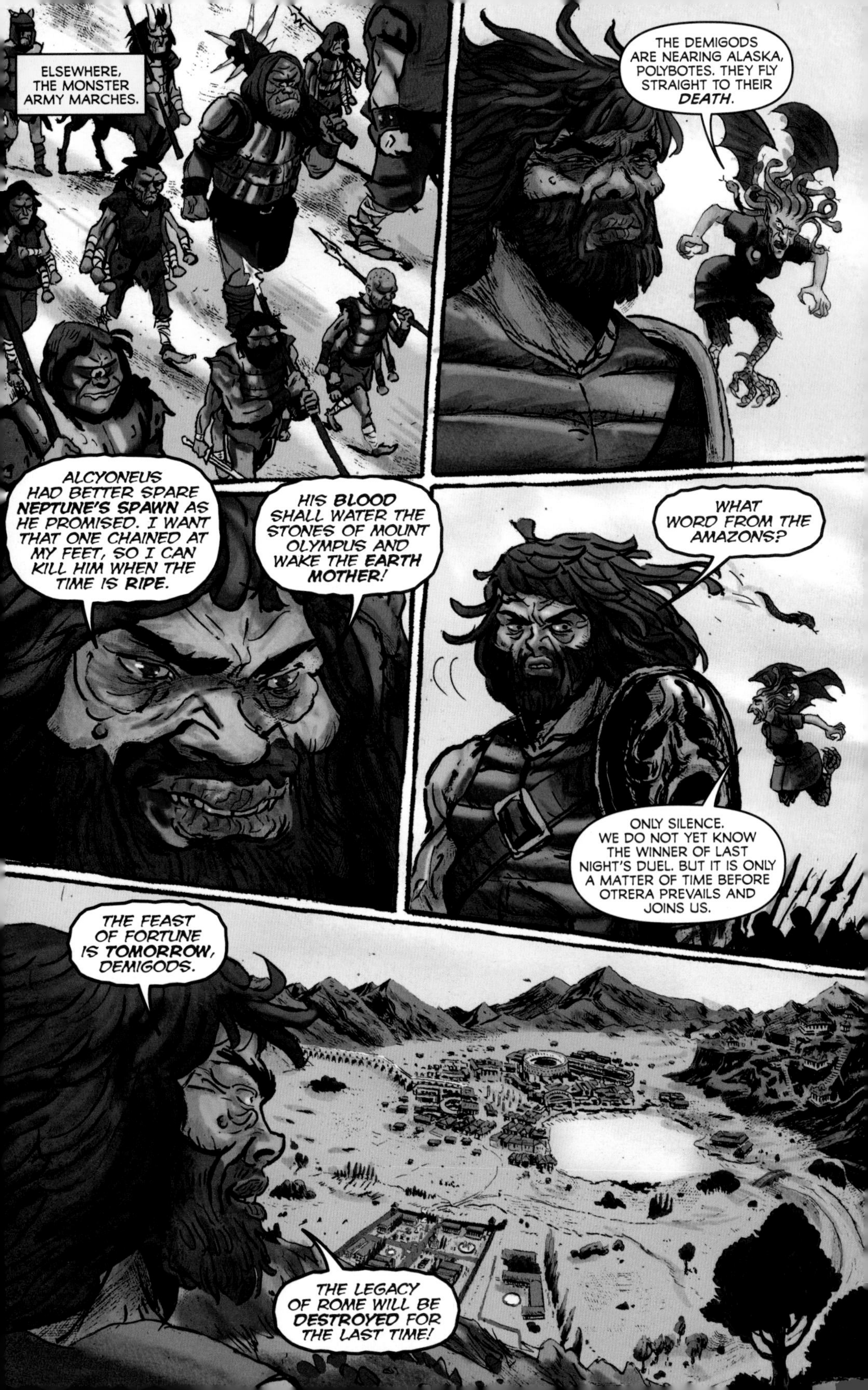

ELSEWHERE, THE MONSTER ARMY MARCHES.
THE DEMIGODS ARE NEARING ALASKA, POLYBOTES. THEY FLY STRAIGHT TO THEIR *DEATH*.
ALCYONEUS HAD BETTER SPARE ***NEPTUNE'S SPAWN*** *AS HE PROMISED. I WANT THAT ONE CHAINED AT MY FEET, SO I CAN KILL HIM WHEN THE TIME IS* ***RIPE***.
HIS ***BLOOD*** *SHALL WATER THE STONES OF MOUNT OLYMPUS AND WAKE THE* ***EARTH MOTHER!***
WHAT WORD FROM THE AMAZONS?
ONLY SILENCE. WE DO NOT YET KNOW THE WINNER OF LAST NIGHT'S DUEL. BUT IT IS ONLY A MATTER OF TIME BEFORE OTRERA PREVAILS AND JOINS US.
THE FEAST OF FORTUNE IS ***TOMORROW,*** *DEMIGODS.*
THE LEGACY OF ROME WILL BE ***DESTROYED*** *FOR THE LAST TIME!*

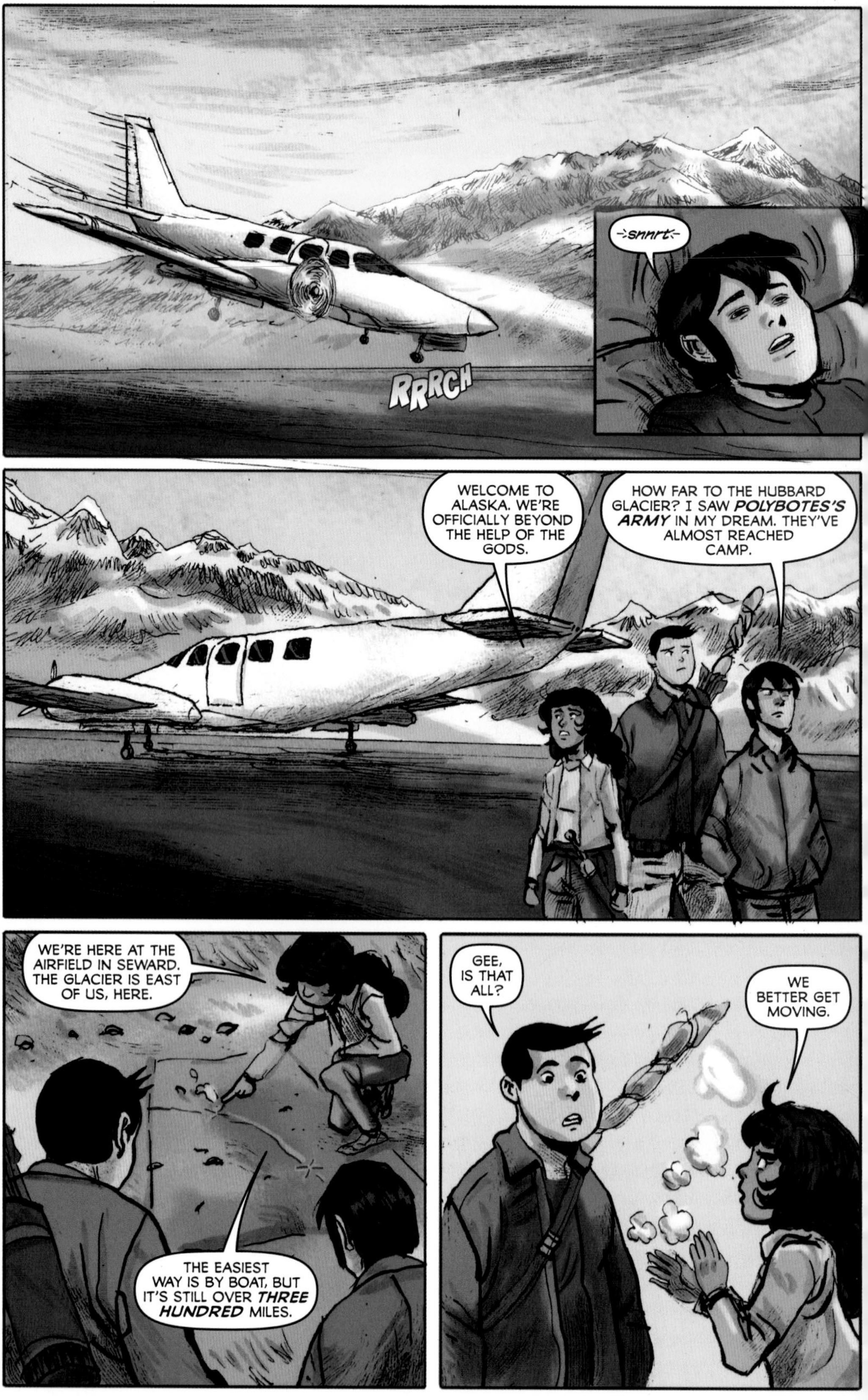
RRRCH
-snnrt-
WELCOME TO ALASKA. WE'RE OFFICIALLY BEYOND THE HELP OF THE GODS.
HOW FAR TO THE HUBBARD GLACIER? I SAW *POLYBOTES'S ARMY* IN MY DREAM. THEY'VE ALMOST REACHED CAMP.
WE'RE HERE AT THE AIRFIELD IN SEWARD. THE GLACIER IS EAST OF US, HERE.
THE EASIEST WAY IS BY BOAT, BUT IT'S STILL OVER *THREE HUNDRED* MILES.
GEE, IS THAT ALL?
WE BETTER GET MOVING.

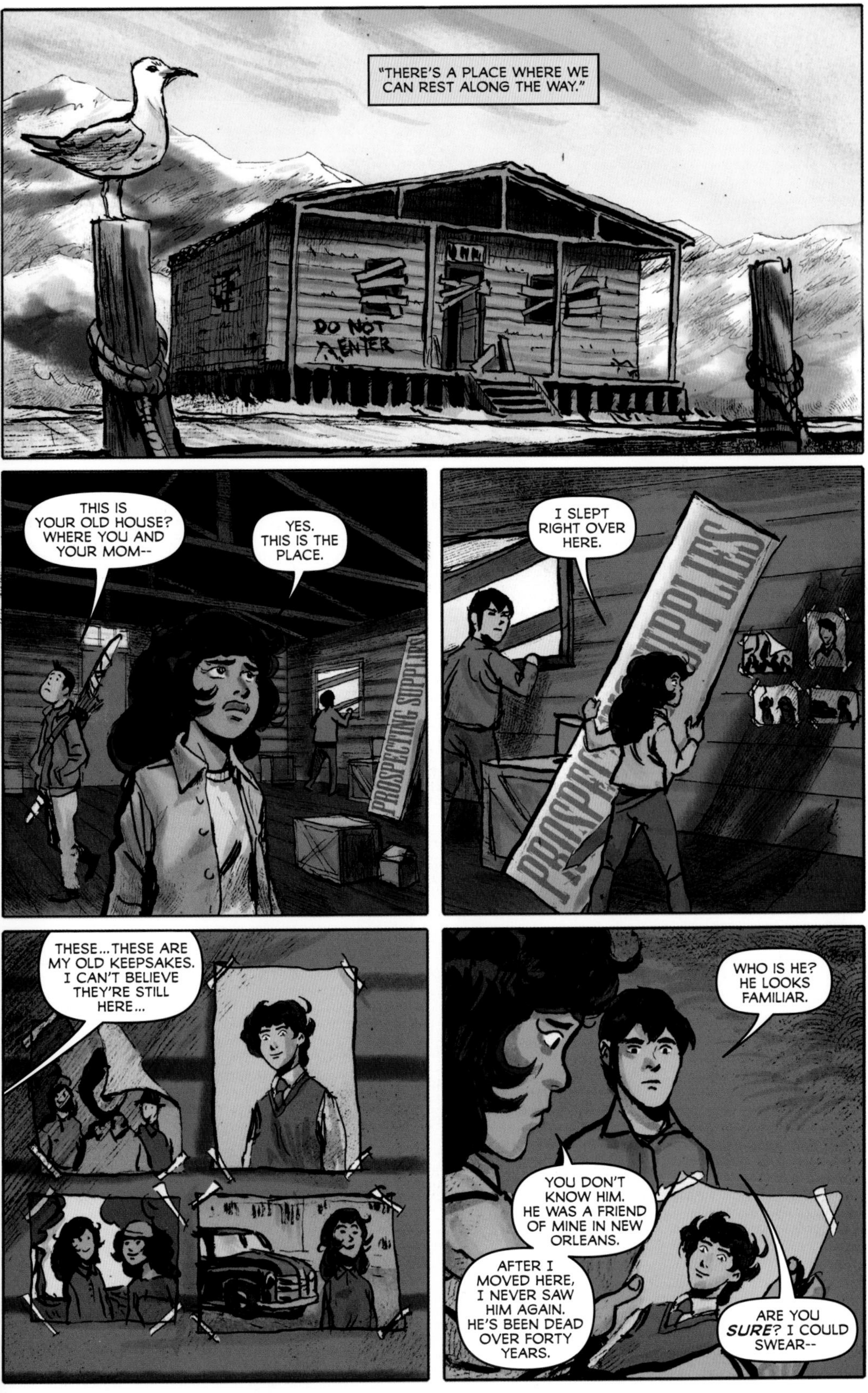
"THERE'S A PLACE WHERE WE CAN REST ALONG THE WAY."
DO NOT ENTER
THIS IS YOUR OLD HOUSE? WHERE YOU AND YOUR MOM--
YES. THIS IS THE PLACE.
PROSPECTING SUPPLIES
I SLEPT RIGHT OVER HERE.
THESE...THESE ARE MY OLD KEEPSAKES. I CAN'T BELIEVE THEY'RE STILL HERE...
WHO IS HE? HE LOOKS FAMILIAR.
YOU DON'T KNOW HIM. HE WAS A FRIEND OF MINE IN NEW ORLEANS.
AFTER I MOVED HERE, I NEVER SAW HIM AGAIN. HE'S BEEN DEAD OVER FORTY YEARS.
ARE YOU *SURE*? I COULD SWEAR--

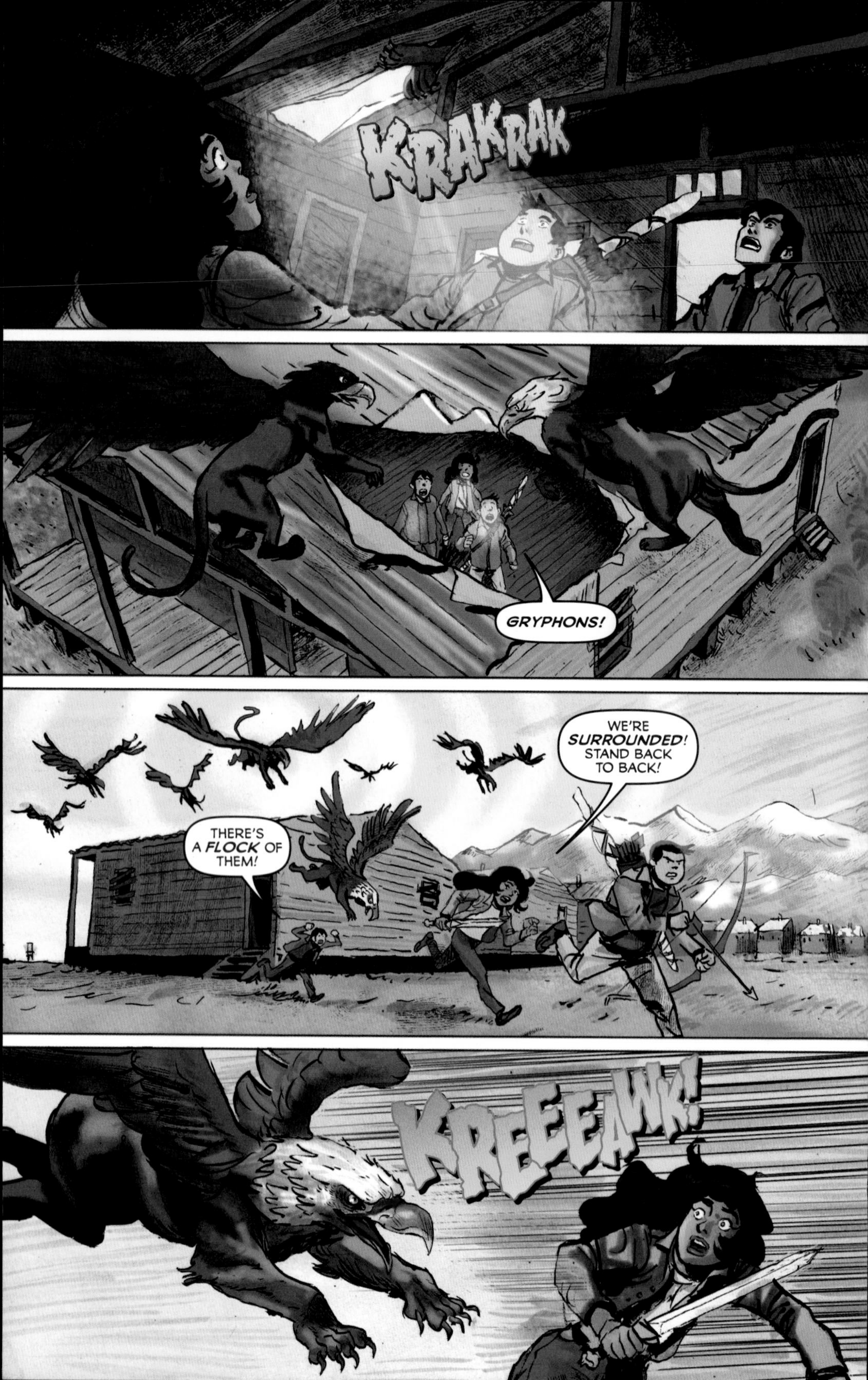
KRAKRAK
GRYPHONS!
THERE'S A FLOCK OF THEM!
WE'RE SURROUNDED! STAND BACK TO BACK!
KREEEAWK!

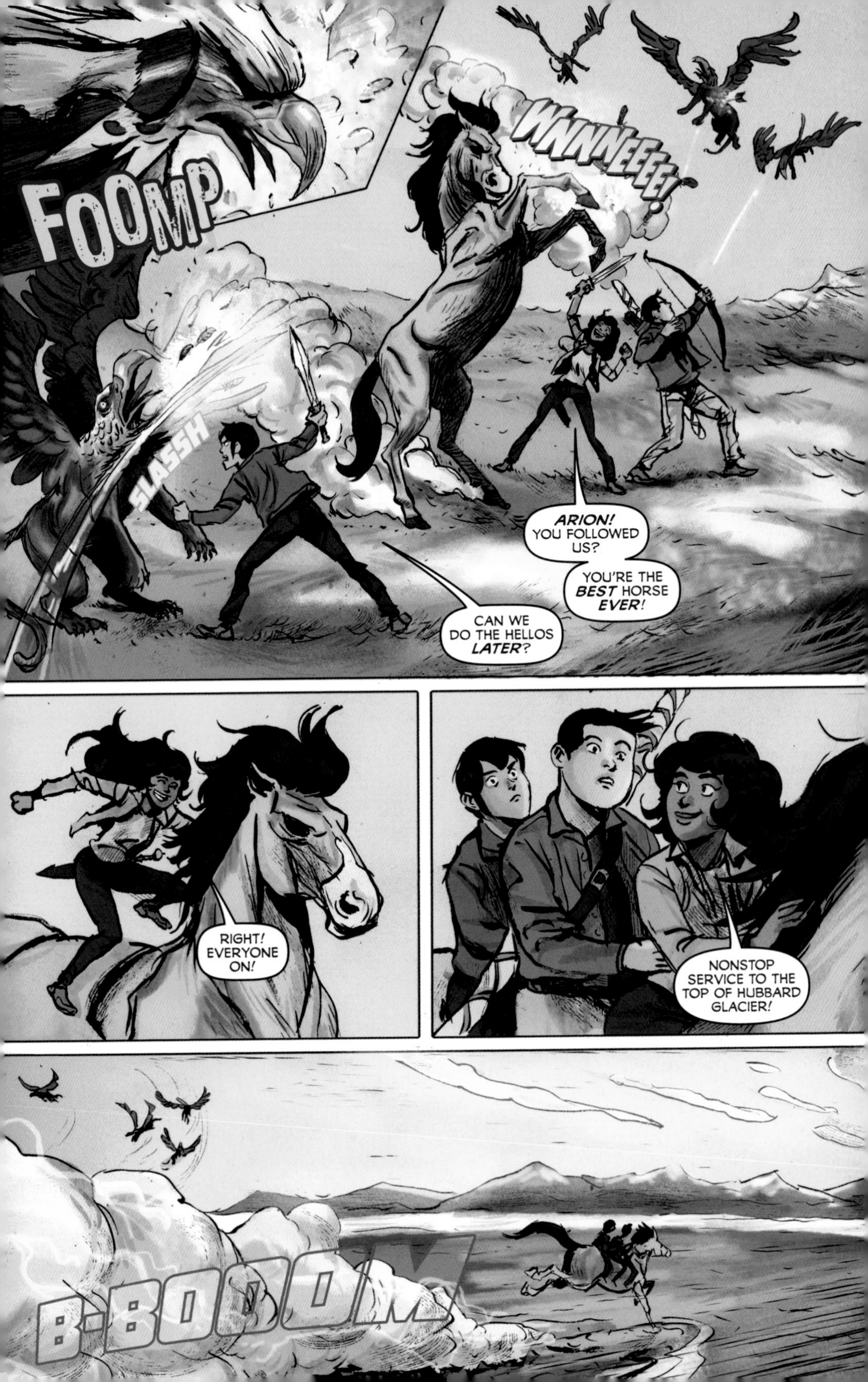
FOOMP
WNNNEEEE!
SLASSH
ARION! YOU FOLLOWED US?
YOU'RE THE BEST HORSE EVER!
CAN WE DO THE HELLOS LATER?
RIGHT! EVERYONE ON!
NONSTOP SERVICE TO THE TOP OF HUBBARD GLACIER!
B-BOOOM

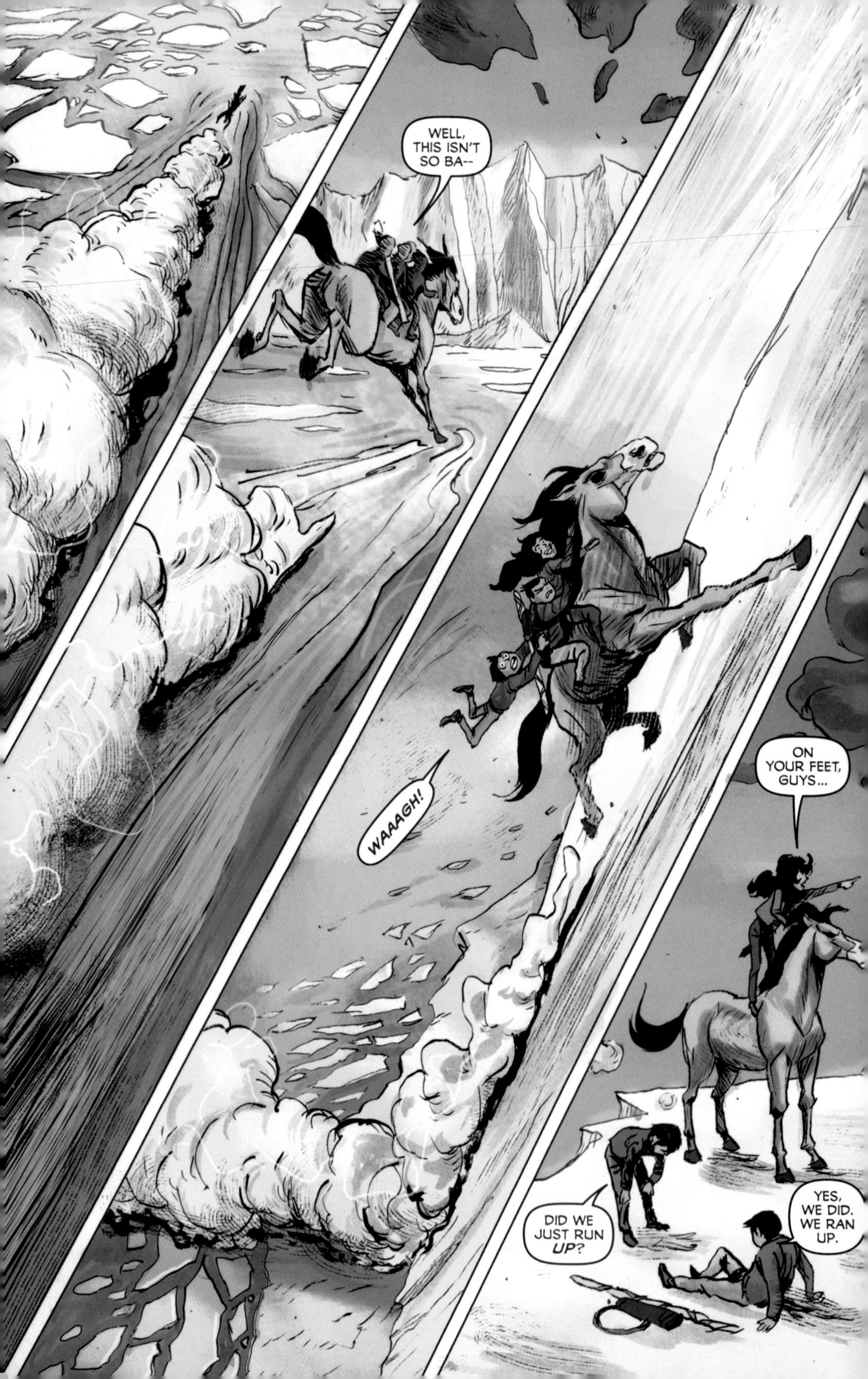
WELL, THIS ISN'T SO BA--
WAAAGH!
ON YOUR FEET, GUYS...
DID WE JUST RUN *UP*?
YES, WE DID. WE RAN UP.

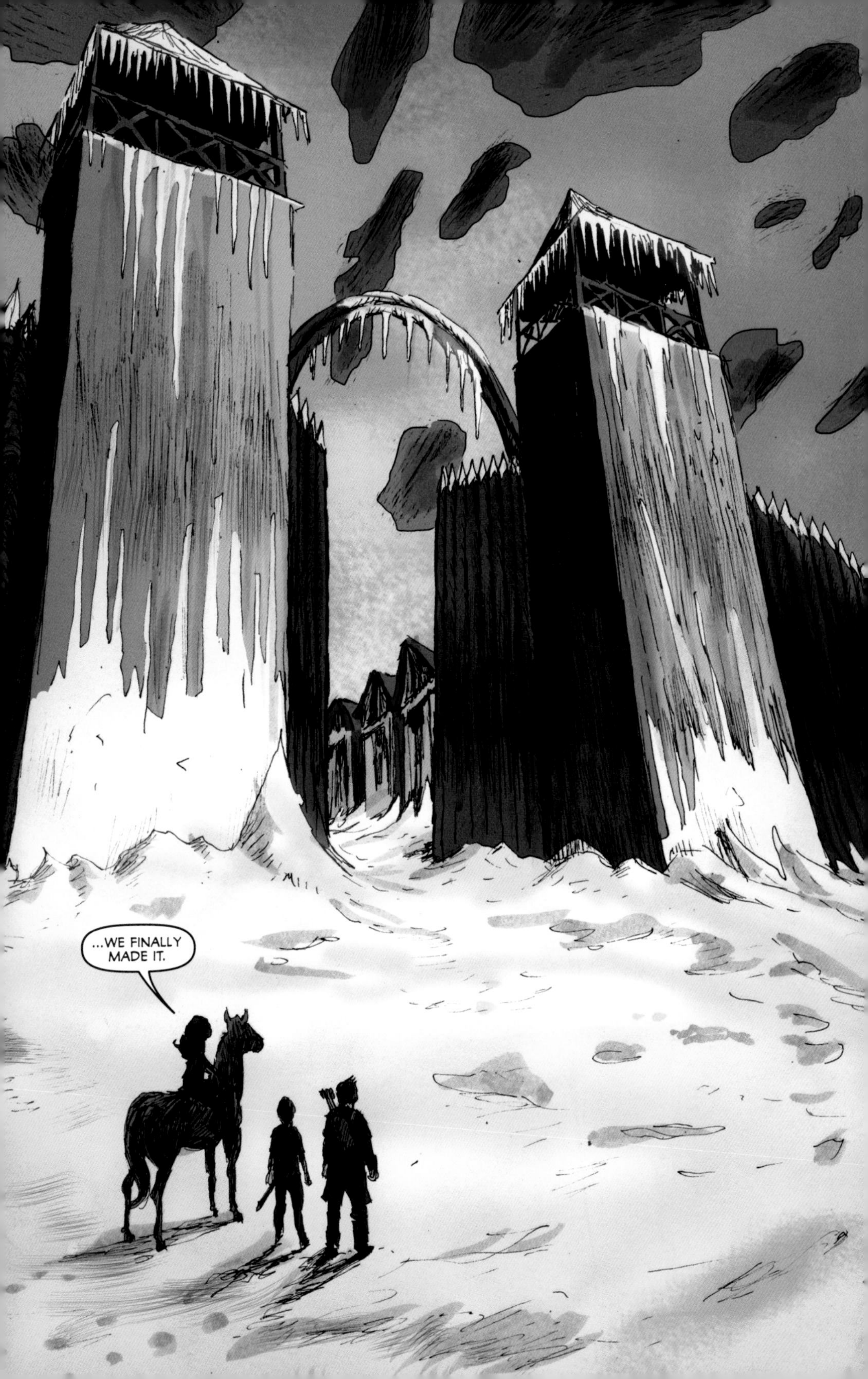
...WE FINALLY MADE IT.

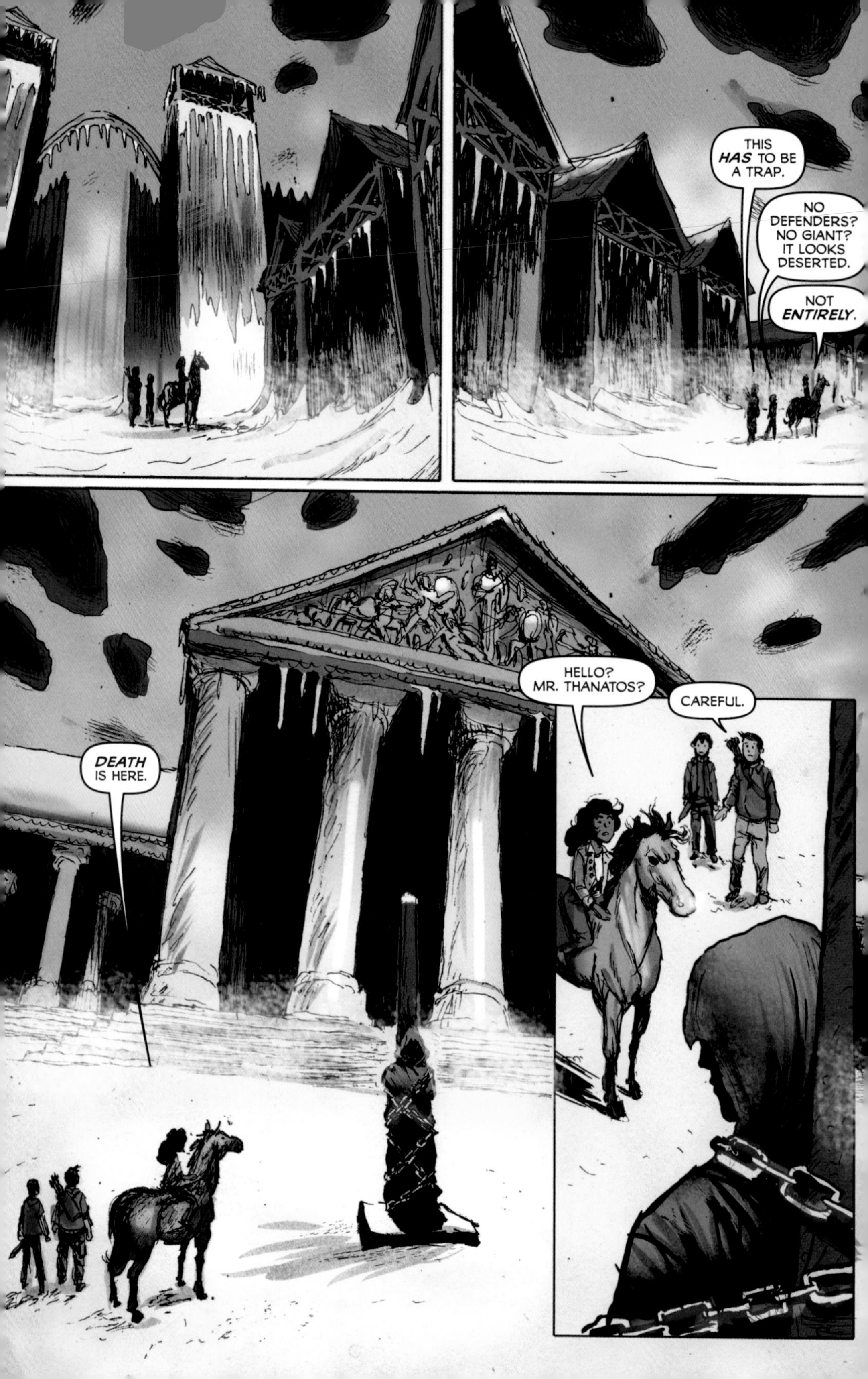
THIS HAS TO BE A TRAP.
NO DEFENDERS? NO GIANT? IT LOOKS DESERTED.
NOT ENTIRELY.
DEATH IS HERE.
HELLO? MR. THANATOS?
CAREFUL.

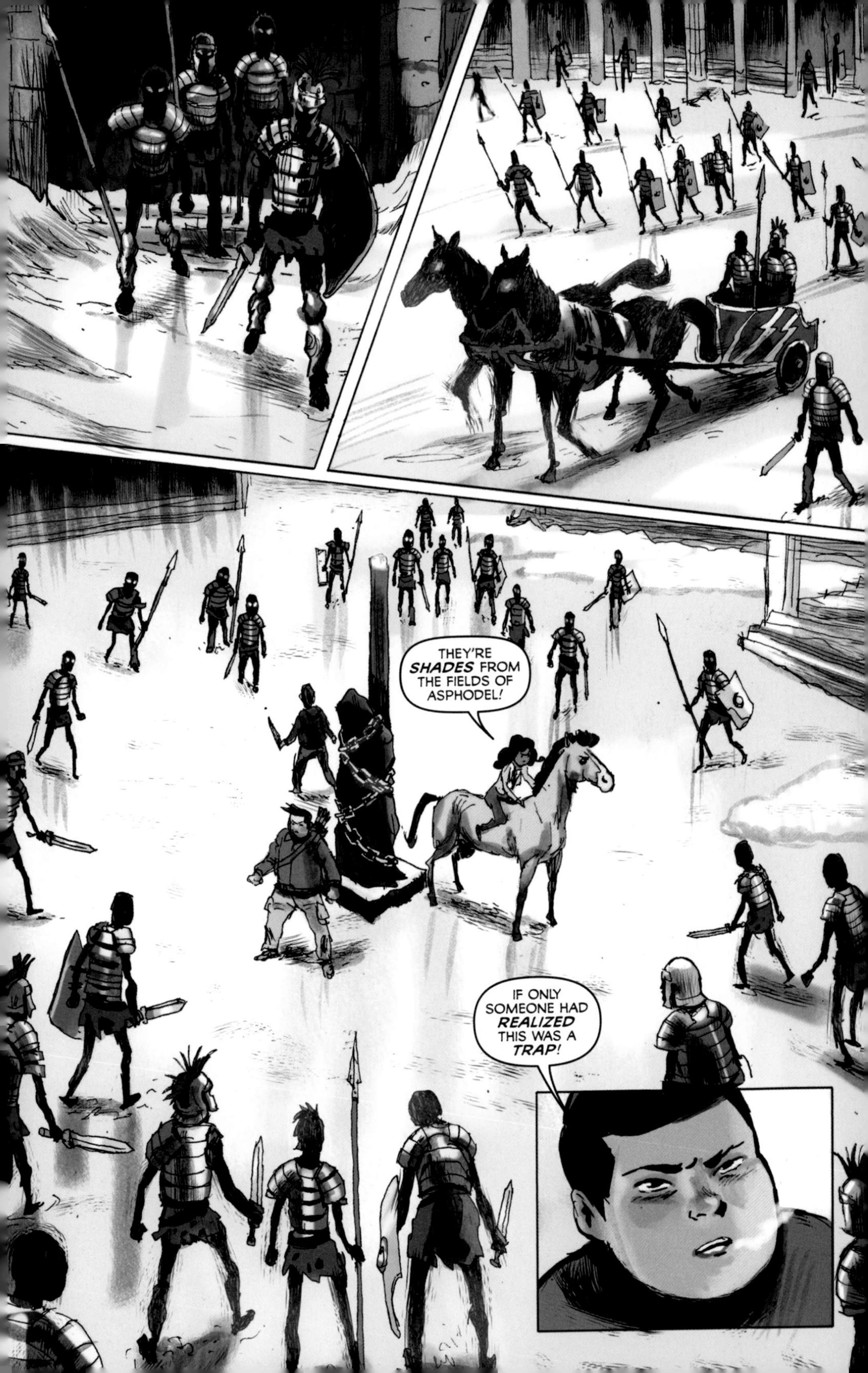
THEY'RE *SHADES* FROM THE FIELDS OF ASPHODEL!
IF ONLY SOMEONE HAD *REALIZED* THIS WAS A *TRAP*!

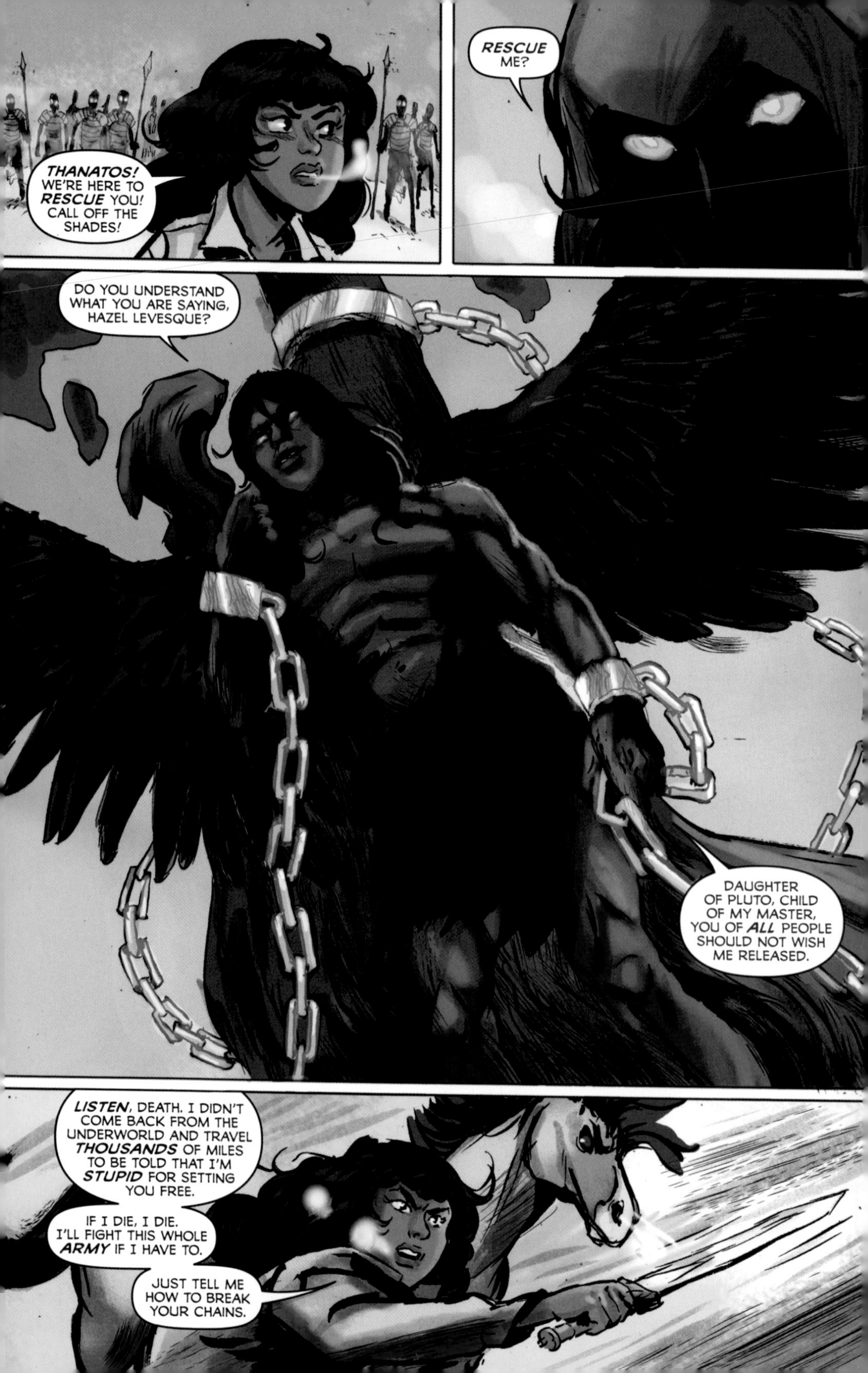
THANATOS! WE'RE HERE TO RESCUE YOU! CALL OFF THE SHADES!
RESCUE ME?
DO YOU UNDERSTAND WHAT YOU ARE SAYING, HAZEL LEVESQUE?
DAUGHTER OF PLUTO, CHILD OF MY MASTER, YOU OF ALL PEOPLE SHOULD NOT WISH ME RELEASED.
LISTEN, DEATH. I DIDN'T COME BACK FROM THE UNDERWORLD AND TRAVEL THOUSANDS OF MILES TO BE TOLD THAT I'M STUPID FOR SETTING YOU FREE.
IF I DIE, I DIE. I'LL FIGHT THIS WHOLE ARMY IF I HAVE TO.
JUST TELL ME HOW TO BREAK YOUR CHAINS.

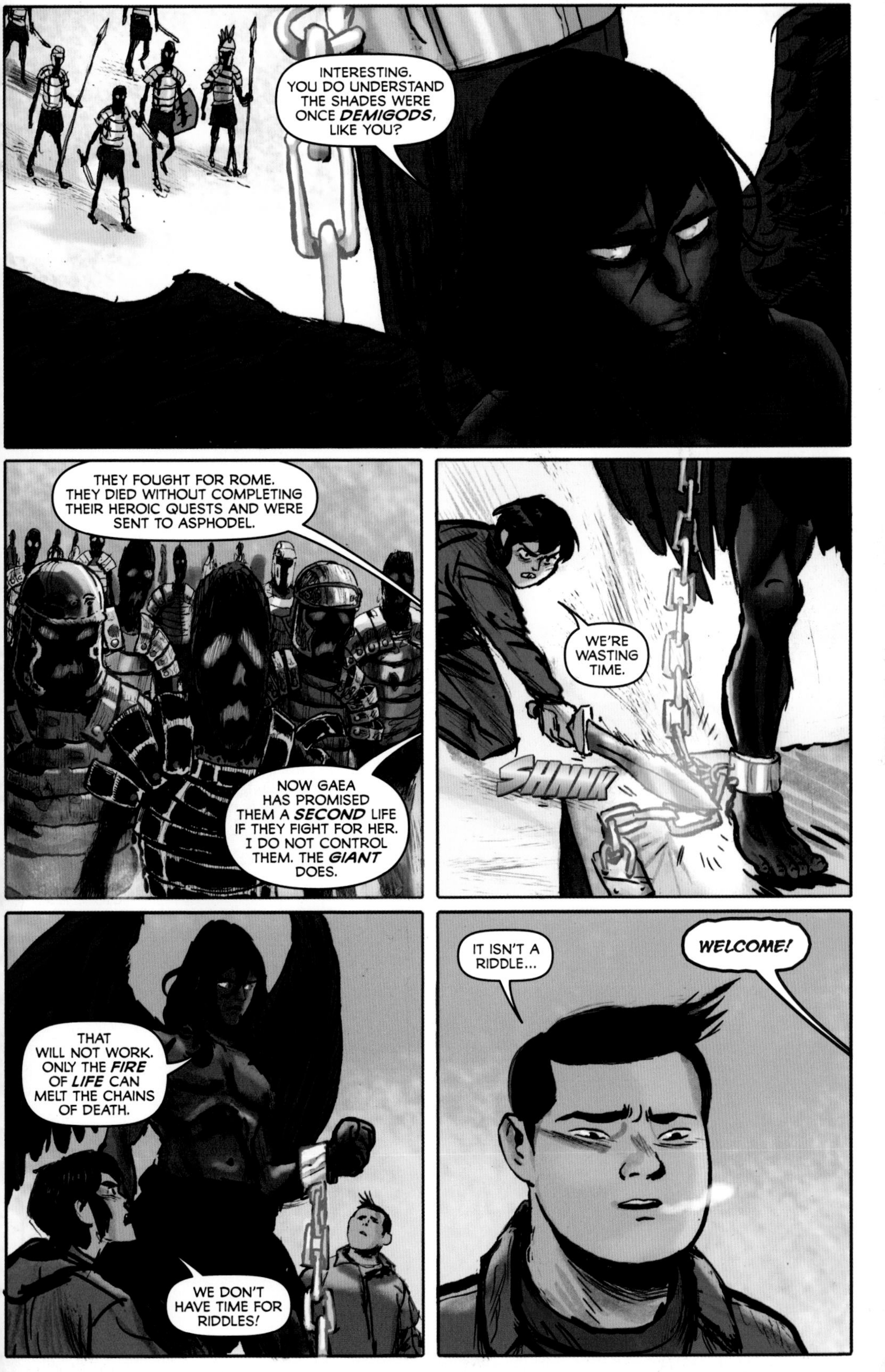
INTERESTING. YOU DO UNDERSTAND THE SHADES WERE ONCE *DEMIGODS*, LIKE YOU?
THEY FOUGHT FOR ROME. THEY DIED WITHOUT COMPLETING THEIR HEROIC QUESTS AND WERE SENT TO ASPHODEL.
NOW GAEA HAS PROMISED THEM A *SECOND* LIFE IF THEY FIGHT FOR HER. I DO NOT CONTROL THEM. THE *GIANT* DOES.
WE'RE WASTING TIME.
SHNNK
THAT WILL NOT WORK. ONLY THE *FIRE* OF *LIFE* CAN MELT THE CHAINS OF DEATH.
WE DON'T HAVE TIME FOR RIDDLES!
IT ISN'T A RIDDLE...
WELCOME!

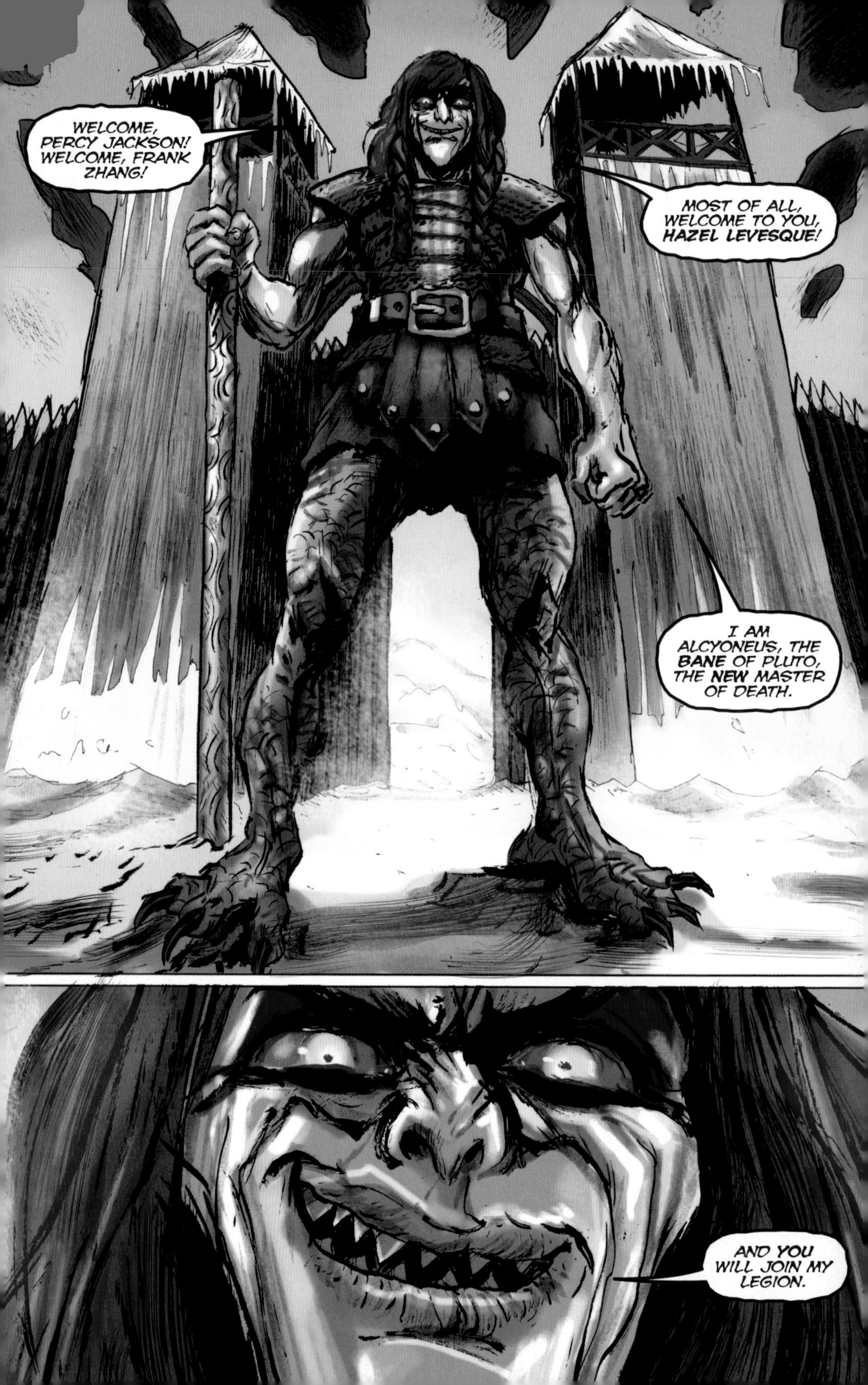
WELCOME, PERCY JACKSON! WELCOME, FRANK ZHANG!
MOST OF ALL, WELCOME TO YOU, HAZEL LEVESQUE!
I AM ALCYONEUS, THE BANE OF PLUTO, THE NEW MASTER OF DEATH.
AND YOU WILL JOIN MY LEGION.

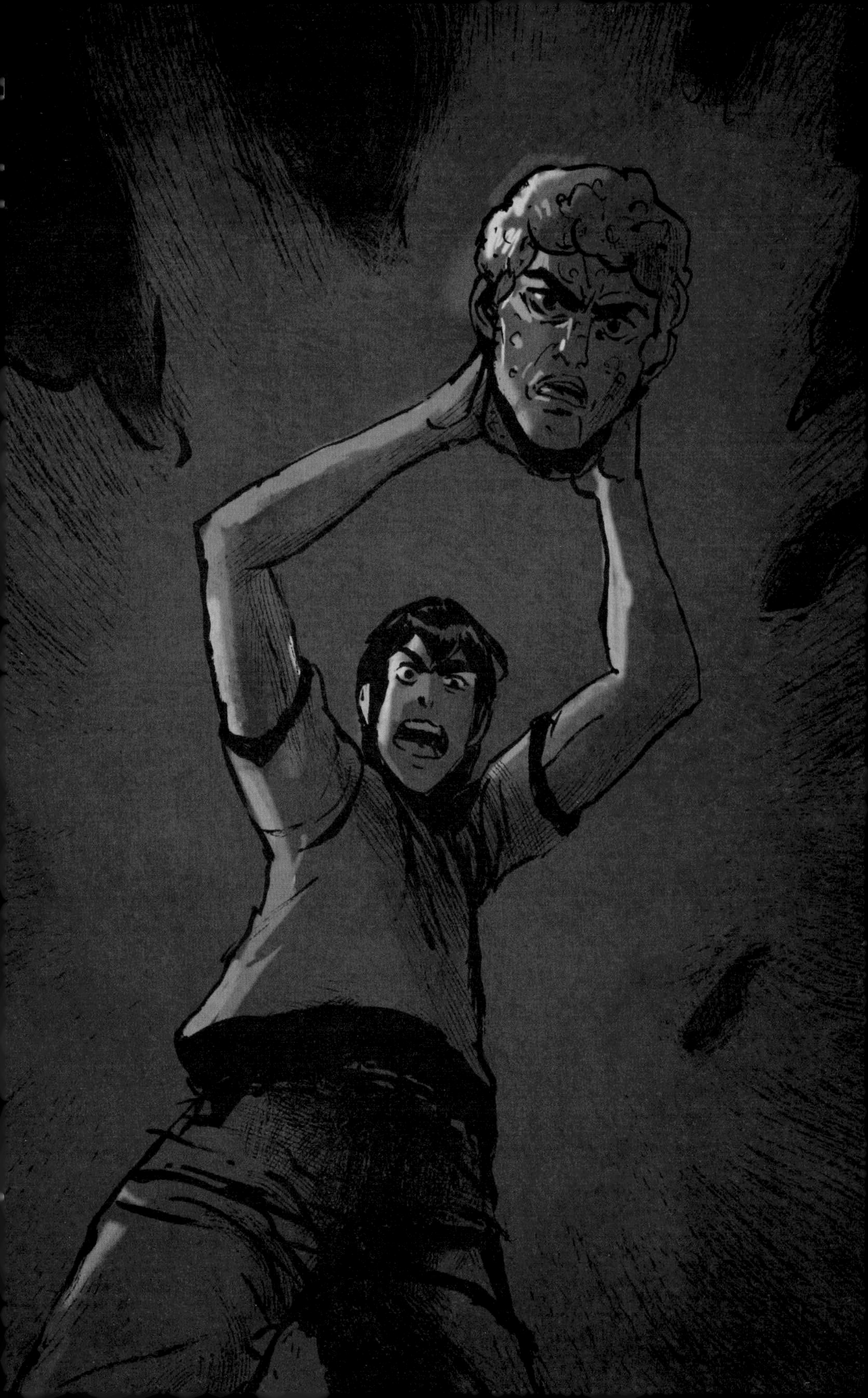

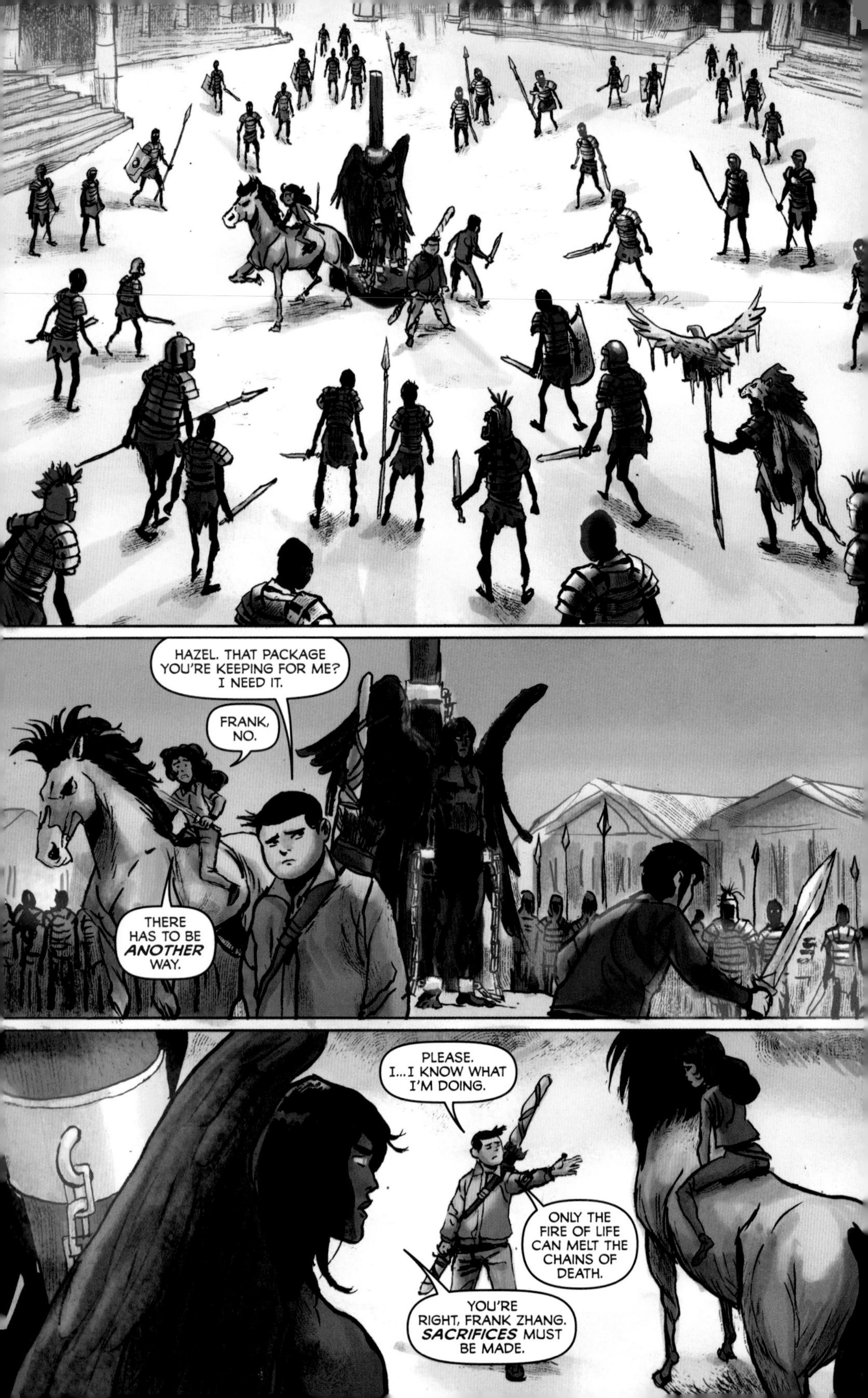
HAZEL. THAT PACKAGE YOU'RE KEEPING FOR ME? I NEED IT.
FRANK, NO.
THERE HAS TO BE *ANOTHER* WAY.
PLEASE. I...I KNOW WHAT I'M DOING.
ONLY THE FIRE OF LIFE CAN MELT THE CHAINS OF DEATH.
YOU'RE RIGHT, FRANK ZHANG. *SACRIFICES* MUST BE MADE.

I'VE FOLLOWED YOUR PROGRESS, *SON* OF *NEPTUNE*.

GAEA HATES YOU ABOVE ALL OTHERS.

YEAH, FLATTERING. BUT I'M A SON OF *POSEIDON*.

I'M SORRY I CAN'T KILL YOU RIGHT NOW, BUT MY BROTHER *POLYBOTES* THINKS IT WILL BE AMUSING WHEN HE DESTROYS NEPTUNE TO HAVE THE GOD'S FAVORITE SON ON A *LEASH*.

I'M FROM CAMP HALF-BLOOD. I *REMEMBER* NOW.

GREEK, ROMAN, IT DOESN'T MATTER. A WEED MUST BE PULLED UP AT THE ROOT.

EVEN NOW, MY BROTHER *PORPHYRION* PREPARES FOR THE *REAL BATTLE*.

HE MARCHES FOR THE ANCIENT LANDS, TO DESTROY THE GODS AT THEIR *SOURCE!*

THE SOURCE... HE MEANS *GREECE*.

NO NEED TO WORRY ABOUT THAT. YOU WON'T LIVE LONG ENOUGH TO SEE OUR *ULTIMATE VICTORY*.

THE DOORS OF DEATH WILL STAND OPEN. THOSE WHO SERVE US WILL NEVER *PERISH*. ALIVE OR DEAD, YOU THREE *WILL* JOIN MY ARMY.

YOU'RE MY BEST FRIEND, FRANK. I SHOULD'VE TOLD YOU THAT SOONER. I HOPE YOU KNOW WHAT YOU'RE DOING.

PERCY, KEEP THE GHOSTS AWAY FROM HIM.

A WHOLE *ARMY*? NO SWEAT.

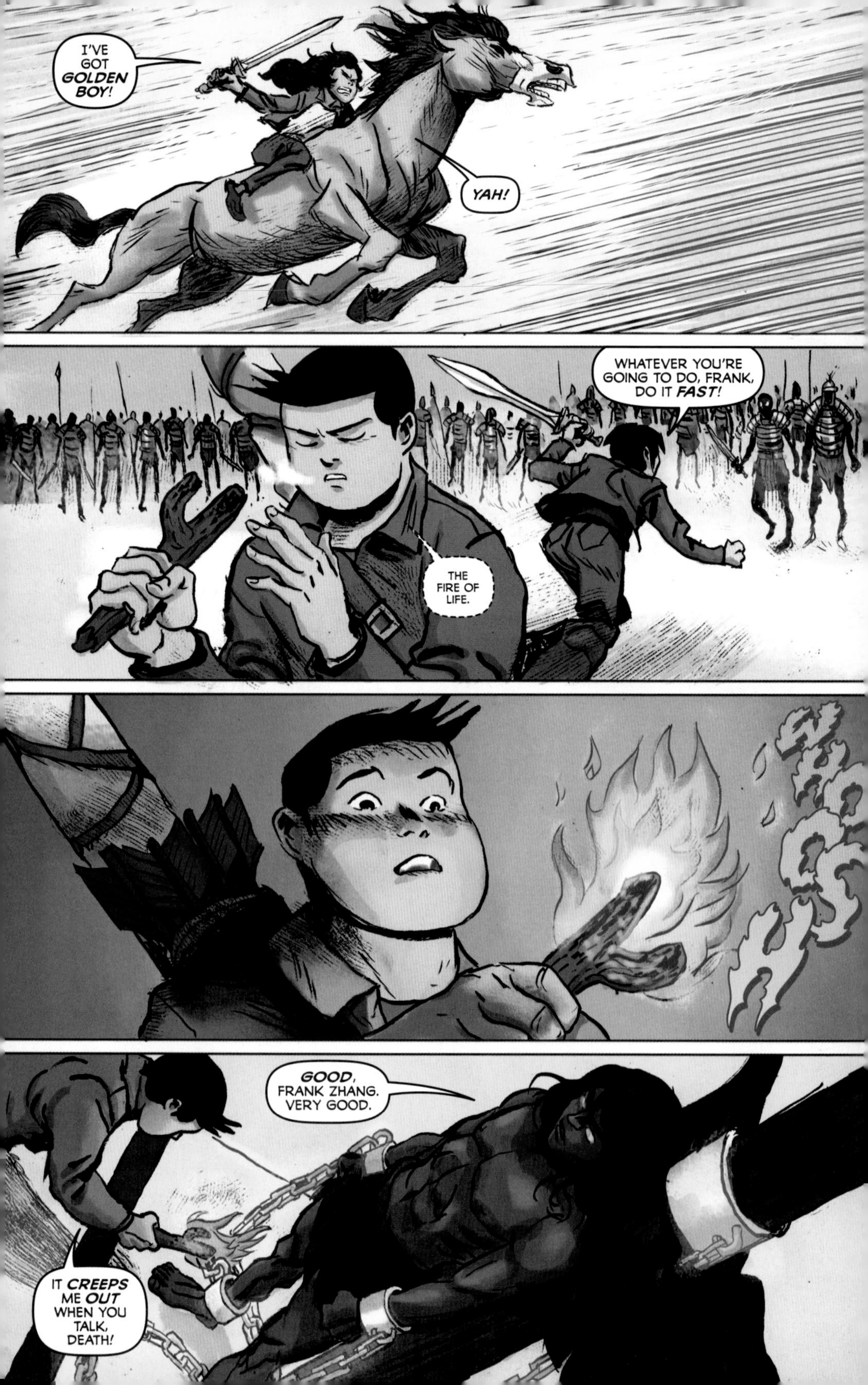

I'VE GOT *GOLDEN BOY*!
YAH!
WHATEVER YOU'RE GOING TO DO, FRANK, DO IT *FAST*!
THE FIRE OF LIFE.
GOOD, FRANK ZHANG. VERY GOOD.
IT *CREEPS* ME *OUT* WHEN YOU TALK, DEATH!

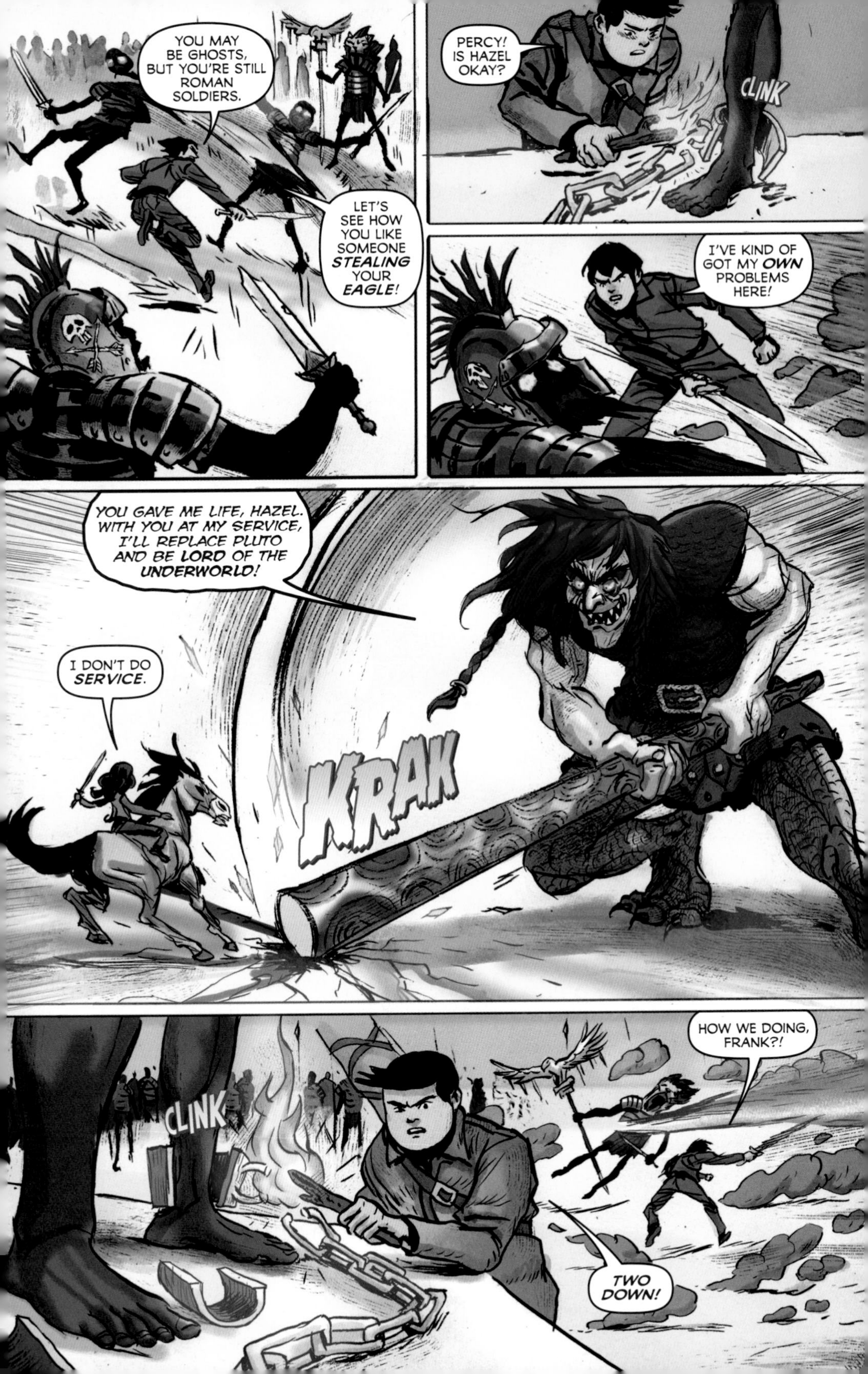
YOU MAY BE GHOSTS, BUT YOU'RE STILL ROMAN SOLDIERS.
LET'S SEE HOW YOU LIKE SOMEONE STEALING YOUR EAGLE!
PERCY! IS HAZEL OKAY?
CLINK
I'VE KIND OF GOT MY OWN PROBLEMS HERE!
YOU GAVE ME LIFE, HAZEL. WITH YOU AT MY SERVICE, I'LL REPLACE PLUTO AND BE LORD OF THE UNDERWORLD!
I DON'T DO SERVICE.
KRAK
CLINK
HOW WE DOING, FRANK?!
TWO DOWN!

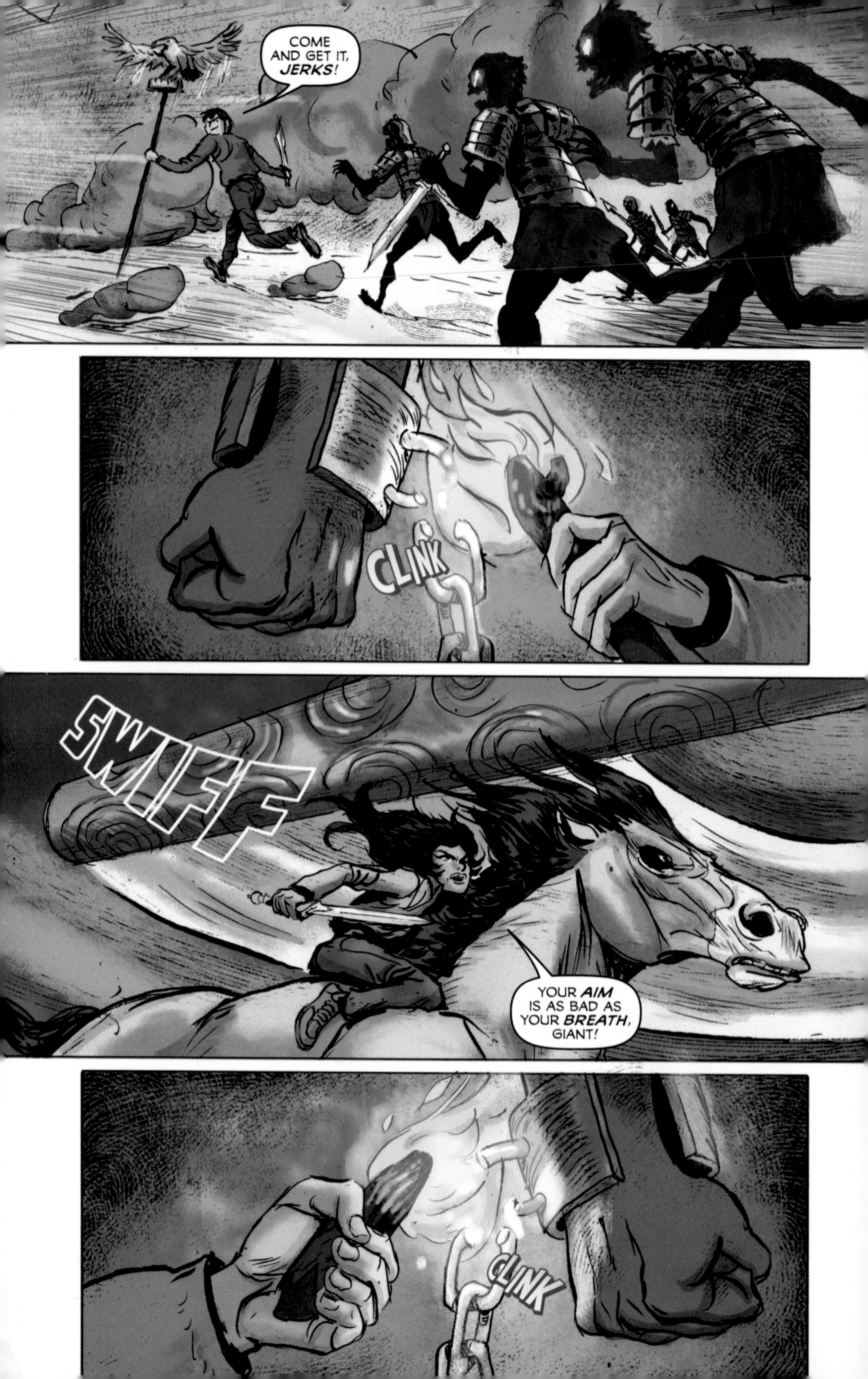
COME AND GET IT, JERKS!
CLINK
SWIFF
YOUR AIM IS AS BAD AS YOUR BREATH, GIANT!
CLINK

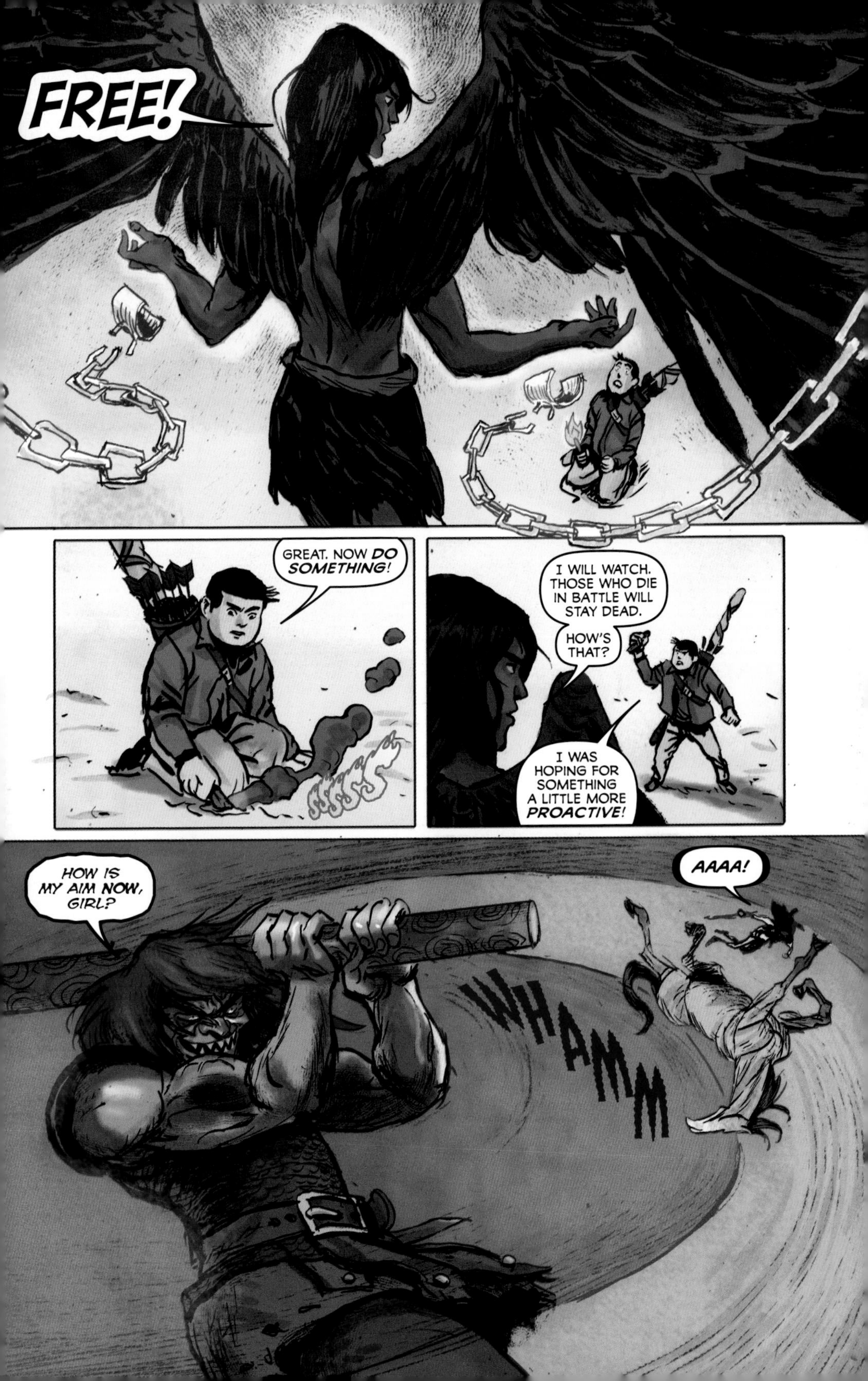
FREE!
GREAT. NOW *DO SOMETHING*!
I WILL WATCH. THOSE WHO DIE IN BATTLE WILL STAY DEAD.
HOW'S THAT?
I WAS HOPING FOR SOMETHING A LITTLE MORE *PROACTIVE*!
HOW IS MY AIM NOW, GIRL?
AAAA!
WHAMM

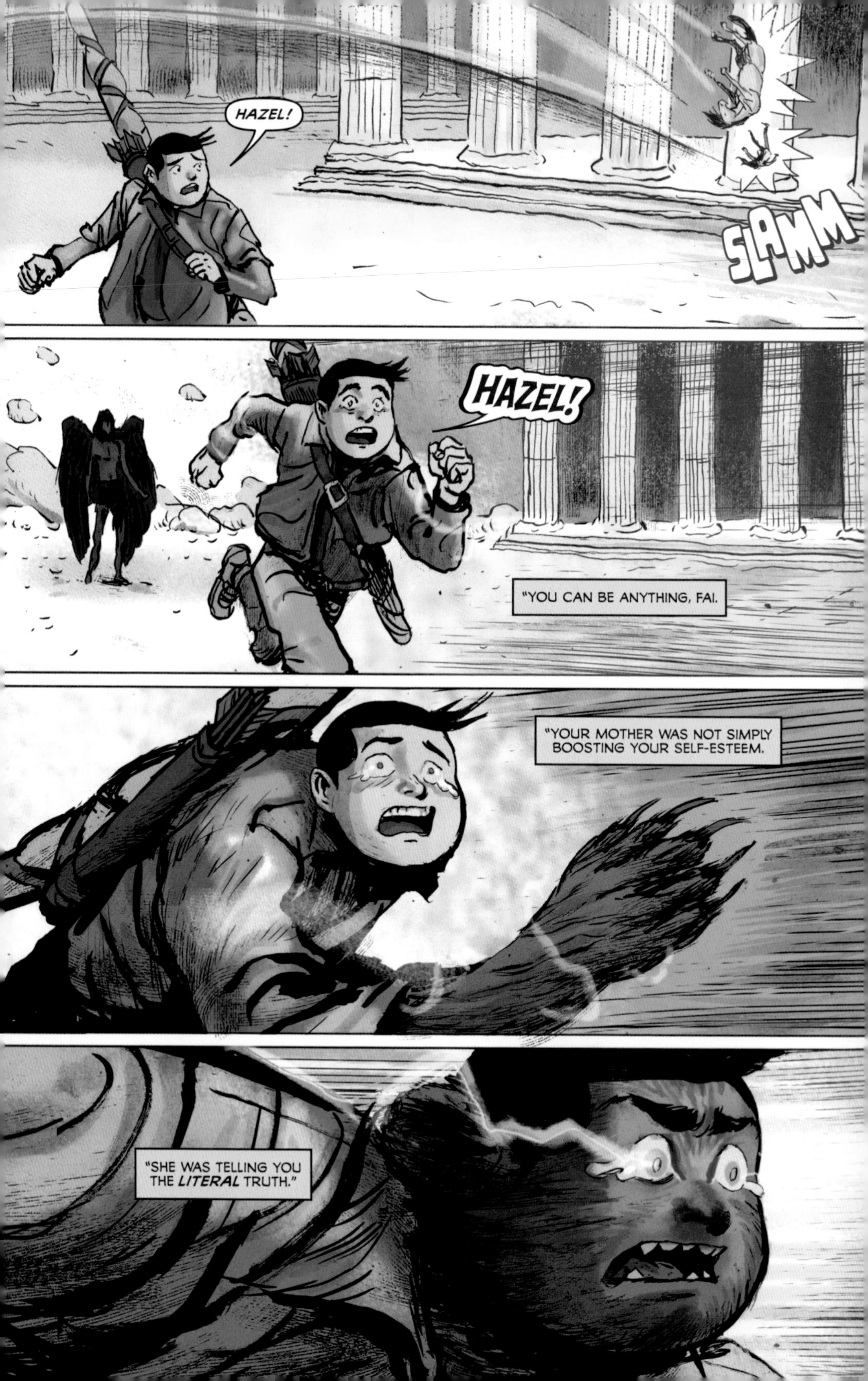
HAZEL!
SLAMM
HAZEL!
"YOU CAN BE ANYTHING, FAI.
"YOUR MOTHER WAS NOT SIMPLY BOOSTING YOUR SELF-ESTEEM.
"SHE WAS TELLING YOU THE *LITERAL* TRUTH."

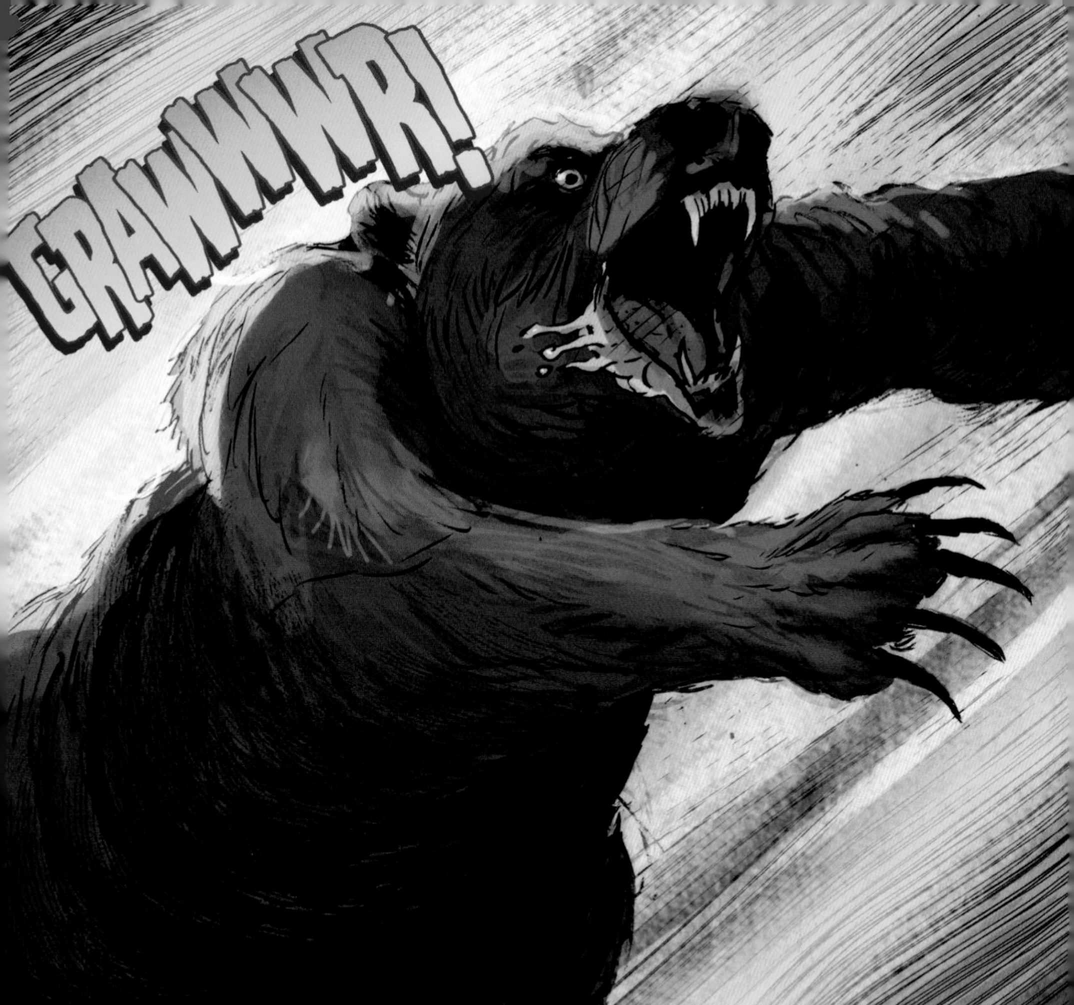
GRAWWWR!

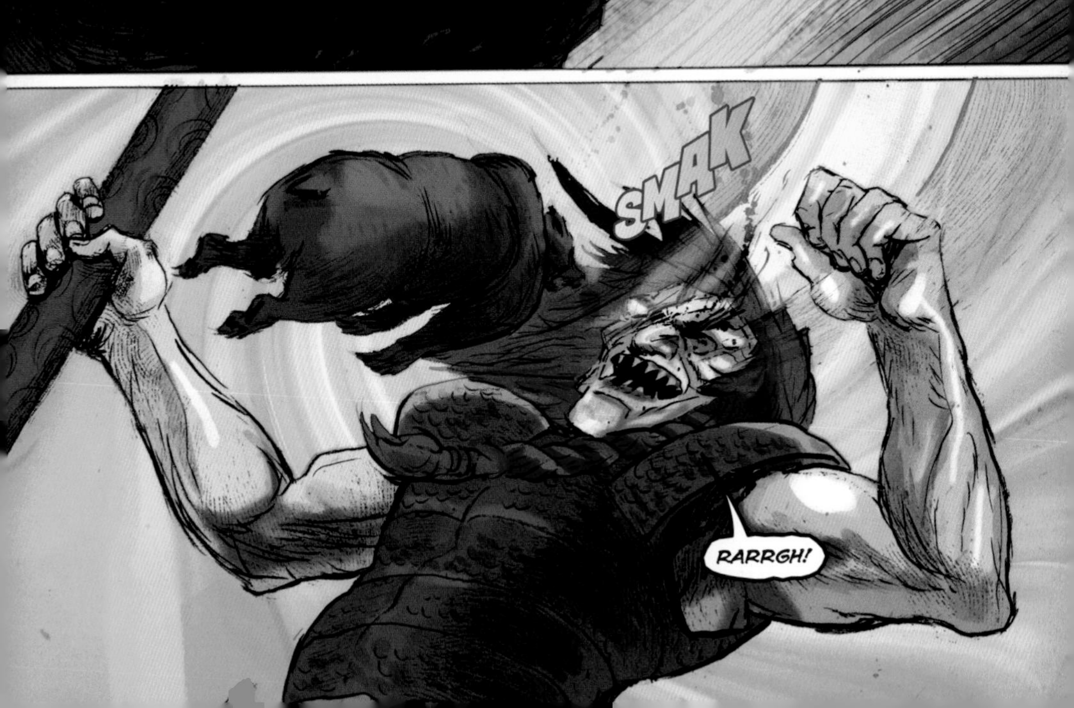
SMAK
RARRGH!

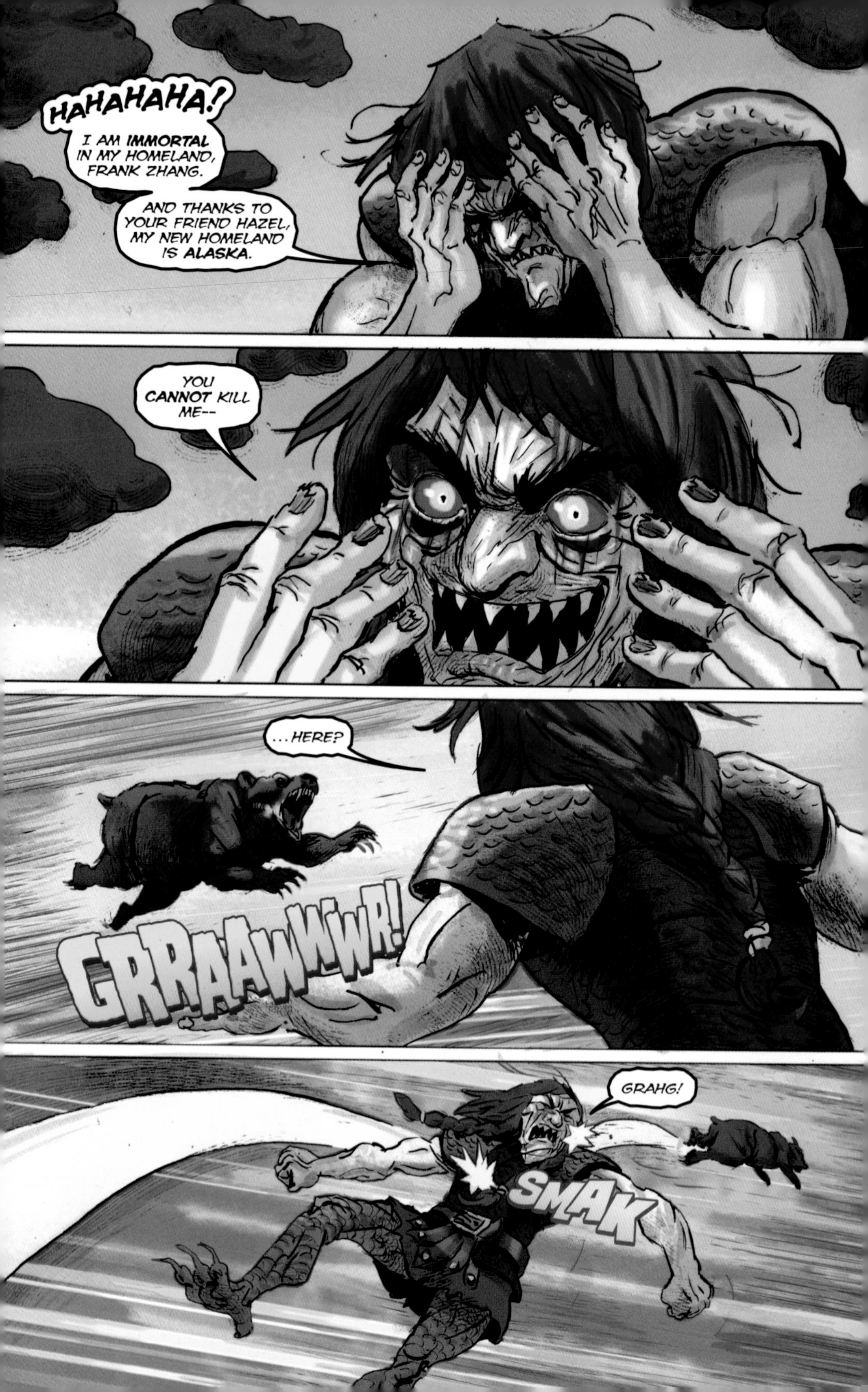
HAHAHAHA!
I AM IMMORTAL IN MY HOMELAND, FRANK ZHANG.
AND THANKS TO YOUR FRIEND HAZEL, MY NEW HOMELAND IS ALASKA.
YOU CANNOT KILL ME--
...HERE?
GRRAAWWWR!
GRAHG!
SMAK

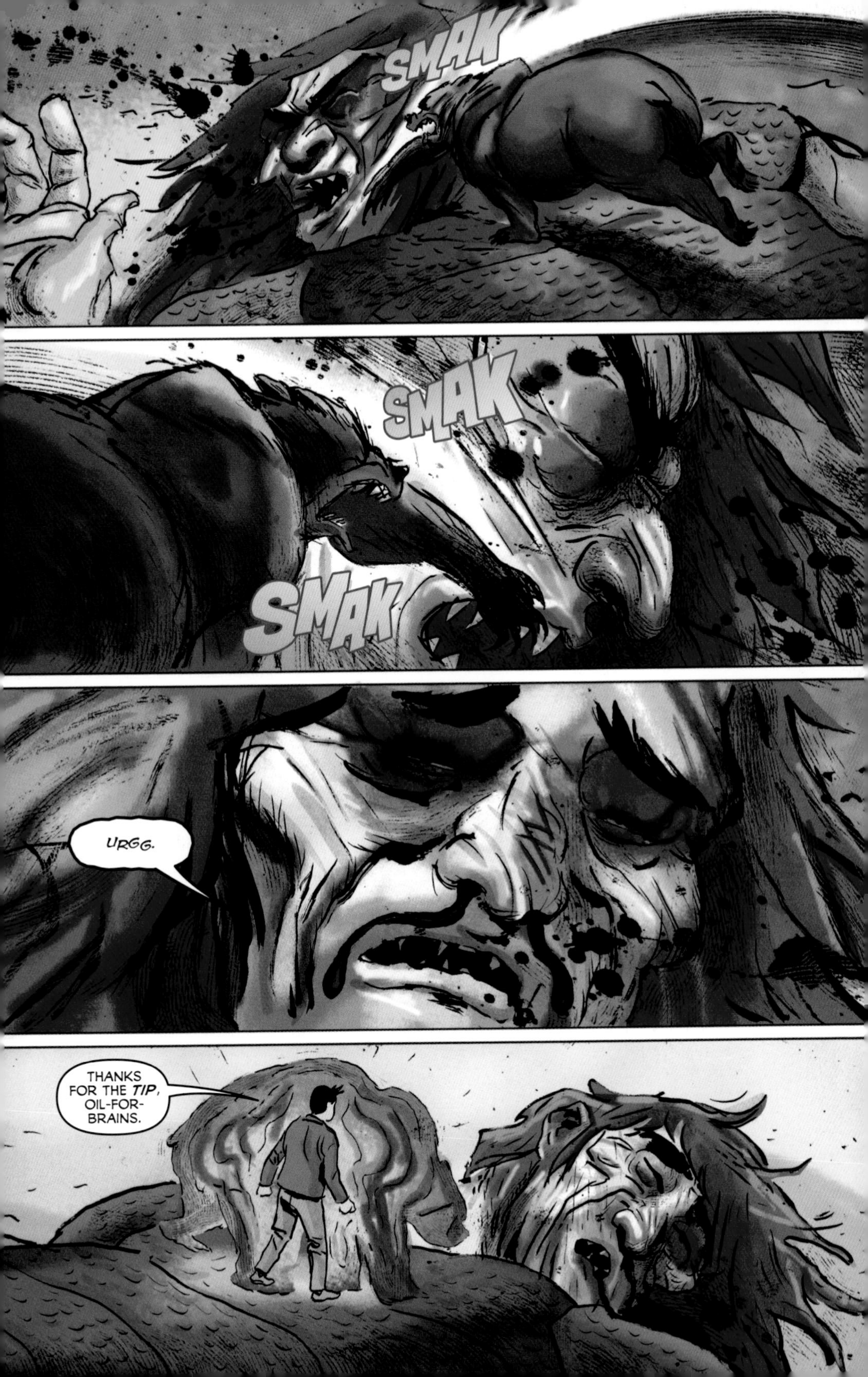
SMAK
SMAK
SMAK
URGG.
THANKS FOR THE *TIP*, OIL-FOR-BRAINS.

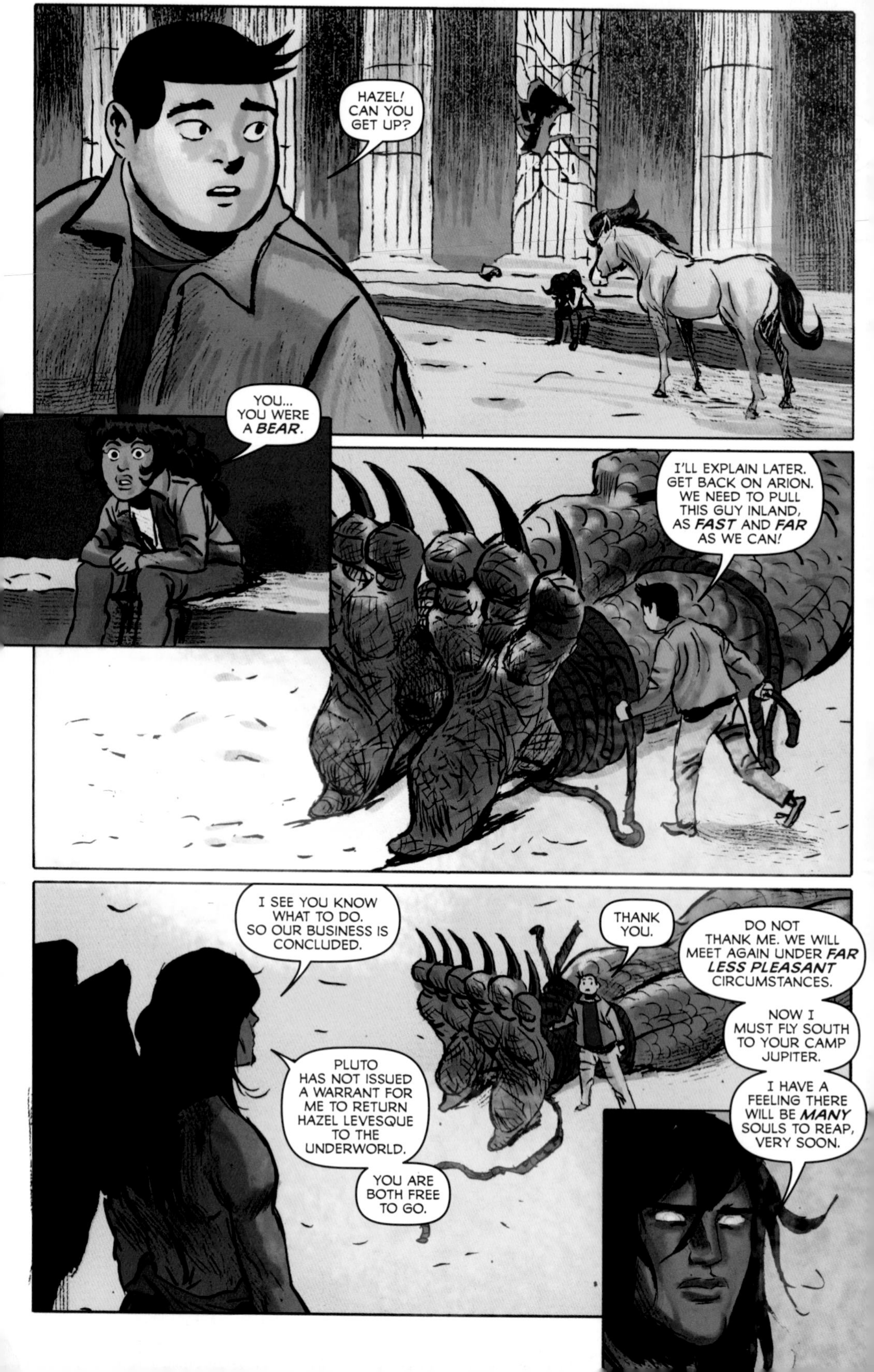
HAZEL! CAN YOU GET UP?
YOU... YOU WERE A BEAR.
I'LL EXPLAIN LATER. GET BACK ON ARION. WE NEED TO PULL THIS GUY INLAND, AS FAST AND FAR AS WE CAN!
I SEE YOU KNOW WHAT TO DO. SO OUR BUSINESS IS CONCLUDED.
PLUTO HAS NOT ISSUED A WARRANT FOR ME TO RETURN HAZEL LEVESQUE TO THE UNDERWORLD.
YOU ARE BOTH FREE TO GO.
THANK YOU.
DO NOT THANK ME. WE WILL MEET AGAIN UNDER FAR LESS PLEASANT CIRCUMSTANCES.
NOW I MUST FLY SOUTH TO YOUR CAMP JUPITER.
I HAVE A FEELING THERE WILL BE MANY SOULS TO REAP, VERY SOON.

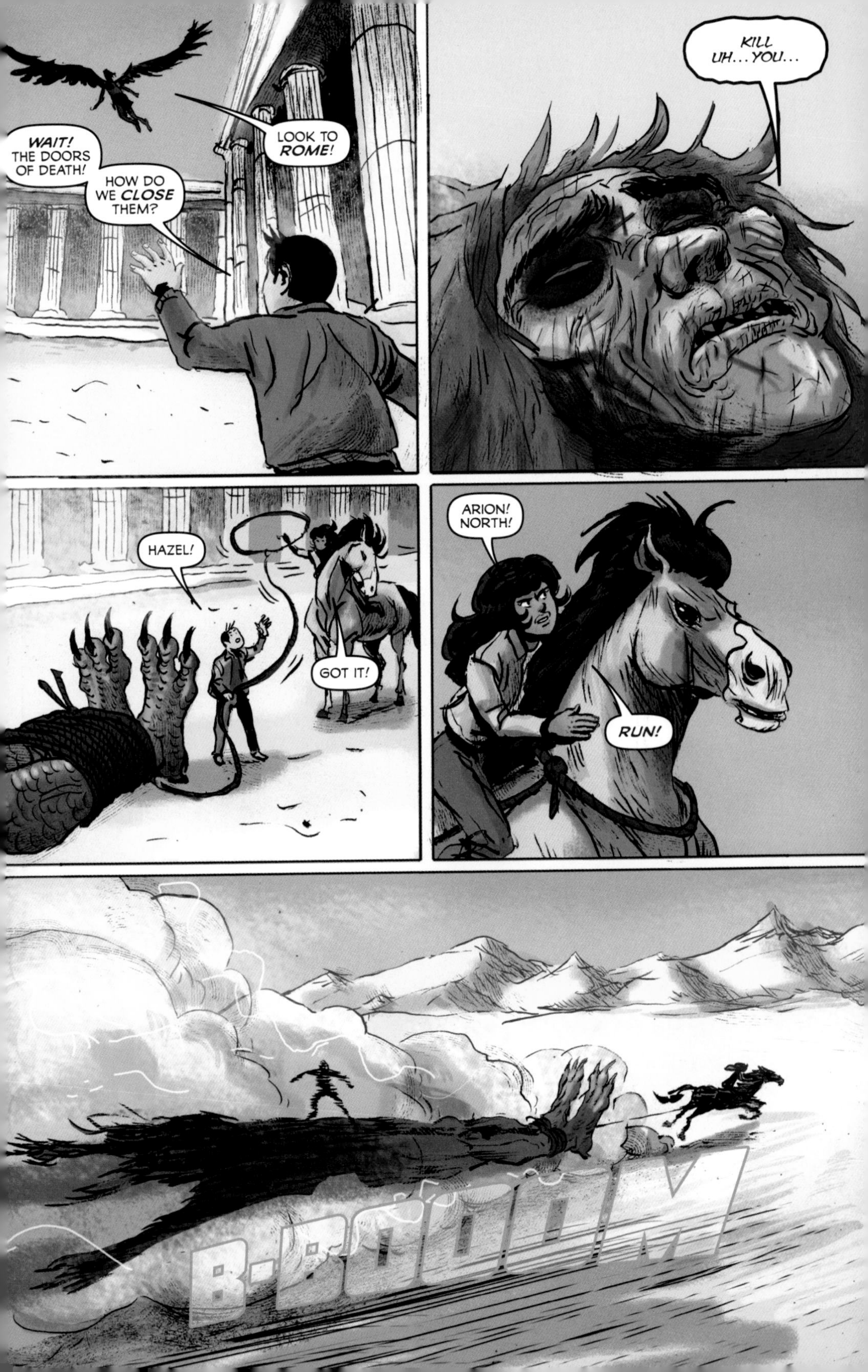
WAIT! THE DOORS OF DEATH!
HOW DO WE CLOSE THEM?
LOOK TO ROME!
KILL UH... YOU...
HAZEL!
GOT IT!
ARION! NORTH!
RUN!
B-BOOM

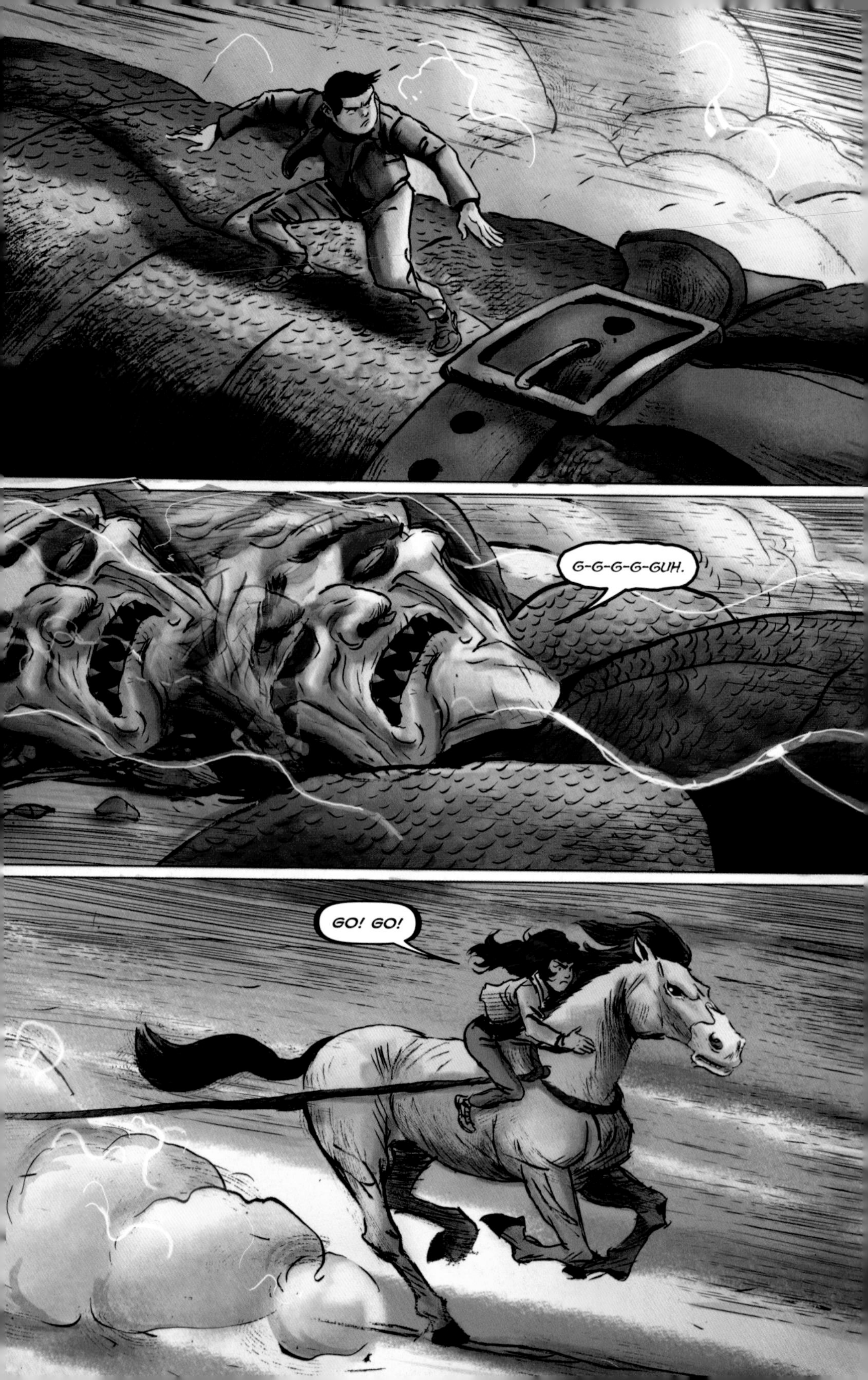
G-G-G-G-GUH.
GO! GO!

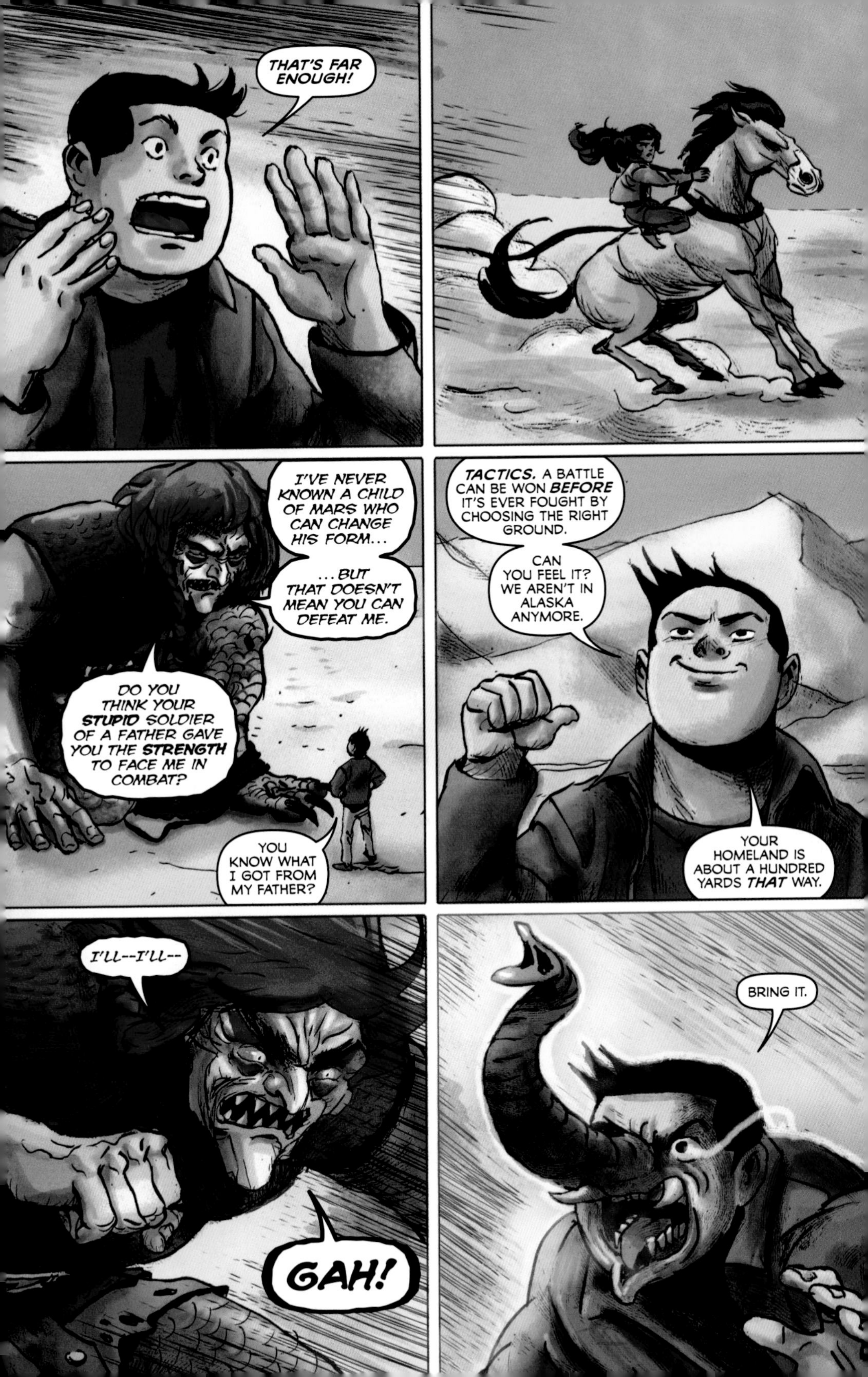
THAT'S FAR ENOUGH!
I'VE NEVER KNOWN A CHILD OF MARS WHO CAN CHANGE HIS FORM...
...BUT THAT DOESN'T MEAN YOU CAN DEFEAT ME.
DO YOU THINK YOUR STUPID SOLDIER OF A FATHER GAVE YOU THE STRENGTH TO FACE ME IN COMBAT?
YOU KNOW WHAT I GOT FROM MY FATHER?
TACTICS. A BATTLE CAN BE WON BEFORE IT'S EVER FOUGHT BY CHOOSING THE RIGHT GROUND.
CAN YOU FEEL IT? WE AREN'T IN ALASKA ANYMORE.
YOUR HOMELAND IS ABOUT A HUNDRED YARDS THAT WAY.
I'LL--I'LL--
GAH!
BRING IT.

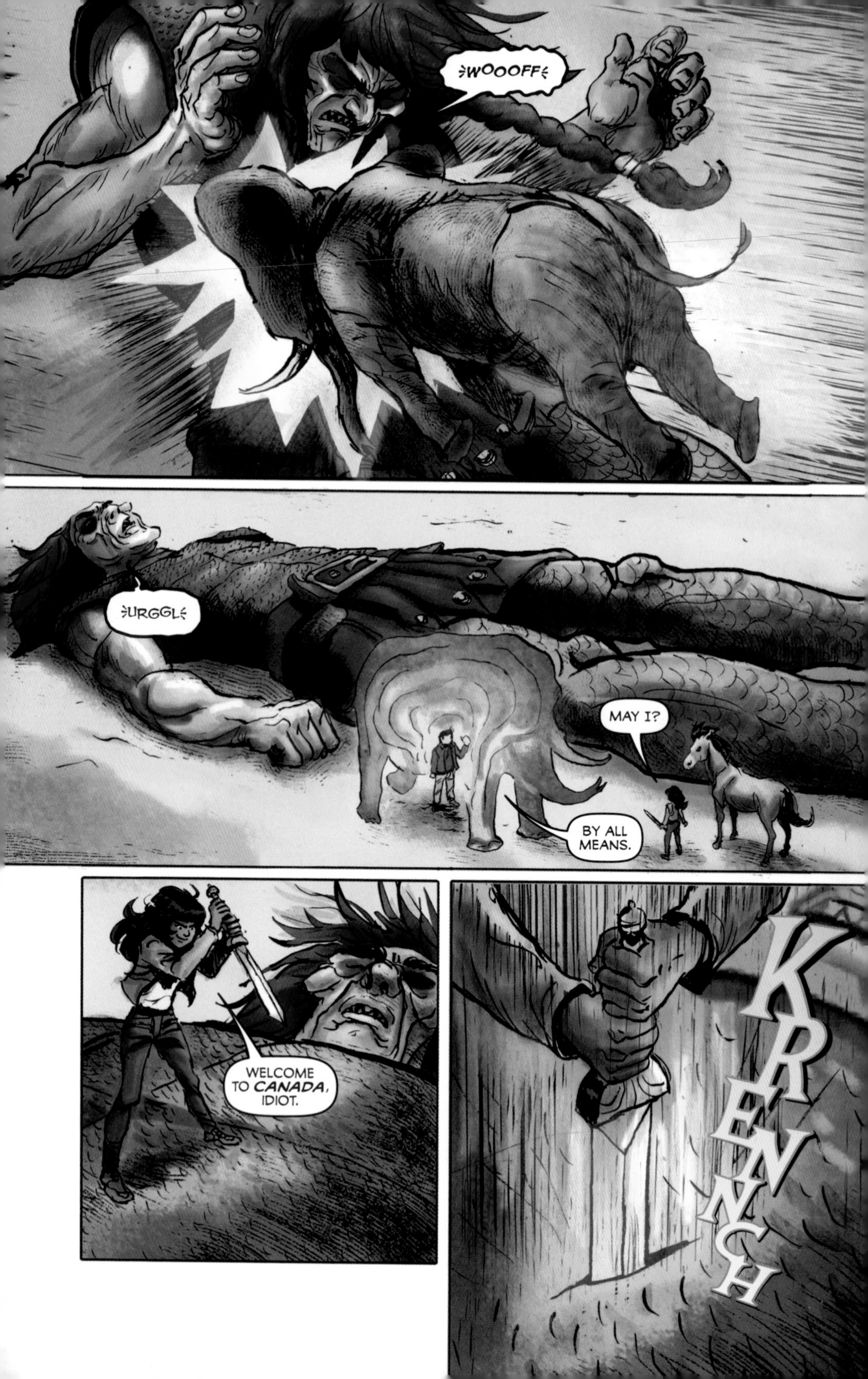
WOOOFF
URGGL
MAY I?
BY ALL MEANS.
WELCOME TO *CANADA*, IDIOT.
KRENNCH

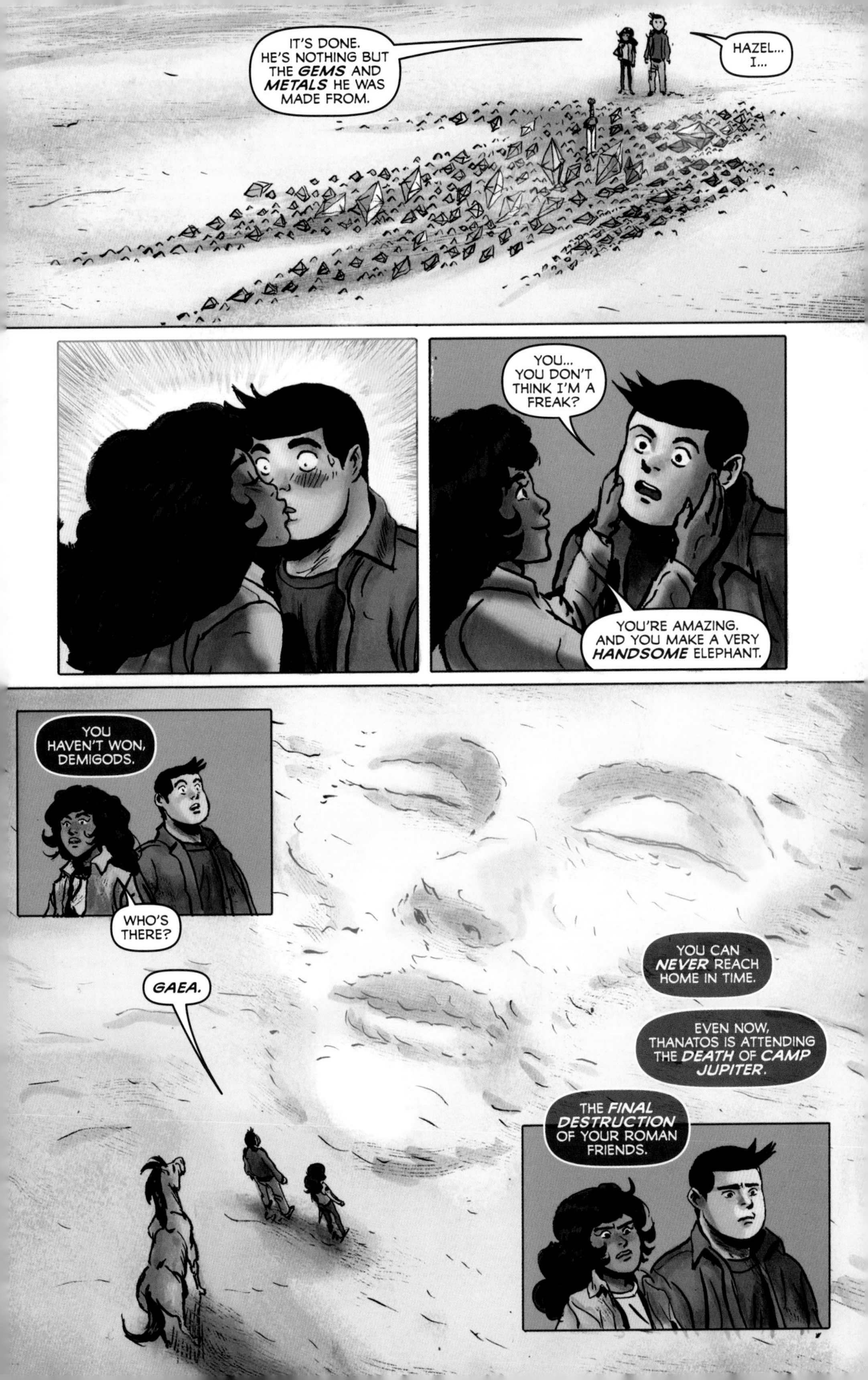
IT'S DONE. HE'S NOTHING BUT THE GEMS AND METALS HE WAS MADE FROM.
HAZEL... I...
YOU... YOU DON'T THINK I'M A FREAK?
YOU'RE AMAZING. AND YOU MAKE A VERY HANDSOME ELEPHANT.
YOU HAVEN'T WON, DEMIGODS.
WHO'S THERE?
GAEA.
YOU CAN NEVER REACH HOME IN TIME.
EVEN NOW, THANATOS IS ATTENDING THE DEATH OF CAMP JUPITER.
THE FINAL DESTRUCTION OF YOUR ROMAN FRIENDS.

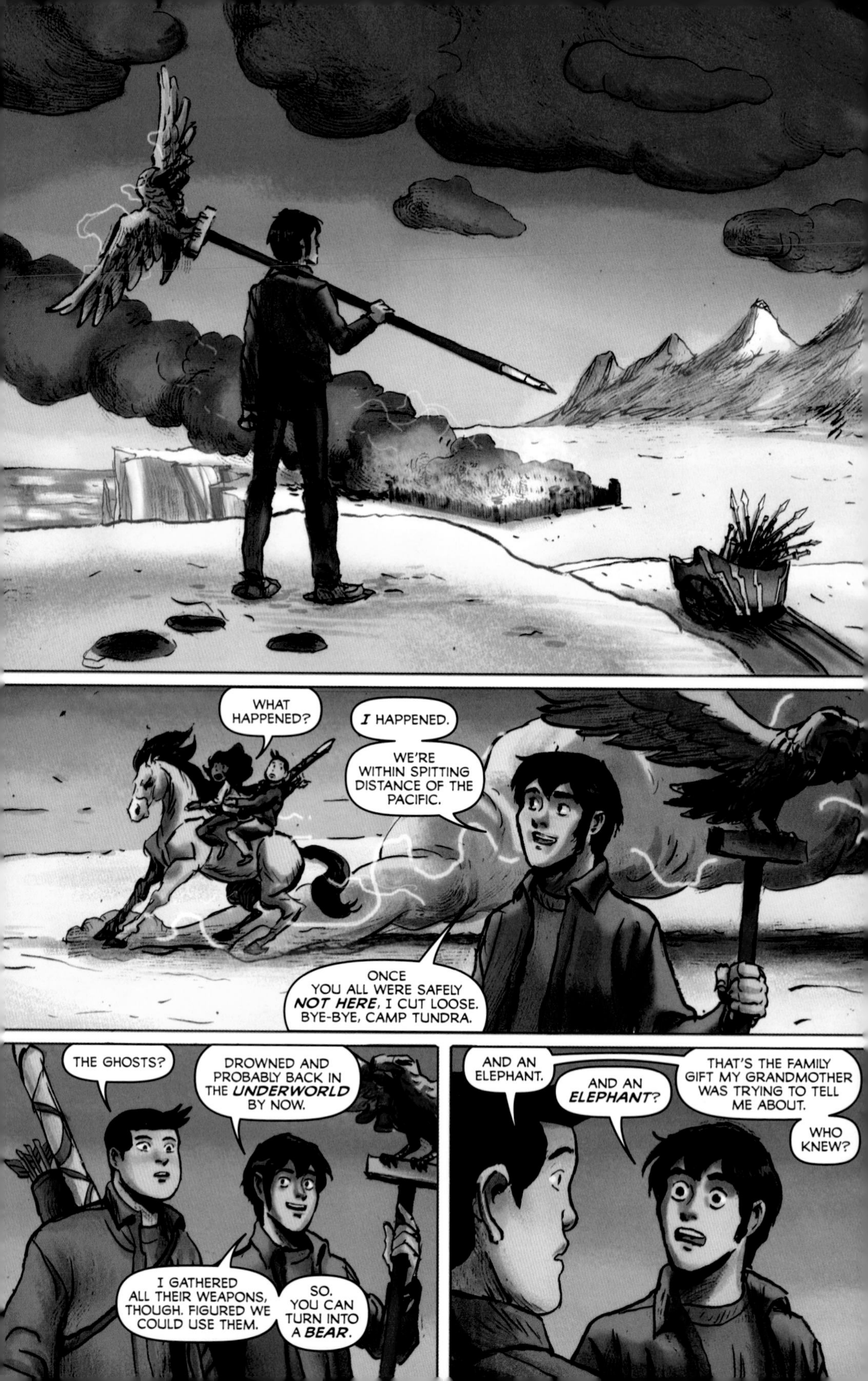
WHAT HAPPENED?
I HAPPENED.
WE'RE WITHIN SPITTING DISTANCE OF THE PACIFIC.
ONCE YOU ALL WERE SAFELY NOT HERE, I CUT LOOSE. BYE-BYE, CAMP TUNDRA.
THE GHOSTS?
DROWNED AND PROBABLY BACK IN THE UNDERWORLD BY NOW.
I GATHERED ALL THEIR WEAPONS, THOUGH. FIGURED WE COULD USE THEM.
SO. YOU CAN TURN INTO A BEAR.
AND AN ELEPHANT.
AND AN ELEPHANT?
THAT'S THE FAMILY GIFT MY GRANDMOTHER WAS TRYING TO TELL ME ABOUT.
WHO KNEW?

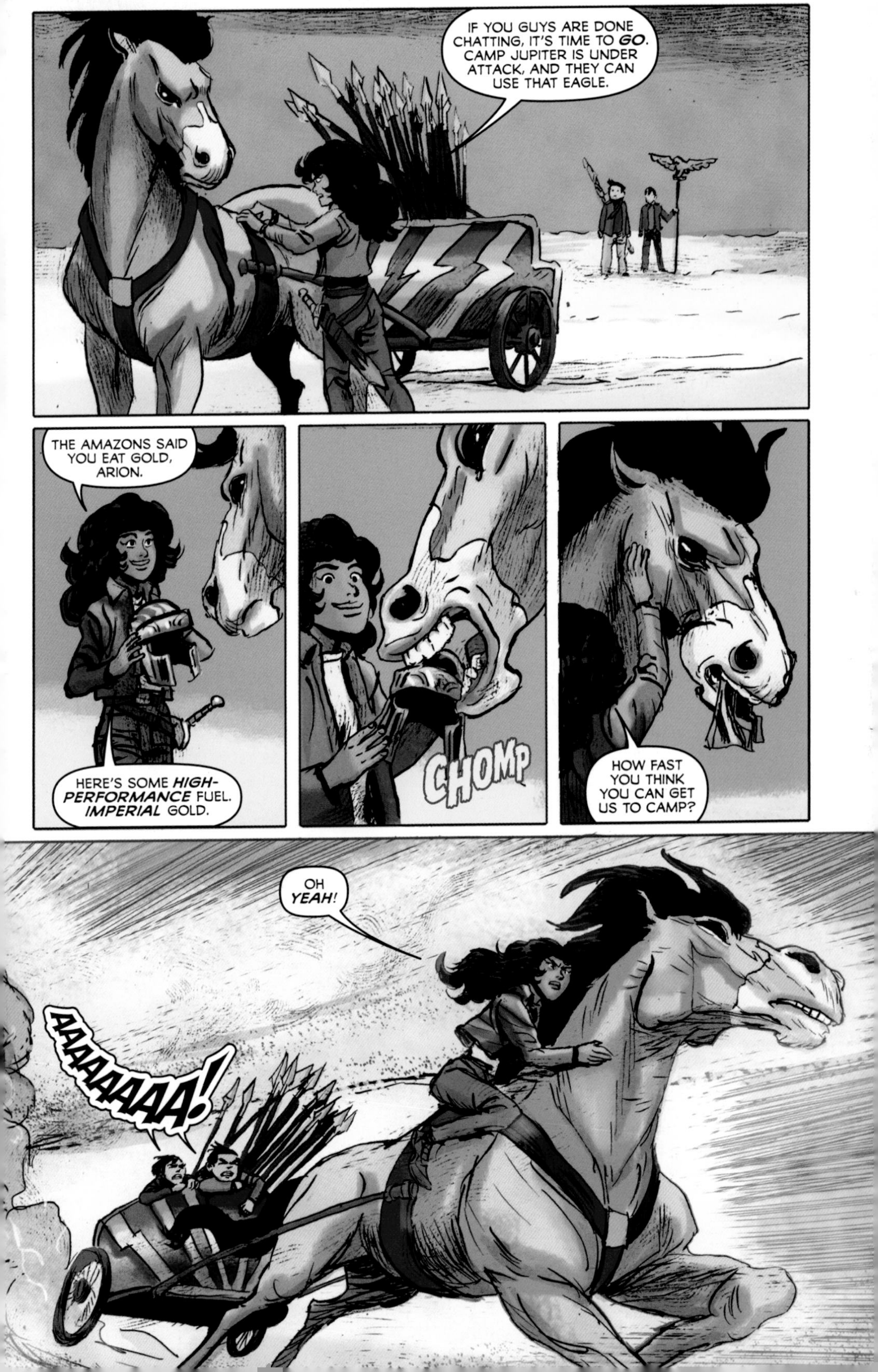
IF YOU GUYS ARE DONE CHATTING, IT'S TIME TO *GO*. CAMP JUPITER IS UNDER ATTACK, AND THEY CAN USE THAT EAGLE.
THE AMAZONS SAID YOU EAT GOLD, ARION.
HERE'S SOME *HIGH-PERFORMANCE* FUEL. *IMPERIAL* GOLD.
CHOMP
HOW FAST YOU THINK YOU CAN GET US TO CAMP?
OH *YEAH*!
AAAAAAAA!

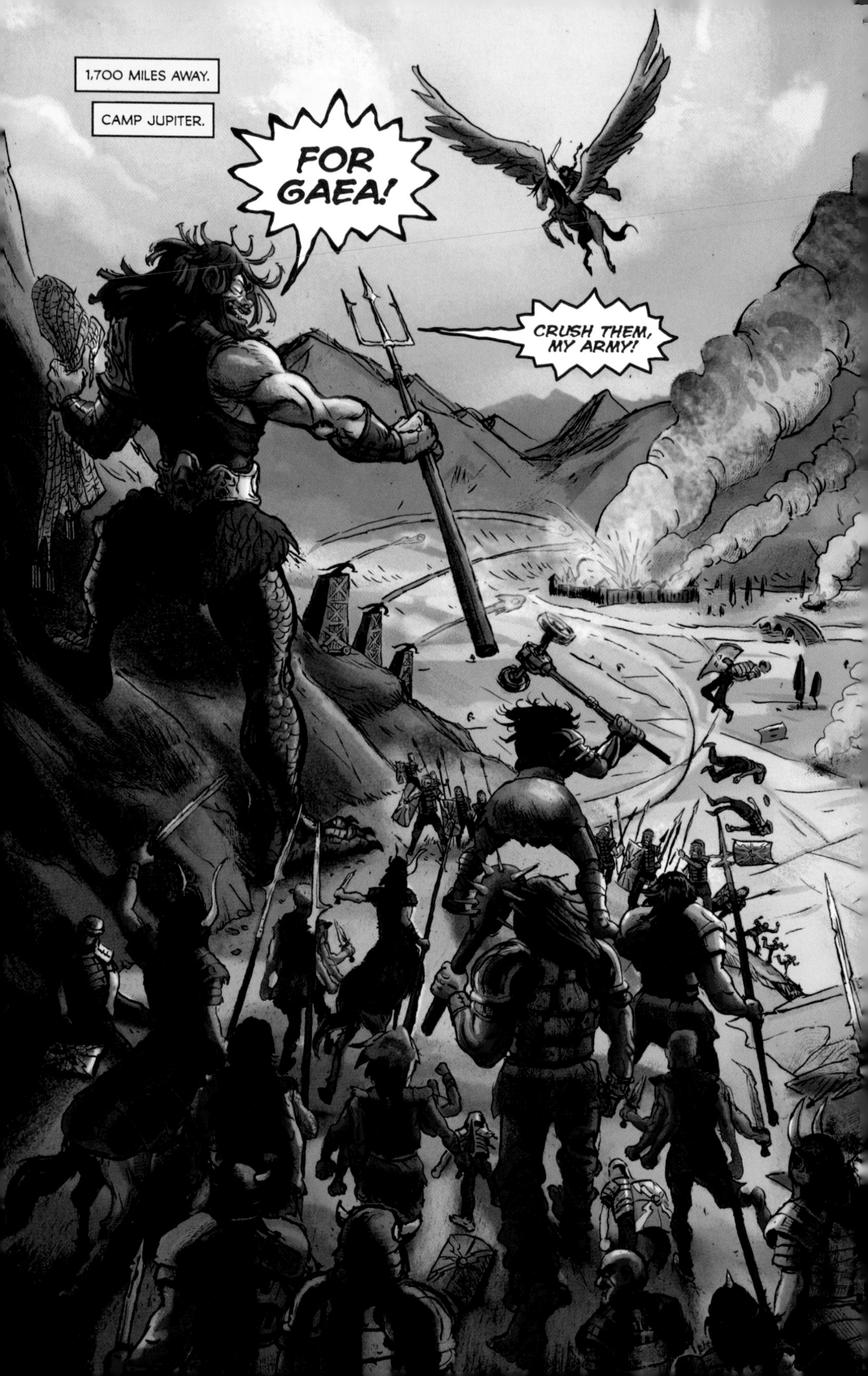
1,700 MILES AWAY.
CAMP JUPITER.
FOR GAEA!
CRUSH THEM, MY ARMY!

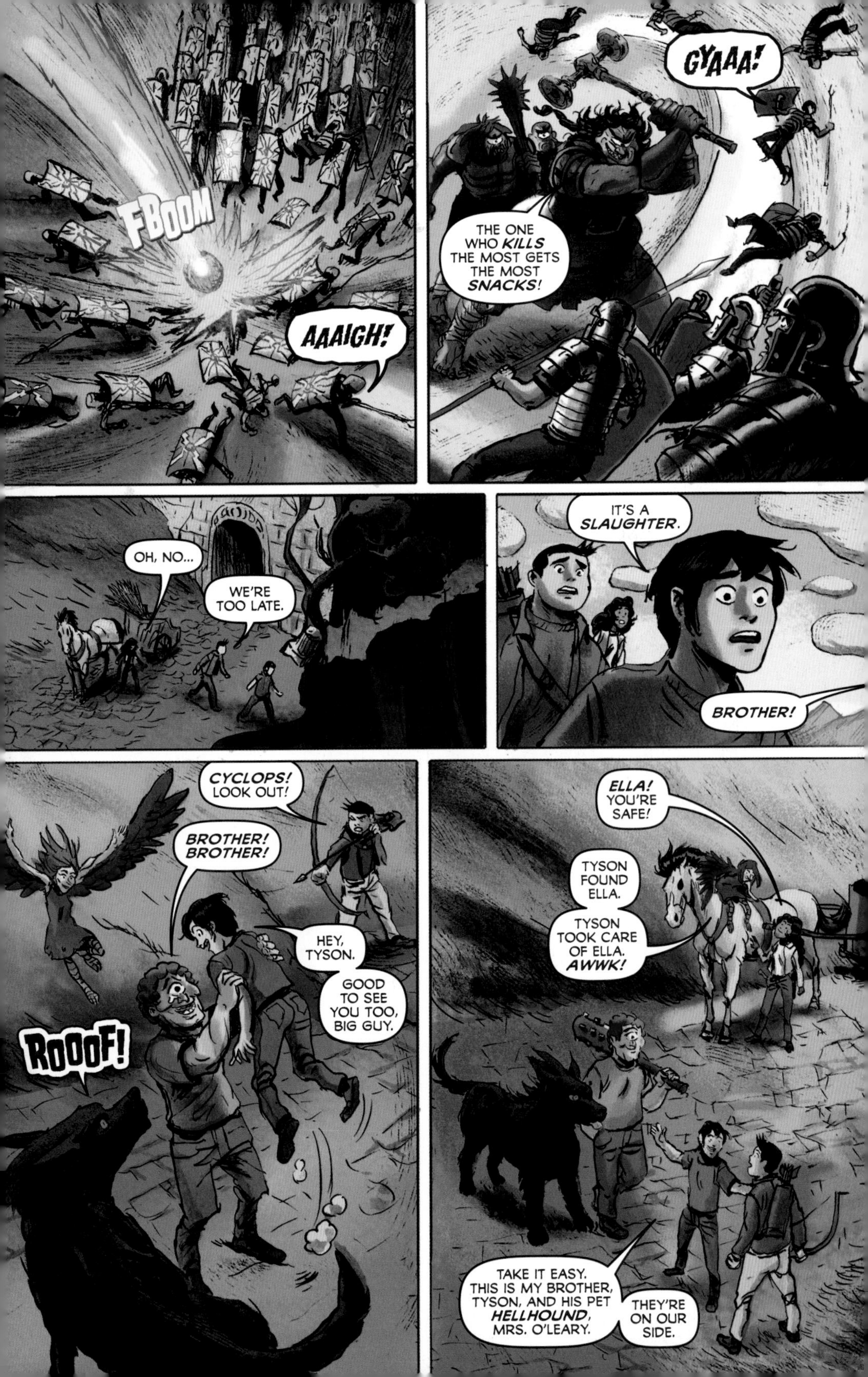
FBOOM
AAAIGH!
GYAAA!
THE ONE WHO KILLS THE MOST GETS THE MOST SNACKS!
OH, NO...
WE'RE TOO LATE.
IT'S A SLAUGHTER.
BROTHER!
CYCLOPS! LOOK OUT!
BROTHER! BROTHER!
HEY, TYSON.
GOOD TO SEE YOU TOO, BIG GUY.
ROOOF!
ELLA! YOU'RE SAFE!
TYSON FOUND ELLA.
TYSON TOOK CARE OF ELLA. AWWK!
TAKE IT EASY. THIS IS MY BROTHER, TYSON, AND HIS PET HELLHOUND, MRS. O'LEARY.
THEY'RE ON OUR SIDE.

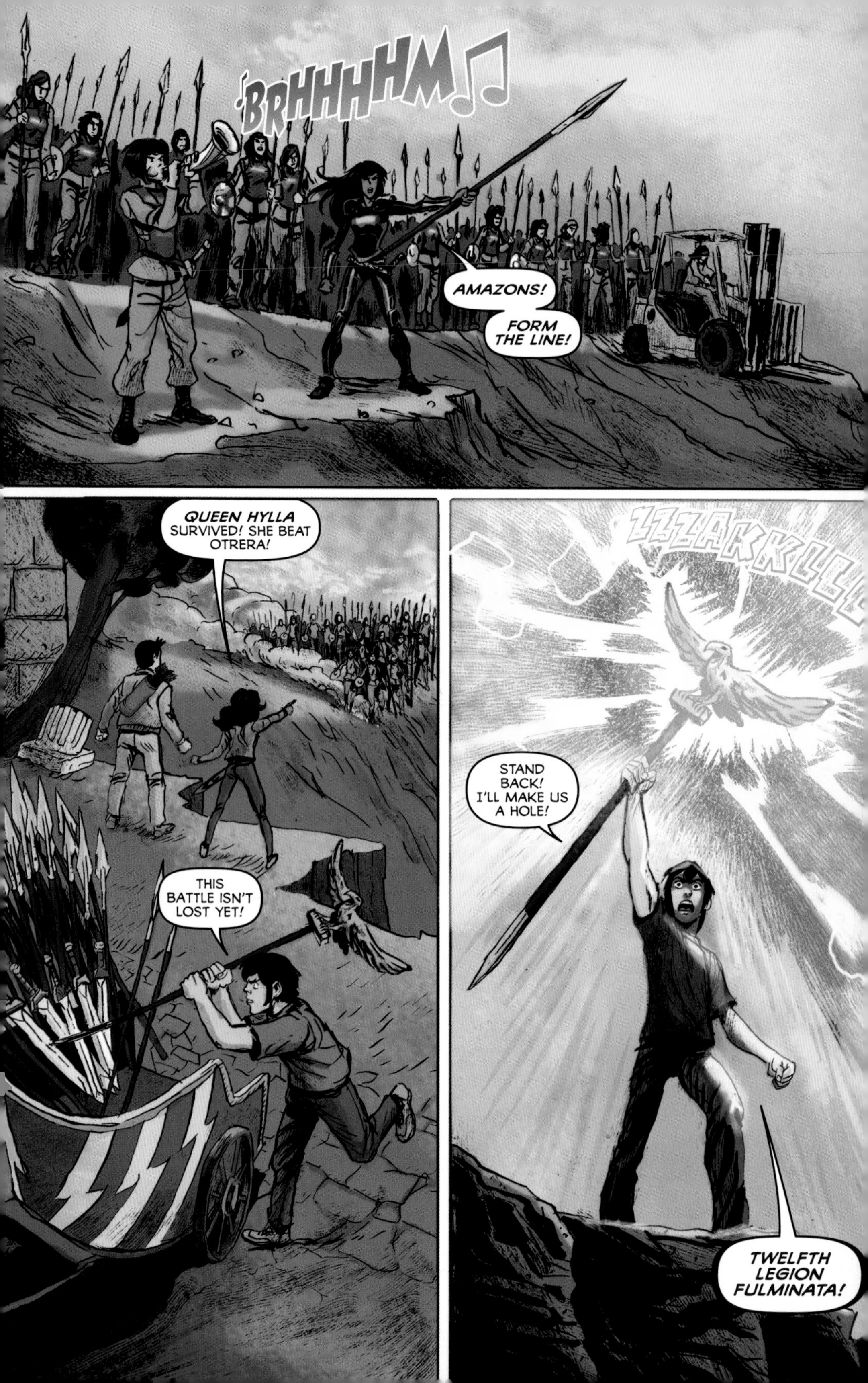
BRHHHHM
AMAZONS!
FORM THE LINE!
QUEEN HYLLA SURVIVED! SHE BEAT OTRERA!
THIS BATTLE ISN'T LOST YET!
STAND BACK! I'LL MAKE US A HOLE!
TWELFTH LEGION FULMINATA!

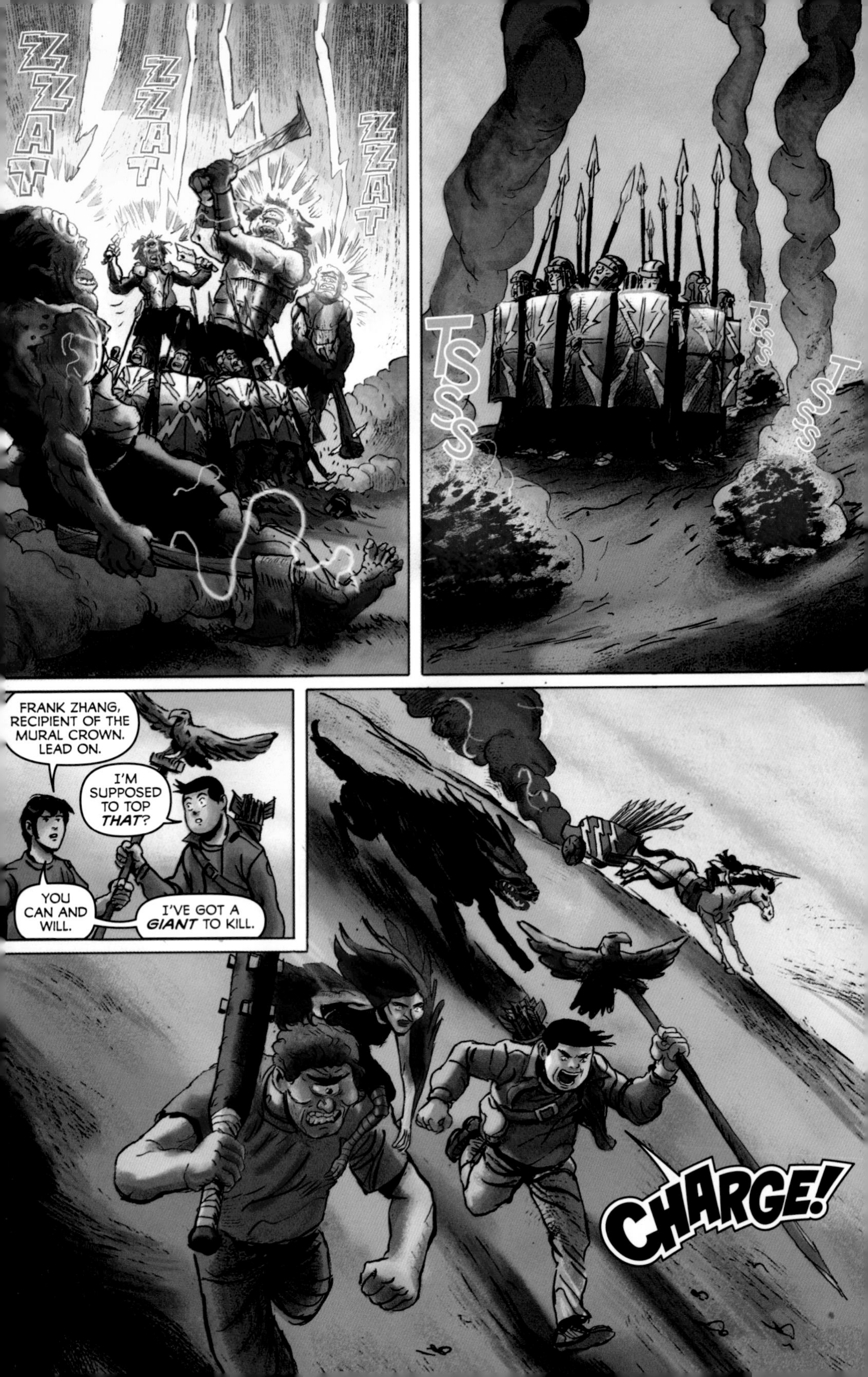
ZZZAT
ZZZAT
ZZZAT
TSSS
TSSS
TSSS
FRANK ZHANG, RECIPIENT OF THE MURAL CROWN. LEAD ON.
I'M SUPPOSED TO TOP *THAT*?
YOU CAN AND WILL.
I'VE GOT A *GIANT* TO KILL.
CHARGE!

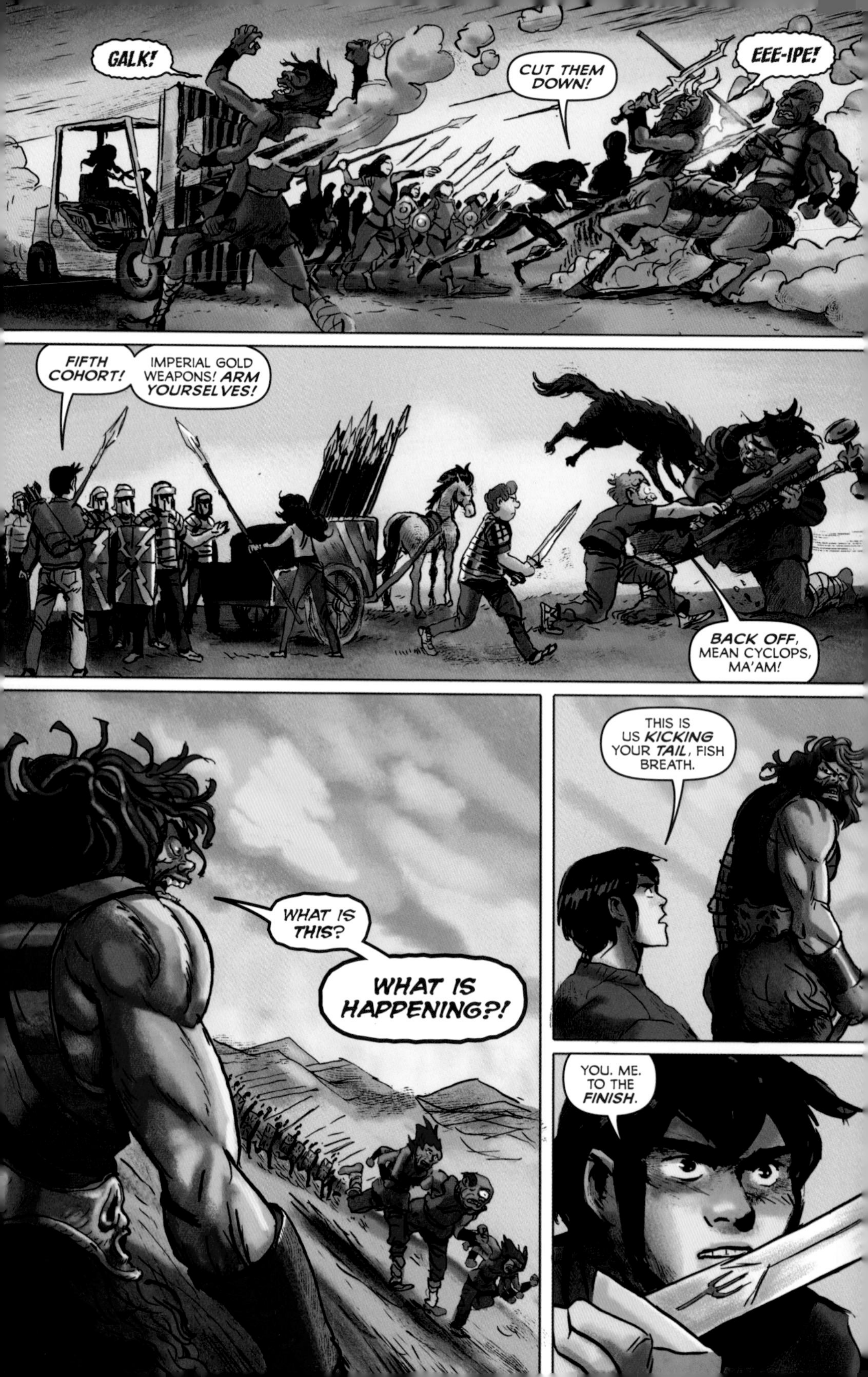
GALK!
CUT THEM DOWN!
EEE-IPE!
FIFTH COHORT!
IMPERIAL GOLD WEAPONS! ARM YOURSELVES!
BACK OFF, MEAN CYCLOPS, MA'AM!
WHAT IS THIS?
WHAT IS HAPPENING?!
THIS IS US KICKING YOUR TAIL, FISH BREATH.
YOU. ME. TO THE FINISH.

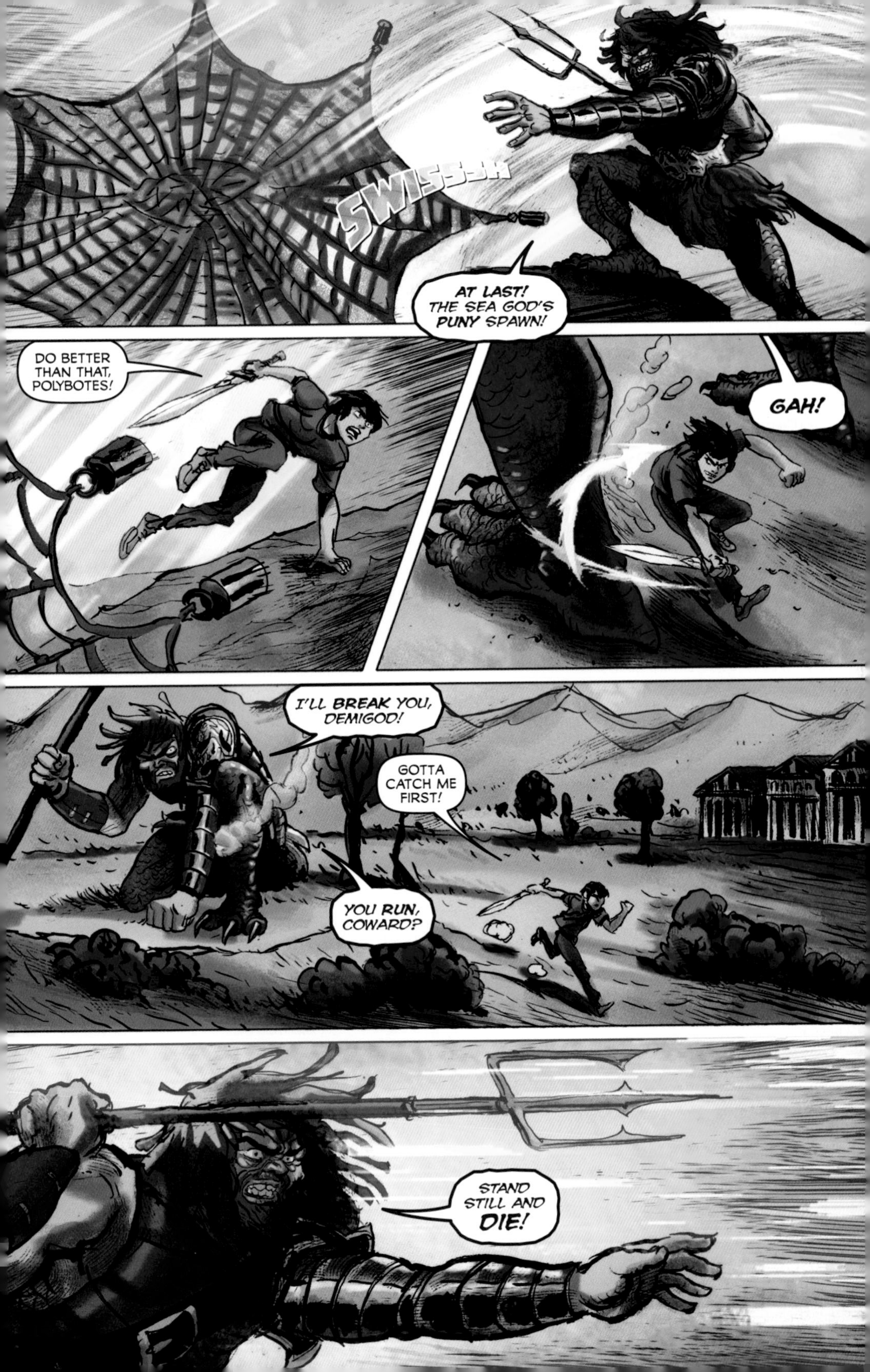
SWISSSH
AT LAST! THE SEA GOD'S PUNY SPAWN!
DO BETTER THAN THAT, POLYBOTES!
GAH!
I'LL BREAK YOU, DEMIGOD!
GOTTA CATCH ME FIRST!
YOU RUN, COWARD?
STAND STILL AND DIE!

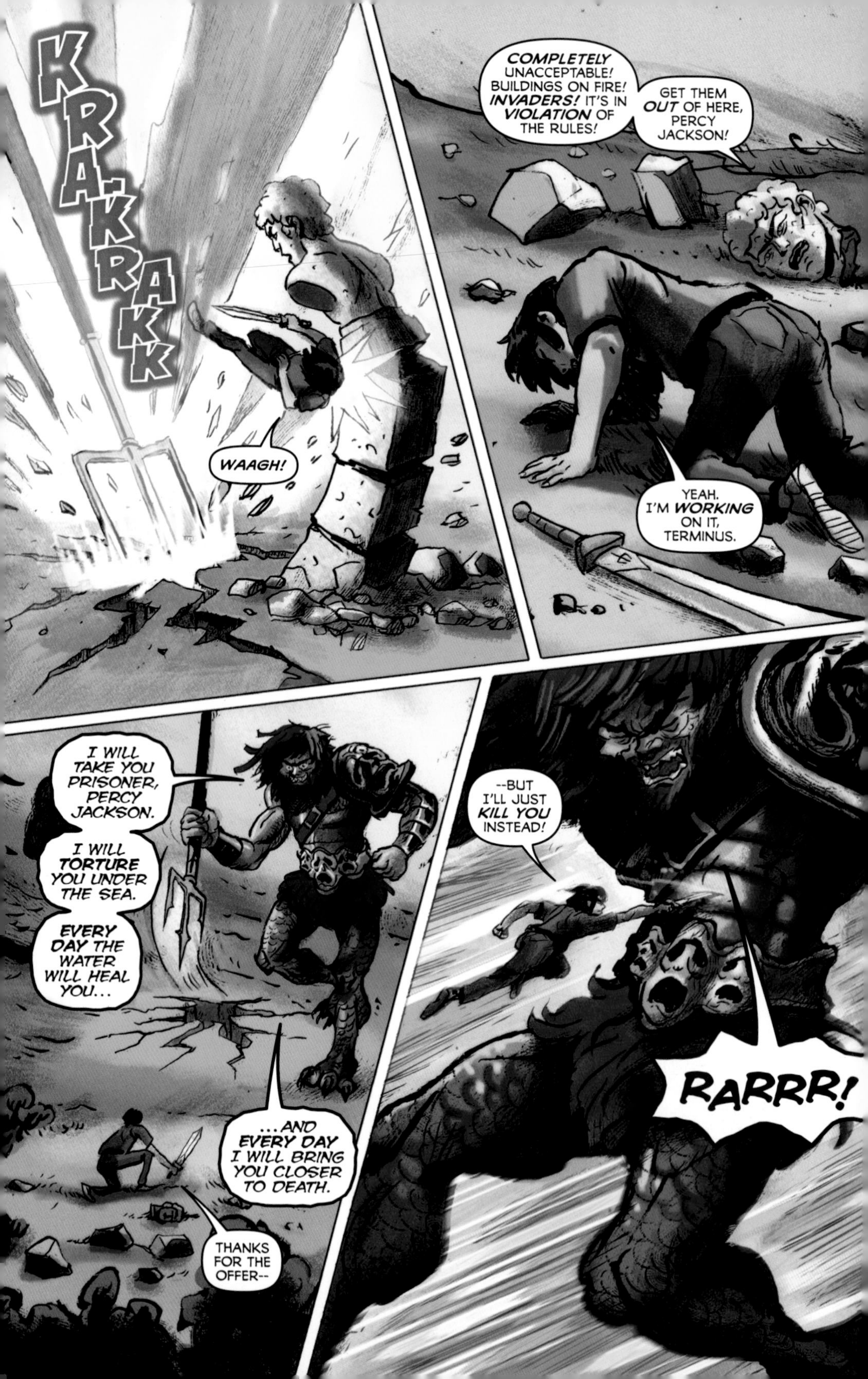
KRA-KRAKK
WAAGH!
COMPLETELY UNACCEPTABLE! BUILDINGS ON FIRE! INVADERS! IT'S IN VIOLATION OF THE RULES!
GET THEM OUT OF HERE, PERCY JACKSON!
YEAH. I'M WORKING ON IT, TERMINUS.
I WILL TAKE YOU PRISONER, PERCY JACKSON.
I WILL TORTURE YOU UNDER THE SEA.
EVERY DAY THE WATER WILL HEAL YOU...
...AND EVERY DAY I WILL BRING YOU CLOSER TO DEATH.
THANKS FOR THE OFFER--
--BUT I'LL JUST KILL YOU INSTEAD!
RARRR!

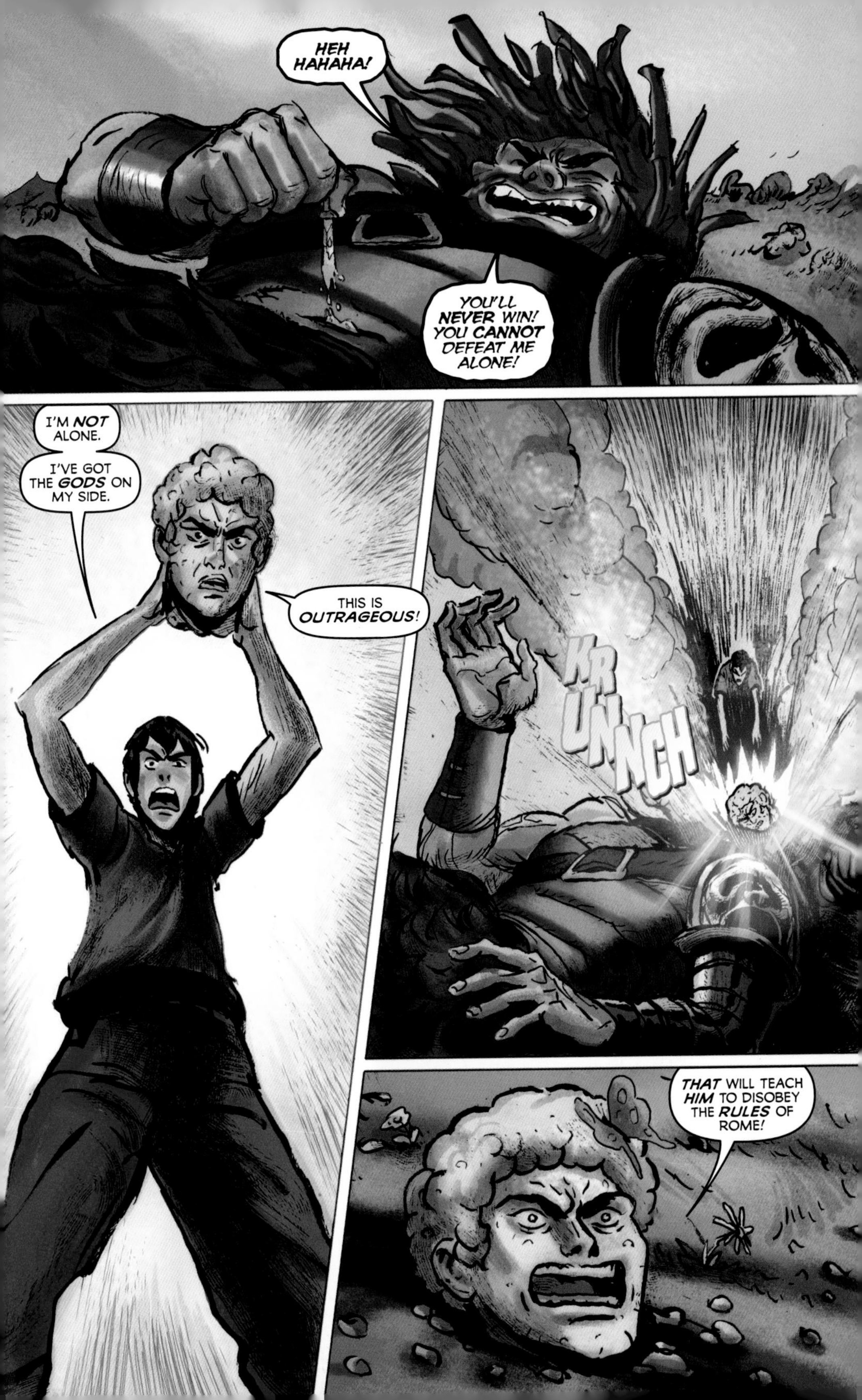
HEH HAHAHA!
YOU'LL NEVER WIN! YOU CANNOT DEFEAT ME ALONE!
I'M NOT ALONE.
I'VE GOT THE GODS ON MY SIDE.
THIS IS OUTRAGEOUS!
KRUNNCH
THAT WILL TEACH HIM TO DISOBEY THE RULES OF ROME!

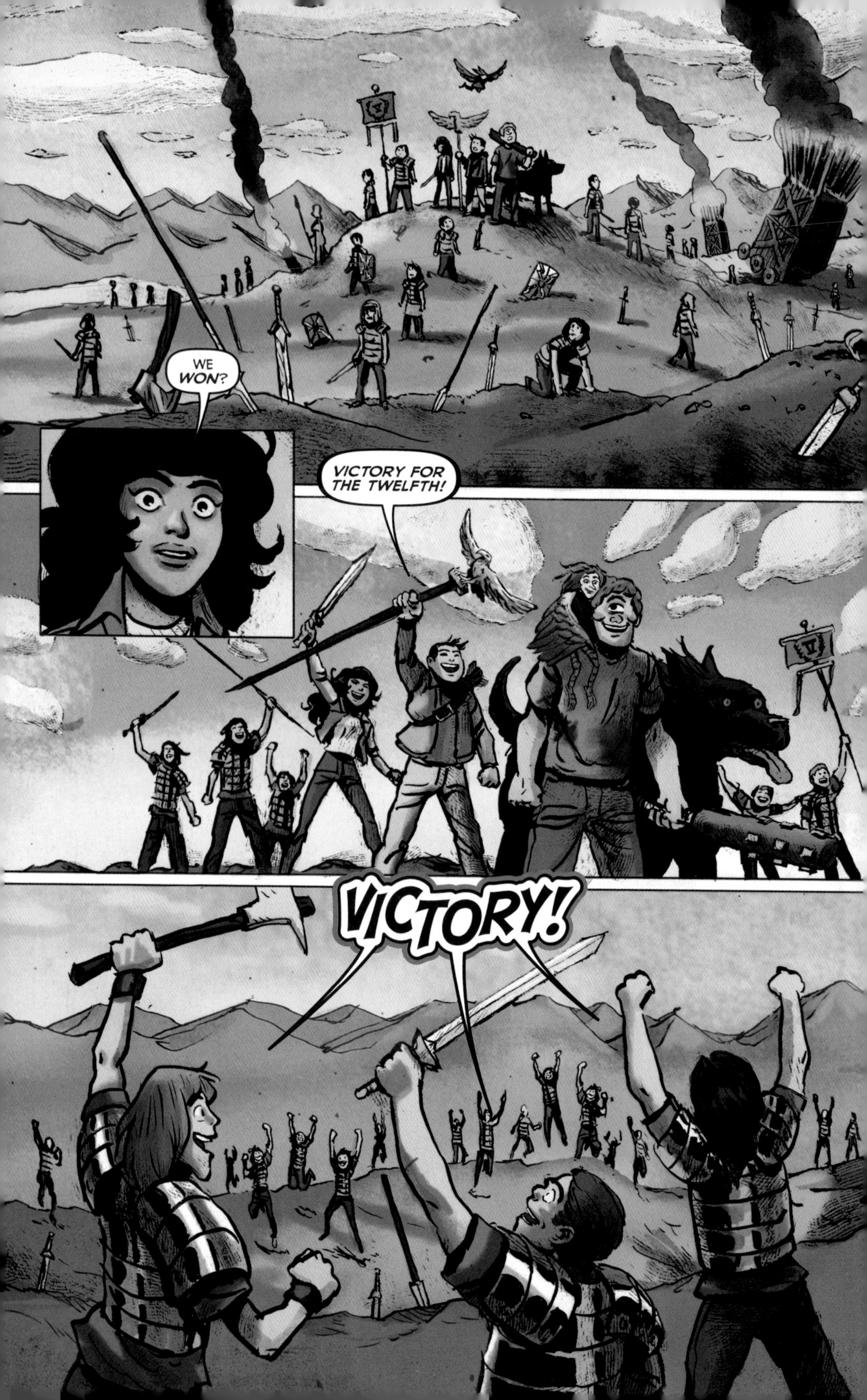
WE WON?
VICTORY FOR THE TWELFTH!
VICTORY!

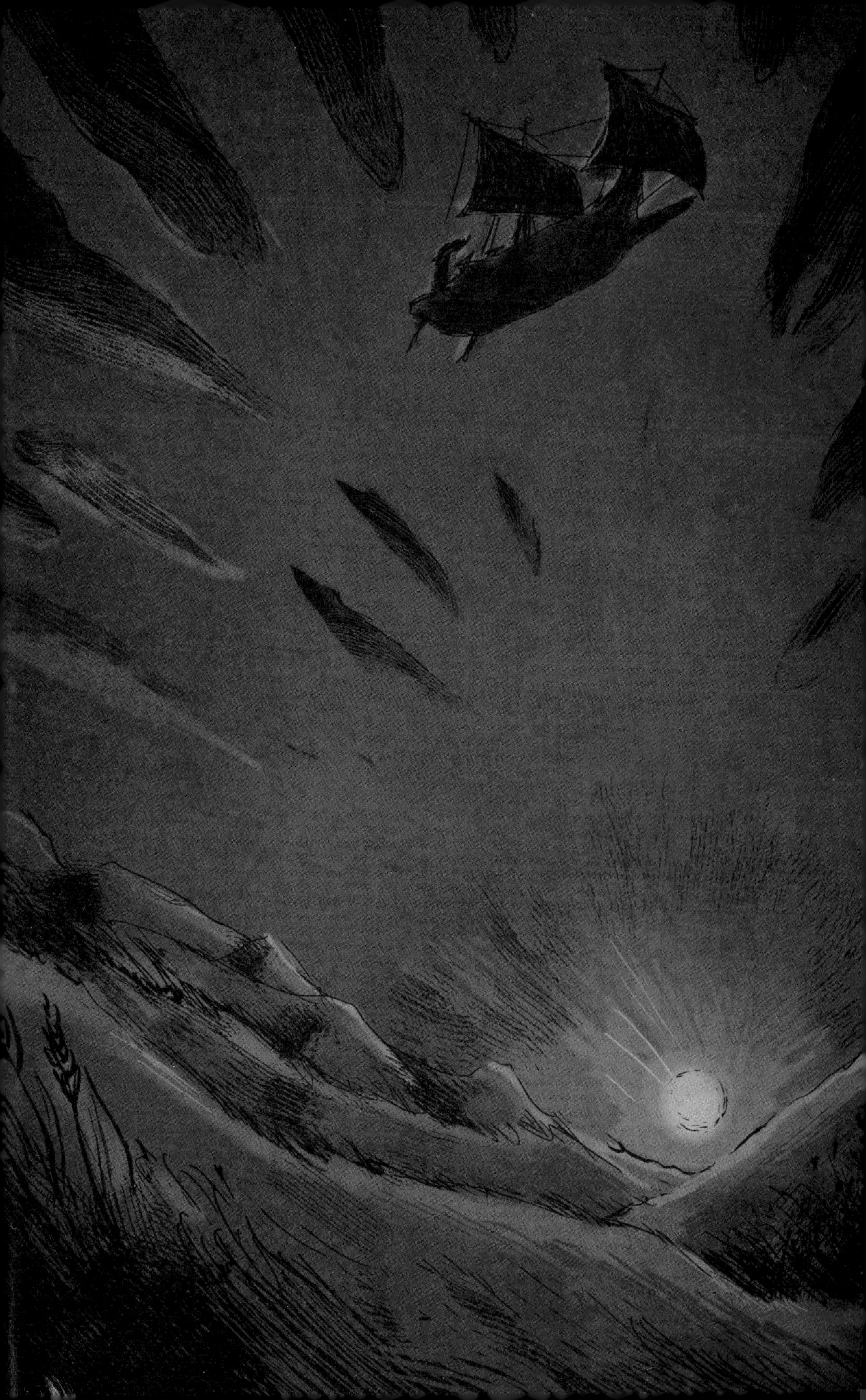

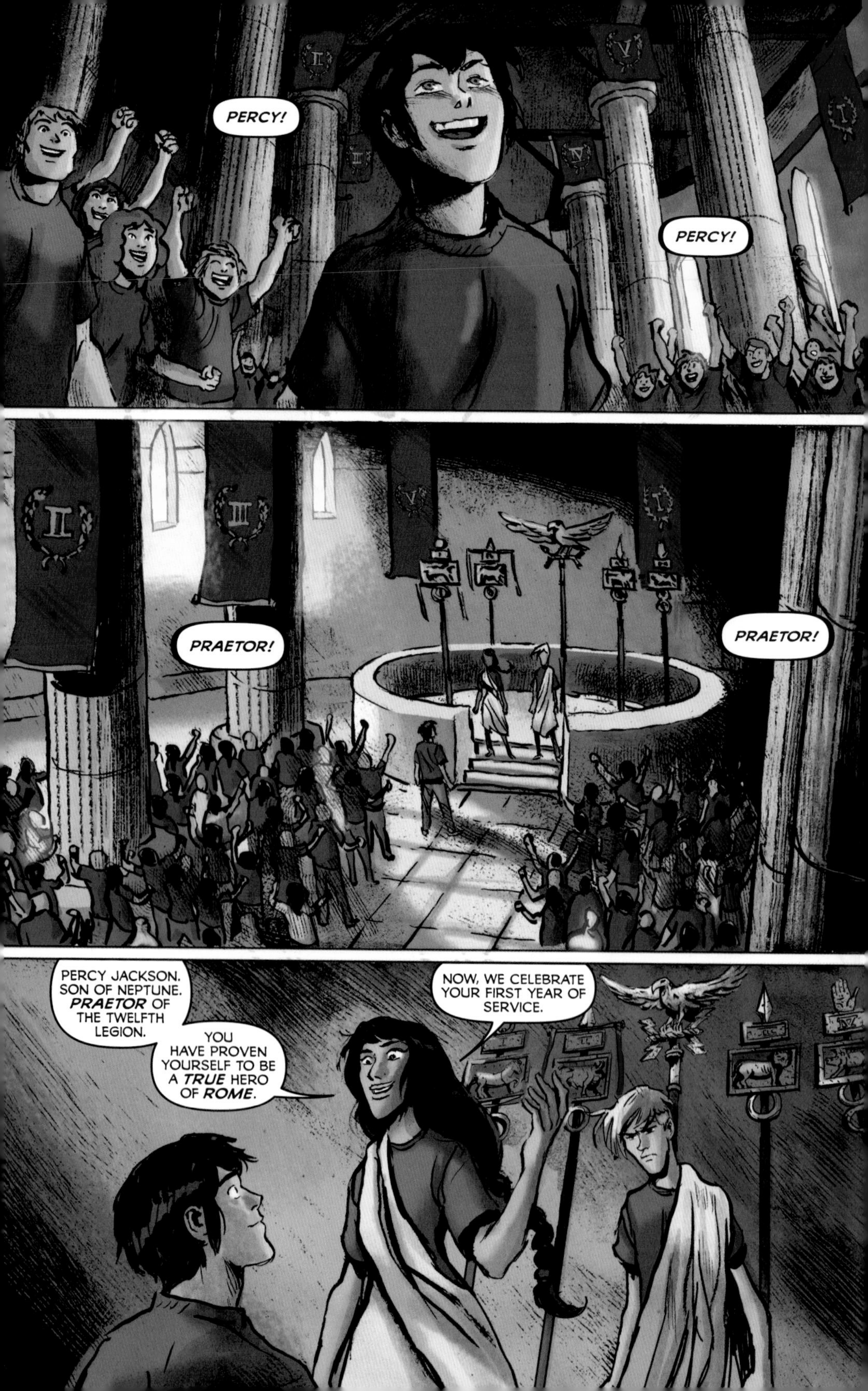
PERCY!
PERCY!
PRAETOR!
PRAETOR!
PERCY JACKSON. SON OF NEPTUNE. PRAETOR OF THE TWELFTH LEGION.
YOU HAVE PROVEN YOURSELF TO BE A TRUE HERO OF ROME.
NOW, WE CELEBRATE YOUR FIRST YEAR OF SERVICE.

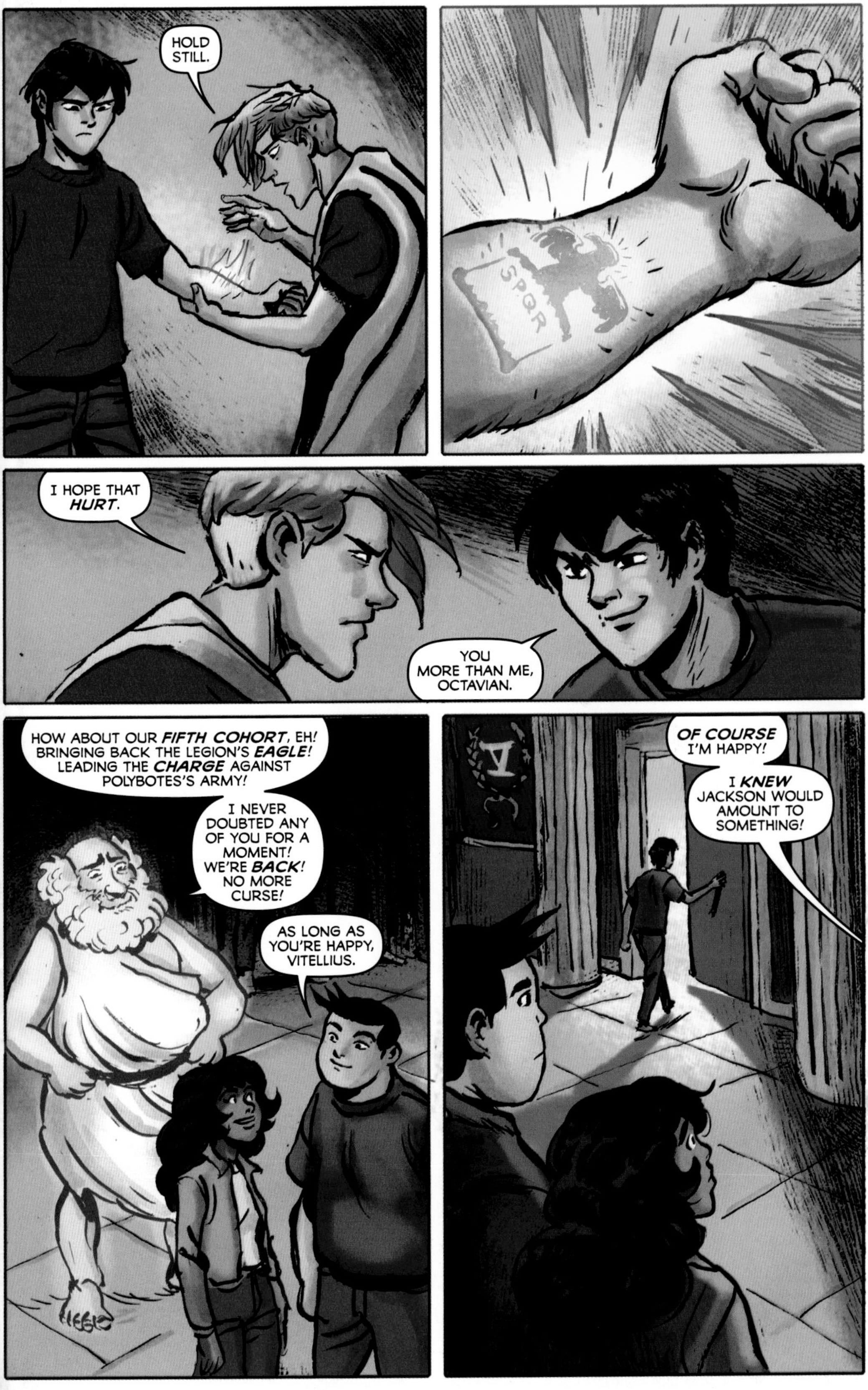
HOLD STILL.
SPQR
I HOPE THAT *HURT*.
YOU MORE THAN ME, OCTAVIAN.
HOW ABOUT OUR *FIFTH COHORT*, EH! BRINGING BACK THE LEGION'S *EAGLE*! LEADING THE *CHARGE* AGAINST POLYBOTES'S ARMY!
I NEVER DOUBTED ANY OF YOU FOR A MOMENT! WE'RE *BACK*! NO MORE CURSE!
AS LONG AS YOU'RE HAPPY, VITELLIUS.
OF COURSE I'M HAPPY!
I *KNEW* JACKSON WOULD AMOUNT TO SOMETHING!

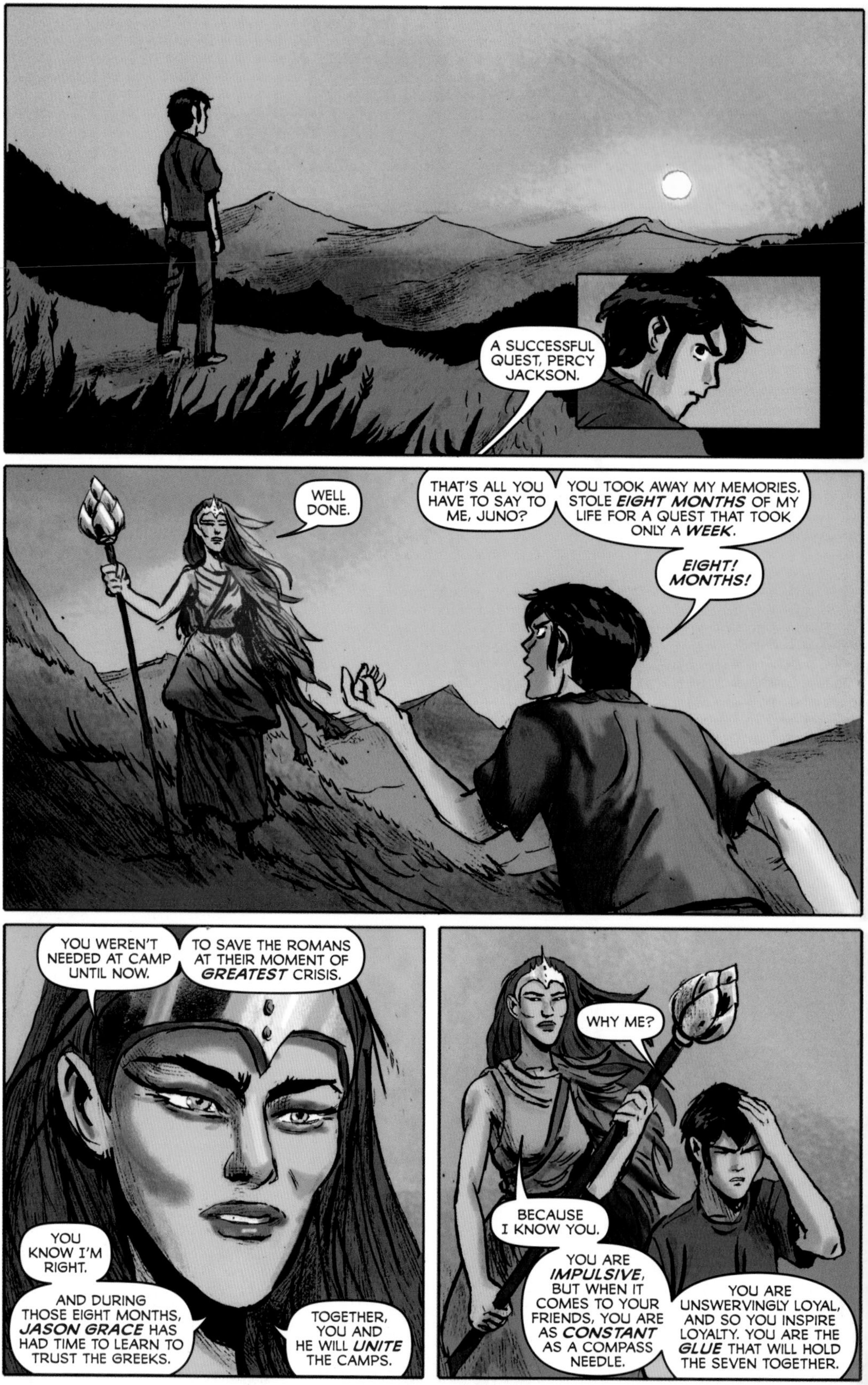
A SUCCESSFUL QUEST, PERCY JACKSON.
WELL DONE.
THAT'S ALL YOU HAVE TO SAY TO ME, JUNO?
YOU TOOK AWAY MY MEMORIES. STOLE EIGHT MONTHS OF MY LIFE FOR A QUEST THAT TOOK ONLY A WEEK.
EIGHT! MONTHS!
YOU WEREN'T NEEDED AT CAMP UNTIL NOW.
TO SAVE THE ROMANS AT THEIR MOMENT OF GREATEST CRISIS.
YOU KNOW I'M RIGHT.
AND DURING THOSE EIGHT MONTHS, JASON GRACE HAS HAD TIME TO LEARN TO TRUST THE GREEKS.
TOGETHER, YOU AND HE WILL UNITE THE CAMPS.
WHY ME?
BECAUSE I KNOW YOU.
YOU ARE IMPULSIVE, BUT WHEN IT COMES TO YOUR FRIENDS, YOU ARE AS CONSTANT AS A COMPASS NEEDLE.
YOU ARE UNSWERVINGLY LOYAL, AND SO YOU INSPIRE LOYALTY. YOU ARE THE GLUE THAT WILL HOLD THE SEVEN TOGETHER.

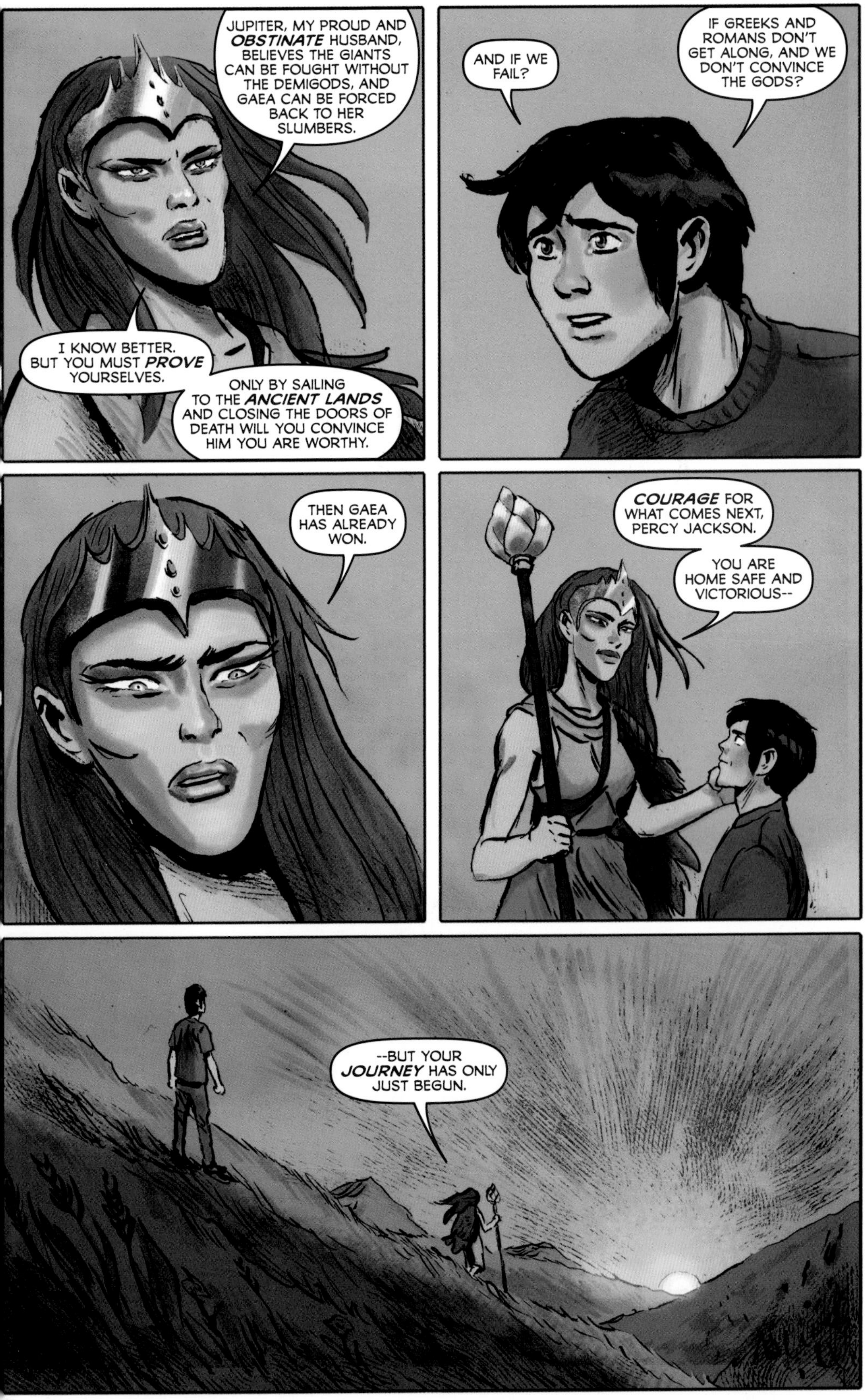
JUPITER, MY PROUD AND *OBSTINATE* HUSBAND, BELIEVES THE GIANTS CAN BE FOUGHT WITHOUT THE DEMIGODS, AND GAEA CAN BE FORCED BACK TO HER SLUMBERS.
I KNOW BETTER. BUT YOU MUST *PROVE* YOURSELVES.
ONLY BY SAILING TO THE *ANCIENT LANDS* AND CLOSING THE DOORS OF DEATH WILL YOU CONVINCE HIM YOU ARE WORTHY.
AND IF WE FAIL?
IF GREEKS AND ROMANS DON'T GET ALONG, AND WE DON'T CONVINCE THE GODS?
THEN GAEA HAS ALREADY WON.
COURAGE FOR WHAT COMES NEXT, PERCY JACKSON.
YOU ARE HOME SAFE AND VICTORIOUS--
--BUT YOUR *JOURNEY* HAS ONLY JUST BEGUN.

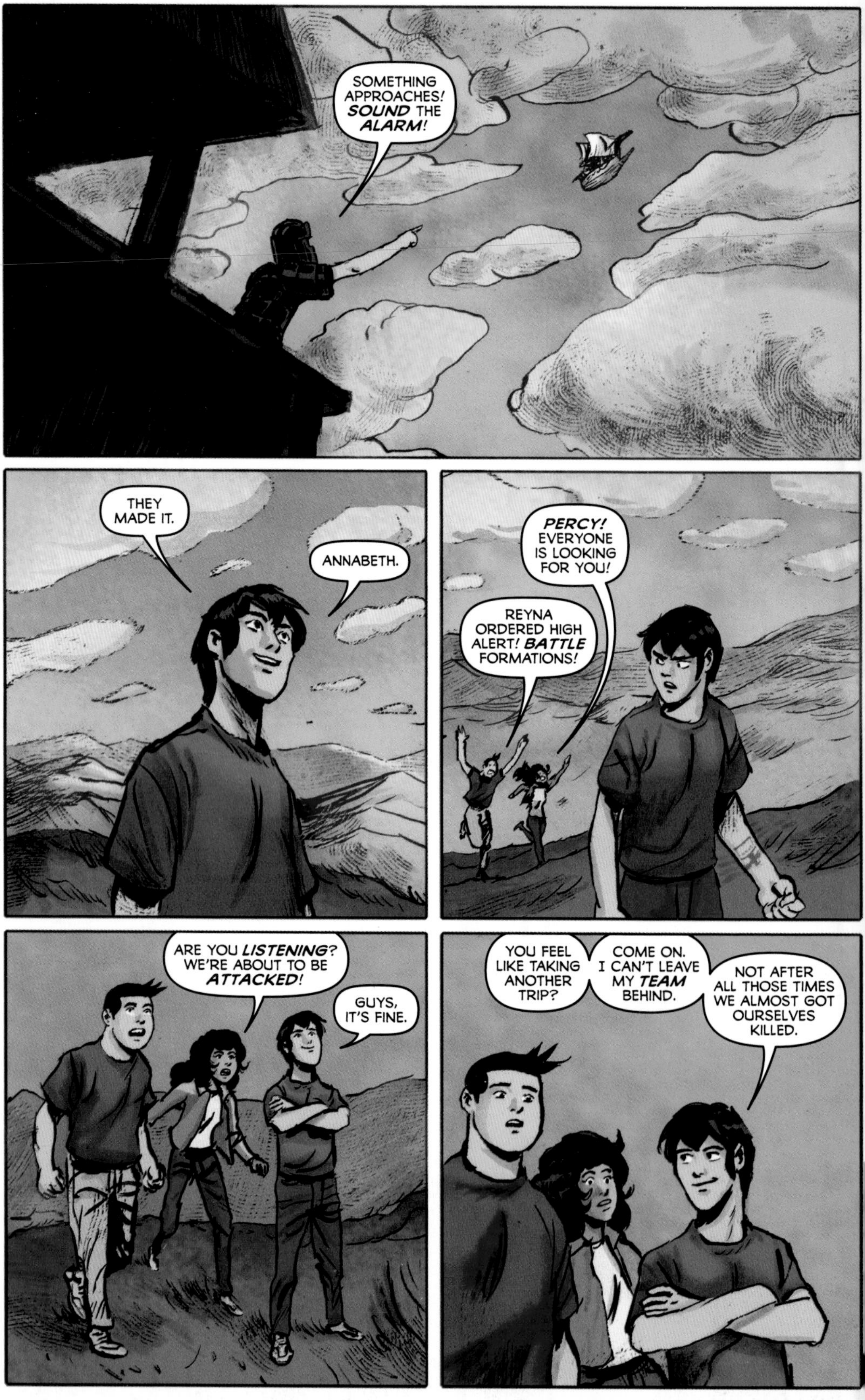
SOMETHING APPROACHES! ***SOUND*** THE ***ALARM***!
THEY MADE IT.
ANNABETH.
PERCY! EVERYONE IS LOOKING FOR YOU!
REYNA ORDERED HIGH ALERT! ***BATTLE*** FORMATIONS!
ARE YOU ***LISTENING***? WE'RE ABOUT TO BE ***ATTACKED***!
GUYS, IT'S FINE.
YOU FEEL LIKE TAKING ANOTHER TRIP?
COME ON. I CAN'T LEAVE MY ***TEAM*** BEHIND.
NOT AFTER ALL THOSE TIMES WE ALMOST GOT OURSELVES KILLED.